TITAN

A Villetti CHRONICLES NOVEL

SARAH BAILEY

Titan Copyright © 2022 by Sarah Bailey

This book is a work of fiction. Names, characters, places, and incidents either are products of the author's imagination or are used fictitiously. Any resemblance to actual persons, living or dead, events, or locales is entirely coincidental.

Please note the spelling throughout is British English.

Cover Art by Sarah Bailey

Published by Twisted Tree Publications
www.twistedtreepublications.com
info@twistedtreepublications.com

Paperback ISBN: 978-1-913217-41-9

This one is for all my degradation kink girlies
Sometimes we just want to be called good little sluts

ONE

Theia

The music pulsed in my ear as I fixed my eyes on a spot on the red velvet upholstered seating in front of me. My body twisted around the pole, performing a routine I'd done hundreds of times. Yet each time gave me a sense of satisfaction unlike any other. Something about being watched made my heart race and my body grow hot. It was my escape from the shit in my life and something I was infinitely grateful for.

There were a couple of men seated at the table closest to my raised dais where the pole I was twirling around sat. The club was relatively busy this evening, but as it was a special club night, it was to be expected. The owner of Desecration, Zayn Villetti, sat in his usual place with women surrounding him, surveying the room as he always did. I'd noticed the way he discreetly did business with his various clients and his under-the-table dealings.

Tonight Zayn had arrived with a guest who looked very much like him, with dark hair, tanned skin, and dark eyes. A younger version of Zayn without the tattoos. I wondered if it was his brother. The staff were aware he had two of them, but no one apart from Remi had been formally introduced to all the Villetti men. Unsurprising when Zayn treated her like his little sister. I spent more time around Liza Royce, who was his manager and ran the day-to-day of the club on Zayn's behalf, than the big boss himself.

I turned my attention away from the club owner and the man I thought might be his brother, focusing back on the men watching me from their table. Their eyes were leering as they spoke in low voices to each other. Something about them made the hair on the back of my neck prickle. All the patrons of Desecration were thoroughly vetted before being allowed entry to the club, but it didn't mean there weren't creeps amongst them. Club nights meant clients could bring guests if they wished. It was their responsibility to keep their friends in order. I hadn't seen these two in here before, so I assumed they were with someone, or maybe they were new. Something told me it was the former. There was no way in hell they'd be let in otherwise. They weren't our normal type of clientele.

One of them nudged the other, who stood up the next moment. He came closer to the dais, his eyes fixed on my body contorting around the pole. It was my first clue that something was wrong.

I didn't falter in my routine, but my eyes narrowed on him. While I might like to be watched, I was not here for a guy blatantly looking at me like I was a piece of meat. It reminded me too much of things best left in the past. There was a difference between being watched for the eroticism of it and being leered over. A huge fucking one I understood all too well. For me, there was safety in being watched in this place where there were strict rules and boundaries everyone had to abide by. It wasn't the same as when people thought you belonged to them, and they could do whatever the fuck they wanted. When people considered you something to be thrown away when they got bored or thought you were of no use to them any longer. But it was never forever. They always came back.

"All right, love?" the man said with a grin.

I didn't answer him. He clearly didn't know he wasn't meant to approach or try to interact with the dancers. We were here to be watched, not touched. If a client wanted a lap dance, they would have to request it via the hostesses who were dotted around serving drinks.

"Cat got your tongue?"

I spun away, knowing if I gave him the time of day, it would only encourage him to come closer. It made me wonder where the fuck the bouncers were and whether they were actually paying attention. Usually, they were good at keeping patrons under control.

My gaze went to Arlo, Zayn's right-hand man, who was in the corner having a heated conversation with Liza. Something was going on, but I had no idea what. It wasn't my business. I was here to dance, not pry into what was happening with my bosses.

The next thing I knew, someone had wrapped their hand around my ankle and tugged at it, almost forcing me off balance. I whipped my head around, finding the leering guy staring up at me with a scowl.

"Hey, I'm talking to you."

I tried to shake him off, but his grip was like a vice. What the fuck was this guy's problem?

"Let go of me!"

He glared at me and opened his mouth to say something else, but he didn't get the chance to. A hand wrapped around his throat and dragged him away from me. His nails scraped across my bare ankle, making me wince and hold on to the pole to stay upright. I watched as the man was thrown back into his seat and a loud thump echoed above the music, followed by a pained howl emitting from his throat. My gaze darted down to the table, finding his hand pinned to it by a knife.

What the...

"Don't touch the girls."

The deep voice belonging to whoever had said those words echoed around my skull. They were quiet, but I heard it all the same. I stared at the man who had dragged the creep away and swallowed hard when I realised who he was.

"Gil, you cannot go around stabbing my patrons," came Zayn's hissed voice as he arrived next to his brother.

"He touched one of your girls."

Zayn looked plain exasperated with the man I assumed was his brother's response.

"I realise that, but this is not how I deal with things."

Arlo joined the fray a moment later, staring down at the man who was whimpering and gesturing to his pinned hand with his other one.

"Do you want me to deal with this, boss?"

His words only made Zayn look even more pissed off. He gestured at the man with a knife in his hand.

"Get rid of him." He pointed at his brother. "And you, come with me."

I didn't know whether to be shocked, amused, or horrified by the scene in front of me. It wasn't the first time I'd witnessed violence, but it rarely occurred in Desecration. Zayn ran a tight ship. It was one of the reasons I'd chosen to work at the club. I had safety here. I could rely on my work colleagues and my bosses to make sure I was unharmed.

Zayn walked over to me, his annoyed expression clearing. I stepped down off the dais to meet him.

"Are you okay?"

"I'm fine, Mr Villetti. No harm done," I replied, not wanting to make more of a scene.

I knew Zayn preferred to deal with anything like this in private. He wasn't a showy man who wanted everything on blast. More like someone who worked behind the shadows and had everyone dancing to his tune without even trying too hard to manipulate them.

His brother arrived next to him. The way he looked at me made me swallow all over again. It wasn't leering nor curious. His dark eyes were almost devoid of emotion, which was incredibly unnerving.

"I'm glad to hear that, but I do think you should take five, okay?"

I nodded. Zayn smiled at me. Then he glared at his brother before walking off toward the private rooms and his office.

For a moment, his brother and I stared at each other. His mouth twitched slightly, and he stepped closer.

"Thank you."

The words erupted from my throat in a rush, not wanting to seem ungrateful that he'd dealt with the man for me. I didn't like being touched by people without my consent. It made my skin crawl. Having someone defend me the way he had meant a lot to me.

He cocked his head to the side but didn't open his mouth. My eyes were drawn to it for some reason, taking in the fullness of his lips and wondering what they would feel like against me.

And now I'm having extremely inappropriate thoughts about my boss's brother!

"Gilberto. Now."

I almost jumped at the sound of Zayn's voice. His brother raised his eyebrow and walked away from me. I turned, watching him make his way across the club with Zayn until they disappeared through the doors to the private rooms.

My breath whooshed out of me. I shook myself, flexing my hands by my sides before I darted away towards the bar and the staff rooms behind it. The moment I was alone, I sat down on a bench and put my head in my hands.

"What the fuck was that all about?" I muttered to myself.

The man who'd touched me would be dealt with appropriately. I wouldn't have to worry about him again. That hadn't flustered me. No, it was Zayn's brother, who he'd called Gilberto… Gil. The way he'd stared at me with little emotion in his expression. The fact he'd so casually stabbed a man in the hand like it meant nothing should terrify me. When you've spent years witnessing violence against the people around you, not to mention against yourself, you get desensitised to it. It became commonplace. Maybe it was why I didn't have any issues working for a man who was the heir to his father's mafia empire.

Zayn had always treated me and his other employees with respect. Almost everyone who worked here had a shitty past they were trying to escape. We were a family. A strange, dysfunctional one, but a family all the same. That was the atmosphere Zayn and Liza always fostered amongst the staff.

Still, I shouldn't have been thinking about how attractive Zayn's brother was or what he could do with his mouth. I mean, sure, I'd always thought my boss was hot with all those tattoos and the way he carried himself, but it didn't mean I was interested in him... or his brother. I wasn't interested in relationships full stop. No one needed my damage, nor did I want to feel like a burden. I was happy alone, working here where I'd found safety in sex work. Where I'd rebuilt myself from the ground up. I still had a few old wounds left to heal, but I was moving forward. That's what mattered the most.

I let out a breath and rubbed my face with both hands. Then I got up and checked my makeup before fixing my hair. I adjusted my clothes as I stared at myself in the mirror.

Time to go back out there and let yourself get lost in the music, in having people watch you perform. That's your happy place, remember? You don't need to think about the past any longer, Theia Louise Nowak. You never have to think about it again.

Turning around, I walked out of the staff room and back into the club. I wasn't going to let this little incident ruin my night. He could go fuck himself. I didn't give a shit if he'd been stabbed in the hand. He wasn't worth my time. And I swore to myself I really wouldn't think about the fact that Gilberto Villetti had seared himself into my mind permanently after he'd come to my rescue, when he didn't even know me.

No, I wouldn't think about him at all.

TWO

Gilberto

THREE MONTHS LATER

M y brother sat behind his desk with a neutral expression on his face. I'd known my whole adult life that Zayn did not want to take over the mafia from our father. Ever since he'd told *Papá* to go fuck himself when I was nineteen. Now our father was dead. Everything had changed. Yet I don't know why I expected his stance on it to have changed in light of recent events.

"You want me to take over his role?"

Zayn nodded slowly, his eyes flickering with emotions I wasn't sure I understood. To be honest, I wasn't good with emotions full stop. They made my skin itch.

"Why?"

My brother let out a sigh before rising from his seat and coming around his desk to stand in front of me. Perhaps he thought I'd respond better if we were on a level playing field.

I'd always respected Zayn for who he was and how he stuck to his principles no matter what. However, what he was suggesting was unorthodox, not to mention would be an incredibly hard sell to our men.

"A Villetti has to be in charge, Gil."

"You're a Villetti too."

He shook his head at me stating the obvious.

"As loath as I am to admit this, you're far more qualified to run the mafia than I am. The men know you. They will follow you far more willingly than me."

"Only because you didn't want to learn or be a part of it."

He reached out and placed a hand on my shoulder. Because Zayn and I were close and family, I allowed it. If someone I didn't know put their hands on me, I would have them on the ground with my boot to their back faster than they could say hello.

"I'm sorry I placed that burden on you. Now you know why. I'm sure you understand my reasons."

I knew all right. Our father had put our mother in a coma and kept her there for nigh on ten years. Her funeral had only been last week. It was something I didn't like thinking about because it made me feel. I didn't like to feel. It made life harder for me.

I stepped back from him and crossed my arms over my chest.

"The head of the family has always run things, Zayn. What you're suggesting goes against everything we've ever known, though I'm hardly surprised you don't want to follow tradition."

"Just because it goes against tradition, doesn't mean it won't work."

Zayn wanted me to be head of the mafia while he remained head of our family and the man who ran London behind the scenes. I understood why. He didn't have time to do everything. I was pretty sure Ari would have his head for it as well. He might be in charge, but his woman was a force to be reckoned with. Even I couldn't deny she was good for my brother.

"You'll have free rein. I won't interfere unless you need me to."

"It doesn't mean I won't still answer to you like everyone else in this city. *Papá* was the only one who didn't bow to you. Now he's gone, and this looks like you're placing me at the head of the table as your puppet."

Zayn looked away, his brow furrowing slightly.

"It wouldn't work like that, Gil. We're family. I trust you, and I know you trust me. Make them eat their words if you have to. Show them you're no puppet whose strings are held by your own brother. You're more than capable of it."

I didn't realise my brother had that much faith in me. Our father certainly hadn't. He might have treated me like his heir in place of Zayn, but it didn't mean he appreciated the way I was. Probably why I'd kept my true self hidden under a mask of indifference for so long. It was the only way to survive Gennaro Villetti.

"You want me to deliberately go against your wishes to prove a point?"

"No. I want you to do whatever it takes to make sure our family remains on top. It's the only way to keep us all safe."

11

SARAH BAILEY

It hardly came as a surprise to me, him wanting to protect us all. What I wasn't expecting was for him to ask me for help in achieving his goal. Zayn rarely asked anyone for assistance, except for Arlo. He dealt with everything himself. Perhaps having Ari in his life had mellowed him out somewhat. He certainly appeared to be more flexible in his approach to things.

"Okay."

Zayn looked at me again.

"Okay? Does that mean yes?"

What other choice did I have in the matter? Zayn needed me to do this for him. I'd been groomed to take over from our father in case Zayn didn't come back into the fold. It wasn't as if I didn't know how to be the mafia boss. I'd never decided whether I really wanted the role or not. I honestly didn't know what I wanted from life. Having a father like Gennaro Villetti meant you didn't get to make decisions about your life. The path was already laid out for you to follow. I wasn't sure who I was now my father was gone, nor who I wanted to be, but I could do this.

"Yes."

Zayn looked almost relieved by my answer.

"Good. I'll leave you to deal with the men. They're getting restless."

The older members wouldn't take kindly to this situation, but I would have to make sure they knew who they answered to.

"And we'll go see Dino and Gian together."

I flinched at the mention of our cousins. They were our great uncle Nevio's children. He had two sons and two daughters, all married with children of their own. Dino was head of their side of the Villetti family. He and Gian were the other two Villetti mafia bosses, though my father had always been top dog. I wondered if that would be me now. They may well resent a twenty-eight-year-old who wasn't even head of my side of the family being more powerful than they were.

Well, fuck them. If I'm going to do this, I'll make sure I remain on top.

"Do we have to?"

I'd already spent more than enough time around them during our mother's funeral. They were far too loud and in your face. I'd never felt comfortable around them, hence why I avoided going to see the other side of the family unless it was strictly necessary.

"Yes. If we're going to make this work, then we need them on board."

I shrugged and dropped my arms.

"Fine."

"I'll let you know when they're expecting us unless there's anything else you want to ask me?"

There probably was, but it could wait. There were a million things I needed to think about and achieve. First and foremost was bringing the men in line before things went tits up. It was a real possibility. I'd deal with the older ones first. If they followed me, the rest of them would get with the program.

"No."

Zayn gave me a nod as if dismissing me. I walked away towards the door and opened it.

"Gil."

I paused but didn't turn around.

"Thank you… for agreeing to this."

"You left me with very little choice."

"You always have a choice. If this isn't what you want…"

I raised my hand and gripped the doorframe.

"What I want is irrelevant." I turned my head slightly. "I'm a Villetti. This is what we do. It's all I've ever known."

I didn't give my brother a chance to say anything more. Dropping my hand, I left his office and shut the door behind me. I didn't move away from the door, staring at the blank wall in front of me and let out a breath. What I'd said was the truth. All I'd ever known was the mafia. It was all I was good at. Zayn didn't understand that part of my life because he hadn't wanted anything to do with it.

Gennaro Villetti had turned me into an efficient and brutal killer. One who wouldn't hesitate to deal with any threat to keep us on top. I wasn't sure if that was the way I wanted to run things going forward, but if I was going to get the men to follow me, I had to be the man they'd always known. The silent but deadly son. But I wasn't the son any longer. I was the leader. And I would make sure I was an efficient one.

I'll try, anyway.

A quiet gasp to my left had my head turning. Standing just inside the double doors that led to the private rooms of the club was a woman. I narrowed my gaze on her, taking in her straight, light brown shoulder-length hair, blue eyes, and slightly tanned skin. She was dressed in a t-shirt and jeans, but as it was the middle of the day, I wasn't expecting anything else.

I know you…

"Hi," she said in her soft little voice that made my palm twitch.

The last time I'd seen her was months ago when I'd visited the club on one of Zayn's special nights. It had ended in disaster and him having a right go at me over stabbing one of his patrons in the hand. I hadn't regretted it. As far as I was concerned, the fucker deserved it after touching this girl. She shouldn't be harassed by anyone. This was her place of work. Zayn took their safety seriously. It's why I'd intervened in the first place. His bouncers had seemed busy. I didn't want it to escalate for her sake.

She stepped towards me, her hands flexing at her sides.

"I didn't get a proper chance to thank you for what you did."

She didn't need to thank me. It was the right thing to do. I didn't like being given praise or compliments for being a decent human being.

I was surprised she even remembered me. She must've seen a lot of people in this place between now and then. I wasn't anyone special in the club other than being Zayn's younger brother. It wasn't as if I came here very often either, but perhaps that would change now I was to be head of the mafia.

When I didn't respond, she came even closer, staring up at me with curiosity in her eyes. Being close to strangers made my skin prickle, but I didn't want her to think I was being rude, so I didn't move.

"You're welcome…"

"Theia, my name is Theia."

"Is that your real name or your stage name?"

For some reason, it made her smile.

"My real one, but if you want to know, I go by Pisces in the club."

I didn't ask her why, since I knew Zayn gave all of his sex workers star constellations as their stage names. To be honest, I didn't even know why I was still here talking to her. There was so much for me to do and think about, but my feet remained in place and my mouth didn't tell her goodbye.

"And you're Gilberto, right? That's what Mr Villetti called you, so I assumed…"

"Yes, however, Gil is my preference."

"Well, thank you again, Gil. I appreciated your intervention more than you know."

She gave me a small shrug and a bright smile. I didn't know what else to say to her. It wasn't often I made small talk with anyone, nor did I get random women thanking me for things. I suppose Theia wasn't exactly random. Still, I mostly kept to myself. It was easier that way. Getting to know people was a struggle for me.

Theia was looking at me as if she expected an answer. I could admit she was an attractive girl with a pretty face. I didn't find myself attracted to her, but it wasn't anything new for me. It was rare I found anyone interesting. It didn't stop me from being intrigued by her. This close, I noticed her eyes were more of a blue-grey. It was unusual. She was… I didn't know. There was something about her. And I didn't like that.

"I need to go."

"Oh, of course," she said, her face falling slightly. "I'm sorry if I took up your time."

"It's fine. I hope you don't get harassed by anyone else."

Turning, I started towards the back door to leave the club. I didn't look back, relatively sure I would see disappointment or some other negative emotion on her face. I didn't have time to deal with it from someone I didn't know.

Are you running away from a woman you find intriguing right now, Gil?

Yes... yes, I fucking well was. And I didn't care what it meant. Not when my life was about to get a whole lot more difficult now my brother had decided I was the next mafia boss rather than himself.

THREE

Gilberto

My fingers tapped against my thigh as I sat behind my father's desk in the office where he conducted much of his mafia business. The building was an old printing factory that had been converted into *Papá's* base of operations not long after he took over. It was my place now. At least, it would be officially when Zayn had dealt with our father's estate.

I didn't feel much like a mafia boss, despite being flanked by the only person I trusted outside of my own family. Well, I trusted Zayn. Enzo was a different matter. Right now, he was completely off the rails and neither I nor Zayn knew what to do about his antics. I'd ignored it. He was an adult, and I wasn't his fucking keeper any longer. Besides, I had more important shit to worry about, like being in charge of the *famiglia*.

"You going to tell me what this is about?" Edric asked when I didn't say a word.

My eyes were fixed on the door, waiting for the two men who would make or fucking break this situation, Gennaro's longest-serving members, Matteo and Salvatore.

"This is about Zayn giving me the keys to Gennaro's empire," I said after a minute, turning my attention toward my best friend.

Edric raised his chestnut eyebrows, his hazel eyes widening slightly behind his wide-framed glasses.

"Your brother wants you to be in charge?"

I inclined my head.

"Well, fuck."

I'd known Edric Russell since I was a teenager. His father was a minor member of the mafia, but as we were the same age, he was often in my company. He was the loud one out of the two of us. Always getting up in people's faces, rarely backing down from a fight, and regularly getting in trouble. That was my chestnut-haired friend. I was constantly shaking my head at his antics, but he was loyal to a fault. Probably why I let him stick around me for so long. Now, I would need his loyalty more than ever.

"I'm promoting you to my second-in-command effective immediately," I told him as the door opened to admit the older men.

I caught Edric's startled expression before my eyes were drawn to Matteo and Salvatore, who were both looking around the room with suspicion in their eyes. If I knew anything about my friend, it was his adaptability. However, I'm not sure he was ready for me to place him above everyone else in the chain of command. It would ruffle feathers, considering Edric was relatively low down in the pecking order. By all accounts, I should have given it to Matteo or Salvatore, but I didn't trust them as far as I could throw them.

"Where is Zayn?" was the first thing Matteo said.

The question rubbed me up the wrong way. My palm flattened against my thigh, my teeth gritting in my mouth, but I remained outwardly calm.

"He isn't here."

"I thought we were having a meeting about the new leadership."

"We are. If you'd take a seat, I'll explain everything."

I waved at the two chairs in front of me. Edric shifted next to me, leaning closer and lowering his voice.

"Are you sure about this, Gil?"

"Don't question me in front of them," I murmured under my breath.

Edric straightened immediately, his back going rigid. I needed him to shut up and give me his silent support. If they even got a whiff, there was any dissent, Matteo and Salvatore would be on me in a second. This had to be handled the right way, or we'd face an uphill battle. It was bad enough that I was about to tell them I was in charge now. If Edric didn't stand by me, I wouldn't have any allies or someone to watch my back.

Salvatore was the first to sit down, giving me a slight nod. He was the more measured one of the two who liked to know all the facts before he made a decision about anything. Matteo remained standing as he crossed his arms over his chest. I'd been Gennaro's second-in-command for the past five years. Salvatore and Matteo had been his *capodecinas*, who I should have been in charge of, but my father had supervised everything I did. His standards were sky high. I'm not sure I ever really met them.

I wanted these two to remain in their positions if possible. They had the most sway over the men they were in charge of.

"Matteo."

"I'm not sitting down until you tell me what is going on. Gennaro has been dead long enough. We can't afford to sit around like fucking lemons any longer. Zayn should be here doing what he is supposed to. That little upstart has always thought he was better than us. No wonder he sent you to deliver the news."

I leaned forward, linking my hands together and setting them on the desk. Matteo denigrating my older brother pissed me off. Zayn was family, and no one disrespected a Villetti in my presence without consequences.

"We aren't here to discuss my brother," I told him, keeping my voice calm. "I'm in charge now, and I expect you to respect my position."

Matteo blinked, his greying eyebrows shooting up into his hairline. Salvatore sat back, his eyes roaming between me and Edric as if he was assessing the situation.

"You?"

I tapped a finger on the desk.

"Yes, me. This *famiglia* is mine now."

"Are you seriously telling me your brother decided you—"

I put my hand up, silencing him.

"I'm telling you, this is my house and if you want to remain *capodecina*, I suggest you sit the fuck down and shut up."

Matteo's mouth dropped open. I'd never spoken to him that way in my life. To be honest, I kept silent for the most part. Speaking out against my father wasn't worth the hassle. It was easier to fly under the radar and do as you were told. Now, they were going to learn I wasn't going to take it easy on them if they stepped out of line.

Zayn told me to run things my way, make them understand I wasn't a puppet and could hold my own. It was the only thing I could do under the circumstances. Be my own man and show them my worth.

"If you think I'm going to let you talk to me like that, you have another—"

Matteo didn't get much further than that. No, he was dead within moments of the gun going off with a shot right between the eyes. The gun was now sitting on the table in front of me after I'd pulled it out of the drawer of my desk and fired. Not only had the piece of shit disrespected my brother, but he'd also been unwilling to listen to me. I didn't have time or the inclination to deal with him any further. He was better dead than alive to me at this point. If anyone else wanted to mouth off at me, they would meet the same fate. They should all know better. I was Gennaro's most ruthless killer, after all. When *Papá* wanted to make an example of someone, he gave them to me.

Matteo dropped to the floor in a heap, his lifeless eyes fixed on the ceiling. Neither Salvatore nor Edric said a word. I sat back in my chair and crossed my hands over my chest.

"Do we have an understanding about who is in charge here, Sal?" I asked, turning my gaze to the man still sitting watching me with a neutral expression on his face.

He inclined his head.

"We do, boss."

I didn't smile.

"Good." I rubbed my fingers together. "Edric will be my underboss and you will answer to him. We will need someone to replace Matteo, so I want you to give me a list of potential candidates. And get the men to deal with him." I waved at his body. "We'll compensate his family for their trouble." I glanced up at Edric. "Make arrangements for me to see his wife and give her my condolences before the funeral. Find out her favourite flowers and send them on my behalf too."

Edric gave me a slight nod but kept his mouth shut. I was sure he would speak his mind once Salvatore had left.

"I need to know everything that has happened since Gennaro's death. I want you to report to me tomorrow. You're dismissed."

I waved at Sal, who stood and eyed Matteo with an unreadable expression.

"Yes, boss."

Neither Edric nor I spoke as he left the room. He was back a few minutes later with a couple of men. They dragged Matteo's body out. Sal gave me a nod and shut the door behind them.

I sagged in my chair and rubbed my temples. It wasn't how I wanted any of this to go, but after Matteo had opened his mouth, I saw red. I'd become like my father, who was ruthless to the extreme. It kind of made me sick.

"Well, I'd say that went better than expected."

I looked up at Edric, who had leaned against my desk and was giving me the once over.

"You think?"

"If your aim was to be the next Gennaro, you succeeded. He'd have probably shot Matteo sooner, but I guess you wanted to give him the benefit of the doubt or something."

"I'm not him."

"You sure about that?"

I didn't glare at Edric, but I wanted to. Deep down, I knew I was nothing like Gennaro Villetti. I could be ruthless and uncompromising, but only because it was who he taught me to be. Someone with little to no emotion who killed without compunction. That's the man I'd displayed. I wasn't entirely sure I liked him... or if I wanted to be him.

"Doesn't matter. What's done is done."

It wasn't like I could change the outcome now. Matteo was dead. It was a necessity. I had to live with it.

"Well, you could have warned me long before they walked in that you wanted me to be your underboss, Gil. I'm pretty sure no one, including Sal, wants that."

"I only care if you do."

He broke out into a grin and waved at the door.

"Being in charge of that old fuck? Sure thing. I'll make sure the rest of them don't piss you off too much."

"That's because you'll piss them off instead."

Edric winked.

"Bingo."

I rolled my eyes and stood up from the desk before wandering over to the window which looked out over the rest of the building. A few men were sitting at desks and some others chatting near the kitchen area. It felt strange that I was now in control of all of this. I had the power.

"Do you think I can do this?"

"You killed a guy for disrespecting you, Gil. Pretty sure that qualifies you as a mafia don."

"Don't call me that. I hate that term."

It reminded me too much of my father and my conflicting feelings towards him. I still hadn't dealt with the fact he was the reason my mother had been in a coma for almost ten years, and now she was in the ground. It wasn't the first time I'd buried my feelings because processing them felt like an uphill battle.

"All right, boss, calm down."

I wanted to throw something at his head, but I remained where I was, watching the men. Edric had a habit of rubbing everyone up the wrong way. I was used to dealing with his shit.

"Are you quite done being a cunt?"

"Maybe."

"Good. We have work to do, and I don't need you messing shit up for me."

I turned my head to look at him. Edric had sat in my place behind my father's desk with his legs up on the table. I almost told him to knock it off, but it wasn't worth it.

"You know you can count on me."

He was probably the only one outside of my immediate family I could rely on. I didn't want to ask Zayn for help. He'd put his faith in me. I had to deliver. This was only the beginning. Getting the men on board was one thing. Telling our family about this would have to be handled more delicately. Zayn might be optimistic about Dino and Gian's reactions, but I wasn't. In fact, I was pretty sure they would be unimpressed with his decision to put me in charge of the mafia.

TITAN

He'd sent me a text earlier to let me know we were expected at Dino's tomorrow night for dinner. I had to prepare for that, on top of the fact I'd killed one of my *capodecinas* and now had to appoint someone else. Fuck knows who Sal would suggest. All I knew was I couldn't trust a single one of them.

The only thing I had going for me right now was the fact Edric would stand by me. But even he didn't understand the pressure of being a Villetti. What it meant to be a part of this family. And even though I'd made him my second, it didn't mean he would ever comprehend the responsibility Zayn had given me to protect our family and keep us on top.

I don't know if I can live up to your expectations of me, Zayn... just like I never lived up to Papá's ones for me. If I fail at this... I don't know what I'll do.

I wasn't good at anything else. The only thing I'd ever been capable of doing well was killing. And really... I wasn't proud of that achievement.

Not one bit. Not at all.

FOUR

Gilberto

Zayn pressed down on the doorbell as we stood outside Dino's house. I glanced down at Ari, who was tucked into his side. I hadn't realised he was bringing her, but it shouldn't surprise me. He'd included Arianna in most aspects of his life since our father's death. And he'd told me in no uncertain terms I was to "make an effort" with her. It wasn't like I was going to ignore his girlfriend or anything, but he knew I wasn't good at making friends. It was a miracle I even had one in Edric. Then again, he was pretty insistent, forcing his way into my life and making a place for himself in it.

"How are you, Gil?" Ari asked, turning her head to look up at me.

"I'm fine."

I caught Zayn giving me side eyes.

"How about you?" I added.

"I'm okay."

"Just 'okay'?" Zayn asked, looking down at her with a frown.

"Your family is kind of intense."

He chuckled and rubbed her side. No doubt he'd warned her about them at our mother's funeral. The wake had been a lively affair. I'd found an excuse to hide in the corner with Enzo, who'd sulked the whole time. Being forced to make small talk was my idea of hell. I used my younger brother needing me as an excuse to avoid it. Enzo had done nothing but complain about everything under the sun. I was safer listening to him than dealing with my extended family.

The front door opened, revealing a tall woman in her late forties with a blonde bob, brown eyes, and pale skin. Her lips were bright red as usual, and she was dressed impeccably.

"Evening, Pippa," Zayn said.

She didn't smile at him. I'd never known Dino's wife to smile at anyone. Her disdainful attitude towards everything and everyone made me wary.

"Hello, Zayn, Gil." Her eyes went to the third one in our party. "And Arianna. It's nice to see you again."

She didn't sound thrilled about it, but I wasn't going to comment on it.

Pippa stood back to allow us in, giving us air kisses as we walked into the house. We went straight through into the dining room, finding Dino, his two children, Vincenzo and Vedetta, and Gian. They all had dark hair, dark eyes, and tanned skin, like most of the Villetti clan. I almost ground my teeth at the sight of Vincenzo. He pissed me off every time I saw him with his smug attitude. Not to mention he definitely fancied himself a ladies' man. I thought he was a dick who shouldn't get within ten feet of a woman. Zayn felt the same way. He told me he'd rejected our cousin's application to become a member at Desecration.

Why the fuck is he even here? He doesn't live with his parents. And why didn't Zayn warn me?

I glanced at my brother, but he wasn't paying attention, too busy saying hello to everyone. I nodded at all of my cousins but didn't speak. This whole thing made me uneasy as fuck. Zayn was acting like everything was normal when we were about to drop a bombshell on Gian and Dino. I hoped he wouldn't announce it during dinner. The whole family didn't need to be involved. It was a wonder Dino hadn't also invited his sisters, Legra and Carlotta. Their dining room was certainly big enough to accommodate the entire Villetti clan.

Pippa encouraged everyone to sit down when she came through with a clap of her hands. I ended up sandwiched in between Gian and Ari. She didn't look particularly pleased to have been separated from Zayn, who was sitting across from us.

"Is this going to turn into the dinner from hell?" she murmured.

"Probably," I said, keeping my voice low.

She glanced up at me.

"Thanks for the heads-up. I was suspicious as fuck when Zayn told me about this."

Typical Zayn.

"You didn't immediately assume it was a nice family dinner, then?"

She snorted before putting her hand to her mouth and passing it off as a cough. Zayn gave her a sharp look across the table as if to tell her to behave herself. Ari's eyes were full of mischief like she knew something I didn't. I wasn't sure I even wanted to know in all honesty. Their dynamic was... interesting, to say the least.

"Considering all of the Villetti family gatherings I've been to have ended in an argument, I'm going to say no," she whispered, leaning closer to me, "unless you've already forgotten, Legra got into a fight with her husband at Noemi's wake and threw her martini in his face."

How could I forget? It was an absolute mess.

Ari raised her eyebrows at me. I looked down at the table, trying my best not to smile. I wouldn't tell Zayn I liked his girlfriend because she was blunt to a fault. I preferred people who were honest and upfront. I didn't have to interpret their intentions.

We didn't say anything further because dinner was served. Dino waved at everyone to start when all the plates were placed down. I picked up my fork, staring down at the dish and wondering what on earth was in it. Pippa was exacting about what she served. No doubt it was the latest fad that was going around or something.

"So, Gil, how're things with you? I imagine you're helping Zayn deal with everything," Gian said, nudging my shoulder.

I almost glared at him for touching me. Why couldn't people respect my personal space?

"They're fine."

"And you're okay with him taking over?" He huffed. "Honestly, I'm surprised he even managed to bring everyone in line."

"Then you don't know Zayn very well," I muttered.

Gian thankfully didn't hear me as he continued talking.

"But I'm impressed all the same. For such a young'un, he's done well for himself."

Zayn was thirty-four, hardly a "young'un," but I supposed to Gian, who had turned fifty-two not too long ago, he was.

"How are your children?" I asked, interrupting his talk of Zayn because I really didn't want to have a conversation about my brother's takeover of London.

Gian started going on about Nino and Roche, his sons, and how they'd taken well to their roles underneath him. Roche was my age and Nino was thirty. He had two younger daughters, Neryssa and Etta, but Gian rarely waxed poetic about them. Unsurprisingly, some members of my family were sexist pieces of shit. I wasn't a fan of their attitudes towards women. Despite the man our father was, I had never bought into his views on that matter. Neither had my older brother.

For the rest of dinner, I was stuck listening to Gian prattle on about his sons while Ari kept giving me these 'are you as bored as I am' looks. It was the only thing that carried me through this fucking farce, knowing I wasn't the only one who didn't want to be here. Afterwards, Zayn suggested to Gian and Dino that we should retire to Dino's office.

Dino poured us all a glass of whisky. I took mine but didn't drink. I rarely did, preferring to keep a clear head. Zayn gave me a significant look as he stood by the fireplace. Gian stared out of the window over the garden.

"So, what's this about?" Dino asked before he sipped from his tumbler.

"As you're family, I wanted to extend to you the courtesy of informing you about the leadership change now our father is no longer with us."

Dino frowned.

"We assumed you would take his place."

I placed my tumbler down on the side table, knowing Zayn was about to stir shit right up and I was in the middle of the brewing storm.

"Gil was his second and therefore he has taken Gennaro's place." He waved a hand. "I will remain head of our family, but Gil will lead his men and take over his mafia interests."

You could have heard a penny drop in the ensuing silence. I glanced at Gian. His back was stiff, and he didn't turn around. Dino, on the other hand, was staring at Zayn as if he'd grown two heads.

"Am I hearing you correctly?" Dino asked, taking a step towards Zayn. "Did you really just say you're giving Gil our cousin's empire?"

"Yes."

Dino blinked.

"Are you fucking insane?" He jabbed a finger in my direction. "If you don't want it, you should give it to me or even Gian, not your younger brother. What the hell does he know about running an empire? Nothing. Gennaro barely let him do a thing."

Zayn remained calm despite Dino's outburst, but I could see the irritation lingering in his dark eyes. I, on the other hand, wanted to shrink back into the corner. I couldn't as it would show weakness and make Dino's words valid.

What did I actually know about running an empire? I knew the ins and outs of my father's business, but Dino wasn't wrong. I hadn't been allowed to manage anything. *Papá* ran it without my input or help. No doubt if he'd lived, he would have given me more responsibilities as I got older, but he was gone. I had no choice but to step up.

"Are you questioning my decision about my *own* family?"

"I'm questioning whether you should even be head of your family if you're planning on sticking him in charge."

"I see."

Zayn calmly placed his tumbler on top of the fireplace before walking over to me and placing his hand on my shoulder.

"Gennaro took over from Massimo when he was not much older than Gil. He is more than capable of being a leader. I'm disappointed you don't believe in either of us, but we're not going to stand here and take your insults."

He gave Dino a dark look.

"Jealousy is an ugly look on you. Gennaro didn't give you his empire, he gave it to *me*. If I deem my brother worthy of the position, then it's my choice. My *famiglia*, my rules."

Technically, our father had been intending to change everything and make me his heir, but Zayn had killed him before that could happen. Something I didn't blame my brother for. Our father was a monster. And one I had mixed feelings about at this point.

Zayn looked at me.

"Let's go."

Gian turned around. He looked incredulous, as if Zayn speaking to them that way rubbed him up the wrong way.

"Running away, are we?"

I stepped away from Zayn toward our cousins. If I didn't say something I would look like I was incapable, just like Dino had said. I didn't want to appear weak by allowing my brother to do all the talking.

"You two can stand there and act like you're better than me and Zayn, but you're just sad old men playing at a young man's game. Watch your backs."

I didn't even look at them as I turned and walked out, nor did I wait for Zayn. I left Dino's house. Panic started to set in. My hands were sweaty, and my mind was running riot.

Fuck. What did I do?

Never in my life would I ever have imagined I'd call my cousins out like that. I rarely spoke my mind to anyone but my brothers. Making enemies of Dino and Gian was a fucking terrible idea. Why had Zayn thought I could do this? I couldn't do this. I wasn't a leader. I didn't know what the fuck I was playing at.

"Gil."

I hadn't gone anywhere after I'd stepped outside of Dino's house. My head turned, finding Zayn standing on the doorstep with Ari behind him.

"I don't know why you believe in me, especially not after… that." I waved at the house. "They're never going to accept me."

Zayn dug his hands in his pockets and walked down the front steps until he was level with me. We were of a similar height.

"You think I care what they have to say about it?"

I didn't respond.

"I wouldn't have given it to you if I didn't think you were capable, Gil. You can do this."

I shook my head.

"I wish I believed you."

I walked away because I couldn't stand the fucking look in his eyes. It was as if Zayn couldn't comprehend why I thought so little of myself. He didn't get it. No one fucking got it. Hell, even I didn't understand myself. I had no clue who I was without my father guiding me along the path he'd laid out. And it was really fucked up.

I got in my car and set off, not even knowing where I was going, only that I needed to get away from my family. On instinct, I started to make my way home, but I got about halfway, stopped at a red light, and stared at the road like it had the answers. Only it didn't have any.

I didn't want to go home. I didn't even want to be around myself.

Who do you want to be around, then, Gil?

A certain blue-grey-eyed girl with light brown hair popped into my head completely unbidden. I didn't know why. I'd only met her twice. And I'd told myself I didn't need a complication like a woman in my life. Especially not one who worked at Zayn's club. It would only lead to trouble.

Would it?

My life was already flipped upside down and turned around. Why would I need more craziness in it?

My warring thoughts didn't explain why, when the lights turned green, I changed my destination. And why I drove straight towards trouble instead of far, far away from it.

What the fuck am I doing here?

I asked myself that a thousand times as I pulled up at the car park near Desecration, got out of my car and walked along to the club. As I didn't want to alert too many people to my presence there, I made my way in from the back where the offices were. I wandered down the hallway where the private rooms lay and into the club itself. My eyes darted around the place. It was relatively busy tonight, so no one paid any attention to me.

The moment I spied Remi standing by the bar, I made a beeline for her. She looked up when I approached, her green eyes widening.

"Well, fancy seeing you here."

I didn't have time for small talk. Remi knew better than to engage in it with me anyway. She was Zayn's pseudo little sister. I'd known her as long as he had, but we weren't remotely close in the way they were.

"Is Theia, I mean, Pisces working tonight?"

Remi's eyebrows shot up.

"Do I even want to know how you know her real name, or why you're asking for her?"

"Is she here?"

She glanced around before moving closer to me and lowering her voice.

"Yes, but it still doesn't explain why you want to know."

For some reason, I felt relieved she was here. At least I hadn't come all this way for nothing, even if I still didn't know why exactly I was here. It didn't matter. What did matter was getting Remi to do something for me without anyone else finding out.

"This isn't me being a weird creep. She told me what her name is because we've met."

"Okay. I wasn't thinking you'd been creeping on her or anything, Gil. I know you're not like that."

I took a deep breath.

"Can we talk in private?"

Remi blinked, then looked around before taking me by the arm, pulling me away from the bar and leading me into the corridor where the private rooms were.

"I need a favour," I said as we came to a standstill.

She frowned.

"What kind of favour?"

"Can you enter me into the system under an assumed name and get me a private session with Theia? I don't want anyone to know I'm here."

I don't think Remi was expecting me to ask for that. She stared at me like I'd gone crazy. I had, but it was beside the point.

"You want me to... well, this... I had no idea you were into—"

I put my hand up.

"I'm not into anything, Remi. I don't want any of the stuff the club offers. I only want to talk to her."

She opened her mouth, closed it, and then frowned.

"You want to *talk* to her? You do realise this is a sex club, not a therapist's office, right?"

This was probably the most embarrassing situation I'd ever been in. I wasn't interested in doing anything sexual with Theia. I merely wanted to see her. I wanted something to take my mind off everything that had happened in the past twenty-four hours and the shitshow my life was turning into. It might be insane for me to want to see a sex worker, but whatever it was about Theia that intrigued me when I'd seen her last had led me here. I intended to find out why the fuck she had been my first thought when I'd asked myself who I wanted to be around.

"I'm aware of what happens here."

"I'm just checking because, you know, I wasn't expecting *you* to turn up here asking for a session with one of the girls. Enzo has been banned from doing so since he works at the club, but Zayn never said anything about you."

No fucking surprise Zayn had vetoed Enzo getting private sessions here.

"You can't tell him about this."

She crossed her arms over her chest.

"Let me get this straight. You want me to give you access to the club under a fake name so you can talk to Theia and not tell your brother anything about it?"

"Yes. I'll pay for the session, obviously, and whatever the membership costs."

"I never thought I'd see the day *you* asked *me* for a favour, but okay, I'll do it."

I thought for a second she might tell me no and dob me into Zayn, but no, Remi was going to do me a solid.

"Thank you."

"Come on, we'll go down to Zayn's office since he isn't here, and I'll get you all set up." She dropped her arms and shook her head. "You owe me for this, though."

"Anything you want, I'll do it."

She started towards Zayn's office. I followed along behind her.

"I'm not even going to pretend to understand why this is such a big deal for you and why it has to be Theia, but whatever.

"You can't tell her it's me either."

She turned her head.

"Anything else his majesty wants me to do that's completely fucking batshit crazy?"

"No, that's it."

She rolled her eyes and shoved open the doors towards the offices at the end of the corridor.

"I'm going to get in so much trouble with Zayn when he finds out about this," she muttered.

You and me both, Remi. You and me fucking both.

FIVE

Theia

I stepped out onto the club floor after taking my break as Remi sidled up next to me with a tentative smile on her face. As far as I knew, I had no specific clients tonight, so I was due to mingle with the patrons of the club and perhaps take my turn on the pole.

"Did you want something?"

"I have a new client for you," she said with fake enthusiasm.

New clients turned up all the time requesting my particular range of services, so this wasn't unusual. However, Remi's demeanour was. Her eyes darted about the room as if she had a secret.

"Okay. Do you have the details for me?"

She shook herself and handed the tablet in her hands over to me. I scanned the requirements, wanting to see what they'd requested.

"Um, why are you giving this to me when they haven't actually picked the service they want? Didn't you show them how it works?"

There was literally just the name, with nothing listed as their preferences. It was super fucking weird. Why would they request me and not say what they wanted?

"He, um, would prefer to tell you himself."

"Are you telling me you're sending me in to see a new client blind?"

She gave me a half-smile and a shrug.

"Kind of."

Remi knew better than this. All the hostesses did. The clients were thoroughly vetted, so I shouldn't be worried about it. I shouldn't... but I was.

"You promise he doesn't want anything weird or stuff I don't do? The client is a he, right?"

She nodded profusely.

"I promise it's totally legit. He doesn't want anything weird, and yes, it's a guy."

I handed her back the tablet after memorising his name. Curiosity got the better of me. While I could refuse a client if I wished, especially a new one, I wasn't in the habit of doing so. After all, this was my job. I got paid to give clients what they wanted.

"Okay. What room?"

"Four... your usual one. Figured that was best."

"Thanks."

I gave her a nod and walked away towards the doors leading to the private rooms. Glancing back before I went through, I noted Remi watching me with a worried look on her face. If she was fucking with me, I'd be pissed.

When I reached room four, I took a deep breath, put a smile on my face, and opened the door. I didn't look around the room as I shut the door behind me.

"Hello, Mr—"

I stopped dead in my tracks as I turned and took in my new client. The last person I expected to see was sitting on the bed with a neutral expression on his face.

What the actual fuck is he doing here?

"Gil? I... oh god, I'm so sorry, I'm in the wrong room, aren't I? Shit, I'm going to kill Remi."

I put my hand over my mouth, wanting to stuff the words right back in.

Jesus fucking Christ, what the hell just came out of your mouth?

Gil blinked slowly, making things ten times worse. I had no idea what he was doing here, if I was in the right place, or what was happening.

"Hello, Theia."

I dropped my hand from my mouth.

"Hi."

He stood up and took a step towards me.

"You're not in the wrong place. I asked Remi not to say anything about who I was."

Considering I'd only met this man twice, and he was Zayn's brother, the fact he'd requested to see me had me trying hard not to let my jaw drop. The last time we'd been in the same space, he couldn't get away from me fast enough. I thought I'd offended him even though I'd merely thanked him for saving me from that handsy guy months ago.

"You're my new client?"

"I guess you could call me that."

Okay, this is completely unexpected and totally left field, but okay. I can do this. I'll find out what he wants and give him what he's paying for. No need to be flustered or completely thrown off by his presence, Theia. No need at all.

Who the fuck was I kidding? I was completely thrown. It didn't help that the more I looked at Gil, the more I wanted to know what was going on inside his head. Plus, the man was absolutely gorgeous. It was seriously unfair how attractive the Villetti brothers were.

I'd met Enzo, the youngest, as Zayn had given him a job at the club. He was the complete opposite of my boss, though. Always flirting with everyone and generally being a bit of a nuisance. It made me wonder why on earth his brother had hired him in the first place.

I'd told myself I shouldn't find my boss or his brothers hot, but it didn't change the facts. They'd been blessed with a good set of genes.

Don't think about that now. You have a job to do.

I stretched my fingers out, taking a deep breath before diving straight in.

"Okay, I'm sure Remi went over my services with you and what I do."

Gil looked slightly alarmed by my statement. I didn't know why.

"Your services?"

"Yes. It's why you're here, right?" I stepped closer to him. "If you want to make yourself comfortable, we can start…"

I waved at the seating area across from the bed. Gil remained rooted to the spot, his dark eyes widening with every word I said. Not wishing to make things any more awkward, I pressed on.

"Okay, well, to start with, I want to make it very clear that I don't allow physical contact between myself and clients. Remi should have told you that, of course, but I always like to reiterate it."

He didn't look like he knew what I was talking about.

Fucking Remi! Why the hell didn't she prepare him? This isn't like her. I'm so going to kill her.

"I'm guessing this is your first time. Maybe we can start with a private dance. Does that sound good to you?"

He merely stared at me.

"No? Not what you're here for? You want the full show?"

"Full show?" he repeated back, with confusion lacing his voice.

"I cater to those interested in voyeurism, so a full show would entail me pleasuring myself for you. You're obviously welcome to do whatever you like during it, other than touch me."

A look of pure fear ran across his features.

"What? No, I don't want… that's not… I really don't want you to do that." He ran a hand through his hair, looking distinctly put out by the whole thing. "I'm not interested in anything sexual with you, Theia. It's not why I'm here." He let out a sigh and looked away. "I just want to talk to you, that's all."

For a moment, I had no idea what the fuck to say as I tried to process what he'd told me. Why the hell was he in his brother's sex club if he didn't want anything sexual? This had to be some kind of fucking joke.

You are a dead woman, Remi. I'm going to have your head for this.

"You just want to… talk?"

He looked at me again.

"Yes."

"This is a joke, right? You and Remi have cooked up some stupid prank to play on me?"

He frowned and took another step toward me.

"No, it's not. You have me confused with Enzo. I don't do pranks."

It was the type of thing I imagined Enzo doing. I would have never imagined his brother would ever do something like this, nor did Remi. She couldn't stand Enzo and his antics.

"Listen, Theia, I'm sorry. I should have stopped you before you started talking about your services and told you what I wanted. That's my fault."

Too fucking right, it's your fault. Jesus, this man is giving me whiplash.

"I want someone to talk to and because of things going on in my life, I need it to be confidential. I know you can't talk about it outside this room."

He was right. None of us talked about our client's personal business. Zayn made us all sign non-disclosure agreements. I wouldn't have said anything to anyone, anyway. I didn't have a lot of friends. The only people I saw were my work colleagues. I kept to myself outside of my job for good reason.

It didn't make this any less weird. Him wanting to talk to me, that was. Surely, he had other people he could speak to as opposed to a sex worker.

He's paying for your time, Theia, so you need to give him what he wants. Don't forget that.

I had to put my big fucking girl boots on. It was strange, but at the end of the day, Gil was a client and if he wanted to talk, we could talk. It was completely out of the ordinary for me, but the fact I didn't have to perform for him made this less awkward. If I was going to be completely honest with myself, the thought of him watching me touch myself aroused me way more than it should. I enjoyed performing for my clients or I wouldn't do this sort of work. I didn't find any of them attractive. But Gil? He was a different matter entirely.

"Okay. If that's what you want, I can do that."

His face cleared of all emotion.

"Are you sure?"

I smiled at him, not wanting to betray my inner thoughts. The ones about how disappointed I was that he didn't want to watch me. They were entirely fucked up.

"Of course, we're all about making sure our clients are happy here."

He rubbed his hand over his shirt and looked around the room. It was time I got on with my job.

"Why don't you come sit next to me over here?"

I moved over to the sofa, sat down, and patted the seat next to me. He stared at my hand like it might physically harm him.

"I'd rather not be that close."

I didn't know whether to be offended or not.

He's a client. Why the fuck are you taking this personally?

I knew why. I was attracted to him, and he didn't want what I'd assumed he would as a paying client. I had to get my act together before I derailed his session further.

"You can sit wherever makes you comfortable, Gil. I can move if you'd like?"

He shook his head.

"No, it's okay. I don't need you to."

He paced away, digging his hands into his pockets. He didn't talk for a long moment. I tried not to fidget while I was waiting for him to start. I rested my hands on the sofa, and then immediately moved them to my lap.

How the fuck do I behave right now?

This was so far out of my comfort zone. I knew what to expect from clients. I came in, did my thing while they got off and then went on my way. There were other scenes I did with my colleagues, all of them centred around voyeurism, but they had to be booked in advance so we could organise everything. Performing was easy for me. His only wanting to talk made me feel like a fish out of water. It had never been something I did. My colleagues could be chatty with their clients, but me? I was strictly business. My past made it difficult for me to form friendships, let alone give someone the "girlfriend experience." My clients knew not to make small talk other than explaining what they wanted me to do for their sessions. It worked for me and them.

"I don't know where to start," Gil said after several minutes had gone by.

"You could tell me about your week?"

He glanced at me, his eyes taking on an assessing look as if he was stripping me bare with them. My skin prickled all over. I rubbed my legs, trying to ward off the feeling. Why the hell was I so affected by him? I shouldn't be attracted to this man… but I was.

"What do you know about my family?"

"Um, well, I know they're like, you know, a mafia family."

I wasn't sure if it was the correct answer or not. It was common knowledge amongst the staff that Zayn and his brothers had been the sons of Gennaro Villetti, the mafia kingpin, who'd died not long ago. I'd never looked up anything further about their family because, in all honesty, it didn't matter to me. I knew Zayn was a good man. He'd given me somewhere safe to work, so whatever his family did wasn't really my business.

"Okay. Good… that's good."

He didn't say anything further, making me wonder why he'd even asked. Gil rubbed his face and dropped his gaze to the floor. He took a breath, seeming to steel himself.

"Zayn gave me our father's empire to run." He met my eyes again. Pain radiated out of him, slamming into me like a ton of bricks. "And I don't want to disappoint him, but I don't know what the hell I'm doing."

SIX

Theia

When Gil turned up in this room to see me, the last thing I'd imagined dealing with was him confessing he had no idea what he was doing when it came to running his now-deceased father's empire. I didn't know exactly how his world worked, but I knew the eldest was expected to take over from the previous boss. So why had Zayn given it to his brother?

"Do you even want to run the mafia?" I asked, wondering if it was the right thing to say or not. Honestly, I didn't know how to respond to his admission or why he was here in the first place. He said it was because he needed someone who could keep his confidence, but surely, he had other people in his life he could talk to about this... didn't he?

Gil cocked his head to the side.

"It's not a question of what I want. It's what he needs me to do for our family, so I have to. That's what it means to be a Villetti. To be part of the *famiglia*. You do what the head of the family asks of you, no matter what. That's what *Papá* taught me. It's the only life I know."

I might not understand why he had to, or his family, but by fuck did I relate to the lack of choice he had in the matter. It reminded me of things best left in the past and made my skin itch. I rubbed my legs again, trying to dispel the sudden chill washing over me. I hated feeling out of control. Hated it so goddamn much.

Don't think about it. Don't do that to yourself. It's in the past, remember? You're safe. You're perfectly safe here. No one can hurt you.

I didn't notice Gil coming closer to me until his body was right in my eyeline. My eyes darted up, meeting his dark ones. He leaned closer to me, looking at my face like there was something wrong with it.

"You've gone pale."

I opened my mouth to say something, but words failed me. The bluntness of his statement coupled with his closeness had me trying to catch my breath. I didn't know what it was about this man, but I was definitely not immune to him by any stretch of the imagination. In fact, the urge to slide onto the floor and kneel at his feet was gnawing at me in the most disconcerting way. My hands wanted to reach out and touch him. To know what he looked like underneath his well-tailored clothes.

What the actual fuck?

I'd never felt that way about another person before. And it had certainly dispelled my past from my brain. How the fuck could I think about that when Gil was standing a foot away from me, staring at me like I was a puzzle he couldn't figure out? I mean, of course, I'd been attracted to people before, but this visceral reaction I had to him was confounding me.

"Theia?"

"I… I'm fine," I choked out, not wanting to concern him any more than I already was.

"You don't look fine. Do you want me to get you some water? Is there any in the room?"

He straightened and looked around. I wasn't sure what to say or if I should stop him. He strode off a moment later towards the bedside table that doubled up as a small fridge with water bottles and other drinks inside it. I watched him extract a bottle and bring it back over to me, opening the cap as he went. He shoved it in my face, forcing me to take it. The slight brush of his fingertips had me swallowing as my skin lit up with the feel of him.

"Drink."

I did as I was told, clutching the bottle to my chest after I'd taken a large gulp. He probably thought I was a complete idiot now. This was the worst session I'd ever had with a client. Even the first time I'd done this was nothing compared to what was happening right now. At least then I knew what to expect. I understood the assignment. Right now, I had no fucking clue what to do, say, or how to act. Gil had well and truly thrown me right off course. What was even worse was the fact he was still watching me with no emotion on his face.

What is with this man?

"Better?" he asked when I didn't say a word.

I dipped my head in agreement, still holding the bottle like it would save me from him. Gil wasn't a physical threat to me. His presence was dangerous to my composure. And that was possibly worse.

"Do you want to talk about it?"

My mind couldn't compute what he'd asked for a second because it was ridiculous, him catering to me when he was paying for my time. I stood up, shoving the bottle at him. Gil looked a little startled but took it and screwed the cap back on.

"No. I should apologise for my behaviour. This session is for you, not me, and I'm not giving you what you need."

He frowned. This man was actually impossible to read. No wonder I was so all over the place when he gave nothing away.

"Theia."

Damn it, why does my name sound so good on his tongue?

I shouldn't have even told him my real name, but I never imagined he'd want to see me at work like this.

"Yes?"

"You're not doing anything wrong. I should apologise for springing this on you. It wasn't my intention to make you uncomfortable."

Now I felt worse. He wasn't making me uncomfortable, he was throwing me off-kilter, and it wasn't his fault. It was mine. I was the one having an inappropriate reaction to him.

"You're not."

"No?"

I shook my head and looked at my hands.

"No, I'm honestly a little… thrown by this is all. I don't get clients wanting to just talk to me, you know."

He nodded slowly as if he got what I was saying.

"I should've let Remi tell you it was me and what I wanted instead of springing it on you. That wasn't fair of me. I didn't think… I just… I need not to be in my own head."

He looked a little powerless as if the weight of the world was on his shoulders and he had no clue how to handle it. It tugged at my heartstrings. Life had clearly dealt him a rough hand the way it had me. It made me want to do something to make things easier for him.

"Then let me make it better," I murmured, staring up into his brown eyes that were so full of helplessness it made my bottom lip tremble from the intensity of his gaze.

I stepped closer to him. He flinched but didn't tell me to move away.

"Come sit with me and you can tell me what happened to make you feel so out of control, okay?"

He inclined his head, even though he looked a little scared by my suggestion. I went to sit back down and patted the fabric next to me. It took him a second to take a seat, leaving a large space between us. Getting him to sit made me feel like I'd made some semblance of progress in bringing this back on track.

Gil stared down at his hands resting in his lap. His shoulders were tense as if this whole thing made him incredibly uncomfortable. I imagined talking to a relative stranger wasn't easy, even if he'd sought me out.

"When you saw me coming out of Zayn's office… that's when he told me he needed me to take over from our father. I had to get our… my men in order. And it didn't go the way I planned. It's not normal for the second son to run things. It should be the eldest, so no one is happy about it, our cousins especially. We saw them this evening, and that went to shit too. But Zayn still has all this faith in me, and I don't understand it. I didn't have enough time to learn how to be a leader from our father before he died. I have these huge shoes to fill, and I don't know if I can."

He sighed and rubbed his hands on his thighs.

"Telling you this isn't easy for me. I never talk about how I feel. I couldn't. *Papá* would have seen it as a weakness. I can't afford to look weak to anyone, Theia. I have to show I'm strong or I'll leave myself and my family open to attack. So that's why I'm here… my head is all messed up over this and I don't want to feel right now."

Gil raised his head and met my eyes.

"Have you ever not wanted to feel?"

I almost snorted.

"Every day."

"How do you deal with that?"

I licked my lip, a movement he followed with his eyes before I swallowed.

"I do this." I waved around the room. "It's my escape from the world."

I don't know why I admitted that. It wasn't like I was going to explain my past to him. No one knew the truth about it. I didn't trust anyone enough. They might look at me differently knowing I'd been taken when I was twenty and abused so thoroughly for two years, I didn't know who I was any longer. I was still trying to work it out now, despite the fact it'd been four years since I'd escaped.

Gil cocked his head to the side as if curious by my statement but didn't ask me to elaborate. Something I was thankful for.

"And it helps?"

I smiled.

"Yeah. I like my job too. I wouldn't do it otherwise. Your brother has made this a safe space for all of us."

His lip twitched slightly.

"He told me why he opened the club, so I'm happy to hear you feel safe here. That's what he wants."

A lot of people in this world looked down on sex workers, but Gil didn't seem to be remotely fazed by my work. It made me relax slightly. I'd been on edge since I'd walked into the room. I didn't think he judged me for it, considering he was here to talk to me, but you never knew what people's personal opinions were.

"I take it Zayn doesn't know you're here."

"No."

"Well, your secret is safe with me… and as for the whole 'not wanting to feel' thing. I don't really have any advice other than to find something that takes your mind off things." I looked down at my hands. "I hope I've managed to do that for you."

He didn't respond for a long while. When I looked at him, Gil was frowning. For a man who wasn't particularly expressive - at least, I hadn't known him to be in the time I'd been around him - it felt odd to see his face contorted in such a way.

"Would it be too much to ask to see you again like this?"

I had not been expecting him to ask to see me again. This whole fucking session had been a disaster as far as I was concerned, but maybe I had given Gil what he needed. It was paying work even if it wasn't what I usually did.

"I'd be okay with that."

There was a flicker of hope in his eyes at my acceptance. It made my heart beat a little faster.

"Thank you."

"You're very welcome."

He stood up before rubbing the back of his neck. Gil was ready to leave, which was okay with me. I didn't know if I could keep calm for much longer, anyway. He'd shown me a vulnerable side to him I'm not sure anyone had ever got to see before. In sex work, you got to see a lot of people's vulnerabilities, but this wasn't the same thing. A man I didn't know had trusted me with his fears about his new role. It was a big fucking deal to me. I wasn't sure how I felt about it. Not when he made me flustered in a way I hadn't been in a long time.

"I'll see you soon, I guess."

Gil stared at me for a minute. My skin prickled. He turned around and walked out of the room. I sat there, wondering what the fuck I'd agreed to. I said it was okay for us to see each other again like this. Was that even a good idea?

Probably not, but you can't take it back now.

I sighed and rubbed my hands over my face. It was time to go find Remi and give her a piece of my fucking mind. She and Gil had ambushed me. She could have told me it was our boss's brother.

Standing up, I walked over to the door and ripped it open, intending to find her, but much to my surprise, she was right outside with an apologetic look on her face.

"You have some explaining to do."

"I know."

"And you owe me for this, big time."

Remi nodded, her green eyes intent on mine. I linked my arm with hers and dragged her down the hallway back to the club so we could go to the staff room. We were going to have a little talk about this shit, because there was no way in hell I was letting her get away with what she'd just pulled. No way at all.

SEVEN

Gilberto

Edric and I stared down at the mutilated body left just inside the building. I arrived a few minutes ago to speak to Salvatore about the potential *capodecina* candidates when Edric intercepted me with a grim look on his face. He hadn't said much as he led me over to the side door near the back of the old factory that served as our headquarters.

"Do we know who this is?" I asked when he didn't volunteer anything.

"I haven't looked that close."

Stifling the urge to roll my eyes, I squatted down to get a better look. I'd seen worse done to a person. Hell, I'd done worse, but I didn't like to think about the things I was capable of. Some things were better left in the past. It included everyone I'd killed in my father's name.

His hair was matted with blood and half of his head had been caved in. There was bruising around his eyes and all along his bare torso. Cuts had been made to his chest, and his nails had been torn from his fingers. It was clear he'd been tortured before he died.

"I don't think this is one of ours, unless you recognise him."

Edric came closer, flinching at the gruesome sight.

"No, and I know everyone, so unless he's a brand new recruit, fuck knows where he came from."

I glanced up at my second. Edric was trying to find his feet in his new role, just as I was. The past week hadn't been easy on either of us with trying to keep the men in line. And now there was this.

"Get Sal. Maybe he knows something we don't."

Edric looked relieved to be getting away from the dead man. I shook my head and rose back to my feet as he jogged away to get my *capodecina*. He could be a tad squeamish, but he would have to get over it. I'd seen enough violence and death to last a lifetime. None of it fazed me. Edric hadn't been involved in that side of my father's mafia interests. He would have to learn if he was to survive this with me.

There was something that had confounded me, though. It was the fact I could not stop thinking about *her*. I hadn't suddenly found myself attracted to Theia or anything. I merely wanted to know her. To see what drove her as a person. To understand her. And I had honestly never wanted that in my life. People tended to seek me out and wanted to get to know me, not the other way around. I didn't understand my intrigue. It wasn't like me to find another person strangely... fascinating.

It was also disconcerting knowing I had revealed far too much to a woman I barely knew. I didn't think Theia wouldn't keep my secrets, but it was the first time I'd even admitted my fears out loud. Well, there was one I'd held back on… the fact I didn't know who the fuck I was without Gennaro. Didn't want her to think I was completely incapable of performing my new role. I had to pretend I knew exactly how to handle everything. I sure as fuck didn't know what to do about this situation with a dead body turning up on my doorstep.

My eyes darted around the space by the side door. It wasn't covered by cameras. No doubt how they slipped it in here without anyone noticing. I'd get them to check the outside footage to see if it caught anything. Then I'd up security. If this was the beginning of our problems, I wanted to get ahead of it.

Edric returned with Salvatore five minutes later. Both of their mouths were turned down. Edric kept his distance from the body while Salvatore walked right up to it. He looked over at the man for a minute, then turned to me.

"This is one of your cousin Dino's men."

What the fuck?

"Are you sure about that?"

Sal nodded, his eyes turning dark before he stuck his hands in his pockets.

"I know most of them by face if not name."

I hadn't talked to my cousins since the dinner at their house. Neither had Zayn, not that he'd been asking me for updates or anything, but we'd spoken yesterday.

This did not bode well. Dead bodies turning up was a bad omen. It being one of Dino's men made it infinitely worse.

"Find out his name, then get rid of him. I don't care how, just get the body as far away from us as possible. You two will deal with this personally. This stays between the three of us. No one else gets involved. Is that understood?"

Sal's expression didn't change.

"Yes, boss."

I glanced at Edric, who gave me a nod. If my cousin found out one of his men had been dumped at my headquarters, there would be hell to pay. Given Dino was already pissed at me and Zayn, there was no way I wanted to bring another shitstorm from him down on us either.

"Good. Get it done."

I turned and walked away. Edric caught up with me as I strode towards the security room.

"Gil."

"What? And make it quick. You have a body to deal with."

"This isn't good."

"I know that."

I shoved open the door to the security room and turfed out the man inside. Taking a seat at the desk, I set about bringing up the footage from last night.

"Close the fucking door, Edric," I barked when I noticed he was standing in the doorway.

I heard him close it and come closer.

"What happened when you saw Dino and Gian?"

I hadn't told him about the dinner. I'd come in the next day, gathered everyone together and calmly told my men if they were to step out of line, I'd put a bullet in their heads personally. They all knew about Matteo by now, so it didn't come as a surprise when none of them pressed the subject. I didn't have time for dissent amongst the ranks.

"They aren't happy Zayn made me boss, so I told them they were sad old men playing a young man's game and walked out."

Edric snorted.

"You actually said that to them?"

"Yes."

He burst out laughing and slapped the desk.

"I wish I could have seen their faces. I bet they were raging."

"Mmm."

I hadn't stopped to look, knowing they would have been seriously unimpressed by my words. I'd been too busy freaking out over the whole thing. Edric didn't need to know I felt incapable of doing this. No one except Theia could know.

"Do you think he has anything to do with this? Dino, I mean," Edric asked after he'd settled down.

They wouldn't kill one of their own and dump them here to start trouble. Dino was more fucking sensible than that. At least, I hoped he was.

"I don't know. The only thing I do know is this is a problem we need to stay far away from. Go help Sal, Edric. We'll talk after."

He remained where he was for a moment as I searched through the security footage from outside.

"Are you sure you don't care where we take the body?"

"I need it not to be linked back to us, okay? We had nothing to do with it, and I don't want this to set off a war between me and Dino."

"Okay. I'll deal with it."

He didn't say anything further as he left me to continue looking for any clues, shutting the door behind him. I stared at the screen, skipping through the tape to see if anything happened. It was about three in the morning when people appeared in the shot. I let it play out, watching as they brought the body to the side door. One of the men had picked the lock. They took the body in, shut the door, and left. I watched it twice more for good measure. It explained how they'd got in, but they were all in black and wearing masks, so I had no idea who the fuck they were. Not to mention it was dark. We didn't have lights around that side of the building.

Sitting back, I rubbed my face in frustration. This was shit. I didn't have time to wallow in it, though. I made a copy of the footage before doctoring it. No one else needed to find out about this. It wasn't the first time I'd had to cover up dead bodies and erase the evidence. However, it was my first time as a leader. I'd been doing this job for a week and things were already fucked.

Stuffing the memory stick I'd put the footage on into my pocket, I walked out to speak to the security guy and get him to have the men install more external lights on the sides of the building along with cameras directed at all the side doors. He didn't question it, but I could see he was surprised by my request. I wasn't going to take any chances with this. If one body had turned up here, who was to say another wouldn't.

I went up to my office, shut the door and walked over to the safe where I deposited the memory stick. Taking a seat behind my desk, I tipped my head back as my eyes went to the ceiling.

"What the fuck is my life coming to?" I muttered and rubbed my temples with my fingers, feeling a headache building behind them.

I'd have to take the memory stick home with me. It was safer there than here. In fact, anything related to this incident was safer away from the building. We didn't know who was behind this or why. It didn't make any sense to me.

Why would anyone want to sow discord between me and my cousins? Did they know there was already an issue? How could they? Only me, Gian, Dino, and Zayn had been in the room when we told them about the new arrangement.

I wasn't going to call my brother and tell him about this. He'd expect me to deal with it. This was my house now. I was the boss, even if I didn't feel much like one.

She appeared in my thoughts again. I shook myself, rubbing my head harder to dissipate the memory of her telling me to let her make it better. Being in Theia's presence made me feel calmer. I wanted to be near her. To be her friend.

Dropping my hands, I reached into my pocket and dug out my phone. I sent a text before I could think too hard about what I was doing. A few minutes later, I had a response. It made me smile despite myself. This was a bad fucking idea. All of it was, but I couldn't bring myself to care. For once in my life, I was following my desires rather than allowing someone else to dictate everything.

He's gone. You don't have to be the man he tried to mould you into if you don't want to. You can be your own person.

I didn't know how to be me when I was unsure of who I was inside. Maybe she could help me with it. Something drew me to her as if a part of me recognised a fellow lost soul. I wanted to tug on that thread. Unravel it. Dissect it. Learn all the secrets hiding underneath. And maybe talking about my life would help me in return.

I needed to find out who Gilberto Villetti really was. No doubt it was the only way I'd survive this. I could feel something brewing. A cold sense of dread wormed its way underneath my skin. This body turning up was only the beginning. Zayn's takeover and the subsequent death of our father had consequences no one could predict. I was unsure which ones would come knocking at my door. Unless I could get a handle on this quickly, we'd all be going down together. And I couldn't afford to allow that to happen under any circumstances.

It was time to do some digging, find out who the fuck had the audacity to drop the dead body of one of my cousin's men at my doorstep, and stop them from ruining everything.

EIGHT

Theia

My head was stuck in my locker as I'd just got into work when I heard a voice calling my name. I pulled back and looked over at Gael, who was standing a few feet away. His wavy auburn hair was swept back into a bun and his blue eyes were shining as he smiled at me.

"Hey, you okay?"

He gave me a quick nod before coming closer.

"This was left for you."

I took the envelope he offered to me, trying not to frown at it. My stage name was on the front in swirly handwriting along with the address of Desecration.

"Who gave it to you?"

"Morgan."

Morgan was one of the security men who kept clients in order. He was a big fucker with a tattooed scalp who intimidated everyone who didn't know him. In reality, Morgan was the kindest soul I'd ever met, and never got violent. He merely kept the peace.

"Oh." I stuffed the envelope in my locker, not wanting to open it in front of Gael. "Did you see that client has requested another foursome scene? The same one as the last time."

"Uh-huh. You ready for it?"

It was scheduled for the weekend. The client had been very specific in their requests last time we performed for them a few months ago. It was one of those cases where we never saw who was watching us, but it never bothered me and the boys. It was our job to cater to their desires. To create the perfect scene for their pleasure.

"As I'll ever be."

He nudged my shoulder before planting a kiss on my forehead.

"You were magnificent. Will and Cas said as much."

I snorted. Gael, Will, and Cas, better known by their stage names Lynx, Aries, and Pegasus, were the only three men in the club I engaged in scenes with. We trusted each other implicitly. I got on with almost everyone who worked here, but it didn't mean I was okay with engaging in sexual acts with them. We all had our boundaries.

"I'm sure, especially Cas. He got to call me a dirty little whore, suits his degradation kink down to a tee."

Gael laughed.

"Don't start pretending you didn't like it too."

I batted his arm before turning away to pull tonight's outfit out of my locker so I could change. Having checked my client list, I decided on something a little more demure than my usual short skirt, tight top, and skimpy underwear. No doubt it was

Remi who slipped the name 'Jordan Brown' onto the list. That was Gil. I was equal parts nervous and excited about seeing him.

"I'm admitting nothing."

"Yeah, okay, Theia. You keep telling yourself it isn't one of your proclivities. I'll just be over here knowing the truth."

As Gael retreated to his locker, I threw one of my high heels at his head. It missed, making me curse. He grinned at me from over his shoulder. The little shit was always giving me a hard time. He knew me far too well. Both Gael and I had been through some incredibly difficult shit in our past. I never talked about mine, but he'd opened up to me about his own. Most of the sex workers here had had a bad time of it. It was the thing that bound us all together. We knew what it was like to hit rock bottom and have to dig ourselves back out of it.

I changed into my chosen outfit of a little black dress with a matching black underwear set, before slipping on my heels after Gael tossed me the one I'd thrown at him. He left with a wink after he'd changed, and I was alone in the staff changing room.

Taking out the envelope he'd given me from my locker, I sat on the bench and opened it with trembling fingers. I set it out on my lap and stared down at the small keyring charm that was in the envelope. Dread and horror settled into my stomach. It should be innocuous, but to me, it wasn't. No, the charm signified the worst experiences of my life. It was a raven. It brought back images of the room I'd been held in for two years with the raven painted above the door. A symbol I'd seen plastered all over the fucking building.

Who the fuck sent me this?

I pushed the charm back into the envelope and took a deep breath. I stood up and stuffed it into the back of my locker before slamming the door shut. There was no time to think about it. I had to get to work. It would make me forget about it and keep me from falling apart until I got home.

You can do this. You're safe here, don't forget that. You're fucking safe, Theia.

No one could get me in Desecration. No one.

I strode out of the staff room. There was no need to freak out. It was merely a stupid charm. It didn't mean anything.

It means everything and you know it.

Instead of allowing my fears to get the better of me, I dived into work and before I knew it, I'd seen three clients and now I was sitting in room four awaiting my fourth one. The one I was most nervous about. I'd told him it was okay for him to have more sessions with me, but it'd been a week since I'd seen him. I thought perhaps he'd changed his mind.

The moment he entered the room, my breath got caught in my throat. Did Gil know what kind of effect he had on people? Probably not. He appeared completely oblivious to my admiration, not that I'd tried to make it obvious or anything.

Today he was in a black shirt and dark chinos with smart black boots. His hair was wind-ruffled, and his dark eyes roamed across me with no emotion in them.

"Hello, Theia."

I bit my lip before smoothing the skirt of my dress over my thighs.

"Hi."

He looked back at the door before moving closer.

"Should I call you Pisces? I should have asked last time."

I smiled and shook my head.

"No, it's okay. Please call me Theia."

If it had been anyone else, I would have insisted he use my stage name, but the thought of not hearing him say Theia in that deep voice of his made me feel sad. I wanted to hear him whisper it in my ear over and over because I was clearly fucking insane when it came to Gil Villetti. I was making concessions I never normally would for someone I didn't know very well.

He dug his hands into his pockets. It shouldn't be sexy, but his sleeves were rolled up and I could see all the corded muscles of his forearms.

Dear fuck, I'm so screwed.

"Okay."

He came a little closer to me. I tried not to fiddle with my clothes, wary of how I came across to him.

"I wasn't sure I would see you again," I admitted when he didn't say anything.

He gave me a shrug.

"I wasn't sure either."

I couldn't help my smile. The fact he had come to see me made me irrationally happy. I could watch him and not feel guilty about it. We'd be talking, so I had the perfect excuse. It's what I told myself, anyway. It was okay for me to admire him from afar.

"Have you been okay?"

Gil moved over towards the bed and stared down at it. I was sitting across from it on the sofa.

"Not particularly."

"Is it the same thing or did something happen?"

"Something's always happening in the mafia, but yes, things have gone from bad to worse."

I didn't know if I should ask him what had occurred or not. He was very blunt about his feelings last time, but today felt different. I couldn't put my finger on why.

He turned his head and looked me right in the eyes. I swallowed hard at his gaze. It was stripping me of my defences all over again. Like he had some strange power over me. My heart pounded in my chest and the sound of it rang in my ears.

"Can I ask you something?"

"If you'd like…"

He walked up to me, keeping his eyes pinned to mine. I fought against the urge to rear back and press myself against the sofa. It wasn't fear, but the knowledge Gil was deadly. I'd seen him stab a man in the hand without a second thought. He would do it again.

I'd noticed last time he was here that he was constantly checking his surroundings as if alert to any threat and poised to strike if one presented itself. Even as he stared at me now, I could feel his attention was on the door too, making sure the room was still secure.

"Do you ever wish time would stand still for one minute so you could just breathe? I feel like I never get the chance to breathe."

"You can do that now if you want."

If I answered his question with the truth, it would open me up to old wounds and long-buried memories. A past where all I wanted to do every day was breathe fresh air and yearned for freedom.

He didn't respond to my statement. I rubbed the sofa with my fingers, feeling the leather under the tips, and wondered why I wanted to spill my guts to him despite all of my fears.

"Yeah, I have felt that way," I finally said in a barely audible voice.

He nodded slowly.

"I think someone is trying to stir up trouble between me and my cousins."

The sudden change of subject had me struggling with my composure. Gil's mere presence gave me a riot of feelings, ones I couldn't keep up with.

"Oh?"

He paced away, tearing a hand from his pocket and rubbing his stubbled chin with it.

"If I tell you exactly what happened, it would be including you in something illegal and dangerous, so I'm not going to do that. I don't want to put you at risk."

He turned to me again.

"I don't know if I made the right decision today." He put a hand on his chest. "It was my call. I had to make it as the boss, but I keep going over in my mind what I could have done better. If I handled it right. And I can't ask my father what to do any longer." He sighed and dropped his hand to his side. "Not that he thought anything I did was ever good enough. Not one of us was good enough for him."

"You mean you and your brothers?"

He opened his mouth and closed it again before looking away.

"And my mother... she wasn't either."

I didn't know a single thing about their mother. No one ever talked about her.

Do I ask? Does he want to talk about her?

"But that's not the point," he continued, "I have all this responsibility and no fucking clue if I'm making things better or worse."

A part of me felt relieved I hadn't been given the chance to press the subject, but the other sensed Gil had deep-seated wounds courtesy of his father. And they involved his mother too. It was something I would have to keep in mind and ask him about at a later date. Maybe it was wishful thinking on my part that I might get to understand what was going on underneath his hardened exterior. He might be admitting his fears to me, but it didn't mean I really knew what made him tick.

I wanted to distract him from his warring thoughts. To make it better for him. And the only way I knew how to do that was by using my body. But the way I wanted to use it with him was not how I did things here. I would be on my knees for him with his fist buried in my hair as he watched me with those cold, expressionless eyes of his and told me to suck his cock with my dirty little slut mouth.

I hate Gael for being right about my kinks. Now all I can think about is Gil degrading me with that deep voice of his.

I shouldn't want that. Not with a man who was my client, even if he merely wanted to talk. I had strict boundaries with clients for good reason. Here I was wanting to throw those out the window, all because I was attracted to him in the worst way. And it was so completely and utterly fucked up.

NINE

Gilberto

The way Theia was staring at me with a slight blush on her face had me wondering what on earth was going through her head. When I'd caught her expression, it unsettled me, and I had no idea why. I'd been busy stewing over the fact I'd almost told her the truth about Gennaro. Then I'd looked up, and the world stopped. My brain fucking stopped because of *her*. This woman I'd sought out for a second time purely because I wanted to see her. And it completely baffled me why she had this effect on me.

"Theia."

She blinked, then shook herself before her eyes met mine.

"Sorry, I was listening, I swear."

I stepped closer, no longer having the desire to talk about my own shit. The emotional upheaval of it was making me itch all over. I didn't want to delve into my feelings toward my father. No, I wanted to know things about Theia and why she got this faraway look in her eyes sometimes.

"Remi never told me exactly what you do here. I didn't ask her, but you talked about your services."

Her hands rubbed over the sofa as her expression turned wary.

"I did."

"Would you tell me what they are?"

I wasn't going to ask her to do anything, but I was curious about what she provided for clients. She talked about voyeurism, something I'd never really understood. Then again, I didn't think I truly understood sexual attraction. Well, on a theoretical level I did, and I had experienced it once, but nothing ever came of it.

Her blue-grey eyes widened before her hand went to her chest, rubbing the bare skin showing above her dress.

"I can show you if that's what you want."

"Yes… please."

She frowned before she stood up and walked over to the bedside table where a tablet rested. Picking it up, she flicked through it before she extended her arm out, offering it to me. I ate up the space between us, coming to a standstill right in front of her, and took it. My eyes didn't immediately drop to look at the screen. They remained on hers. Theia chewed on her bottom lip.

"Do you enjoy it?" I asked.

"What?"

My eyes darted down to the screen, reading through the list.

"Being watched."

All of her services involved her performing for other people with strictly no touching. There were various solo sexual acts she'd engage in for a client's viewing pleasure, like masturbation and the use of toys. Then there were scenes she did with others, including tailored experiences to the client's particular tastes.

"Yes," she said, her voice coming out breathy as if the thought of being seen was something she desired above all else. I tucked that piece of information away to examine later.

"Is it not just a performance for you?"

Theia scrunched her face up and looked away.

"It is, and it isn't."

"In what way?"

Her hands rubbed at her dress, and she turned her face towards me again. A dark look fell over it.

"Why are you asking me this? Do you want to know if I fake it for clients? That going to make your decision of what service you want easier or something?"

Her words sounded pained and angry as if she was offended by my questions. Did she think I was judging her line of work? I didn't have anything other than respect for what she did. I was merely curious about what drove her, what she enjoyed and why she chose to do this.

"No, I told you I'm not interested in that."

She crossed her arms over her chest.

"You sure about that? You said you wanted to talk to me, but I don't remember it including asking me invasive questions about myself."

Well, shit, I think I've upset her.

How could I make this better? I didn't want to hurt her or make her angry, but what if I kept saying the wrong thing? This was exactly why I didn't make friends with people. They always took the things I said the wrong way and misconstrued my intentions. I didn't know how to handle it. It was easier not to talk. No one would misunderstand me if I stayed silent.

I couldn't take that way out here. Not if I wanted to learn more about her. Maybe if I was honest about my intentions, she would see I wasn't trying to be insensitive.

"I want to know you."

Incredulity crossed her features, making me take a small step back.

"To know me? Why on earth would you want that? I'm a sex worker, Gil. I get paid to fuck. That's all anyone ever wants from me."

Why on earth would people only want that from her? She was a person. Her work didn't define her. Not in my eyes.

"I don't want to have sex with you, Theia. I'm not attracted to you like that."

She threw her hands up. Her eyes became ever more pained as if I'd hit a nerve.

"Oh well, thanks, that makes me feel so much better about myself."

I put a hand out to her, realising what I'd said had come out the wrong way. It wasn't my intention to come across as insulting. She was a beautiful woman. Me not being sexually attracted to her didn't take away from that fact. It didn't work like that for me.

"No, that's not what I meant…" I took a breath and steeled myself. "Theia, I'm demi."

She blinked, her expression turning confused.

"Demi?"

"Demisexual."

I'd known since I was a teenager I was different, but it was only more recently I'd found a word to describe it.

"I don't experience sexual attraction without having an emotional connection with someone. I never have."

Theia took several steps back until she bumped into the wall behind her. Her hands went to it as if she needed to steady herself.

"Oh… I didn't… that's… oh… oh!"

"I really do just want to talk to you. The fact you're a sex worker doesn't change anything for me. I respect what you do."

Her eyes went to the floor and her face clouded over as if the realisation I genuinely wanted to know her without sex being involved was an odd concept for her to wrap her head around. She let out a sigh and rubbed her face before pushing off the wall.

"I feel kind of stupid I accused you of all that shit. I'm so sorry."

"There's no need to be sorry. You didn't know. I've never told anyone."

Her eyes darted up to mine.

"You haven't?"

I shook my head.

"As if I was going to admit to my very traditional father who raised me in his image, I don't feel sexual attraction the way he thinks we're all supposed to."

Theia smiled and gave me a small shrug.

"I suppose he wouldn't have approved."

"No, it would have only made him even more disappointed in me."

Her expression turned sad.

"He was disappointed in you?"

I rubbed my chest, a sudden pain overtaking it with the memories of the way he spoke to me. How he made me feel small and like I could do nothing right. How he'd complain about Zayn's insolence and how he hoped I never turned out like my brothers. I'd tried so hard to make him proud of me, but he never was. Gennaro was a monster, like Zayn had said. He was nothing but cruel to everyone around him. And he'd tried to make me as cruel as he was. He told me it was the only way to be a leader. The only way a Villetti stayed on top. I wasn't sure I believed that any longer… or if I ever had.

"I don't think I ever made him proud."

She released a breath and looked as though she wanted to reach out to me, but she didn't.

"I know how that feels."

"You do?"

"I'm estranged from my parents. They treated me like shit, so I moved to London when I was eighteen to get away from them."

The idea of anyone treating Theia like crap, let alone her parents, was abhorrent to me. My mother had been nothing other than a doting parent, a complete contrast to my father, but I understood the pain of parental disappointment and being treated as though you were nothing.

"That can't have been easy."

She gave me a sad smile.

"No, but I've never known life to be anything but difficult."

I handed her back the tablet. She placed it on the bedside table and let out a sigh.

"I feel like I've been fucking this up ever since I met you," she said after a moment. "So you genuinely just want to talk to me?"

"Yes."

She shook her head.

"Okay."

Stepping closer to me, she bit her lip and rubbed her fingers together at her side.

"Can I ask you something?"

I dipped my chin as if to say "yes."

"You said you respect what I do... did you mean that?"

"Why wouldn't I?"

"A lot of people look down on sex workers. And it makes it impossible to have relationships, not that I even want one, but they get all hung up on the 'sex with other people' business, you know."

People and their judgemental attitudes were something I knew all too well. My father judged everyone and deemed most people unworthy of his attention. Zayn told me how *Papá* felt about Ari. I didn't understand it myself. Her upbringing didn't make her any less "worthy" of Zayn. She clearly loved my brother without reservation. If she was who he wanted to be with, who was anyone else to tell him otherwise?

"It's your job and your choice. It's not the same, anyway, is it? Like sex at work and sex with a partner."

"It's not. At least, no one I've had that conversation with says it's the same. I wouldn't know, though. Every time I tried to have a relationship, it failed. I decided I was happier alone."

She moved away from me, walking towards the sofa, and taking a seat.

"One guy I work with has a girlfriend. They have very strict boundaries and open communication. I wish more people were that understanding."

I made my way over to the sofa and sat down on the other end. She pulled her dress down her legs as if self-conscious about how short it was. It didn't make a difference to me what she wore. It was her mind that had my attention.

"You don't have to answer this if you don't want to, but have you ever… you know?"

Her cheeks went a faint pink at her question.

"Yes."

"Was it with someone you actually felt attracted to?"

I shook my head. I'd never slept with anyone I felt attracted to, having only ever experienced sexual attraction once with someone I had a bond with when I was a teen. However, I'd never told her how I felt, as I was afraid of ruining our friendship. Didn't matter, anyway. She met someone and it put an end to anything else.

"Attraction, desire, and arousal are separate things, so it's not as if I can't have sex with someone I'm not attracted to… I don't want to. Not any more."

Theia cocked her head to the side.

"Any more?"

I looked at the floor.

"It was easier to convince my father I was normal if I…"

I didn't finish the sentence. I didn't have to because she looked horrified at the suggestion I engaged in sexual activities to prove to my father I was the man he wanted me to be. He was gone. I didn't have to force myself into situations I didn't want to be in. At least not that way. The mafia life wasn't something I could escape from.

"I'm not going to lie. The more I hear about your dad, the more I think he was a shit parent and a bit of a dick."

Rationally, I knew Gennaro hadn't been a good father to me, Zayn, or Enzo, but he was the only one I'd ever known. The only person I'd ever tried to please. And now I was repeating the same fucking cycle with my older brother, trying to please him too. It was why I was even here in the first place, talking to Theia and wanting to know her. I wanted to escape my life and all its expectations… especially the ones I'd placed upon myself.

"We don't have to talk about him, you know. Not if you don't want to. I'm guessing he's a difficult subject for you," she said when I didn't respond to her statement.

I put my hand to my jaw, running my fingers along it before I let out a long breath.

"He is."

My eyes were drawn to my watch. Our time together had gone on longer than I realised.

"Do you need to go?"

I looked over at Theia, who was staring at my watch.

"I think so."

She smiled and stood up, smoothing her dress down.

"Then I guess I'll see you next time… whenever that is."

I didn't move for a long moment, merely watched her fidget under my gaze. Leaving made me feel things I didn't want to think about. Theia gave me a small pocket of peace away from my chaotic life. I knew the moment I left, anxiety would plague me, and I'd be sucked back into the fucked up world I inhabited where people lived and died by my decisions.

Standing up, I shoved all of my emotions back into their locked box and nodded at Theia. She watched me leave. I could feel her eyes on my back. The last thought I had before I disappeared from Desecration into the night was that I couldn't wait a whole week to see her again. And that was the most perplexing part of all.

TEN

Theia

My mind was a riot of so many emotions that by the time I got out of work, my head was spinning, and I had no idea what to do with myself.

As most of us lived in the same building, one owned by Zayn, who gave us reduced rent as we worked at the club, we tended to walk home together since it wasn't far from Desecration. I caught up with Remi, who was at the head of the pack, and linked my arm with hers. She looked up at me with a frown. Remi mostly kept to herself outside of work, never wanting to attend the parties we sometimes held around each other's flats. She was friendly with everyone, but I sensed she had a hard time opening up to anyone who wasn't Zayn.

"You okay, Theia?" she asked when we were within a few feet of the building, and she tried to pull away.

"Do you fancy an after-work drink at mine?"

Remi raised her eyebrows as she dug into her pocket for her key fob.

"Um… why?"

I'd never invited her to mine before, but honestly, I was so fucked up over what happened this evening. I didn't know who else to turn to.

"I need someone to talk to and you're the only one who knows about… *him*."

For a moment, Remi merely stared at me. Then she pulled away and put her fob on the sensor. The door buzzed to let us know it was open. I grabbed a hold of it and tugged the door open, waving at her to go first. The others weren't far behind us, so I waited for them, watching my colleagues pour into the building. I walked in and let the door shut behind me. Remi was waiting by the lifts, fiddling with her coat sleeves, when I arrived next to her.

"By him, you're talking about *Jordan*?"

"Yes."

Remi looked up at the ceiling as the lift doors opened. She shook her head and moved inside. I followed her, standing at the back after I'd pushed the button for my floor.

"Okay, but you have to promise you're not about to grill me about what I know."

"I promise."

I hadn't planned on asking Remi what she knew about the Villetti brothers. No one else knew Gil was my client, although I used that term loosely since he wasn't interested in my services as a sex worker. I couldn't talk to Gael, Cas, or Will about the situation, even though I was the closest to them out of anyone. Remi was the only one who knew the truth. It made it safer to discuss the situation I was in with Gil.

When we got to my flat, I unlocked the door and walked in before kicking off my shoes and hanging up my coat and bag. The post was sitting on the mat, which Remi stepped over before shutting the door. I picked it up and took it into my open-plan living area, dumping the letters on the kitchen island. Most of the flats had a similar layout. An open-plan kitchen/living area just off the lobby, a bathroom, and a bedroom. Some of the flats were two or three beds, but I had a one-bed place.

"What would you like?" I opened the fridge and peered inside. "I have beer, white wine… or I could mix you a gin and tonic."

"You drink beer?"

I tugged two cans of beer out of the fridge and set them on the counter before closing the door and turning to her.

"They're grapefruit beers. Radlers."

Remi stood in the doorway, looking a little awkward as she took in my flat. I picked up a can and held it out to her. She came closer, taking it from me and looking over the label.

"Thanks."

I picked up my own and wandered into the living area, flopping down on the sofa, and let out a sigh. It had been a long night, but I couldn't sleep yet. Not with *him* occupying my mind.

Remi came over and took a seat before cracking open her beer. I watched her take a sip, cock her head to the side and then take another. I opened my own and gulped down a quarter of the can before setting it on the coffee table.

"I think I'm screwed."

Remi looked over at me, her green eyes assessing my face for a moment.

"Why?"

"Well, he really does just want to talk."

Her lips curved into a smile.

"That's a bad thing?"

"No, it's not. It's weird, but it's not bad."

"Then why are you screwed?"

I curled my legs up underneath me and looked over the top of the sofa at the small dining table I had behind it.

"Have you seen him?"

"Um, yes."

"No, I mean, have you *seen* him? It's not fair. No one should look that hot without having a warning label attached to their collar."

For a moment Remi said nothing, then she shifted and let out a snort.

"You have a crush on Gil. Well, that complicates things."

There was no point in disputing the fact. After what he'd told me about himself today, I felt confused and guilty at the same time.

"Oh no, it's way more complicated than that. Fuck, I shouldn't tell you this."

"You know I'm not going to say anything. I'm already complicit in this shit as it is. What's one more secret?"

I felt bad about Remi being forced to keep this a secret, but at the same time, she was the one who agreed to it with Gil. It hadn't been my idea.

"I'm ridiculously attracted to him. I've never felt this way about anyone, let alone a client."

I picked up my can again and sipped at it. Admitting my feelings to someone was foreign to me, but Gil had well and truly ripped the rug out from underneath me tonight. I was floundering in the dark.

"It's bad because he *is* a client, and we all have strict boundaries with them. You're not supposed to have feelings."

"True, but it's not like you're acting on them."

She was right. I hadn't. I'd merely thought about it. That wasn't a crime. At least, it hadn't felt like one until…

"Gil told me he's demi. He literally doesn't have any interest in me sexually, and I honestly don't know what to do with that."

I placed my can down again and buried my face in my hands. That was my real problem. The guilt I felt the moment he told me was all-consuming. Me thinking about him in a sexual way felt wrong when he couldn't see me that way.

"He's… oh… that explains a lot."

I dropped my hands and looked at her.

"It does?"

"Yeah, Gil is totally oblivious to female attention. He really doesn't like people touching him, at least people he doesn't know. I've never seen him date anyone, and I've known the Villettis basically my whole life."

I'd observed him not wanting to be in close proximity. He'd basically run away from me the second time we met. Fucking hell. Remi was right. His behaviour made so much sense now I knew about his sexuality. It didn't make me feel any less shitty about lusting after him. It only made me feel so much worse.

"Now, do you see why I'm screwed?"

Remi sipped her beer.

"I mean, you could refuse to see him if it's that much of a problem."

"I can't do that."

She gave me a look.

"And why not?"

"He doesn't have anyone else."

I sounded ridiculous, but the knowledge I was the person he'd turned to made me feel special. And it fucked with me too. I'd never met a man who didn't view me as a sexual being. Even my work colleagues viewed me through a sexual lens because of the nature of our work.

"You know that sounds a little crazy, right?"

"He's a paying client."

"So? It doesn't mean you're responsible for him."

"I didn't say that."

Her phone went off. She checked it, made a face, and looked down at her beer.

"Mmm, okay, Theia, whatever you say." She stood up and gave me a knowing look. "Listen, I'm going to head to bed. I know he's a paying client, but you don't have to help him with whatever he's going through, okay?"

I nodded, unsure of how to respond. She eyed me for a moment longer before walking away towards my hallway.

"And don't feel too bad about finding him attractive," she threw over her shoulder. "You're allowed to like him even if he can't feel that way about you too."

How the fuck did she know I'm feeling bad about it?

The front door slammed a minute later. I sat there staring at the wall in front of me before sighing and hauling myself up off the sofa. Wandering into the kitchen, I set my can down and rifled through the letters I'd dropped on the counter. One of them stuck out. The handwriting was familiar and made the hair on the back of my neck prickle.

Ripping it open, I turned the envelope upside down and shook it, making a small note fall out on the counter. I set the envelope down and stared at the words.

I bet you're loving all those paying clients,
aren't you? You tried to deny you liked what
we did to you, but don't worry,
we know better now.
Once a whore, always a whore.
Enjoy it while you can.

Sickness coiled in my stomach. I put a hand to my mouth before dashing towards the sink and promptly throwing up. It was violent and unforgiving. I set my forehead on the counter when I'd expelled everything, breathing heavily, and rubbing my stomach.

They know where I work. They know where I fucking live!

I'd forgotten about the charm they'd sent to the club earlier after my session with Gil. I knew who it was. The men who'd held me against my will for two years. Who'd subjected me to things I didn't want to think about. I didn't want to remember.

"No, no, no, no, no."

I could hardly breathe as I sunk onto the floor and curled up into the foetal position.

"They can't hurt me. They can't. It's in the past, it's all in the past," I told myself over and over, even though I didn't believe it.

How the hell had they found me? It had been four years, and I'd been so careful. This was my worst nightmare coming to fruition. And yet they were just words. They hadn't approached me or tried to take me again. Maybe they were taunting me. They couldn't possibly think they'd get to me here, could they? The club was one of the most secure places in London. The same for this building we all lived in.

I hated not knowing. It made me feel so out of control. I'd worked so hard to get my life on track. To heal from what they'd done to me. And now, here I was curled up in a ball, all because I'd received a few fucking messages.

I don't know how long I lay there as I attempted to calm down and breathe again. When my heart finally stopped racing so hard in my chest, I uncurled myself and got up off the floor. Grabbing a hold of my beer, I downed the rest, threw the can in the recycling, and walked into my bathroom. Despite the late hour, I took a long, hot shower, washing away everything until I felt relatively human again.

When I got out, I dried myself and put my pyjamas on. I pulled a bag out of the top of my wardrobe and packed it with essentials. It would be my 'just in case I had to run' bag.

After I'd got done with that, I placed it back on the top of my wardrobe, turned out all the lights in my flat and got into bed. Then I cried myself to sleep because everything about today was too much for me to think about

ELEVEN

Gilberto

I wanted to throw something at the wall, but I remained where I was as Salvatore calmly explained to me another body had turned up on our doorstep. This time, it was one of Gian's men. I'd spent the morning talking to Salvatore about the potential new *capodecinas*. Now I had this shit to deal with.

What the fuck was my life coming to?

It didn't help that I hadn't slept properly after my internal battle for the third night in the row over wanting to see Theia again. Apparently, that was another fucking issue I had to contend with. I was running on empty. And it wasn't good at all.

My first instinct was to tell Sal to get rid of this body like we had done the last one, but I took a minute to evaluate the situation.

Who was killing my cousins' men and leaving them on my doorstep?

Why were they doing it?

What did they hope to gain?

There were too many questions I had no answers to. None of this made any kind of sense.

"What should we do with this one, boss?" Sal prompted me when I didn't speak.

I stared at the body. He'd been tortured the same way as the first one. I assumed it had been done by the same people.

"Where did you put Dino's man?"

I hadn't asked Edric where they'd taken him. He'd been particularly moody when they got back. I hadn't wanted to bring it up then. He was back to cracking jokes the next day, so I assumed he was fine, and it was handled. He had to get used to dead bodies. They came with the territory.

"The Edmonton safe house."

"You took him to one of our safe houses?"

"It used to be a mortuary. Edric thought it would be better if we kept a hold of him."

Edric wasn't entirely wrong. I had to give him credit for that decision. He'd been thrown in at the deep end like me. To know he'd stepped up to his new role as my underboss gave me a sense of relief. Even if everyone had questioned my decision, having a loyal man at my back was important to me.

"Take this one there as well."

"Yes, boss."

"Do you know where Edric is?"

Footsteps sounded on the concrete behind me. This body had been dumped outside by the bins.

"Here… and we have a situation, boss."

I turned around, finding my second walking up to us with a dark look in his hazel eyes. He adjusted his glasses before nodding at Sal.

"What situation?"

"Your cousin is here and wants to speak to you."

Seriously? I cannot catch a fucking break today.

"Which one?"

Edric gave me a smile, which made me incredibly suspicious given he'd come up to us looking like hell itself was about to descend on the world.

"Nino."

Gian's eldest. Why the fuck was he here? I swear to fuck this day was only getting worse by the second.

"Okay. You and Sal deal with the body and I'll go speak to him."

I wasn't going to let on to Sal that I was about to lose my ever-loving shit over this. Edric was looking at me like he knew, but that little shit was far too astute about my moods. Besides, these two needed to get this guy out of here before my cousin saw anything he shouldn't.

I turned around and walked away before he saw anything else. Didn't need him questioning what was going on with me. I had no fucking clue how I'd begin to explain why I was all fucked up. Adults were meant to have their shit figured out by now. They should know who they are, but I had no fucking clue. Here I was at twenty-eight having an identity crisis. It was the worst timing imaginable when I was now head of the fucking mafia.

I found my cousin standing around with my men near the front entrance. Nino was shorter than me, his hair a lighter shade of brown than the rest of us because he took after his mother, and dark eyes.

"Gil."

"Nino."

I waved toward the stairs leading up to my office. He followed me up there without question. I shut the door behind us and walked over to the window, staring out over my building without really seeing it.

"What can I do for you?" I asked when he didn't say anything.

"*Papá* and Uncle Dino aren't very happy with you and Zayn."

Tell me something I don't know.

"I'm aware."

I wanted to know what he wanted before I asked any further questions. If he was here to give me shit, I'd tell him to fuck off out of my sight. Today was not the day for dealing with my family or their drama. I had more pressing shit to get on with, like working out why the fuck someone was killing their men and dumping them at my headquarters.

"I'm not here to give you a hard time, Gil."

I turned and looked at him.

"No?"

He took a step towards my desk.

"I don't care what they think about you taking over. It's between you and your brother. I'm more concerned about the trouble we've been having."

"What kind of trouble?"

He sighed and took a seat in one of the chairs in front of my desk.

"Several of our shipments have gone missing. Like they've straight up dropped off the face of the planet. It's been going on for a couple of months, but *Papá* won't do shit all about it. Well, he keeps telling me he and Uncle Dino are handling it, but clearly fucking not, if it's still happening. Now our men are disappearing too. I said we should inform you, but they told me they want nothing to do with you and to mind my business."

He looked over at me with concern written all over his face.

"We need help, Gil. Regardless of what they say, you're still family. If we can't even keep our own affairs in order and we go down, it looks bad on every Villetti regardless of what *famiglia* we belong to."

He wasn't wrong. It wouldn't reflect well on any of us. Dino and Gian had said I was too young to run shit when they were out here looking like incompetent fools.

Fucking hypocrites.

"They don't know you're here."

"No."

"And you want my help."

"Yes."

I moved away from the window and sat behind my desk. This was an unexpected turn of events, but when had anything been fucking straightforward since I'd taken over?

What would Gennaro do?

He'd probably take over their *famiglias* to prove them wrong after they'd insulted him. He was ruthless... but was I? I didn't know if I could do that to my family, even the ones who didn't think I could do this role. It didn't sit right with me. I wasn't Gennaro. I couldn't be. After my last conversation with Theia, it made me think about how much of a terrible father he'd been to me. How I'd had to hide my identity because I knew he wouldn't approve of it. He'd left me feeling like I wasn't good enough. Like I couldn't do anything right even when I pretended to be someone else. And maybe that was the problem. Maybe I had to be myself... if I could work out who he was.

"They can't find out I've asked you," he added when the silence had gone on for too long.

"Well, considering we're not on speaking terms, it shouldn't be a problem."

"Does that mean you'll help?"

"It depends on what exactly you'd like me to do."

"Find out who is behind this."

It wasn't my responsibility, but the fact I was dealing with two fucking dead bodies belonging to their men had me wanting to get to the bottom of this. I was involved whether I liked it or not.

"I'll need the details of the shipments and the names of the men who've disappeared."

"Of course."

"I need your full cooperation too."

He nodded slowly.

"You have it."

"And when this is over, you won't challenge me if I decide your father and Dino are no longer worthy of their roles."

Nino paled slightly at my words.

"I won't."

"Good. Then give me the information and I'll see what I can find."

And hopefully, make this shit go away for me too. I don't need dead bodies littering my fucking headquarters.

It would kill two birds with one stone if I dealt with this. Plus, I'd show my fucking idiot cousins how wrong they'd been… and maybe live up to my brother's faith in me.

Nino stood up and took something out of his bag before sliding the pages across my desk.

"Thank you for this. I wasn't sure if you'd help."

"We're family, Nino."

He gave me a nod. I might not think highly of my extended family, but they were still Villettis. Family mattered in my world. It came first. My father had drilled it into our heads from a young age. We were loyal to family until they weren't, and the only way to deal with disloyalty was with death. It was why I'd killed Matteo the day I'd taken over. Why I would execute anyone else who decided to fuck with me. Whoever was behind this shit with my cousins would die by my hand. That was how it had to be.

Nino came around my desk and explained what was on the papers to me before he left. I sat back and stared at them, wondering where to start first. I'd have to wait for Edric and Sal to get back. Then we could discuss where we would go from here.

I pulled out my phone and stared down at the messages between me and Remi. If I went to see Theia again, what the fuck would that even mean? I shouldn't be having this dilemma over a woman I was paying to speak to. She was there for me to unburden myself. And yet it didn't feel like this was a transactional relationship. Not when I was with her. That was fucked up. I couldn't blur the lines even if I wanted to be her friend.

You don't know how to be friends with someone, Gil.

The only person I'd ever maintained an actual friendship with was Edric, but he'd forced that on me and refused to accept anything less. I wasn't going to tell him I'd paid a sex worker to talk to me. I would never hear the end of it.

Quit overthinking this shit. If you want to see her, see her. It's as simple as that.

GIL: IS THEIA WORKING TONIGHT?

It took several minutes before I got a response.

REMI: YES… SHE'S DUE TO DANCE, BUT YOU CAN SEE HER AFTER.
GIL: OKAY. IS ZAYN GOING TO BE THERE?
REMI: NO, HE'S TAKING ARI OUT TO DINNER TONIGHT.
GIL: LET HER KNOW I WANT TO SEE HER.
REMI: NO PROBLEM. SHE GOES ON AT NINE.

She didn't elaborate about when Theia would be finished, but I imagined it wouldn't be longer than an hour.

Was I going to arrive at nine to watch her? I had no fucking idea. Maybe it would help me understand Theia more. She said she liked to be watched. The last time I'd been in the club on one of Zayn's special nights, I hadn't paid attention to the dancers. Well, I'd noticed the guy harassing her, but I wasn't focused on what she was doing. Maybe if I paid attention this time, it would help me see why she enjoyed it. I wanted to understand her desires, as they were a big part of her world.

I tried not to question why I was so interested in her, even though my intrigue was concerning. I'd told myself I was going to do something for me. Discovering who Theia was inside would be for me. Worrying about this when I had much larger concerns at hand was ridiculous. If seeing Theia helped me, I should just fucking do it. She was the one thing in my life that felt good. And considering I hadn't been able to sleep properly since I last saw her, maybe she'd quieten my chaotic mind enough to help me drift off. I wouldn't know unless I went to the club.

Go watch her… learn about her… let your curiosity guide you, Gil. You know you want to.

I did. I really fucking did… so I would.

TWELVE

Gilberto

The moment I entered the main club floor, Remi was on me with a knowing look in her green eyes. I frowned, wondering what she wanted. Not like I'd told her I was coming early to watch Theia before our session.

"You here to collect your favour from me?" I asked before she could say a word.

She gave me a grin.

"Of course not."

"Then what do you want?"

"You're here to watch her."

She wiggled her eyebrows, making me want to throttle her for the look in her eyes. I was not here for anything other than curiosity, despite what she might think. Theia was perfectly aware that I sought friendship from her. Remi's opinion of this situation wasn't relevant. It was between me and Theia.

"What's it to you?"

"Nothing. Just be careful with her, Gil."

"What's that supposed to mean?"

She looked over at the poles where two girls I didn't know were dancing.

"She has a soft heart, so don't hurt her."

I didn't get a chance to respond. She took me by the arm and dragged me towards the seating area near the poles.

"Sit here. You'll have the best view."

Remi flounced away, leaving me staring after her. What did she mean? I had no intention of hurting Theia. How could I? I was paying for her time. She was getting something in return for me talking to her. She probably didn't even think about me outside of work, anyway. She had no reason to. I was merely a client to her.

I don't know why the thought disconcerted me as I sat down on the bench Remi had indicated behind a table. I shouldn't feel like it was more than that between us.

Checking my watch, I noted it was just before nine. I was always early for everything. Being late rubbed me up the wrong way.

A minute later, one of the girls came around and asked me if I wanted a drink, so I ordered water after she scanned my membership number from this app Remi made me download on my phone. You could also use it to book sessions, but Remi had told me it was safer for me to go through her if I wanted to remain relatively anonymous. My brother was probably aware I'd joined under a fake name. He clearly had cameras around this building as he took security seriously. I didn't want to think about it or address the situation. He hadn't told me I couldn't see the girls at his club, even though he'd banned Enzo. He likely didn't think he had to when it came to me.

The two girls who were dancing finished up their sets. They stepped down off the raised podiums and walked towards the bar. My eyes fixed on the door behind it where I knew the staff room lay.

The moment Theia walked out, I was instantly aware of her. Her light brown hair was tied back into a ponytail. She was wearing a black underwear set with a red harness over the top of it that criss-crossed across her body. Her black heels were sky high with little red details. She walked across the room like she owned it and demanded everyone's attention.

I barely noticed the girl setting down the water on the table in front of me. I was too busy watching Theia step up onto the dais in front of me. She took a hold of the pole and surveyed the room. Her eyes didn't linger on me, almost as if she hadn't taken anything in, but she was doing it for effect. The music changed. The dark, sultry beat pumped through the speakers, making my skin prickle. Theia spun around the pole once, her body undulating with the music. She slid her other hand along the front of her body. Then she hooked a leg around the pole and things really began.

The way she moved transfixed me. How she spun around the pole with such elegance. The way she contorted her body, drawing attention to its curves and edges. There was a certain confidence to her like she knew everyone's eyes were on her. I couldn't look away to check, not wanting to miss a single second.

Letting go of the pole, she was bent backwards, placing her arms out with her legs above her, hooked around the pole as she spun. For a split second, her eyes landed right on mine. I could see the way they widened at the sight of me. Remi would have told her I was coming to see her tonight, but I doubt she'd been expecting me to watch her performance.

The atmosphere shifted. Theia's attention was on me as she continued to spin and extend her body out. There was a certain intensity to her performance that hadn't been there before. She grabbed hold of the pole again, changing position as she moved one leg down and held it with her free hand as the other extended upwards. I hadn't realised how flexible Theia was, but I should have known, given she was a pole dancer and a sex worker.

My hand went to the glass in front of me, taking a hold of it and bringing it to my lips. She shifted, landing on her feet on the floor before spinning around the pole and undulating her body with the beat again. Her free arm extended outwards as her leg hooked around the pole. She rocked to the beat, almost as if she was putting on a show just for me, which I didn't know how to interpret or react to. Why would she have changed things up because I was there? There was no reason for it.

I set the glass down after taking a sip, my eyes never leaving her body. My feelings towards her hadn't changed, but I admired her ability and the strength she must possess to perform this routine. It was easy to see how much she enjoyed herself as she did it. The way her eyes twinkled at everyone's attention. How she played up to it.

Her attention went to the rest of the room as she continued to dance, but it kept drifting back to me every so often, almost as if to make sure I was still watching. As if I could drag myself away now. Theia had this way about her that demanded all of your attention. She could be fully clothed right now, and I'd still want to watch her every movement. The lines she made with her body were beautiful.

When she finished her first routine, she moved straight into a second one. It was less intense, the beat slower and more sensual, but no less engaging. I don't know how much time had passed while she danced. My entire focus was on her. Every inch of this woman who intrigued me far more than she should.

When she finally finished her set, she smiled at me before she stepped down off the podium and moved toward the bar. I sat back against the bench and rubbed my hands along my thighs. It was then I realised my body had reacted to the sight of Theia dancing. It made me lean forward and adjust myself, cursing under my breath. I was uncomfortable with the involuntary arousal my body displayed. I didn't feel any desire to touch myself or for sex. This shit happened without me wanting it to.

What did I do with the knowledge my body had found Theia dancing arousing when I didn't feel attraction towards her? I hadn't even considered it sexual when I was watching her, so this was awkward. How on earth would I face her now?

It took several minutes for it to go down. The whole time I was wondering what the hell I was going to do. Theia had seen me. She knew I was there. I couldn't run away. She might know something was wrong. Usually, I could act like nothing was bothering me, but something about Theia had me turning to honesty every single time. I didn't want to lie to her.

Enzo had told me I was brutally honest on far too many occasions. He didn't appreciate it, but he was a little shit, so I didn't care about hurting his feelings. I did care about Theia's feelings and opinion of me.

You don't have to tell her your dick got hard watching her dance, Gil. No one needs to know about that. It didn't mean anything.

I had to get my shit straight. She might not have thought anything of me having watched her performance. She wasn't going to question me on whether I'd got aroused by it. I'd merely tell her I was curious and leave it at that. Didn't need to be a big deal.

Standing up, I downed the glass of water before walking toward where Remi was hanging out at the bar. She looked up at me when I approached with a smile.

"She's quite something, isn't she?"

"Yes."

"Room four. She'll be along soon."

I gave her a nod and decided not to question her about what she'd said earlier. Instead, I made my way to the room. I sat down on the sofa, putting my hands in my lap as my eyes darted about the place. It was where we'd met the last two times. Maybe it was Theia's regular room. I hadn't asked.

The longer she took to arrive, the more nervous I felt about the whole situation. I shouldn't feel so out of my element, but I wasn't good at navigating relationships with other people. Especially not women. I mean, I was fine with the girls I'd known for a long time, like Remi and Enzo's best friend, Alissa. I was still getting to know Ari, but she wasn't hard to get along with. She reminded me of Edric in a lot of ways. They had similar temperaments.

Theia entered the room, diverting me away from my churning mind. She'd put on a black silk robe and her feet were bare.

"Hey," she said with a smile as she shut the door and padded towards the sofa.

She took a seat on the other end from me as if conscious of how much I liked my personal space.

"Hello, Theia."

She fiddled with her ponytail for a moment before looking at me. I didn't know what to say now she was here. Should I bring up the fact I'd watched her dance? Or should I move on to why I was actually here... my fucked up day. I didn't really want to talk about it now. There wasn't much I could say that wouldn't draw her further into my world. I'd told her I didn't want her to be involved in the illegal nature of it.

"You watched me dance."

I rubbed my thigh, not quite relieved she'd brought it up, but glad I hadn't needed to make the decision myself.

"I did."

"I didn't think you'd be interested in that."

I gave her a shrug and looked away.

"I was curious. People come to watch you, so I wanted to see what that was like."

I didn't want to tell her it was so I could understand her better. I never knew how people would take the things I said. And I was feeling self-conscious after my involuntary reaction to her.

"You could have asked me to dance for you here, Gil. I would have."

I rubbed the back of my neck. Getting a private show from her would feel too intimate. And now I knew how my body would react, there was no fucking way I wanted to draw attention to it.

"No. That's… I don't want that."

I glanced at her. Theia didn't look put out by me refusing, but I did wonder if she thought I was being rude.

"You're very talented. I've never seen anyone move the way you do. It was an experience."

It wasn't a lie, but I wanted her to know it had nothing to do with me thinking she was bad at dancing. I was mesmerised by it.

"Well, thank you. I appreciate that."

I gave her what I thought was a smile, but who the fuck knew. Why did I feel so weird about the whole thing? Being here with her gave me far too much anxiety, even though every other time I'd been around this woman, her presence had calmed me.

"Did something happen today?"

"Why do you ask?"

She shifted closer, her blue-grey eyes intent on my face.

"Isn't that why you're here? To talk to me about what's going on?"

I swallowed.

"Or would you like me to distract you, Gil? Tell me what you need."

I watched her lean towards me, placing her hand down on the leather sofa between us. She was much too close. My skin grew hot. I rubbed my arm. I didn't know what I needed from her. Last time I'd wanted to talk, but today, after seeing her dance, I wasn't sure if I could.

"I don't know. I don't know what I need." I waved at my head. "There's too much... I can't..."

Understanding formed on her features. She gave me a tentative smile, but thankfully didn't move any closer.

"Then let me take care of you."

Take care of me? What... what are you going to do?

THIRTEEN

Theia

Gil looked so afraid. His dark eyes were wide and unblinking. I didn't know why he was acting so oddly today. He didn't seem like himself. Sweat had formed along his brow like this whole situation was making him anxious. And it bothered me. This was meant to be a place he could feel safe. Where he could open up.

I didn't want to press the subject of him watching me dance. He hadn't wanted to talk about it. That much was clear by the way he'd reacted when I brought up giving him a private dance. I'd asked about his day to change the subject, but it only distressed him further. Now all I wanted to do was make that look in his eyes go away.

How can I make this better for you, Gil? I want to. I want to take care of you so fucking bad.

The days had passed slowly since the last time I'd seen him. I'd attempted to distract myself from those fucking notes I'd received by dancing every night on the podium at the club before I saw clients, having switched shifts with one of the other regulars. It was the only way I could escape the reminders and the fear they would come for me.

Now Gil was here and my whole fucking being was consumed by this man all over again. I couldn't stop thinking about him. I wanted to know him. To understand him. He wasn't like anyone else I'd ever met. He didn't want the things other men did from me.

"Take care of me?" he asked in a quiet voice laced with confusion.

I was fully aware Gil needed to be approached with caution and care. Remi made it clear he required his personal space, especially with people he didn't know. I wasn't a stranger any longer, at least not completely. Everything inside me screamed to soothe him somehow.

"Yes. I think you need me to take your mind off whatever is going on up there."

He didn't respond. A furrow appeared on his brow as he looked away. If only I could smooth it away with a simple touch.

Are you really going to go there, Theia? What about your own boundaries?

If it had been anyone else, I wouldn't have ever considered crossing my no-contact boundary. And I probably shouldn't be thinking about it now, considering how I felt about him. I couldn't leave him like this, though. It felt wrong. He needed something to get his mind off whatever was bothering him. The fact he'd come to see me dance had to mean something, didn't it?

"Gil… would it be okay if I held your hand?"

I watched him swallow hard at my words, but he didn't look at me.

"I don't know," he whispered.

"Would you be willing to try? We can stop if you feel uncomfortable."

What about you? Are you going to feel uncomfortable?

I had no fucking clue, but holding hands was relatively simple, wasn't it? I couldn't think of any other way to comfort him.

"Why do you want to?"

"Do you want the honest truth?"

He nodded and stared down at his hands in his lap.

"Correct me if I'm wrong, but you want me to provide you with a safe space to talk and give you friendship, right?"

I'd assumed he wanted a friend after he'd said he wanted to know me.

"Yes."

"When my friends are distressed, I comfort them. I don't think you'd want me to hug you, so I'm asking if you'd accept something smaller and less intrusive."

Gil's teeth scraped across his bottom lip as if he was contemplating my words.

"Doesn't that violate your no-contact rule?" he asked after a long moment.

"I'm making an exception... just this once."

Quite honestly, I'd make all the exceptions for you, Gil. I'd let you touch me everywhere, but you don't want that, so I won't admit it to you.

He shifted in his seat, then he slowly moved his hand until it sat next to him with his palm face up. His eyes were on it like he couldn't quite believe he was saying yes to me touching him. I didn't hesitate in gently placing my hand on top of his. His skin was warm. The contact sent tingles running up my arm, but I tried not to focus on that. Instead, I left my hand on his and waited to see his reaction.

Gil let out a shuddering breath and closed his eyes. He didn't attempt to move away or even tell me to stop. His hand twitched when I laced our fingers together. He'd let me touch him and neither of us was running away. I was okay with this. I was jumping up and down on the inside. He felt good. It felt so fucking good.

"Does this feel okay?" I asked him, keeping my voice soft.

He didn't open his eyes, but he inclined his head. His chin dropped to his chest, his shoulders slumping as if a weight he'd been carrying around had shifted. Feeling bold, I let go of his hand before turning and sitting cross-legged so I could face him. I cradled his hand with one of mine and used the other to stroke lines down his palm with the tips of my fingers. Gil let out another breath, but he didn't move otherwise. He let me stroke his hand without a word.

"I have a big scene to prepare for tomorrow," I told him, wanting to further distract him from his thoughts.

"You do?"

"Mmm."

Gil didn't open his eyes, but he got more comfortable and rested his head back against the wall.

"Tell me about it."

There were certain details I couldn't reveal to maintain client confidentiality, but I didn't think Gil would talk about what I told him to anyone else. He wanted to know me. My job was a big part of my world.

"It'll happen in room ten as it is purpose-built for voyeurism. It's been split into two with a two-way mirror in between. The client can see in, but the performers can't see them. The client room is stocked with a multitude of toys and anything else they could need. They can ask to see pretty much anything they like."

The whole time I was explaining, I kept stroking his palm. Gil seemed to relax further under my touch, his body practically melting into the sofa. It made me happy. It was difficult to see him distressed when I had no idea how to help him.

"There are different forms of voyeurism. Some people like to be in the room with you and some prefer the anonymity."

"Which one do you prefer?"

His question made me pause in my stroking. He cracked an eye open.

"Don't stop," he murmured.

"You like that?"

He nodded and closed his eyes again. I resumed stroking his palm and took a moment to recognise the significance of this moment. This man who didn't like people up in his personal space was allowing me to soothe him. Me. A girl he didn't know that well.

Fuck... I was blurring so many lines here and I couldn't bring myself to care. He didn't feel like a client to me. He never had. He knew me as Theia, not Pisces. It was always destined to be different because of that simple fact.

"Did you mean what do I prefer when people watch me?"

"Yes."

I bit my lip.

"If it's a solo scene, I prefer them to be in the room. I like seeing their eyes on me. It makes me feel good. But in group situations, I prefer the voyeur room."

"Why is that?"

If I told him the truth, it might lead to more questions. Ones I didn't know if I could answer truthfully. And yet I also didn't want to keep things from him. I found myself wanting to trust Gil. He made me feel... safe. It was crazy since we were still getting to know each other, but the fact his interest lay with my mind and not what my body could offer made me feel secure.

"The only people I feel comfortable being intimate with are a few of my work colleagues. I can pretend no one else is there if the clients aren't in the room."

"Is that why you have the no-contact rule? You don't feel comfortable with random people touching you."

"One of the reasons."

"I can understand that. I feel the same way."

"You're letting me touch you."

He rubbed his face on his shoulder but didn't open his eyes.

"You're not a random person, Theia. Not to me."

My heart squeezed painfully in my chest at his words. For Gil, it was a huge admission. I was someone to him.

His tortured soul was beautiful to me. He made me feel things I thought I was incapable of. I wanted to be there for him, and not as someone he was paying, but as me, Theia Nowak. I wanted to be in his life. I was so hopelessly gone for Gil Villetti, it was ridiculous. What the fuck was happening to me? I didn't want anyone. And I *wanted* him so badly, it fucking hurt.

This whole thing was alien to me. Being around a man I had feelings for who couldn't feel that way about me. The only thing I could be was his friend. It had to be enough. I didn't resent Gil for the way he was. I merely wished things were different... or did I? Maybe it was a good thing, him not feeling attracted to me. It made me realise I wasn't as okay as I thought after everything that had happened to me. I'd spent so long healing from all the trauma and pain, but I continued to assume men wanted one thing from me.

My body.

Gil didn't want me for that. It was a revelation and had me sitting in some very uncomfortable feelings towards myself and the world around me.

Was I really so broken that I only saw value in my body and what I could do with it? Did I think that was all I had to offer other people, especially men? How could I think that about myself?

And yet it wasn't entirely surprising.

When you get sex-trafficked and forced to please men you find abhorrent, it worms its way into your psyche. The idea you're only good for one thing and one thing alone. It's all they ever told me. I was a whore who needed to do what she was told. Years of abusive language, rape, and sexual assault changes a person. You can't go back to who you were before. You have to find a new version of yourself underneath all those layers of trauma. I could only be glad I was taken away from that life. It allowed me to heal. Working here at Desecration helped with that too. And now I'd met Gil, I realised I had to do some more soul-searching.

"Theia."

My attention went back to Gil, who had opened his eyes and was staring right at me.

"Yeah?"

"Would you want to watch?"

It felt so strange to be asked what I preferred when I was always the one making sure my clients' needs were taken care of.

Being the watcher was never something I'd ever considered, but voyeurism and exhibitionism went hand in hand. They were two sides of the same coin.

"Other people? I could see that being hot, but I wouldn't want to be in the room with them."

My eyes went to Gil's palm. I watched my fingers as they moved across it. It was relaxing for me too, especially after all the stress I'd experienced because of the letter and the charm. This was far more effective than dancing had been. He represented safety and security.

"This big scene you have. Is it something you've done before?"

"Yeah. I was super nervous the first time, but I'll be fine. I trust them, my work colleagues. We're a family, you know. We take care of each other." I concentrated harder on my fingers. "There'll be four of us, so it's a lot to coordinate."

Telling the man I was obsessed with I'd been in scenes involving three other people made me nervous.

"I can imagine it is."

I looked up, finding his expression neutral. Gil could be impossible to read.

"You're not weirded out by that or anything?"

"No. It's your job. If you didn't want to do it, you wouldn't."

I don't know why I kept questioning whether he was okay with the things I did. It was hard not to have that reaction when so many people judged you for being a sex worker. I had to stop being so worried about what he thought. After all, Gil hadn't judged me so far. He'd been far more understanding than anyone else I'd met outside of Desecration.

I decided I would be honest with Gil, no matter the consequences. Deep down, I felt like I could trust this man with anything. And it was quite possibly the scariest thought I'd ever had.

FOURTEEN

Theia

I shook my head and smiled, not wanting to alert Gil to my internal debate. It wouldn't do to let him know I was far too attached to him for my own good.

"I'm sorry I keep asking if you're okay with what I do. Guess I'm so used to people looking down at me for being a sex worker. Having someone be okay with it outside of my work colleagues is new to me."

Gil frowned.

"Even your clients think that way?"

"Not all of them, but with some of them, you can tell if you met them outside of the club, they'd definitely look down on you."

Without warning, his hand closed over mine, trapping my fingers against his palm.

"I hate that you have to deal with such judgements, but I also understand. People determine your worth and value on what you do for a living. They think it defines who you are as a person. I have to deal with it too." His hand tightened around mine. "I'm seen as the second son of Gennaro Villetti, a man who was never meant to take the reins while my older brother still lives. They judge me as unworthy of being the new mafia boss, but they don't see me… they don't see Gil, just as they don't see Theia."

His words tore a hole in my chest. He understood what I went through because he dealt with it too. Being seen only for your labels and not who you really were inside. And fuck if it didn't make me relate to him all the more.

"I see you."

His eyes darted away. The grip he had on my fingers was borderline painful, but I didn't protest. I honestly didn't care. The fact he was touching me made up for it.

"Do you?"

"Yes… you're Gil to me. I don't see the mafia boss, I just see you."

He didn't say anything for a long minute, as if he was weighing up my words to find their merit. I hadn't seen him outside of the club. I didn't know what his life was like nor what he had to deal with other than what he'd told me.

"I don't know who Gil is."

"What do you mean?"

He loosened his hold on my fingers but didn't let go.

"I told you my father had a lot of expectations I didn't live up to. He raised me to be a ruthless killer. Someone who doesn't feel emotions or remorse for what he does in the name of our *famiglia*. It's the only way I know how to be." Gil's eyes met mine again. "Then there's Zayn, who expects me to do what is best for the family. Rule the way I see fit. He's nothing like my father. He cares even if he doesn't always show it. I feel like I'm stuck between two opposite forces... and neither of them are me. They're not Gil. I don't know who I am underneath the labels given to me by my father and my brother."

No wonder he needed someone to talk to. Struggling with your identity and who you were inside was no walk in the park. I kept my hand in his, wanting him to know I was here. The things he'd admitted to me tonight were fucking huge. It made me appreciate this man even more than I already did. It felt like a privilege to be allowed access to his most vulnerable parts. It made me want to give him mine in return.

"You're trying to find yourself while also trying to navigate your new role."

"Exactly."

"I can see how difficult that would be."

He dipped his head in agreement before biting his lip. My eyes were drawn to it. The fullness of his mouth made me swallow hard. I shouldn't be imagining what it would be like to kiss him. Guilt flooded me immediately. This attraction was not something I could afford to have. It didn't stop me from feeling it. The only thing I could do was not act on it. Not allow it to consume me entirely.

"Things got a whole lot worse today. My working theory is that someone is deliberately trying to create trouble between me and my cousins. I have to work out who is behind it. They're my cousins once removed from my great uncle's side. They have their own *famiglia*."

"What exactly is *famiglia*? I know it means family, but I get the impression there's more to it when it comes to the mafia."

Gil removed his hand from mine. I felt bereft of his touch immediately.

"It's what we call our mafia family. I'm the boss or the *capo*, then I have an underboss and below him are the *capodecinas* who basically look after a section of their own men. That's how it works for me and my cousins, anyway."

He demonstrated it with his hands before settling them in his lap and giving me a half shrug.

"So you each have a *famiglia*."

"Yes, but Zayn is still the head of my side of the family. It includes me, Enzo, my aunt Martina and her three daughters. At any other time, there wouldn't be a separation, but Zayn doesn't want to run the mafia. He never wanted it and he has enough on his plate already, so he entrusted it to me. Dino and Gian don't like that at all. Going against tradition is simply not done in our world. At least, not until Zayn decided he no longer wanted to follow in our father's footsteps. I can see why and where he's coming from. I think things need to change, but it's up to me to prove I can do this… that I can be a leader."

The weight resting on his shoulders was a heavy burden to bear. I understood now why he was so troubled. Why he felt like he had no one else to turn to. Gil was enduring this by himself. He couldn't afford to let anyone else in. And didn't that fucking hit. I'd never been able to confide in anyone about my past. Especially not now it had resurfaced.

"Would it be weird if I said thank you for trusting me with this?"

"I don't think so."

"Then thank you. It means a lot to me. And I want you to know I'm not just saying that because you're my client. I like spending time with you."

Fuck, why did you say that? You shouldn't admit that shit to a client, Theia!

I'd already established Gil wasn't a client to me. He was someone I wanted in my life, regardless of whether he was paying for my time.

"I like spending time with you too."

He smiled as he said it, making my heart flutter in my chest. Then he looked down at his watch, and I knew our time was over.

"You have to go."

He stood up.

"Yes."

I nodded, getting up to follow him to the door. I opened it and we walked out together. He paused outside and looked down at me.

"I'll see you soon, okay?"

I tried to smile at him even as my heart protested at him leaving.

Quit it! You cannot get any further attached to this man.

Who was I kidding? Gil was all I could think about. I never knew when he was going to request a session. It made me treasure every moment he was here with me.

"Yeah."

He reached up and ran his knuckles along my cheek. My breath caught at the contact.

"Stay safe, Theia."

Dropping his hand, he turned and walked away towards the back entrance. He never came around the front, not wanting to bring attention to himself since he was Zayn's brother. I watched him leave and tried not to freak out. He'd stroked my damn cheek. My hand went to it, trying to memorise the feel of his skin against it. To savour it for as long as I could.

Shaking myself, I turned around and was about to walk back to the club when I noticed someone leaning against the wall behind me with a smirk on his face.

"So, you and my brother, eh?"

Enzo shoved off the wall and came closer. Gil's younger brother looked like him, except for his dyed blonde hair. Not to mention his personality was nothing like Gil or even Zayn. He drove most of the staff crazy by constantly making jokes or flirting with them. He knew better than to try that with me. I didn't usually give him the time of day.

"There is no me and your brother."

"No? You telling me I didn't see Gil leaving your room?"

"Of course not, but what you saw is not what you think. He's not a client, and you definitely need to keep your mouth shut about it."

Enzo merely shrugged.

"If he's not a client, what's he doing with you?"

"He is, and he isn't. And I mean it, Enzo, this has nothing to do with you."

He came closer.

"A secret tryst between you two. How exciting."

I wanted to smack him around his fucking head, but I remained where I was and tightened the belt around my robe.

"It's not a secret tryst. We're just talking."

He put his hands up.

"Okay, I believe you, but if it's not a secret, why are you so concerned about me talking? I take it Zayn doesn't know about this."

I crossed my arms over my chest.

"Of course, he knows. He has cameras all over Desecration."

I wasn't stupid enough to think Zayn was unaware of his brother visiting me.

"Listen, I have no interest in getting in between whatever this is. Gil can do what he wants. He would literally kill me if I did anything to piss him off. My brothers are both fucking crazy. I was just curious, is all. I meant no harm."

I had no idea whether to take him at face value or not, but I had better things to do than talk to Enzo.

"You sure about that?"

He rolled his eyes.

"What? About my brothers being crazy? Fuck yes. I get lectures from Zayn almost daily and Gil… well, let's just say he's fucking brutal and doesn't sugar-coat a single thing."

I could readily believe that about Gil. His blunt honesty had been a lot to take at first, but I was getting used to it. It was refreshing in a lot of ways. I didn't have to worry about where I stood with him. He was very clear about it. I was the problem in this scenario with my inappropriate feelings towards him. I hoped he never found out. It would make things supremely awkward. He might not want to see me. I couldn't abide by it.

"I meant about not saying anything."

"Oh. I'm not going to say a word, don't worry."

"Okay, well…" I waved in the direction of the club. "I need to go."

He stepped aside and swept his arm out.

"As the lady wishes."

I ignored him and walked away. As long as he kept his mouth shut, it would be fine. Not that I actually trusted Enzo. He hadn't given me a reason to.

When I got onto the club floor, I looked around and found Remi leaning against one of the tables. I stalked towards her. She didn't notice when I came to a standstill next to her. I looked across the room, following her line of sight. A man was sitting on one of the velvet upholstered benches on the opposite side of where we were standing. He had light brown hair, a scar on his face, and was covered in tattoos. The way he looked at Remi sent a shiver down my spine. There was an intensity to him that made me nervous.

Why the hell is he staring at her so hard? That's kind of fucking creepy.

"Who is that?" I asked.

Remi jumped at the sound of my voice and whipped her head around to me. She had a guilty look in her eyes like she'd been caught doing something she shouldn't.

"No one."

I didn't believe that for a second, but I wasn't going to question her about it in the club in full view of the man and everyone else. Grabbing her by the arm, I tugged her away towards the staff room.

"We need to talk."

FIFTEEN

Theia

R emi didn't protest as I dragged her through the
door behind the bar. Not only was I going to find
out why she was looking at that guy, but I also
needed to discuss my encounter with Enzo.

I let go of her when the door swung shut. She looked at me
with wide eyes. I wasn't going to let her get away with shit.

"No one? He was staring at you pretty fucking hard for
being *no one*."

Her cheeks went pink, and her eyes darted away.

"He's just a guy, okay?"

The whole time I'd known Remi, she'd never dated. Will
told me men were intimidated by her because she came across
as aloof. Not that he was interested in Remi as he had a
girlfriend, but Cas had been when they first met. She put a halt
to that pretty quickly. I didn't blame her, as Cas was flaky at
best when it came to the opposite sex. He put his time in at
work, but outside of it, he wasn't one to commit.

"Are you seeing him?"

"No. I mean, he's asked me out a ton of times. I kept saying no, but he's persistent. I kind of said yes this time."

I thought I'd heard her incorrectly at first, but no, Remi definitely told me she agreed to a date with whoever this guy was.

"You're going on a date? That's a first."

"It's not a date! I'm only going to hang out with him, that's all. Anyway, aren't you finished for the night? I assume you're done with Gil."

Technically I was. I needed to go change and find out where Gael had got to. He'd agreed to walk home with me as he was finishing around the same time. I wasn't taking any chances now I'd had those fucking notes.

"Yes, but I need you to do something first."

She rolled her eyes and crossed her arms over her chest.

"What do you want this time?"

"Can you text Gil and tell him Enzo knows he's visiting me?"

Remi's eyebrows shot up.

"Enzo knows? Oh well, you two are fucked then."

"He swears he won't talk, but that's not the point. Gil should be aware his brother knows in case he wants to do something about it."

Remi gave me a look. I was asking a lot of her with all of this shit between me and Gil, but I had little choice in the matter.

"You can ask me for his number and tell him yourself. Would be far fucking easier if the two of you communicated with each other yourselves."

"What? No. I can't do that."

"And why not?"

I looked away, rubbing my arm with one of my hands. It wouldn't be right. He hadn't agreed to it. There was no way I would go behind his back to get information on him. It was a total invasion of privacy.

"He's a client."

"He's not a client to you, Theia. Don't forget, I know how you feel about him."

"It's still not okay. If he wants to give me his number, he can do it himself."

She shrugged and dug her hand into her pocket.

"Fine. Suit yourself. I'll let him know, but I suggest you work out what the fuck is going on between the two of you, because I'm telling you right now, this is going to end badly if you don't."

I didn't ask why or what she meant by it. I already knew I was going to end up broken. My feelings were engaged. There was no turning them off now. I was the stupid one for having them. For wanting a man I couldn't have.

"Thank you."

"You're welcome. I'll see you tomorrow."

I walked towards the staff room, trying not to feel despondent. Seeing Gil had given me such a high. Now I was crashing back down to earth with Remi's words. Why the fuck had I told her about my feelings for Gil?

"Hey, girl, you ready?" came Gael's voice the moment I got into the staff room. He poked his head around the corner and frowned. "Oh, guess you need to get changed."

"Give me two minutes."

I made a beeline for my locker, opened it, and tugged out my clothes. Considering Gael and I had been intimate, I didn't care about him being there while I changed. I was ready to be home at this point. It had been quite the night.

We linked arms together as we left via the front door after I'd changed, and we'd made our way through the club.

"So, how was your evening?" he asked, raising an auburn eyebrow.

I was about to answer when I stopped dead in the street. Leaning against the wall outside was Gil. He pushed off it when he spied me.

What the…

We'd only said goodbye less than fifteen minutes ago, and here he was. I didn't know what to do with myself.

"Theia."

His deep voice almost melted me into a puddle of goo right on the fucking pavement like some kind of lovesick fool. I swear I was going to give myself whiplash from my emotions this evening. They were all over the place.

"Um, hi, what… what are you still doing here?"

I could feel Gael staring at me. He didn't move from my side. If anything, he held onto my arm tighter, as if he was guarding me against the man in front of us as Gil came to a standstill. There was no need for him to become an overprotective bear, but Gael had always looked out for me. And no doubt he knew this was Zayn's brother. Fuck, I was going to have to explain what was going on to him. What a mess. First Enzo, then Remi giving me shit, and now Gael was about to lecture me too.

"I was leaving, but I got Remi's text. I wanted to check if you were okay and that my brother didn't upset you."

"Oh… I'm fine."

Gil didn't look entirely convinced. He glanced over at Gael, then back at me.

"I'll talk to him. Make sure he doesn't bother you again."

"You don't have to do that."

"I do."

I shifted on my feet, expecting him to say goodbye now he'd checked up on me, but he didn't. Every second that went by, it grew even more awkward.

"Well, we're just going home, so… uh, did you want to walk with us?"

I couldn't read Gil's expression, but I could certainly read Gael's. He looked like I'd lost my fucking mind. Well, I already knew that. When it came to Gil Villetti, I wasn't remotely sane, but I was sort of okay with it.

"Okay."

The fact he agreed had my heart racing in my chest. As if it wasn't already going crazy from his mere presence.

I turned to Gael and gave him a pleading look when he didn't immediately let go of my arm. He let out a little huff and released me before walking off in the direction of our building. Gil stepped up beside me and we moved off at a more sedate pace.

"Is he okay?" Gil asked after a minute.

"Yeah, he will be."

"I hope I haven't made things awkward. I just know what Enzo is like." He rubbed the back of his neck. "He's going through some shit, so I wanted to make sure he didn't give you a hard time."

I waved a hand.

"No, it's fine. I appreciate that, but he really didn't do anything bad other than complain about you and Zayn."

Gil's eyes narrowed.

"What did he say?"

"That you were both crazy, Zayn is lecturing him every day, and you're brutally honest about everything."

He snorted and shook his head.

"Well, that's nothing new. Enzo has always been overdramatic."

I didn't respond, unsure of what else to say. We walked in silence for most of the rest of the way. I wanted to reach out and hold his hand, but I didn't. It wouldn't be about comforting him like I had in the club when he was distressed. It was my selfish urge to get closer to him. One I had to curtail. It was getting out of hand.

When we got to my building, Gael was waiting by the door. He leaned against the building with his arms crossed. Gil turned to me, ignoring my friend entirely.

"I know I shouldn't have waited for you, Theia. It crossed a line, and I'm sorry."

I stepped closer to him.

"No, no, it's okay. I understand why."

He reached into his pocket and tugged out a small scrap of paper.

"Take this."

I put my hand out, and he placed it in my palm before enclosing my fist around it. The touch of his skin had me swallowing. He stepped back, dropping his hands to his sides.

"If you need anything, use it."

He smiled, looked at Gael for a moment then inclined his head at me. I dropped my hand to the side, turned and walked over to where Gael was standing.

"Let's go in."

Gael eyed Gil for a long moment before he turned and used his key fob to unlock the door. We went inside the building together. I glanced back to find Gil watching us as if he was making sure I was safely inside.

"Is that who I think it is, Theia?" Gael asked when we reached the lifts and I hit the button.

"The big boss's brother, yes."

"Do I even want to know what you're doing with him?"

I sighed as the lift arrived. We walked in. Gael pressed the button for our floor.

"He's kind of a client, but not really, since he only wants someone to talk to. And no, I can't tell you more than that. I realise it looks really fucked up to you, but I promise, Gil is safe."

He gave me a look that spoke volumes. Gael didn't think I was being smart. I agreed with him on that front, but it didn't mean I trusted Gil any less. He wouldn't harm me.

"Theia…"

"I know, I know, I get it. Please don't look at me like that."

"I hope you know what you're doing."

As if I ever knew what I was doing in life but being around Gil felt right. I didn't want to sever the budding connection between us.

When Gael left me at my door as his flat was further along from mine, he hugged me and told me he'd see me tomorrow for the foursome scene. I hadn't forgotten about it, but my attention had been consumed by Gil for the entire evening.

I looked at the scrap of paper in my hand. He'd given me his number. I didn't know what to make of it, so I put it in my pocket to deal with later. Gil had thrown me for a loop enough this evening. I didn't have the energy to unpack him being outside the club, nor him giving me his phone number and telling me to use it if I needed anything.

I unlocked my door and noticed the postman had been. I picked up the single letter and shut the door behind me. My fingers shook as I recognised the handwriting. Tearing it open, I read the note and swallowed.

> *We hear you've been fucked by three men*
> *at once. You're really pushing the boat*
> *out there, but we always knew what*
> *type of girl you are. A whore.*

The fact they knew about the scene I'd done months ago made me sick to my stomach. I didn't understand how. There were only a few people who were aware. I didn't think any of them would have said a word about it. It meant there was a leak somewhere, but it's not like I could accuse anyone outright when I had no clue who it would be or why.

Instead of getting worked up about it, I took the letter into my kitchen and stuffed it in a drawer I rarely opened with the other one. I'd brought the charm home and put it in there too. That way, all of this shit was in one place.

Fuck knows what I would do. It's not like they'd tried to do anything else to me other than scare me with these letters. And I certainly wasn't going to ask for help when it came to this, either. I hadn't told anyone what happened to me. They didn't understand the hell I'd been through. I might have been rescued by an unknown benefactor and given somewhere to stay to rebuild myself, but it didn't mean I trusted anyone.

You trust Gil.

That might be true, but this was my deepest, darkest fucking secret. I wasn't yet ready to open up that part of myself to him. Talking about my trauma didn't come easy to me, no matter how much I'd healed from it. It didn't matter if I had a safe space at Desecration to explore those things that hurt me the most. People didn't openly discuss those things. After sexual trauma, you could become hypersexual. It was a normal response to what had happened to me. And the more I thought about it within the context of Gil and me, the more I realised my hypersexuality was something I needed to deal with.

I was not an object. I was a person. And it was about time I started treating myself like one.

SIXTEEN

Gilberto

I flexed my hand as I walked into Desecration via the back door. Zayn had given me the code for it a long time ago and kept me informed when it changed. I was trusted to come and go as I pleased. It felt strange being here during the daytime.

I'd stayed away over the weekend as I knew Theia had a big scene. Besides, Edric and I had a lot on our plate now we were looking into who was killing my cousins' men and the missing shipments. Well, we'd been making a plan of how to approach it. Currently, we didn't have any leads, so we didn't have a great deal to go on other than the two men in our mortuary safe house and the documents Nino had given me. I'd set Edric to look into the shipments in the meantime while I decided what the next steps were.

Theia hadn't used my number, not that I expected her to. I didn't know why I gave it to her. The moment I found out Enzo had spoken to her, it made my protective instincts flare.

I didn't want him harassing her. It was why I'd crossed a line and sought her out as she left the club. I had to make sure she was okay.

Enzo hadn't been pleased when I cornered him the next day at our father's former house before he'd gone to work. I'd arrived first thing to make sure I caught him. He told me to go fuck myself after I'd demanded to know what he'd said to Theia. I made sure he wasn't going to say a word to Zayn. Not that I thought my older brother didn't know about my visits to his club, but that wasn't the point.

I'd warned Enzo to stay away from Theia. He thought I was being a dick, but he was the one acting out and kicking up a fuss every time Zayn asked him what he wanted to do next. He had a secure job at Desecration, but my younger brother wasn't exactly the most responsible out of the three of us. I half blamed myself for it since I'd been the one who'd taken care of him when *Mamá* was put in a coma. He was only fifteen, and me, nineteen. It was a fucking recipe for disaster since *Papá* demanded more of my time after Zayn left. I did my best with Enzo, but he wasn't exactly easy to deal with when we'd been left motherless. Not only did I not know how to manage his pain, but I had no idea how to confront my own.

Zayn's office door was open, so I walked straight inside, finding him sitting behind his desk with Arlo behind him and my aunt, Martina, sitting in front of them. I closed the door behind me. When Zayn told me we needed a family meeting, I had expected to find him and Enzo, not our aunt. She was my deceased Uncle Orsino's wife. He'd been murdered a year ago, but we had no idea by whom. My father hadn't done anything to find his killer. The two of them had been at odds for years. None of us knew why.

"Good, you're here. We can start," Zayn said after he glanced at me. "Someone attempted to abduct Sofia last night while Martina and the girls were coming home from dinner."

I'd barely walked a few steps into the room, but his words made me pause.

Why would anyone try to abduct my cousin?

"Is Sofia okay?" Arlo asked with a frown.

"Yes, she's fine," Martina replied, but her voice shook on the words. "We were all rattled by it, but we're no worse for wear."

Zayn laced his fingers together on his desk.

"Things are a little unsettled in our world right now, so perhaps you're being targeted because of it, but I can't be sure."

Martina inclined her head. It was a precarious time for all of us now Gennaro was dead.

"They need protection," I said without preamble.

Zayn glanced at me. He knew I was right. Martina and the girls might not be a part of the mafia life, but they were Villettis. We couldn't allow anyone to harm them.

"They do." His gaze went back to our aunt. "Do you agree, Martina?"

"If it's what you think we need," she replied, looking at the three of us.

"I don't want anything to happen to you or the girls. Until we can establish who is behind this, I want to know you're safe. All of you."

"Then I'll accept whatever protection you give us."

"The girls will have to agree to it as well."

"They won't have a choice."

Martina smiled at Zayn. She had always been a practical woman, so I was hardly surprised she'd agreed. Not to mention she was protective of her daughters, Verona, Sofia, and Rina. There was no way in hell she'd let anything happen to them after her husband had been murdered.

"Good. Well, I'll have to see who I can send…" He paused, turned his head, and gave Arlo a knowing look. "You can go."

"Me?" Arlo asked, sending a slight glare Zayn's way.

"Yes. You can manage the men for me as well." Zayn turned back to our aunt. "Would you be okay with Arlo staying with you while we find out what's going on, Martina?"

Zayn turned back to our aunt with a more measured expression on his face, unlike the smirk he'd thrown at his best friend. I was in no doubt it had everything to do with Rina. It'd been obvious to me for years she was completely enamoured with Arlo. I might not be good at relationships, nor could I tell when someone liked me, but I could certainly see it in other people. Rina was constantly watching him with this dreamy look on her face.

"Of course, we can make room somehow," Martina replied. "I'm sure the girls will love having you there."

I wasn't so sure about that. Verona would probably hate it, but she hated everything and everyone. She'd been a bitch to Ari the first time they'd met, but Zayn's girlfriend had put my cousin in her place. My first impression of Ari had been cemented that day. She was outspoken and wasn't afraid to give anyone hell for trying to give her a hard time. And it was exactly what our family needed… not that I would ever admit it to Zayn.

"Good. Well, that settles it then." He turned to Arlo. "I trust you will investigate everything thoroughly and find out what's happening. I'll leave you and Martina to arrange details."

"Of course." Arlo stepped around to the other side of the desk. "Martina, shall we?" He waved towards the door.

She stood up and followed him out. I was left looking at my brother, who had levelled his gaze on me.

"How are things?"

I dug my hands into my pockets.

"Fine. Is that all you needed?"

He leaned back in his chair.

"You'd tell me if something was wrong, right?"

Was I going to tell Zayn about the shit I was dealing with?

No. Not in a million fucking years.

"If I need you, I'll ask for your help."

I wasn't going to lie, but this enabled me to skirt around telling him the truth. He'd told me I wasn't going to be his puppet. He needed to let me do things my own way.

"Fair enough. Have you spoken to Enzo recently?"

"I saw him over the weekend. Why?"

He let out a sigh before reaching up to rub his temples.

"Ever since I told him the truth about *Mamá*, he's been driving me up the fucking wall. I understand he's hurting, but I don't know how to get through to him."

I shrugged, unsure of what else Zayn expected. Enzo didn't want our help. I'd learned a long time ago my little brother would do as he pleased, regardless of my intervention. Besides,

I was relatively sure he was suffering even more without Alissa, Arlo's sister, who'd been his best friend their entire lives. She was refusing to speak to him. I had no fucking clue what he'd done, but knowing Enzo, it couldn't have been anything good.

"Enzo is going to do whatever he wants, Zayn. That's who he is. We can't hold his hand if he doesn't want us to."

He looked away. Family was one of the few things that got Zayn worked up. He rarely let anything rattle him, but when it came to me and Enzo, Zayn couldn't hide behind a wall of indifference. He cared about us too much.

"He's lost."

"I know."

My brother shook himself before placing both hands on his desk. Enzo wasn't the only one who was lost. I was too, but I couldn't admit it to Zyan.

"I can count on you if I need any help with Martina and the girls, yes?"

"Of course."

"Good. I have other things to get on with. I'm sorry this was so short, but I wanted to keep you in the loop."

I nodded at him before I left. Family always came first, even before the mafia.

As it was during the day, I wasn't expecting to see anyone I knew in the club. However, the door to Liza, Zayn's club manager's office, opened at the same time I walked out of Zayn's. Theia strolled out. She was in jeans and a slouchy jumper. When her head turned and she saw me, her eyes widened.

"Oh… hi, Gil."

I abruptly shut Zayn's door, not wanting him to overhear my conversation with her. Then I walked towards her, making her eyes widen even further. The urge to be close to her drove me.

"Theia."

I don't know why my heart started to beat faster when she smiled at me.

"Visiting Zayn?"

I inclined my head, unsure of what to say now I was standing in front of her.

"Well, I'm sure you're busy. I should let you go."

The thought of her leaving made me want to throw something. What the fuck was wrong with me today? I needed to get my shit together. If I wanted to see her, I had to ask.

"Are you around tonight?"

"It's my day off. I dropped in to speak to Liza about my shifts." She stared up at me with questioning eyes. "We could do something now though if you wanted?"

"Now?"

"Mmm, like go for coffee."

When I didn't immediately tell her no, hope bloomed in her expression. I wasn't sure if we should see each other outside of the club. I had already crossed a huge line by waiting for her last time. Then again, Theia had trusted me to walk home with her. And she was the one offering to do something with me.

"Only if you're free. I wouldn't want to impose on your time. I know you're busy."

I'll be free for you, Theia.

"I'd like that."

"Yeah?"

I nodded. To be honest, I needed to get back to work, but something inside me was baulking at the idea of not getting to spend time with Theia. Edric could hold the fort. I hadn't told him how long I'd be. Not like Zayn had said exactly what this family meeting was about.

"Shall we?"

She waved at the back door. I nodded again and the two of us left together. She grinned up at me when we left the alleyway as if she was pleased I'd agreed to spend time with her.

"Are you sure you're okay about seeing me outside the club?" I asked when we got near the café she was taking me to.

It was probably a bad idea for us to hang out like this. I no longer cared about that. Not when she looked so happy to be doing this with me. I wanted to make sure she was okay with it.

"I wouldn't have asked if I wasn't." She gave me a small shrug. "You're not exactly a regular client."

"I know but—"

"I want to spend time with you, Gil, and it's just coffee."

She gave me a wink before she pushed open the door to the café. And I was left feeling like this wasn't *just* coffee. It was the start of something else between us, but I didn't know what.

SEVENTEEN

Gilberto

I followed Theia into the café. It was decorated in pale greens and had a huge counter with all sorts of baked goods. She got this wide-eyed, excited look in her eyes when she approached it and spied all the cakes. The sun streamed in through the large windows. Her hair caught the light, making her look almost ethereal. It gave me a strange feeling in my chest. One I didn't know how to interpret. All I knew was Theia's blue-grey eyes were twinkling, and I couldn't stop staring at her.

"What do you want to drink?"

It took me a long moment to register she'd asked me a question.

"A black coffee."

Theia bit down on her lip and turned to me.

"Would you care for something sweet too?"

Why would I want something sweet when I have you?

Where the fuck did that come from? I was pretty sure my brain was playing tricks on me right now. I shoved all my weird fucking thoughts away and concentrated on answering her question.

"You can choose something for me."

Theia clapped her hands together and moved over to the till to order for us. I watched her talk animatedly with the woman behind the counter before she paid and came back over to me.

"Let's sit."

She moved through the tables to the back. There was a free table with a comfortable-looking sofa. She patted the seat next to her when I reached her. I sat down, placing my hands on my lap as I did so.

What the hell are you doing here, Gil?

I couldn't remember the last time I'd ever gone out to coffee with anyone. In fact, I don't think I ever had. My life had been filled with the mafia and my family, not going on coffee dates with women. Not that this was a date. Definitely not. We were friends. Did friends do this type of thing together? And if we were friends, why the fuck was I staring at her hand resting on the sofa next to her thigh and wishing she would stroke mine with her fingers again?

"You're thinking awfully hard over there."

My eyes darted up to Theia's face. There was this soft smile there that made me swallow. There were far too many alien feelings twisting up my insides. We were outside the safety of Desecration where there were rules to our meetings. Ones Theia and I had thrown out the window the last time we saw each other when she held my hand.

"Why are you okay with seeing me outside of the club?"

She sat back against the cushions and dragged her teeth across her bottom lip.

"We're still on that? Okay… the honest truth is, I feel safe with you." She rubbed her chest with her fingers. "My past is pretty fucked up, so finding safety in another person is a big deal to me. You see me for me, not Pisces, but Theia." Her eyes darted away. "Being vulnerable with someone is difficult, but I want to be… with you." Her chin dropped to her chest. "I guess what I'm trying to say is I would like to be your friend for real, not because there's a transaction between us. And I'm hoping this isn't scaring the shit out of you right now, because admitting it is scaring the hell out of me."

I didn't get a chance to answer right away as the waitress brought over our drinks and cakes, placing them on the table for us. Theia's cheeks had gone pink, and she steadfastly avoided my gaze. The moment the woman left, she picked up her coffee and hid her face behind it.

"I'm not scared, Theia."

"You're not?" she whispered.

"No." *At least, I'm not scared of you wanting to be my friend. The other stuff I'm feeling, yeah, I'm fucking terrified of that.* "I thought I only needed someone to talk to, but I think I actually need a friend."

"Do you not have any friends?"

I shrugged.

"I have one. He forced me into being his friend, though."

Theia snorted and placed her mug back down.

"Forced you?"

I rubbed my thigh.

155

"If you met Edric, you'd understand. He's the opposite of me. Brash and in your face, but he's also smart and incredibly loyal." I couldn't fight the smile forming on my lips. "He's annoying, but I don't know where I'd be without him."

She leaned closer.

"So I'd be your second friend?"

"I guess so."

"Well, I'm honoured."

The way she smiled had me swallowing all over again. Had her smile always been that cute? She looked different outside of the club. There was no wall or line drawn between us. It made her seem freer. Like she could be herself and not the carefully constructed image she portrayed as Pisces. I'd seen her this way when I'd walked home with her, but it was amplified now. And I liked it. I liked her. It was the only explanation I had for the rapid thudding of my heart behind my ribcage. Well, it didn't make sense for me to experience this about a "friend." I'd never wanted to be this close to Edric. The only time I'd felt this about anyone was... *oh fuck*... *no, it can't be that, can it?*

I wasn't sure I was ready to face what my brain spat at me. Instead of dwelling on it, I decided to change the subject.

"What did you pick for me?"

Theia blinked, then looked over at the cakes.

"The lemon drizzle."

"Why's that?"

Her eyes darted back to mine.

"Because you're sweet and sour."

Her lips curved up into a smirk as a burst of laughter fell out of my mouth without warning. I rarely laughed. Theia was doing something to me. Making me want to be in her space at all times. To have her say stupid shit to make me smile. It made me feel lighter than I had done in years.

"I don't know whether to take that as a compliment or an insult."

"Definitely a compliment. I happen to like sweet and sour things."

"Did you want a bite of my cake, then?"

Before she could say a word, I reached over, dragged the plate towards me and sliced a piece with my fork. Theia's eyes went wide as I brought it up to her mouth.

"You should try it first."

I waited, not saying a word until she opened her lips and let me slide the cake inside. Her pupils dilated as I drew the fork out of her mouth. My eyes were on it, watching her chew and swallow. I couldn't remember ever being interested in another person's mouth the way I was with hers right then.

And yet you want to deny what's happening here. If you admitted it, you wouldn't be so confused right now.

"Good?"

"Very," she murmured.

"What did you get?"

"Carrot cake."

"Should I feed that to you as well?"

She licked the cake crumb off her lip.

"Please."

Leaning over the table, I sliced a piece of her carrot cake and brought it up to Theia's mouth. She accepted it with this timid look in her eyes like she wasn't sure whether this was appropriate or not. I think we threw appropriateness out the window when I agreed to get coffee with her.

I set the fork down, stole hers, and picked up my cake. I sat back and tried it myself.

"You're right, this is really good," I said after I'd swallowed. "The perfect choice."

She smiled and shrugged, her cheeks going bright red this time.

"I'm glad you like it."

I smiled, put my cake down, and sipped my coffee. It took a few minutes for Theia's blush to disappear from her face. During that time, she sipped her drink and ate more of her cake. I wondered what was going through her head.

Was she as confused by this as me?

She said she wanted to be my friend, but did she want more than that?

Did I?

I wasn't good at this shit. At reading other people and whether they liked me or not. I'd never had to before. Not like this, anyway. I didn't have a frame of reference to go on. The foreignness of it made my skin itch. It wasn't as if I could ask anyone else about it, either. The thought of what Edric would say if I told him… well, it didn't bear thinking about in all honesty.

You're on your own here.

Before I could dwell on it further, Theia looked at me with curiosity in her eyes.

"Is your friend also involved in the mafia?"

"Edric? He's my second-in-command. I needed someone loyal to me. I don't trust anyone except for him and my family… and now you."

Her smile made my heart do that racing thing again.

"I trust you too… and I really mean that. There are things I've never told anyone before, but a part of me wants to tell you."

"What things?"

Her eyes turned sad.

"Things about my past. That's not a conversation for today, though. I need a little more time."

The fact she even wanted to confide in me was humbling. I didn't want to read too much into it. Then again, maybe I should. Theia meant something to me. More than something. I couldn't get her out of my head.

"I understand."

She sipped her coffee and placed it down.

"Tell me more about Edric."

"Are you sure you want to know about him?"

"Of course, I'd like to know who my competition for your best friend is."

She grinned to let me know she was joking.

There's no competition, Theia. I care about you in a completely different way from him.

"Well, okay, if you insist."

I spent the rest of the time we were at the café telling her about the idiotic shit Edric had got up to when we were younger. Like the time he broke his wrist trying to impress a girl while drunk. He'd climbed up a tree and fell out of it. He wasn't known for being sensible when we were teenagers.

As much as I wanted to spend the rest of the afternoon with Theia, I had to get back to my headquarters, so we left after we finished our coffee and cakes. I walked her home as she didn't live far. She smiled at me when we reached the front door.

"Are you still going to visit me at the club?" she asked as she dug in her handbag for her keys.

"Yes, if you're okay with that."

"Of course, but maybe we can also do this again too."

I stepped closer to her. My hand came up without me thinking about it. I brushed a hair out of her face before dusting my fingers over her cheek. She swallowed, her blue-grey eyes intent on mine.

"Let me know when you'd like to."

"Gil—"

The front door opened, and Remi stepped out. Her eyebrow shot up when she saw us. I stepped back from Theia, dropping my hand and flexing it as I did it. The loss of contact made me feel odd.

"Hello, you two."

"Hey, Remi," Theia said, her voice pitched higher than before as if we'd been caught doing something we shouldn't. She looked at me with wide eyes. "I should go. I'll see you soon."

Theia darted inside, leaving me alone with Remi, who was staring at me with conflicting emotions in her eyes.

"What?" I asked.

"What indeed? I could ask the same of you. Pretty sure I warned you not to hurt her."

I frowned.

"What makes you think I'm hurting Theia? We were just getting coffee."

Remi shook her head.

"Are you really *that* oblivious?"

"I don't know what you're getting at."

She crossed her arms over her chest.

"Don't get her hopes up only to crush them, Gil."

Now I was seriously confused. What the hell was she trying to tell me? I wasn't doing anything with Theia other than trying to be her friend... and work out why I was having these new feelings for her all of a sudden.

"I'd rather you tell me what you mean than make cryptic comments about what I'm doing."

"Do you like her?"

"Of course I like her."

Her lips thinned.

"No, I mean, do you *like* her, Gil? As in, do you have romantic feelings for her?"

Do I what?

I was about to say no, but everything that had happened today made me pause. I couldn't dismiss it out of hand without thinking about it.

"Romantic feelings?"

"Yes. Listen, don't get mad, but Theia told me about your sexuality. You've spent a lot of time together and now you're going on coffee dates outside of the club, so excuse me for questioning whether your feelings towards her have changed in light of those circumstances. It's okay if they have, but you have to understand I'm trying to protect Theia."

I wasn't mad that she'd told Remi. I hadn't realised the two of them talked about me. It wasn't an issue. Remi could keep a secret, as evidenced by her staying silent about me visiting Theia at the club.

"Why would you need to protect her from me?"

She gave me a sad smile.

"If I tell you the truth, I'll be breaking her confidence, so I'm going to need you to answer the question first. Do you have romantic feelings for Theia?"

I looked away as my chest tightened with each breath I took.

"I don't know the answer to that."

For a moment, she said nothing. I turned my gaze back to her, finding Remi looking at me with a pensive expression on her face.

"The fact you don't know says a lot more than you realise." She sighed and dropped her arms from her chest. "I have to get to work. Think about it for me, and when you do work it out, tell her the truth. She deserves that from you."

Remi didn't give me a chance to respond, not that I even knew what to say, and left me standing in front of the building with a million thoughts racing through my mind. The most prominent one being... was Remi trying to tell me Theia had romantic feelings towards me? And if so, what the fuck was I going to do about it?

Work out if you have them for her, like Remi told you to. It's the only thing you can do at this point, Gil... you don't have anything to lose, but if you fuck this up with Theia, you'll regret it.

EIGHTEEN

Theia

My heart pounded so fucking hard in my chest, I thought I was going to die any minute. My skin felt all clammy, and I no longer knew how to function properly as I leaned against the mirrored wall of the lift.

What the hell just happened?

I could have sworn Gil had flirted with me at the café, which was crazy because it was the opposite of being friends. He didn't want more than that. He'd told me as much. So why the hell had he fed me cake, smiled at me, and actually laughed? I made Gil Villetti laugh. I had to be in an alternate timeline right now. None of this made any sense. Not the way he'd been in the café, nor the way he looked at me when he stroked my cheek outside. I couldn't have seen affection in his eyes. And to think if Remi hadn't interrupted us, I might have blurted out the truth of my feelings because, in the moment, I wanted us to be something we couldn't. That was the worst part of all. I could have made an absolute fool of myself.

I buried my face in my hands and groaned out loud. No one else was in the lift to witness my breakdown, thankfully. This was a nightmare. One I didn't know if I wanted to escape from. On the one hand, I was losing my mind over this man. On the other hand, I was revelling in his attention.

You're so screwed up, you know that, right?

I didn't only like Gil because he was attractive. He was blunt, yes, but he was smart, protective, understanding, and wanted to do what was best for everyone, to the detriment of himself. The last part I wanted to work on with him if I could. He didn't need to run around trying to live up to everyone else's expectations. He needed to be himself. He was good enough all on his own. I wished he could see it.

The lift arrived on my floor. Gathering myself, I made my way out and along the hallway to my front door. I unlocked it and stepped in. A lone letter sat on the welcome mat. I sighed, shoving the door closed before I picked it up. It didn't contain an address, just my name. It immediately made me suspicious as I carried it through into the kitchen. I placed my handbag down on the counter and ripped open the envelope. Dread settled in my stomach when I read the note.

You've been such a bad girl, haven't you?
It's lucky for you we've missed our favourite
fuckdoll, so we won't punish you... much.
Be seeing you very soon, whore.

I set the page down. Then I turned away and leaned my back up against the counter, taking several deep breaths. I tried to convince myself everything was okay, but I knew it wasn't. Nothing in my life was okay right now.

Here I was trying not to have a panic attack because the men from my past were back. And I was confused as fuck over Gil's behaviour today. The man I shouldn't want. The one who made me trust him without having even tried.

I wanted to cry. I wanted to tell him everything. Throw myself at his mercy and let someone else take care of me for once in my life. But I wouldn't. It wasn't in my nature. I already owed so much to one Villetti for giving me a safe haven. I couldn't owe anything to Gil. Not with the life he was involved in.

You can still tell him about your past, though, Theia. He won't judge you or make you feel lesser for it.

Would it make me feel better? I'd carried this burden for so long. Until I met Gil, I thought I was okay. I thought I had a handle on everything. But I didn't. My view of myself was so fucking skewed. He never asked me to re-evaluate myself, but I had, all because he didn't want me the way almost every other man I'd encountered since I was rescued did.

I was worth more than being an object of sexual desire. In the short time of being around this man, he'd shown me that. He *saw* me. I didn't know how much I needed to be seen by someone else. To be seen as me.

I wiped away the stray tear falling down my cheek. More slid down my face. I couldn't prevent them. Everything was a mess, and all I wanted was comfort. For someone to listen and tell me it was okay. I wasn't broken. What those men had done didn't define who I was for the rest of my life.

Rationally, I knew those things. I didn't need validation from anyone else. When you've lived with so much pain for so long, wasn't it human to want to share it with someone? To know you're not alone? All I'd done for the past four years was feel alone. I'd isolated that part of myself from everyone I knew. I didn't want to hide it any longer. Not from him.

Wiping my eyes with my sleeve, I tugged my phone out of my pocket and sent a message.

THEIA: I KNOW I SAID I WASN'T READY TO TALK ABOUT MY PAST, BUT I THINK I NEED TO.
THEIA: OH, THIS IS THEIA, BY THE WAY.

I'd added his number to my contacts over the weekend after debating with myself whether I should. He'd given it to me. Told me to use it if I needed anything. Well, I needed him, so I would have to wait and see if he was okay with it.

I stuffed the offending letter in the drawer along with the others and made myself some herbal tea before taking it over to my living area. Curling up on my sofa with a blanket over me, I put on some mind-numbing TV show to distract myself from everything.

I was beginning to think I wouldn't get a response from him when my phone buzzed. I picked it up from the coffee table and stared at the screen.

GIL: OKAY. JUST TELL ME WHEN AND WHERE.

It was straightforward and to the point. Totally Gil. It made me smile, then I burst into tears all over again. It was stupid to feel grateful he was willing to be there for me.

THEIA: TONIGHT AT MINE, BUT ONLY IF YOU'RE NOT BUSY.
GIL: I CAN BE THERE AT NINE.

I sent him the number of my flat before dumping my phone down beside me and reaching for the tissue box. Settling back down after wiping my face, I focused back on the TV while I waited for evening to come.

When nine rolled around, I'd had dinner, a quick shower and changed into something more comfortable. Not like I was out here trying to look my best for him when I was an absolute mess inside. The buzzer went, and I let him up. When I opened the door a few minutes later, Gil was rubbing the back of his neck.

"Hey, come in."

I stepped back, allowing him to walk inside. He let me take his coat and hang it up before following me into my living area.

"Do you want a drink?"

"No, I'm okay," he said, watching me with a neutral expression on his face.

"Well, make yourself comfortable."

I waved at the sofa in the living room before I fixed myself a drink. A strong one because I was so fucking nervous. It had felt like a good idea to open up earlier, but now I was going back and forth with myself over how wise it was to spill my darkest secret to him.

Don't act like you don't need this, Theia.

I sighed as I carried my gin and tonic into the living room and took a seat on the sofa on the other end from Gil. He stared at the space between us with a frown but didn't comment on it. I decided not to question why. I was too busy fretting over what I was about to tell him.

"Did something happen?" he asked after a moment.

"No. I couldn't stop thinking about it after I brought it up earlier."

His eyes narrowed as if he didn't quite believe me.

"I see."

I stared down at my glass before I downed the whole thing and set it on the coffee table. Then I took a deep breath.

"I was kidnapped, and sex trafficked six years ago when I was twenty."

The words came out in a rush. It was the only way I could get them out. My eyes were on my fidgeting hands. They were clammy, so I wiped them on my thighs, but it didn't stop the fear rippling under my skin.

I'd told someone the truth.

I'd admitted it.

Fuck.

It wasn't until I felt two hands covering mine and stilling their movement that I let out a shuddering breath. My eyes darted up and met Gil's dark ones. He'd moved closer, and our thighs were almost pressing together. His face was expressionless, but there was emotion swelling in his eyes. Something that looked a little like anger mixed with understanding. It made me want to spill the whole sorry story and not leave a single thing out.

"They held me for two years in a cold, dark room with no outside windows. The door had a window. There were bars across it like I was in a prison. I was fed three times a day to keep me from starving to death, but I got so thin because they never gave us enough."

My voice was unsteady, but I knew I had to keep going. The way he held my gaze made it impossible not to.

"At least once a day they took me out to… to do things to me." I swallowed. "At first, I fought, screamed, and told them no. It didn't stop them. It went on and on. I lost track of time and space in that place. It was hard not to. They told me it was to break me in, to make me obedient." A lone tear slid down my face. "And it eventually did. That's when it got worse."

I choked on my breath, letting more tears make tracks along my cheeks.

"They gave me to their clients, and they… they…"

Gil's hands squeezed mine, reassuring me it was okay.

"They hurt me. Sometimes it was just one of them, sometimes more. I can still remember it all so vividly. Every painful, excruciating moment of those two years of my life. I thought it would never end. That they'd never let me go. Every day I wished for freedom, but it never came. They broke me into tiny little pieces, and I started to believe them when they told me I was a whore. That I wasn't worth anything else."

I closed my eyes, trying not to allow the images to flood my mind. The way they laughed as they raped me repeatedly like it was a fucking joke. How they told me it was all I was good for. I would never be anything but a whore. A piece of meat for them to fuck whichever way they pleased. They dehumanised me to the point I no longer knew myself. Until I was a shell.

"Then one day I was being taken to visit a client. They had me in the back of a van with a blindfold on. They never let us see where we were going. I don't even know to this day where I was held, but that's not the point. I thought it was like any other day, except during the drive there was a loud bang outside. The van screeched to a halt. Then there was shouting and the sounds of fighting. I could have sworn a gun went off. The next thing I knew, my blindfold was pulled off and there was a woman. She told me I was safe."

I opened my eyes and stared at Gil. There was pain in his eyes like he was horrified by the story I was telling him. It was horrifying, but there was hope too because I'd got out of there. I'd been set free.

"To this day, I still don't know her name. I don't know any of the names of the people who rescued me. All I know is she took me somewhere safe. After a few months of nursing me back to health, they introduced me to Liza, who set me up here and told me when I was ready, I had a place to work, but only if I wanted to. I didn't have to worry about anything for months. They gave me access to a therapist, but I never took them up on that offer. I did, however, start working at Desecration as a hostess. Then I became a dancer. And two years ago, I started sex work as a way of taking my power back from the people who'd hurt me."

I let out a sigh and looked down at our joined hands.

"However, I'm beginning to see that because of the abuse, I suffer from hypersexuality. Even though I found an outlet at Desecration where I felt safe, I also see I cut myself off from relationships and making real connections with people. All I've ever felt good for is what I can do with my body. Meeting you

170

has made me see I'm worth more than that. I deserve more than being treated like a sex object for men's pleasure. And it's time I stopped treating myself like that's all I am too."

NINETEEN

Theia

I didn't know whether admitting the part about him was a good idea or not but being honest felt right. The burden I'd been carrying around had lifted. I'd finally told my story out loud to another person. Someone I trusted with it. Who made me feel safe enough to be myself without fear of judgement or reproach.

When Gil let go of my hands, I looked at him, but he was busy pulling tissues from the box on my coffee table. I swallowed when he turned back to me, took hold of my chin, and mopped up my face without me saying a word or asking him to. Gil's attention was solely on drying my eyes for a long moment. He lowered the hand containing the tissues but didn't release me. He stared into my eyes, making my skin prickle all over from his scrutiny.

"Thank you for trusting me with your past. Sometimes I feel like saying sorry is kind of meaningless, but what I will say is, in my eyes, you are strong, brave, and resilient. And it's okay if you're still healing from your traumas. I understand and will never think less of you for it."

My hands curled around my thighs to keep from reaching out and touching him. He was so close, and his words hit me in the chest, making more tears spill down my cheeks. He wiped one away with the pad of his thumb.

"Theia…"

The way he said my name was almost too much for me to handle. His deep voice was laced with concern.

"Thank you," I whispered.

His expression softened a fraction.

"For what?"

"Being here and listening."

He dropped his hand from my face and grabbed another tissue.

"I want to be here for you."

My heart squeezed as he handed me the clean tissue. He dumped the others on the coffee table. His eyes darted around the room as if he was taking in our surroundings.

My living space had white walls, but I'd adorned them with black and white photographs of dancers. There were accents of blue and grey on the sofa, the cushions, and the rug under the coffee table. I'd never thought to buy a great deal of stuff or really make my flat into a home. Nowhere felt like home to me. Not after two years had been stolen from me. And no matter how safe I felt here, there had always been the lingering threat of them finding me again. Now the threat had come to fruition. Yet… I still couldn't bring myself to tell anyone about it. At the end of the day, if they came for me, I'd run. I could never go back. I'd rather die.

"Have you had a sexual interaction with someone that was just for you?"

I wiped my face with the tissue he'd given me, shoving away my morbid thoughts.

"What do you mean?"

"You started sex work to take your power back, which I support by the way, but I'm questioning whether you've ever had sex be about you rather than what the client requests of you."

My eyes darted away as I considered his question. I couldn't be sure why he was interested, but I wasn't going to lie to him about it either.

"Once... but it was also sort of work-related."

"How so?"

Did it feel weird I was about to admit to my only sexual interaction outside of the club in the past four years to a man I wanted to have sex with but couldn't? Yes... yes, it fucking well did. But I'd told Gil about the darkest parts of my past. This was tame in comparison.

"I wanted to start doing voyeurism scenes with a partner, but I hadn't been with anyone intimately since... well, you know." I waved a hand. "One of my friends at the club offered to help me. He doesn't know about my past, just that it was bad." My cheeks grew hot. "Actually, it's the one you sort of met. I felt safe with him, but it wasn't a passionate thing, it was more of a 'help me get over this fear of being touched even though I really want to be touched' thing because, you know, hypersexuality mixed with trauma."

Gil cocked his head to the side as if he was evaluating my words and making a mental calculation about them in his head.

175

"There are only three guys at the club I do scenes with and it's maybe like once or twice a month. We're all just friends, and we take boundaries very seriously. Everyone at the club does."

I don't know why I felt the need to tell him. It wasn't like we were anything other than friends, so it shouldn't matter what I did at the club with other people. It shouldn't make a difference, but to me, it did matter that he knew. I could tell myself a million times over we were friends, but it didn't stop me from wishing there could be more between us.

"Would you want an experience that's all about you?"

"Who wouldn't?"

"That's not an answer."

I fiddled with the bottom of my t-shirt.

"Of course I would, but I'd have to feel safe with them, and they'd have to be okay with giving me the things I want."

"What would those be?"

Now I was questioning why the hell he was asking me these things. Gil had been very insistent about wanting to know me. I could put it down to that, but there was something else to all of this I couldn't put my finger on.

"Well, you already know I like being watched. I'd like it if they told me exactly what to do, and praised me for it when I pleased them, but at the same time, I want to be…"

I swallowed. The only person who knew about my kinks was Gael, and he'd given me shit for this one because I wouldn't admit it. Gil hadn't judged me so far, but I couldn't help being apprehensive all the same.

"Be what?"

"Degraded," I whispered. "Just not the word 'whore.' It reminds me of... them."

Gil's expression didn't change as I admitted these things to him. I wasn't sure what he made of my desires. Honestly, this whole conversation was making me have seriously inappropriate thoughts about him. Ones I'd banned myself from having. How on earth could I help it when he was asking me questions about my sexual preferences?

I want to sink down on the rug between his knees and rub my face all over his thigh. I want him to watch me touch him. And I need him not to have any emotion on his face as I make him come.

"Thank you for telling me."

My mouth opened and closed. My thoughts were giving me way too many feelings and him only saying "thank you" to my confession like it was an everyday conversation we'd been having was the icing on the cake. Not wanting him to see the emotions I was sure were written all over my face, I jumped up and grabbed my empty glass before making my way over to the kitchen. I fanned my face as I stood with my back to him. I set about mixing myself another drink, taking a large gulp when I was done.

"Theia."

I whipped around to find him standing right behind me. My back knocked into the counter as I tried to contain my surprise. How the hell had he snuck up on me?

"Yes?"

"Did I upset you by asking you all those things?"

"No. Not at all. Just not used to anyone taking an interest in my... preferences."

No way in hell I was upset with anything he'd said to me. More like confused and aroused at the same time. Both were very disconcerting when he was standing so close to me. I could practically feel his body heat radiating off him.

What did I do to deserve this torture? I want to be near him, but it's fucking painful at the same time.

"I want to know everything about you."

"Everything?"

"Yes."

I shouldn't be surprised with all the questions he'd asked me, but I was.

"Do I get to know everything about you in return?"

"If you'd like."

He stepped closer, making me hold my breath as he reached around me. The next thing I knew, he'd handed me the glass of gin and tonic I'd made. I sipped it, staring into his dark eyes as I tried not to react further to his proximity. It was impossible, of course, but I had no other choice.

"You told me you didn't want me involved in your mafia life."

"It's dangerous."

"I think you're just as dangerous."

He smiled.

"Maybe I am. If I told you what I've done for the *famiglia*, there'd be no going back."

My fingers tightened around the glass.

"Who am I going to tell? I barely speak to anyone outside of the club."

He leant a hand on the counter and tipped his head down.

"I trust you, Theia. I'm just not sure you're ready to hear it, and honestly, it's for your own safety that you don't know."

My chest grew achy as did other places I didn't want to think about with him so close.

"Is everything else fair game?"

"Yes."

I smiled and sipped my drink.

"Okay… do you like cats?"

He blinked as if my question was entirely unexpected. I wasn't going to ask him anything super personal. He might have asked me those things, but I felt awkward considering what he'd told me about himself and his sexuality.

"Do I like cats?"

"Yes. I've always wanted a pet, but I can't have one here."

"I guess so. My cousin Rina has cats. For some reason, whenever I go around my aunt's house, the two of them always seek me out. Rina thinks they like my energy, whatever that means."

The thought of two cats following Gil around and him being completely confused by their attention was too adorable for words.

"You're the cat whisperer."

He snorted and shook his head, taking a step back from me.

"Hardly."

"I can imagine you being the Pied Piper of cats. All of them following you home and you shutting them out in the cold because they're giving you too much attention."

Gil laughed before rolling his eyes.

"You're right about the last part."

I finished my drink, and grabbed a bottle of wine from the fridge, along with a single glass. I checked to see if he wanted something, but he refused again. We made our way back over to the sofa. I asked Gil about his childhood with his brothers, and he obliged me with stories of Enzo's and Zayn's antics. I wanted to get off the more charged topics of conversation we'd been having. It was nice to see him smile as he reminisced about his younger years.

By the time I'd finished the bottle, it was getting late, and I was a little drunk. When I got up to walk him to the door, I almost tripped over the rug. Gil caught me by the arm and steadied me. I stared up at his face, and all I could think about was how attractive this man was. How much I wanted him to take me in his arms and kiss the living shit out of me. Apparently, my thoughts had become unfiltered.

"You have pretty eyes," I said with a giggle, then shoved my hand over my mouth, completely embarrassed by what had come out of it.

Gil merely stared at me for a long moment before he moved closer. The next thing I knew, he'd swept me up into his arms like I was a child.

"What are you doing?" I squeaked.

He didn't answer me. Instead, he carried me through the living room, into the hallway, and down to my bedroom. He adjusted me in his hold so he could pull back the covers, and he placed me in bed. I found myself tucked in the next moment. He straightened and looked down at me.

"Goodnight, Theia."

I didn't know what to do with myself. Gil had put me to bed. It was sweet, him taking care of me in my semi-drunken state even if I had said something stupid.

"Night."

I closed my eyes, and as I drifted off, I could have sworn I felt his hand brushing my hair from my face, followed by his fingers dusting across my cheek. But I could have been mistaken. I was in the land of dreams before I could be sure of anything at all.

TWENTY

Gilberto

The past two days had involved me going back and forth with myself over what I was about to do. After Theia had told me what happened to her, all I could feel was rage. Those sick fucks had stolen two years of her life and subjected her to the worst type of things. She might not have gone into detail about the abuse, but I could imagine well enough. She'd had to heal from so much, and she was still working on herself even now. I could understand how hard it must be. I related to her, what with my own inner fucking turmoil over who I was.

Theia was such a strong woman. I admired everything about her. More than admired, if I was honest with myself. I had feelings for her. Ones I didn't know how to handle, but I had them all the same. And tonight, I'd decided to tentatively act upon them… at least, sort of. This wouldn't be about me. It would be about her.

When I'd asked Remi to arrange this, she'd not asked questions, but I could hear the suspicion in her voice. She told me to work out if I had romantic feelings toward Theia. This was my answer… as unorthodox as it was.

My eyes were on the window in front of me as I sat there waiting for Theia to arrive. This was so fucking alien to me. And yet I was strangely okay about the whole thing too. Maybe it was because I'd be doing it with Theia, who I felt a kinship with. I knew intimate things about her. The bond was there, alive and kicking. I was emotionally involved, and I got the impression she liked me the same way too. I couldn't be sure as I was terrible at working out whether women were interested in me, but she gave it away when she blushed over some of the things I said. Not to mention she told me I had pretty eyes when she was drunk.

The door to the room opened and in stepped Theia, her expression tentative and a little confused. Remi clearly hadn't told her what was about to happen.

"Hey," she said, coming over to the sofa, but she didn't take a seat.

"Hello, Theia."

She was wearing these little black shorts with a black lacy bra. Over that, she wore her red harness. I swallowed at the sight of it. Yes, I'd always thought Theia was beautiful, but now this urge to touch her thrummed through my body. I wanted to explore every inch of her skin almost as much as I wanted to know everything going on in her mind.

"Can I ask why we're in the voyeur room?"

"We're going to watch a scene."

Theia blinked rapidly, then frowned.

"Watch… you and me are going to… watch?"

"Yes."

"A scene as in a sex scene?"

"Yes."

She opened her mouth, closed it, and then opened it again.

"Are you sure *you* want to watch people having sex?"

"Yes."

"Oh."

She looked stumped for a moment. Then she let out a breath before going over to the panel next to the window and pressing one of the buttons. Remi told me it was to signal to the performers when we wanted them to start. I knew Theia would have questions about this whole situation, but I was glad she decided to go with it.

"Come here, Theia."

She walked over and took a seat next to me, staring down at her hands. I tilted my head closer to hers.

"Are you nervous?"

Her eyes darted up towards me, those blue-grey depths filled with an emotion I couldn't read.

"Yes, I mean, no, I mean… I wasn't expecting you to want this when Remi said you requested to see me."

The light in the other room switched on as the door to it opened and in walked a man and a woman.

"This isn't for me. It's for you."

She blinked.

"What? Why would—"

"I want you to watch. Don't take your eyes off what's happening in the other room."

I pitched my voice lower, wanting her to know this wasn't a request. Theia visibly shivered, shut her mouth, and turned her gaze to the other room. I glanced over at the occupants. The man had dark hair, and the woman was a redhead. He was undressing her. I wasn't remotely stirred by the sight, but when I turned my gaze back towards Theia and caught the way she bit her lip, my hand twitched in my lap. The urge to pull her lip from her teeth made my jaw clench.

This is for her. She said she feels safe with you… and you know what she wants.

She shifted in her seat a minute later, her hands rubbing against her bare thighs. I glanced at the scene, finding the two participants were nude, their mouths locked together and their hands exploring each other's bodies. I'd asked Remi to tell them to make it a sensual experience. This scene was for Theia's benefit, not mine.

My eyes went back to her, watching the way her lips parted and her pupils dilated. I might not be able to read people's body language very well, but this… I knew what this meant. I leaned closer until my mouth was almost at her ear.

"Is this turning you on?" I murmured.

Theia almost jumped at the sound of my voice. Her eyes darted over to me, and her hands wrapped around her thighs.

"Keep watching, Theia."

She flushed as her gaze went back to the scene.

"It is," she whispered in a barely audible voice as if scared of admitting the truth to me.

"Then I want you to touch yourself."

Theia let out a choked sound.

"Wh—"

"Run your fingers over your body."

For a moment, I thought she was going to refuse, tell me this was crazy and demand to know what was going on. Her body trembled as she uncurled her hands from her thighs. She placed her fingers on her chest and ran them down the centre. I watched her movements, mesmerised by the delicate way she brushed the tips of her fingers along her bared skin. Her breathing grew more laboured as she continued. This was what she wanted. For someone to tell her exactly what to do. To make it all about her.

"That's it. Now, circle your nipple with your thumb over your clothes."

Her small pant was the most delicious sound I'd ever heard. I almost buried my face in her neck and asked her to moan. Her hand enclosed around her breast and her thumb hovered over it.

"Gil…"

"Are you going to be a good girl and do as you're told?"

Her head bobbed as her thumb brushed over her nipple. Her body rolled slightly. I looked at the scene in front of us. The two of them were on the bed now. He had his face buried between the woman's thighs. Her hands were dug into his hair as her back arched off the bed.

"Do you want someone to be on their knees for you? For them to worship your body the way it deserves?"

"Oh fuck," she hissed, her other hand sliding across her bare stomach. "Yes, I want that."

Without thinking about it, I pulled myself up off the sofa. Theia didn't stop watching the scene, but I knew she was wondering what I was doing. I walked around the sofa and knelt behind her. I leaned over the back, my hands on either side of her, and placed my mouth next to her ear. Now I could see what everyone was doing without having to turn my head.

"Move your other hand lower and slide it under your clothes."

She did as she was told, sliding her fingers under the waistband of her shorts.

"Touch yourself, Theia," I whispered, "I want to watch you."

Her exhale was mixed with a slight whining noise as her fingers came into contact with her pussy. She rubbed herself, letting out more quiet noises of pleasure.

"That's it. Show me what this is doing to you. Show me your fingers."

She dragged her hand out and brought it up. The way they glistened slightly with her arousal made me swallow.

"Take them off."

"My... my clothes?"

"Yes."

She hesitated, her chest stuttering slightly.

"You want to be on display for me, don't you? You want to be my good girl and show me how you pleasure yourself. Unless you want to be something else, hmm? What's the word I'm looking for, Theia?"

The way she squirmed had me wrapping my hands around the back of the sofa. This overwhelming urge to take over and touch her myself was making me a little crazy, but I would stay in control. I had to. Didn't matter if it was the first time in my life I'd ever wanted someone the way I wanted her. Not even my teenage self had felt desire for my friend the way I felt for

Theia. This was for her. All of it. She deserved to know what it was like to have someone make it about her pleasure. Her desires.

"I want to be… to be…"

"Yes?"

"Your good little slut," she whispered.

Whatever she wanted me to call her, I would. And to be quite honest, hearing her tell me what she wanted to be for me was far more arousing than I'd counted on.

"Then you should do as you're told."

Her fingers went to the buttons of her shorts. She flicked them open before tugging them and her underwear down her hips. It had been a long time since I'd seen a woman half-naked. And none of them had made my mouth water the way Theia did when she discarded her clothes next to her before spreading her legs.

In the room in front of us, he'd gone from eating her out to sitting up against the headboard and having her ride him. They'd angled themselves so Theia and I had a perfect view of the way he was sliding in and out of her.

"I want you to fuck yourself the way she's fucking him."

Theia shifted before running her hand down between her legs. Then she was sliding two fingers inside her. She moaned as she began to fuck herself on them, her palm rubbing up against her clit with her movement.

"That's right, look at you on display for me. Does that feel good, Theia?"

"Yes," she whimpered.

"Mmm, I bet it does. You're being such a good little slut."

Her moan and the way her back arched had me swallowing back the saliva pooling in my mouth.

"Show me your breasts," I murmured.

Theia pulled the cups of her bra down with one hand, exposing her nipples to the air. They were hard points on her chest.

"Pinch your nipple."

She did as I told her, panting while she continued to fuck herself on her fingers.

"Are you imagining my hands on you? Touching you the way you're touching yourself?"

"Gil," she whimpered.

I tried not to grind myself against the back of the sofa at the sound of my name on her lips, despite the fact I was aroused. It was painful, this need inside me to do things to her soft little body. Things like pin her down and give in to my baser instincts. It wasn't that I'd never desired sex, but I wanted to know what it was like to drive into someone I was actually sexually attracted to. I wanted to feel it. And this right here confirmed I felt that way about Theia.

It wasn't only about sex, though. I had romantic feelings towards her too. It scared the shit out of me because this wasn't what I expected to happen. I didn't know that by getting to know this woman and finding out her deepest darkest parts, I'd become enamoured with everything about her. It was almost as if a switch had flipped, and it all became crystal clear.

I wanted Theia. I wanted to make her mine… but I didn't know if it would be a good idea, given the state of my life and everything going on in it.

TWENTY ONE

Gilberto

S haking myself out of my brooding thoughts, I focused my attention back on Theia. She was grinding against her hand and moaning as she did it.

"Answer the question, Theia."

"Yes, yes… fuck."

I pressed my mouth right up against her ear, unable to stop myself from touching her in this small way.

"Do you want me to wrap my lips around your nipple? Nibble and bite it until you're panting? Or do you want my mouth lower, hmm? What about buried in your pussy?"

She almost lost it when I said that. I could tell by the way her body shook and the pained moan sounding from her throat. They were the exact things I wanted to do to her. The ones I trusted myself to do. I wasn't sure what would happen if I was given free rein of Theia. How far I'd want to go.

"Both, I want both," she cried out. "Fuck, Gil, I'm... I'm..."

"You're going to come?"

"Yes."

I wanted to see her fall apart. To watch her come undone because of me. The scene in front of us was building up to its final climax too. He had her on her hands and knees now, driving into her as their skin slapped together loudly. We could hear them through the speakers, but I only cared about the sounds Theia was making. Those were the hottest things I'd ever heard in my life.

"Good girl," I whispered, making her shudder. "My good little slut."

She let out a breath. Her body tensed, and her head fell back against the sofa. She closed her eyes, letting out a pant as it washed over her. After a minute, her body stilled, her hands falling away to rest next to her.

When she opened her blue-grey eyes, she stared right up at me with an almost lust-drunk smile on her lips.

"Did you like that?" I asked, my voice gravelly.

"Yes," she whispered.

I reached up and stroked a finger down her cheek.

"I wanted it to be good for you."

She swallowed but didn't reply. I could see the wheels turning in her head, wondering why I'd done this and what it all meant. I wanted to explain, but I found the words didn't come. It was hard for me to express the feelings I had toward her. I might want Theia, but there was still a part of me holding back with all the uncertainty in my life.

Edric and I were heavily focused on searching for these missing shipments. I might have tasked him with it, but he'd asked for my help with a couple of things. This was my family and my business. I would never let him flounder. Besides, I'd spoken to Nino yesterday, and he'd got nowhere with Dino and Gian. They were still acting like everything was fine when it clearly wasn't. It made me incredibly suspicious. Why would they be so blasé about the situation? Probably didn't want to look weak. They were likely afraid of what might happen if they were found out to be incompetent considering their cousin, my father, had been offed by his own son.

With all that shit going on, I didn't want to put Theia at risk. If anyone else found out about my visits to her, it would cause problems for both of us. It wasn't like I could stay away, either. I didn't want to. I'd have to think very carefully about what I did next when it came to me and her.

There was also the fact she'd mentioned she didn't seek out personal relationships. I understood why now, but I was worried she still felt that way. That she might not want this to be something. I wasn't sure if I wanted it or not, either. Fuck, my mind was a mess. I didn't know what the hell to do with all of these things racing through it.

I pulled myself up off the floor, aware I was still aroused, but not wanting to stay down on my knees any longer. Theia raised her head and stared into the other room. They'd finished up while we weren't paying attention and the lights were off again.

"I hope you didn't find watching your work colleagues strange," I said as I discreetly adjusted myself.

"No, it wasn't weird."

She gathered her clothes and put them back on, sliding her shorts up her thighs before buttoning them up. She set her hands down on either side of her body and looked down at the floor.

"So… um, did you want to talk or anything?"

Her voice was hesitant as if she didn't know how to act. I had flipped things on their head. I could admit that, but I had no idea what to say either. I was pretty sure if I didn't get out of there, I might blurt out things I wasn't ready to admit yet. This whole experience had given me way too much to think about.

"I actually have to go."

She turned her head and stared up at me with this sad yet confused look in her eyes.

"Oh… okay."

I leaned down towards her, placing my hands on the sofa.

"We will talk soon, Theia, I promise."

She let out a breath when I stroked her cheek again before straightening.

"Okay."

Leaving her was so much harder than I expected it to be. I wanted to stay, but my brain was far too chaotic. It was making me anxious. I didn't want to talk about something as important as this without a clear head. And I could admit I was scared of what I was feeling inside.

I felt like shit the moment I got home to my penthouse flat, almost like I was a stranger in my own skin.

The moment I'd been able to move out of the family home when Enzo finished school at eighteen, I did. I needed some separation between me and my father. Working with him and being at home with him had become too much, especially with his expectations.

My first instinct was to go straight to my bathroom, strip off and step into a steaming hot shower. I stood under the spray staring at the tiled wall, and all I could think about was her. The way she'd been so willing to do everything I said. How she'd moaned. The way she'd said my name.

My head dipped as my hand landed on the wall in front of me. I let out a breath, my body feeling hot all over and not just from the shower. It was the memories flooding my brain.

"Theia," I whispered, wishing I hadn't been such a fucking coward and ran away the moment I got overwhelmed by what happened.

I want her… fuck, I want her.

Irritation with myself and the lingering arousal had me wrapping my hand around my cock. I let out a harsh pant as I stroked it, wondering what the fuck was wrong with me. Why couldn't I tell her the truth? It wasn't fear that she didn't feel the same way about me, but everything else. I didn't know what to do with these feelings inside me. How to handle my own fucking emotions. I'd never had to. I avoided them, but I couldn't do that when it came to Theia. She was far too important to me.

My hand moved faster, my grip tightening until it was almost punishing. A growl of frustration sounded from my throat. I didn't want to be here in this shower, getting myself off in an angry torrent of emotions. I wanted to be with her. To touch her. To hold her against my bare skin and revel in the feel of hers. To abandon all my stupid thoughts and anxiety. I wanted to give in to the unending need to *fuck* her that had started the moment she'd slid her fingers inside herself for me.

Why did I run from you? Why did I do this to myself? Why did I do it to you? You deserve better from me, Theia.

Her name sounded over and over in my head. It wasn't the one I wanted to hear. No, I needed her voice crying out my name. Again. And again. I could hear it forever and it would never be enough. I closed my eyes and let the images of her carry me under. My grip was bordering on painful, but I couldn't stop now.

"Theia... fuck..." I groaned. "My good girl. My good little slut."

I didn't know why calling her that was arousing to me. Questioning it felt futile. It wasn't as if I'd judged her when she told me she wanted to be degraded. I hadn't expected to want to degrade her. If anything, I wanted to do more... but only if she was okay with it.

I let out a harsh breath as I erupted in my hand. It wasn't cathartic or remotely rewarding, but it was a release I needed after all the pent-up arousal and desire from earlier. It didn't feel good, though. Nothing about this did.

Cursing myself, I washed before getting out and wrapping a towel around my waist. I stood by the sink, placing my hands on either side and stared into the misted-up mirror. My reflection was distorted. I ran a hand through my wet hair, leaving it half sticking up.

"What is wrong with you?"

It felt like everything was fucking wrong at that moment. I wanted to fix this situation. All the shit going on with my family, the mafia and especially with Theia. The only one I could make right was her.

I got dressed and picked up my phone, shooting off a text to Remi.

GIL: IS THEIA STILL THERE?

It took her a few minutes to respond, and by that time, I was already leaving my flat to get in the car.

REMI: NO, SHE LEFT AFTER HER THING WITH YOU...

I checked the time as I got in the car. It was only nine. I'd booked a relatively early session with Theia, as I didn't know how things would go.

REMI: DID YOU UPSET HER? SHE DIDN'T SEEM LIKE HERSELF.

Unsurprisingly, Remi had got straight to the point. And now I felt even worse.

GIL: I THINK SO, BUT I'M GOING TO FIX IT.
REMI: I SHOULD HOPE SO. DON'T FUCK IT UP ANY FURTHER.

I threw my phone into the cupholder, turned the engine on and set off. What was going on between me and Theia was none of Remi's fucking concern. I knew she was worried about Theia, but our relationship was our business.

What relationship is that, Gil?

The relationship I was going to build with her. We'd already laid the foundations. Now I had to stop being a fucking coward about the whole thing. If I wanted her, I had to go get her and make it clear my feelings towards her had changed. I wanted to explore them with her.

Some people might call me crazy for wanting someone like her with the job she did. It was her life. She'd been clear about what she did and didn't do at the club. I wasn't going to dictate shit to her about it. If that's what Theia wanted to do, she had my full support.

My father had taken away my mother's choice. He'd forced her to stay with him in the most brutal and permanent way. I would never do that to someone I cared about. It wasn't in my nature. I might be a killer, but I wasn't heartless or cruel. Not like Gennaro Villetti had been. I was beginning to see that now. It wouldn't be an overnight process, but I had to separate the man he wanted me to be from the man I actually was inside.

You don't have to be Gennaro Villetti… you can be Gilberto Villetti. It's okay to be you. She sees you as Gil. So be him. Don't let your past ruin your future.

I pulled up near Theia's building, paid for parking, and made my way down the street. After running away from her at the club, I could only hope Theia would let me in. That she'd want to see me. I wouldn't be a fuck up this time… at least, I hoped not. I didn't know what would happen when I saw her, and whether I'd manage to get my words out about my true feelings towards the woman I'd become completely enamoured with.

TWENTY TWO

Theia

My hands rubbed my temples as I stared at the ceiling. The moment I got in after leaving the club, I'd taken a shower and changed into my pyjamas. I curled up under a blanket on my sofa and lay there in the quiet, semi-dark, wondering what the fuck had happened. My body was thrumming from the aftermath even now, but it didn't stop me from being confused by his behaviour and actions.

When I went into work today, I'd only had one client on my schedule… Gil. Remi hadn't acted like anything was amiss until she informed me it would occur in room ten, the voyeur room. I'd become immediately suspicious. And to be quite fucking honest, I was right to be on my guard.

The memory of his voice in my ear flooded my senses all over again. I put my hands over my eyes and cursed myself for feeling aroused by it. The only thing that had become clear to me was why Gil had asked me all those questions after my confession about my past. He wanted to know what I wanted. And he'd given it to me. Fuck, had he given me something precious and so fucking fulfilling... until it wasn't any longer. Until he left me questioning everything between us.

Why on earth would he do something sexual with me when he wasn't interested in me that way? He hadn't mentioned anything changing between us. Sure, he'd flirted with me at the coffee shop, but I didn't know if it was because he was more comfortable with me or something else.

The buzzer went for the door. I hauled myself up from the sofa and went over to the intercom. My heart almost stopped when I saw who was at the front door on the little camera. Not even thinking about it, I pressed down to let him up without even saying hello. Gil looked up at the camera for a second before he pushed the door open and walked in.

I stepped back and wrung my hands together. He was here. He was fucking here. Were we going to talk about what happened? I hadn't been expecting him to turn up here. Not when he said he had to go. I assumed it was mafia stuff, but perhaps I'd been wrong.

The moment he knocked, I rushed over to the front door and pulled it open, completely forgetting I was only dressed in a baggy t-shirt and a pair of shorts. My hair was still damp from my shower.

Gil stood there with a pensive expression on his face. I didn't say a word. The sight of him made my heart squeeze painfully in my chest. My hand went to it, rubbing the sore spot. His eyes darted to my movement, narrowing on my fingers before they darkened with an intensity that had me shivering on the spot.

Before I could do another thing, he stepped towards me, pulled the door from my free hand, and shoved it shut behind him. I was backed up against the wall a moment later. Gil's hand went to my face, thumb skating over my jaw while his other curled around my back. I sucked in air when he pressed me against him.

"Theia," he rumbled, the vibrations of his chest running right through me. "*Non riesco a toglierti dalla mia testa.*"

My mouth parted. I had no idea what he said, but the emotion in his voice almost fractured me in two. Had he spoken Italian to me? I don't know why it surprised me Gil would be bilingual, considering I'd heard Zayn and Arlo using Italian to speak privately, but it did.

"Come with me," he all but growled.

He stepped back, took a hold of my hand, and dragged me towards my bedroom. I didn't stop him. I was so fucking undone by the fact he was here, I had no idea what to do with myself. Especially not when he released me by the end of my bed before his fingers were at the bottom of my t-shirt, pulling it up off my body. For some reason, I put my arms up to help him. My shorts and underwear came next, my clothes pooling on the floor below us.

"Sit."

I planted myself on the end of the bed, watching him kick my clothes away before he lowered himself to his knees.

"Can I touch you?" he asked, as if hesitant to go any further without my consent.

I swallowed and stared into his dark eyes. He'd undressed me without a word and yet he was still asking permission to put his hands on me.

201

We should talk. I knew that rationally, but all my thoughts were centred on the fact he was going to *touch* me. Gil Villetti, a man I was so fucking gone over, was going to touch me. Putting the brakes on this to have a conversation was the very last thing I wanted. I let my heart and desires make the decision rather than my head.

"Yes," I whispered. Whatever he was going to do to me, I wanted it.

His hands went to my knees, curling around them as he spread my legs and shifted closer to me. Lifting his hands from my knees, one went to my jaw, tipping my face to the side while the other gripped my hip. He leaned closer until his mouth was hovering over my jaw.

"*Non posso fermarmi. Non posso.*"

I choked on my own breath when his lips pressed against my skin. They were so gentle. He drew them down my jaw. My hands instinctively reached out and gripped his coat lapels when he kissed his way down my neck. His hand slid from my jaw to my neck when his mouth landed on my collarbone.

Gil is kissing me. Gil Villetti is kissing my skin. His mouth is on me. Holy fuck.

"Theia," he breathed my name, almost like a prayer, as his tongue ran down my chest between my breasts. "*Sei mia,* Theia, *mia e mia solo.*"

At this point, I didn't give a shit what he was saying. I didn't want him to stop. Had it ever felt this good to be touched by another human being? I couldn't remember a time when I'd wanted someone the way I desired Gil. His hands and mouth didn't remind me of the bad things in the past. I felt safe surrendering my body and mind to his will. I'd never let the latter happen before, but in the voyeur room, I'd done it. Everything told me to question what he was doing, but I'd shoved it away and let his voice carry me under. Now his touch was doing the same.

The moment his mouth latched onto my nipple, I moaned and arched into him. His grip on my hip tightened as if the sound I'd made was eroding his control. I choked when he bit me. It wasn't hard, but pleasure bloomed all over my chest. His thumb stroked circles around my hip, inching closer to where I'd grown wet for him. I ached for Gil to make my need go away. To sate my desire for him.

"I want to taste you."

His words made me want to combust on the spot. I couldn't speak as he was busy leaving hot, open-mouthed kisses down my stomach. My hands left his clothes and gripped the covers next to me instead. His hands went to my thighs, pushing against them to open my legs further. I watched him stare at my most intimate parts when he reached them. He hovered over my pussy for a long moment, as if taking in every inch of me. Then he used his thumbs to spread my lips before he lowered his mouth to my clit and gave me one long lick.

"*Fuck*," I cried when he latched on and used his tongue to make slow circles around it.

My hand went to his hair. I had to touch him. My fingers curled into the thick strands, gripping them to anchor me to him.

I can't believe his mouth is on my pussy. Why is this so hot? Why is he so fucking hot? I want more. I want him. All of him. Fuck, I need him.

My hips shifted. Gil let go of my thigh to grip it and hold me in place. His other hand slid between my legs, stroking along my entrance in an unhurried motion. He wasn't in any rush with the languid way he circled my clit. The drawn-out nature of it had my body trembling.

"You've been so patient with me. This is your reward for being a good girl," he murmured.

Was it possible to die from a man's mouth? I felt like I was going to expire from the words coming out of his.

"Gil."

"Mmm?"

"Please don't stop."

He only redoubled his efforts. I groaned when he slid two fingers inside me, hooking them upwards and beginning to fuck me with them. He worshipped me with his mouth, and I yielded, letting pleasure carry me under and drown me. My fingers tightened in his hair. My other hand went to his shoulder, gripping it and digging my nails into his coat.

"Oh, oh, fuck, don't stop. Please. Don't. Stop."

My words came out in a jumbled mess, becoming more incoherent by the second. I'd never been particularly vocal during sex, but everything was different with Gil.

Safety. He's safety. You can be you. Let go and just be you.

My body moved against him without my say-so. I went with it, my hips rocking into his face. Not even his grip on me stopped them. I whined his name over and over, begging him to keep going. If this ended, I might cry out of sheer frustration.

He fucked me deeper with his fingers, pressing hard against the spot that had my eyes rolling back in my head. His tongue kept the same pressure as if he knew changing it up would ruin it for me. I was so close, right on the edge of the cliff and waiting to fall into the abyss below.

"Can… can I come?" I gasped.

Why the fuck I'd even asked was a question I didn't want to look too closely at. Gil pinched my side as if to say "yes" since his mouth was busy between my legs. It didn't take much longer after that. I cried his name as the pleasure washed over my body, making me want to melt on the bed.

When it was over, I let go of him and collapsed backwards, pressing my arm over my eyes as my chest heaved. Gil kissed his way down my thigh and pulled his fingers from me. I peered down at him from under my arm and caught him sticking them in his mouth.

Of all that is holy…

He sat back on his heels and looked at me as if he was assessing whether I was okay or not. His mouth parted, but before he could get a word out, his phone went off. Gil frowned and dug his hand in his pocket, drawing it out and staring down at it. He let out a mild curse before he pushed up to his feet.

"I'm really sorry, Theia, but I have to go."

I dropped my arm from my eyes and sat up abruptly.

"What?"

This man had given me delirious pleasure with his mouth and now he was leaving again without explaining a single thing. I didn't know whether to laugh, cry, be pissed off or a combination of all three.

He reached out and ran his thumb over my jaw.

"If I could stay and talk, I would, but it's mafia business and I have to deal with it."

I didn't get a chance to respond because he turned and walked out of my room. It took a second for me to register he was leaving before I got up and ran after him, not caring I was naked.

"Gil!"

He'd reached my front door and was in the process of opening it. He turned his head and glanced at me, his face devoid of emotion.

"You can't just leave after... after that."

He gave me a shake of the head.

"I'm sorry."

I didn't stop him as he walked out the door and closed it behind him.

What the actual fuck?

Turning, I trudged back into my bedroom, picked up my clothes and pulled them on before slumping down on my bed. My hands went to my face, rubbing across it with my frustration. Why had I let him go down on me instead of insisting we talked? I'd been too busy allowing myself to feel rather than think clearly about this whole thing. Gil had a way of making my rational side fly right out the fucking window.

Another knock came on my front door. I jumped up and practically ran to the door, expecting he'd come back as he realised it was fucked up of him to leave. Wrenching it open, I opened my mouth and started to say something when I stopped dead in my tracks.

That's not Gil.

My world flipped upside down on its head. The man standing outside was the opposite of Gil. It was one of my captors. He had an ugly sneer on his face.

"Hello, Theia."

I slammed the door shut so fast he didn't have time to stop me. My hands fumbled with the locks, making sure they were secure as I put the chain on. His fist hammered on the door a moment later.

"I know you're fucking there, Theia. You can't keep me out."

I slid down the door, pressing myself back against it as fear raked up and down my spine.

I should have known they'd come for me. I should have fucking known!

I had to leave. I had to fucking well leave. Run as far away as I could. There was no other option here. I wasn't safe. I wasn't fucking safe.

Panic lanced through me. My heart beat was echoing in my ears, making it hard to think straight.

The banging didn't stop, but I forced myself to crawl away from the door into my living space, where I'd left my phone on the kitchen counter. I dragged it off and fumbled to unlock it. Then I did the only thing I could do under the circumstances. I rang Gil. He'd only just left, but if anyone could get rid of this guy, it was him.

Please pick up. Please fucking pick up!

When the call went to voicemail, I almost screamed, but I held myself together and decided to leave a message.

"Gil, I need you. Please. They found me. They've found me. They're here. Please come back. Please."

They were the only words I managed to get out before the phone dropped out of my hand. I curled up in a ball on my kitchen floor, listening to my worst nightmare hammer against my door, dreading he'd break through and take me away from the life I'd worked so hard to build.

TWENTY THREE

Gilberto

I could have killed Edric right at that second. To say I was frustrated was a fucking understatement. Not only had I not been able to talk to Theia, but now she was probably mad at me for leaving. I'd gone to hers with the intention of telling her the truth about my feelings. Only when I'd seen her did those good intentions fly right out of the window. I'd been so wrapped up in needing to touch her. To give in to my desire to taste every inch of her. And fuck had I. She'd felt so good. Tasted so fucking good. It had been the very best sexual experience I'd ever had. Only then my fucking best friend had gone and made my life difficult.

"Where are you holding them?" I ground out, taking the stairs two by two.

"At the warehouse," Edric replied.

My phone buzzed in my hand. I drew it away from my face to find Theia was calling me. As much as I wanted to answer, I had to deal with Edric first. Besides, I was relatively sure she

was pissed at me. I needed to make this up to her. I would…
somehow.

"Okay, and you're sure they know something?"

"I wouldn't have texted you otherwise. I know you want to
deal with this situation yourself."

He was right. Anything to do with these fucking missing
shipments and my cousins was my personal responsibility. I
couldn't leave it up to my men. I might trust Edric, but this
was family. It required my full attention.

"There's three of them, yes?"

"Mmm, Alvin is the leader. Reckon the other two are just
henchmen."

"Okay, good. Thank you."

Edric let out a little sound of surprise.

"You're thanking me? Well, that's a new development."

I rolled my eyes.

"Shut the fuck up. I'll see you soon."

I hung up before he could reply. That fool needed to stop
giving me shit. I always expressed my gratitude to him. Maybe
not to others, but Edric meant something to me, even if I
never admitted it to him. I wasn't very good with feelings. He
knew that.

I looked down at my phone and found Theia had left me a
voicemail. Clicking on it, I put my phone back to my ear. The
automated voice went on for too long and finally it played the
message.

"Gil, I need you. Please. They found me. They've found
me. They're here. Please come back. Please."

I swear my heart fucking stopped at the panic in her voice.
They'd found her. Who the fuck had found her? It took me a

minute to reboot my fucking brain. There could only be one "they." I ran back up the stairs I'd walked down. If those fucks laid a hand on her, I would kill them myself. In fact, I wanted to fucking kill them for what they'd done to her. Rage built inside me, burning so fucking hot it was like a damn furnace. There was concern there too. For my beautiful, strong, resilient girl who had fought her way back from the worst sort of pain.

I'm coming, Theia. I'm fucking coming for you.

The men and Edric could wait. She was in danger right now. And I refused to let her down again. I'd already done it too many times this evening. She deserved so much more from me.

I could have taken the lift downstairs, but I'd needed a minute to gather my thoughts and talk to Edric. I half regretted the decision because if I had taken the lift, I might have caught the fucking guy before he'd got to Theia.

Bursting through the stairwell door as I reached her floor, I could see a man hammering on her door.

"Hey!"

He looked over at me as his hand raised again. Then he was running away down the corridor, disappearing around a corner the next moment. Every instinct inside me was screaming to go after him, but I had Theia to worry about. She was who I needed to keep safe. I made a mental note of what he looked like before I ran to her door.

I knocked gently, not wanting to scare her any further.

"Theia, it's me."

There was no sound from within.

"Theia, open the door, please. It's Gil. He's gone, and I need to know you're okay."

It took another minute before the locks behind the door turned and she pulled it open. The chain was on the door, so I could only peer through the gap.

"Theia."

She let out a little sob, shut the door, unlatched it, and pulled it open. I was caught off guard when she launched herself at me, wrapping her arms around my neck and burying her face in it.

"Gil," she sobbed.

I stroked her back and walked inside, shutting the door behind us as she clung to me.

"Shh, I'm here. I'm right here."

"Did… did you see him?"

"Yes. He ran before I could do anything."

She held me tighter as if she couldn't let go. Her whole body was trembling. My poor girl was terrified.

"Don't leave me," she sobbed, "please don't leave me."

My heart fucking hurt with her words. As if I would leave her in this state. Not when she was crying and scared out of her mind. I picked her up and took her into the living room, settling us down on the sofa together. I let her cry herself out, stroking her back until she'd settled down and her body stopped trembling.

While she was crying, I thought about what the fuck I was going to do. If those cunts had found out where she was living, they'd be back. This building might be safe, but the fact they'd got in made me think they had help. My brother had made sure his employees had the highest security, but I didn't feel right about leaving her here alone. Not after this.

"I need to tell you something," she whispered into my neck.

"What's that?"

She pulled away and looked up into my face.

"I've known they found out where I am for weeks."

I didn't know how to react to her words.

"You have?"

She nodded and looked away, her face going red.

"They've been sending me letters saying all this horrible stuff, and I've been ignoring it. I didn't want to believe they'd actually get to me. I know it was stupid, but… I'm not good at asking for help."

The fact they'd been threatening her pissed me off even further, but I could also understand why she hadn't told anyone. Hell, it had taken her years to even admit her past to anyone. I did not have time to dwell on the whole situation, though. I still had to deal with these fuckers Edric had found.

"You can show me later. Right now, I need you to put some clothes on and get your stuff together because you're coming with me. I'm not letting you stay here."

Theia blinked, then rubbed her face.

"You're not?"

"No. It's not safe."

She didn't immediately respond. Instead, she crawled out of my lap and used some tissues from the box on the coffee table to wipe her face.

"Okay, but where will I stay?"

I got up off the sofa.

"With me. I'm going to need you to hurry. I still have business to deal with."

She nodded, then got up herself and left the room. I paced her living area, running my hands through my hair. This was a fucking mess, but there was no way in hell I was letting her out of my sight. I walked into the hallway and found her leaving her bedroom with a bag. She'd pulled on a pair of jeans and a jumper. I expected her to be longer. My eyes narrowed on the bag.

"Is that everything you need?"

She nodded.

"I already had it packed."

I stepped closer.

"Why?"

Her eyes darted to the floor.

"I packed it the first night they sent me a letter because if they came for me, I was going to run and never look back."

My stomach dropped to my feet, but I shoved the sickening feeling away.

"We need to go."

I grabbed the bag from her and went over to the door. Theia stuffed her feet into shoes, shrugged her coat on, and went into the kitchen to grab something. She came out with a few envelopes, staring at them with distaste. I assumed they were the letters, so I took them from her, unzipped one side of her bag and stuffed them in. I opened the front door and strode out, looking from side to side to check our surroundings.

"Come."

Theia dashed out, locked up, and followed me to the lifts. We were silent as we rode down and I walked her out to where I'd parked. I dumped her bag in the boot and got in. Theia was already in the passenger seat and had her belt on. I turned the engine on and started off. Reaching over, I put my hand on her knee. She looked at me, but I kept my eyes on the road.

"I'm going to keep you safe, okay?"

She slid her hand over mine and squeezed it.

"Okay," she whispered.

I had to move my hand to use the gear stick, even though I wanted to hold her hand and reassure her. She might have stopped crying, but I knew the incident was still affecting her. I could tell by the stiffness of her shoulders.

She was silent next to me for the drive. My mind was racing at a million miles an hour. What if she hadn't called me when that guy came? What if she'd run? I'd have never seen her again. I couldn't abide the thought of it. It made my stomach churn again. If I didn't have her, I think I might have come apart at the seams. She was the only good thing in my life. The person I looked forward to seeing and couldn't get out of my head.

You're mine, Theia. I won't let you go. I'll protect you from them.

I didn't know when I started thinking of her as mine, but I knew it deep in my bones. No matter what it took, I would keep this woman by my side.

When we pulled up outside the warehouse, I turned to her. She was looking out of the window, her fingers curled together in her lap.

"Where are we?"

"A warehouse the *famiglia* owns."

There were other cars parked outside, one of them being Edric's.

"Why?"

"I have to deal with business first, okay?"

I'd told her that before we left, but maybe she'd forgotten. "Okay."

She opened the car door. I got out too, thankful she hadn't thought to insist on staying in the car. I needed her where I could see her. The fear of losing her was driving me to fucking distraction. However, I also needed to remain focused in order to deal with the situation inside.

I walked around the car and took hold of her hand. She stared down at our joined fingers with wide eyes.

"I hate to ask this of you, but I need you to stay quiet while I do this. It's for your protection and safety, okay?"

She nodded. I drew us to a halt right outside the door and cupped her face with my free hand. She leant into it like my affection was exactly what she needed.

"We'll talk after this and I'll take you home, I promise."

"I know."

I dropped my hand from her face and pulled her inside. She followed me without question. We walked down a short corridor before striding through a pair of double doors into the warehouse itself. It was situated near our headquarters. We used it for our interrogations.

Edric was standing just outside of the pool of light where three men were sitting tied to chairs. There were a few of our men dotted around, watching them. We'd selected a few trusted individuals to help us deal with this issue. They'd all been sworn to secrecy and had been directly assigned to Edric. I still hadn't chosen a new *capodecina*, so Salvatore was taking care of the rest of our men himself. He was more than capable of it, but eventually, I would have to appoint another to reduce his workload.

Edric turned at the sound of our footsteps. His eyebrows shot up when he saw I had Theia with me. I stopped in front of him, watching his eyes dart between us.

"Uh, Gil, who is this?"

"Take care of her and give me your gun."

"What?" he hissed, keeping his voice low.

"Do not try my patience, Edric. She is *mine,* and I expect you to take care of her while I deal with them." I put my hand out. "Give me your gun."

His eyes bugged out behind his glasses at my no fucking nonsense tone. He slid his hand under his bomber jacket and pulled out the gun I knew he had holstered underneath it. I'd left mine in the glove compartment, not wanting to scare Theia by getting it out in front of her. I took the weapon from him.

"Which one is Alvin?"

"The one with the bear tattoo on his arm."

I nodded at him before turning to Theia. Her blue-grey eyes were wide as saucers. I didn't have time to soothe her or sugar-coat what was about to happen next.

"Stay with Edric."

I released her hand and stepped around my best friend into the ring of light. My eyes scanned the three men, who all looked battered and bruised. I spied the one with the tattoo sitting in the middle, so I raised the gun and without a word of warning executed both of his "friends" with a shot right between the eyes. The gunshots echoed around the warehouse. The man in the middle, Alvin, flinched and looked left to right.

"What the fuck?" he barked the next moment.

I walked right up to him and placed the barrel under his chin, tilting his head up.

"I'm not in the mood for interrogation tactics or games. You're going to tell me where the fuck those missing shipments are, or I will make your last hours on earth miserable. And trust me, there is a reason why people fear the name Villetti in this town. You may not have realised who is in power now and that's okay." I leaned closer. "I'd say it's a pleasure to meet you, Alvin, but it's really not. Nevertheless, I'm Gilberto and I used to be Gennaro Villetti's executioner. Now, I'm the boss, so I suggest you decide real fucking fast which way you want to play this."

TWENTY FOUR

Theia

The sound of the gun going off was still echoing in my ears, even as Gil started talking to the man in the chair. I flinched at the noise and the scene in front of me. Two men were dead. Killed by the man I'd become obsessed with. I'd always known Gil was dangerous but seeing him be the mafia boss was an entirely new experience. I had no idea what to think or feel about it.

"So, what's your name?"

I jumped at the sound of the voice next to me. My head turned towards Gil's friend. Edric didn't look anything like how I imagined him when Gil had told me about his best friend and second-in-command. He was tall and lanky, with chestnut hair and hazel eyes behind a pair of wide-framed glasses. The other men in the room looked far more like they belonged in the mafia. They were in black suits and ties. Edric had a few buttons undone on his rather colourful shirt underneath a green bomber jacket and he was wearing beige chinos.

"Don't tell me you're one of those silent types, like Gil. I swear he's a fucking nightmare to get anything out of."

I wrapped my arms around my body.

"He told me I needed to stay silent," I murmured, not wanting to draw attention to myself.

Gil was still talking to the man in the chair, but I tuned it out. Thinking about the fact he'd killed two people wouldn't get me anywhere. The evidence was already in front of me, considering they were slumped in their chairs with bullet holes between their eyes. He hadn't even hesitated. It was like his walls came down the moment he stepped into the warehouse, and he became Gilberto Villetti, mafia boss and silent killer. It reminded me of when he'd stabbed that guy in the hand the day we'd met.

By all accounts, I should be fucking terrified of him, but I wasn't. Gil wouldn't physically harm me. He'd hesitated to even be close to me at first. The memory of what he'd done to me earlier flooded my senses, making my skin grow hot.

Stop it! You can't think about that right now.

Edric tutted next to me.

"Figures. Always so strict, that one. Doesn't let me have any fun either."

I looked down at the floor and tried not to smile. Gil certainly had "fun" with me this evening, though I'm not sure it was the type of fun Edric wanted to have with his best friend.

"I'm Theia."

He put his hand out to me.

"Edric."

I took his hand, letting him shake mine.

"I know who you are."

His eyebrow curved upwards.

"Do you now? He didn't say a word about you. Fucking typical. Such a secretive bastard."

I hadn't expected Gil to tell Edric about me. He was a private person, and while he'd told me about his friend, I was aware he had a hard time opening up to people. It was almost a miracle he'd told me anything about himself at all.

"Edric."

Gil's voice whipped around me. There was a sharp note to it that made my back straighten on automatic. It reminded me of the club where he'd told me in no uncertain terms what he wanted me to do, and I'd obeyed without question. My eyes darted over to him. He was looking at his friend with a neutral expression, but I could feel the undercurrent of annoyance radiating off him in waves.

Edric rolled his eyes and made his way over to Gil. They had a hushed but heated conversation between them for a minute. His friend looked a little forlorn as he came back over and stood next to me. I wondered what Gil had said to him. It was probably about behaving himself around me. I don't know why it gave me a warm feeling in my chest. The same thing had happened when he'd called me his. Did Gil see me that way? I had no fucking clue. We hadn't talked about it. On the way over here I'd thought about saying something, but my mind was still firmly on the man who'd arrived on my doorstep. My captor. I only knew him as H. They all went by an initial in that place, so I didn't know his real name.

I wrung my hands together, shoving the memory of his face out of my brain. It was something to think about later when I wasn't surrounded by Gil's mafia men. Not that they would hurt me. I was pretty sure Gil wouldn't let them get anywhere near me.

"Apparently, I'm not allowed to flirt with you," Edric muttered a moment later. His eyes were fixed on Gil's back, and he was scowling.

"You were flirting?"

"No, but I've never seen him so irate over me talking to a woman before. Normally, he doesn't care who I engage with. You're clearly special to him."

There was only one way I could take that. The fact Gil was acting possessively over me was quite the fucking revelation. We still had to talk, though. I wasn't going to take any of this at face value. Until I heard the truth from Gil's mouth, I would reserve judgement on anything that happened.

A scream echoed around the room, making me flinch again. My eyes went over to the man Gil had been talking to. He'd stepped back, but his men were standing by the guy in the chair. One of them had a pair of pliers in his hand and pinched between it was a tooth. Blood dripped out of the tied-up man's mouth.

"I told you I would make this easy on you if you just tell me where they are," Gil said in a calm voice as if none of this affected him.

"Jesus," Edric murmured next to me.

I glanced at him. He was a little green around the edges. A mafia man who was queasy at the sight of blood was not something I expected. Then again, I didn't think Edric was a typical mafia man. Not from what Gil had told me about his best friend.

I should be bothered by this myself, but I'd already seen so much violence in my life. I was numb to it. Still, they were torturing him for information. It was brutal... but what else did I expect Gil's life to be like? I had no fucking clue. Only that it was dangerous, violent, and unforgiving. Now I was getting a clear picture of his mafia world and why he hadn't wanted to make me a part of it.

They continued to torture the man as he refused to talk. Edric turned his eyes away from the scene. I tried not to watch but found it hard to look away. Seeing Gil wearing this mask was a whole new experience. I could see his father's influence. Gil was shut off... cold and emotionless. And I understood why he had to be.

The floor was awash with blood, fingers and even two toes by the time the man talked. Gil drilled him for everything and put the man out of his misery with a shot to his head. He turned away from the scene after telling his men to clean it up and strode over to us. He gave the gun back to Edric.

"Make sure they do as they're told. I'll speak to you in the morning."

"Yes, *boss*," Edric replied with sarcasm lacing his voice.

Gil didn't react. He merely grabbed my hand and tugged me away. I followed him without question. It wasn't until we were outside, and he'd opened the car door for me, I looked up at him.

"Gil..."

"Get in the car, Theia," he barked before shaking himself. Then he looked away and said in a much softer voice, "Please."

I did as I was told. I wasn't afraid of Gil, but I was worried about what was going through his head. He walked around the car and got in himself. He rested his hands on the steering wheel but didn't turn the engine on.

"I'm sorry. I shouldn't have spoken to you like that."

"It's okay."

He turned to me.

"No, it's not. You're not one of my men. You're..." he faltered and looked down at the hand break between us.

"I'm what?"

He sighed, turned his attention to the windscreen and turned the engine on. I closed my mouth, wondering if he was going to elaborate on what I was to him. At this point, I sure as fuck didn't know. I'd given him more than enough time to deal with his mafia issue. It was time we talked about us... if there was an "us."

"I'm what, Gil? What am I to you?" I asked again when he didn't say a word after a few minutes of driving. "I need you to tell me because I'm confused and... and scared right now."

He rubbed a hand over his face.

"Theia..."

"No. You don't get to Theia me. You ambushed me with the voyeur scene, left before we could talk about it, then you turned up at my flat hours later and... and... well, you know what you did. Then you fucking left me again. I don't understand what's going on. You told me you weren't interested—"

"I like you."

My mouth snapped shut. He liked me? What the hell was that supposed to mean? He was going to have to be a damn sight clearer about his feelings than that.

"I mean, I... fuck." He slammed his hand against the wheel. "I know what I said. I hadn't forgotten about that, but it changed as I got to know you. Everything changed."

It was probably a bad idea to have this conversation in the car, but it couldn't wait any longer.

"Changed how?"

He glanced at me as he stopped at a red light.

"All I want to do is be near you... and not even just near you. I want to hold you tight and never fucking let go. I want you in ways I've never wanted anyone else. You are in my waking thoughts and my fucking dreams, Theia. And it scared the shit out of me, okay? My feelings for you scare me, but I can't stay away." He rubbed his chest with one hand. "I want you in my life. I want you in my bed. I just plain fucking want you. Every part of you."

He turned his attention back to the road when the light went green. I didn't know if I could form a response. I was too shocked by what he'd said to me. While I'd wanted the truth, I wasn't expecting that. The way he'd said he wanted me like it physically pained him to speak the words. That confessing his feelings was difficult for him. But he wanted me. He *wanted* me. Not only as his friend, but more. He wanted... more.

By the time I'd put my fucking head back on straight, we'd pulled up into his building's underground carpark. Gil got out of the car and went around to the boot to get my bag. I climbed out and allowed him to lead me over to the lifts. We rode up to the top floor together, stepping out onto a small landing with only two doors. I wasn't sure what I expected, but it wasn't for him to have half a floor to himself.

Gil unlocked the door and led me inside. It was an open-plan living space with lots of natural light from the big windows. The building looked modern from the outside.

"You must be tired," he said when I didn't speak. "It's late."

I nodded. Today had been taxing for me with all the emotions and crazy shit that had gone on. Gil walked towards a small hallway off the living area. I followed after him. He stopped outside a door and opened it.

"You can sleep here. The bathroom is over there."

He waved at the door next to it. I looked at the room, then back at him.

"Is this your room?"

"No, it's my spare bedroom."

What the fuck?

This man had told me he wanted me in his bed, and yet he was putting me in his spare room? Was he fucking crazy?

"Why are you making me sleep in there, then?"

He blinked, then frowned.

"I thought you would want some space."

I sucked in a breath, my hands clenching at my sides.

"Space? I don't want space, Gil."

"I didn't want to presume anything."

I stepped closer to him. He was out of his fucking mind if he thought for a second I would want to spend the night away from him.

"You listen here." I unclenched my fist and stabbed a finger into his chest. "Not only did you make me come twice this evening, but you told me you wanted me in your bed. What on earth makes you think I would ever want to sleep in the spare room?"

He stared down at my finger. There was a confused, almost puppy-dog-like look in his eyes as if he was baffled as to why I was practically shouting at him over what he definitely thought was him being considerate of my feelings.

"You didn't say anything after I told you that."

"Jesus Christ. Do I need to spell it out for you?"

Apparently, I do because he's looking at me like I'm mad.

I flattened my palm on his chest.

"I *want* you too. I've wanted you since that first fucking day, so no, I'm not sleeping in the damn spare room. And if you don't—"

I didn't get any further. Gil dumped my bag on the floor before he grabbed hold of me and planted his mouth on mine. I was so stunned by the whole thing, I stood there blinking as the man I'd wanted for weeks kissed me like I was his source of oxygen, and he needed me to sustain him for the rest of his life.

TWENTY FIVE

Gilberto

My hand dug into Theia's hair. The other curled around her back to press her body against mine. All I could think about when she told me she wanted me was needing to kiss the angry look off her face. I didn't think she would get so mad at me for putting her in the spare room, but apparently, it was the absolute wrong thing to do.

It took her a few seconds to catch up with me when I pressed my mouth against hers. I think I stunned her into silence, but I couldn't help it. The last thing I wanted was for her to be angry. And I didn't want her to think I wasn't keen on having her with me. If anything, it would have been pure torture knowing she was in the other room.

When she reached out and grabbed a hold of my clothes, her mouth moving against mine, I parted it with my tongue. The moment our tongues met, a moan sounded in the back of her throat. I pressed her against the wall next to us. She felt so good against me. All thoughts of doing anything else but kissing her left my head. I could drown in her mouth.

Her body rocked into mine as her hands left my clothes and dug into my hair instead. I only kissed her harder in response. It was messy, but I didn't care. I'd kiss her until we were both breathless, then I'd only kiss her some more.

"Gil," she moaned against my lips.

The sound was so needy and sent all my blood rushing south. Then my thoughts were consumed by a need to be inside her. I couldn't wait any longer. It had to be now. It had to be right fucking now.

Pulling her away from the wall, I picked her up, my hands cupping her thighs to steady her. She wrapped her arms around my neck and her legs around my waist, allowing me to carry her down the hallway and into my bedroom. I knelt on the bed and set her down, my mouth still glued to hers as I did it. Theia's legs parted on instinct, letting me settle between them. Her body ground up into mine, making me let out a pained groan.

My self-restraint was shot to pieces. I didn't know what the hell came over me, but Theia was my oxygen. The need pulsing beneath my skin. The person I couldn't help but want so reverently, it threatened to undo all of my hard-earned control. Here I was, experiencing the real and oh-so-intoxicating desire for another person I'd never been allowed to indulge in before. And I couldn't get enough of it. Of her. If I was honest with myself, I'd wanted to find a person who would ignite me the way she had. Deep down, I'd craved it with every inch of my fucking being.

"Gil, please," she panted as I kissed my way down her jaw.

"What do you want?"

"You."

My hand went to her jumper, pushing it up her chest as I needed to feel her. Every part of her against every part of me. There was nothing else for it. Whatever exhaustion from the day that had plagued me on the way here was gone. I didn't care to ask her if she was okay after she'd witnessed me execute three men. All I cared about was being in this moment with her. Wrapped up in a bubble of desire.

"Tell me exactly what you want me to do."

Theia helped me strip her jumper and t-shirt off. She wasn't wearing a bra underneath. My eyes were on those perfect breasts, wanting to kiss them all over again like I had done earlier.

"It's not a want," she whispered, "I need it."

"What do you need?"

Her eyes grew hooded as my fingers worked the buttons of her jeans. I wasn't taking my time, even though I probably should savour every moment. I couldn't think about anything but doing this with her.

"Fuck me."

The way she said it was so full of desperation. Did she think I didn't want that too?

"You need me to fuck you?"

"Yes."

"Good, because I need to fuck you too."

Her blue-grey eyes widened slightly at my admission. I didn't think Theia realised just how deep my need to be with her ran.

My hands tugged apart her jeans, pulling them down her hips with little care whether I tore them. I didn't think Theia minded judging by the way she was staring at me. I had to shift back so I could slide off her trainers and socks. Those were dropped off the end of the bed before I pulled the rest of her clothes down her legs, leaving her bare before me.

Pushing off the bed, I got to my feet and stared at her. Did she know how beautiful she was? I admired her curves and edges with clinical detachment before, but now... now the sight of her was just plain damn alluring on every single fucking level. I wanted to indulge in it. But what I wanted more was to be inside her.

My hands went to my clothes, pushing my coat off my shoulders. She watched me with rapt attention, barely breathing, as I tugged my shirt over my head and dropped it to the floor. Her lips parted on a sharp exhale, but she didn't say a word. I didn't have to ask if she was happy with what she saw. It was written all over her face. I might be shit at reading women, but I'd been trying to learn Theia's expressions and what they meant. This one was lust. Of that, I was sure.

I didn't want to take my time with the rest of my clothes, but I did for her. Being the sole focus of her attention didn't make my skin itch in the uncomfortable way it did with other people. It was itching for an entirely different reason. One that I couldn't scratch without her involvement.

When I was as bare as her, I knelt on the bed before crawling over her. She was almost panting, her eyes intent on mine.

"I'm going to take what I want from you, Theia," I murmured as I ran my finger down the centre of her chest. "If you don't want that, tell me now."

Her teeth dug into her bottom lip, but she didn't say a word. Her hands rested at her sides, neither trying to escape her fate nor drag me closer to speed this up. I tried not to smile. She wanted to give up control, just as she had earlier in the voyeur room, and when I'd made her sit on her bed so I could bury my face in her pussy.

Leaning closer, I hovered my mouth over the hollow of her throat. I could almost hear the rapid staccato of her heartbeat.

"You want me to take control, don't you?"

"Yes," she whispered in an almost breathless voice.

"Good girl."

Not wishing to delay this any further, I leant towards my bedside table, ripping the second drawer open. I might have never brought a woman back to my penthouse, but I liked to be prepared for all outcomes. My hands found the box I'd stuffed in there. I was tearing it open and extracting one of the small packets a moment later. Theia watched me without making a sound. I could feel her eyes tracking my every movement. They darkened when I rolled the condom on. Even more so when I leant back over her.

I placed one hand by her head, my fingers brushing over her hair laying on the covers. The other was between us. I gripped my cock and ran the tip through her folds. She let out a breathy moan when the head knocked her clit.

"Do you want this?"

She nodded.

"Tell me."

"I want your… your cock."

"Inside you?"

"Please. I want it so fucking bad."

I lowered my face towards hers until our lips brushed.

"My needy little slut."

She shuddered, then whined as I tipped the head down to rest at her entrance. This was as big of an occasion for me as it was for her. I'd never fucked anyone I'd been sexually attracted to. And I'd never been so turned on in my life.

It would be her first experience with someone she wanted since she was freed.

I took a moment to appreciate the gravity of it all before I shunted my hips forward and buried the head of my dick inside her.

My teeth gritted at the sensation, preventing a groan from leaving my mouth. I almost didn't know what to do with myself. Whether to keep going or to stop and experience this for as long as I possibly could. Theia's hips shifting underneath me saved me from making a decision. She wanted more, so I gave it to her. It was slow, drawing out every second, every inch until she was panting and gripping the bed sheets below us. I wanted those delicate hands on me. Tearing one from the covers, I placed it around my back. Theia's fingers spread out across my skin, urging me on with a small push.

Our eyes were locked together. It was impossible to look away. Our connection fed me. I might revel in the physical intimacy of all of this, but it was the emotional one that caught me first. The way she'd opened up to me and me to her, even though we were both fucking terrified of doing so.

One final thrust seated me inside her. Then I didn't want slow and gentle any longer. I wanted rough kisses, no mercy, and all the beautiful sounds of pleasure she made.

My mouth landed on hers as I pulled back and pushed in again. Her fingers dug into my back, a small moan erupting from her throat. Fuck, she felt so good. I finally understood why so many people were driven half-crazy with lust for another person as I gave it to Theia. Drove into her again and again as if my life depended on it. Because it kind of did. At least, right then, it did. I couldn't pull myself away even if I tried.

Theia turned her face away from mine, her other hand coming up to wrap around my shoulder.

"Harder," she whispered as she buried her face in the covers. "Please. I need it."

I pressed my mouth against her throat.

"Then turn over, and I'll make sure you never forget the feel of me inside you."

She choked on her own breath as I reluctantly pulled away from her. Theia flipped over, presenting herself to me on her hands and knees. I gripped her hip and slid inside her again, unable to help the groan leaving my mouth. When she looked back at me, I saw the heat and need in her eyes, so I gave her what she'd asked for.

Pulling back, I slammed into her, listening to the way our skin slapped together and her almost keening sounds of pleasure. I wasn't gentle as I took her, using her hip as my anchor.

"More," she whined. "Please, just fuck me. I don't care about coming. All I need is this."

I leaned over her and wrapped my hand around her throat, not stopping in pace.

"Do you want me to use you, Theia? Use you for *my* pleasure like a little slut?"

"Yes," she panted, her hands curling into the covers.

"You've been such a good girl, taking everything I'm giving you and asking for more."

My fingers tightened around her throat as I continued to pound into her pliant body. She was arching into me, pushing back to show me how much she wanted it. I pressed my lips to the shell of her ear and kept my punishing pace.

"I want to tie you to my headboard," I whispered.

She moaned. I could feel the vibrations of it against my hand.

"And make you into *my* obedient little slut."

"Gil."

It was a desperate cry, one that spoke to my entire soul. This wasn't only sex. It was healing for her and eye-opening for me. A meeting of two broken people who wanted to find solace in each other without judgement. Without the world intruding on such an intimate moment.

It was then I knew I would have a very hard time ever letting Theia go. And I needed to know if she felt the same way.

"Is that what you want? To be my good little slut and do exactly as you're told? That's what you're going to be if you stay with me. *Mine.*"

TWENTY SIX

Theia

My fingers tightened around the covers I'd bunched up below me. I was a panting mess of emotion and pleasure who couldn't remember her own name as Gil gripped my throat and fucked me into submission. Not that I was unwilling. I wanted this more than I wanted to breathe air. There was a sense of freedom I felt in letting go and giving him the reins. It was my choice. And it was funny how having that simple choice changed everything for me.

I hadn't exactly expected him to kiss me, take me to his bed, strip me off and let me see him in all his glory before he plunged inside me, but apparently, I had underestimated his desire for me. Couldn't exactly blame me for it, given I'd been relatively sure he didn't want me this way until he'd ambushed me at the club. I certainly hadn't been anticipating the mouth on him either. The things he'd said only made me burn ten times hotter. It was everything I'd wanted, and so much fucking more.

"Yes," I whimpered, "I want to be good for you."

I didn't care what I sounded like at that point. The only thing I needed was for him to keep hitting the spot inside me with his cock that sent pleasure skating up my spine. To keep squeezing my throat and calling me his slut in my ear with his deep, seductive voice. Who would have thought a man's voice could do such things to my insides, but Gil's was my kryptonite. I melted each time he pitched it low with a gravelly undertone.

"Do you want to be mine, slut?"

"Yes!"

He pressed a kiss to the shell of my ear.

"Good girl," he whispered, and I swear my arms buckled just from those two little words. "*Sei mia adesso.*"

I was wrong. The best thing I'd ever heard was him whispering in Italian to me in his deep voice, even though I still had no clue what he was saying. It didn't matter. I was too undone to care any longer.

"Please, don't stop."

"*La mia piccola troia è così bisognosa per me.*"

His hand grip on my throat tightened. It wasn't quite depriving me of oxygen, but the lack of it was making me a little lightheaded. It only fuelled the need inside me. I didn't struggle against him or ask him to release me. I sunk deeper, letting all of it carry me under the waves. Here I didn't need to think. The memories of my life before floated away. The only things left were him and I locked together. I never wanted to escape.

If my life's only goal was to worship at the altar of Gil Villetti, I would surrender to him in a heartbeat. It was fucked up. I knew it, but when you've been lost, alone and in pain for so long, finding someone who helped you mend those broken parts was a fucking miracle. He wasn't even trying to heal me and yet being with him soothed me all the same. He might be completely clueless about relationships, but I came alive with him by my side… and now he was deep inside me, making me feel every part of him, just like he'd promised. I would never forget this, nor did I want to.

Gil kissed his way down my neck, releasing the tight grip he had on it, so I was no longer almost choking.

"So beautiful," he murmured against my skin, his hand sliding from my neck to my chest. "I want to watch you again." He pinched my nipple between his thumb and forefinger, rolling it between them and making me moan in response. "I want you bare as you perform just for me." He nuzzled my shoulder, pressing hot kisses along it. "You make such artistry with your body when you dance, Theia. You mesmerise me. I can't look away."

I swear someone should make the things this man said illegal because he had no right being this hot. And he didn't even have to ask. I'd dance for him whenever he wanted. Hell, I'd put on as many private shows as he desired. Performing for Gil would make me happy. It would fuel my exhibitionist streak. When he'd watched me in the club, I'd felt myself come alive. I wanted him to see me for all that I was.

I turned my face so I could meet his eyes over my shoulder. His pupils were blown, giving him an almost sinister appearance, but I liked his darkness. I liked every part of him.

He lifted his hand from my nipple, catching my chin between his fingers and tipping my face towards his. He caught my mouth, kissing me and making me feel alive all over again. When he released my mouth, he let out a harsh pant and pressed his forehead to my shoulder. The force of his thrusts grew more erratic as if he was losing a battle with himself.

"Theia," he ground out through his teeth. "Fuck!"

The way he shuddered against me had my heart racing. He groaned my name again like it was torn from his throat. Like I'd made him come undone. And it was more than I could take.

I was in serious danger when it came to Gil Villetti. He was breaking apart all of my walls and bulldozing over them. Yet, even so, I wasn't scared because he was my safe place. He'd given me everything I'd asked for. Everything I'd yearned for in another person, even if I'd never allowed myself to admit it.

He pressed a kiss to my skin, then wrapped his arm around me, rolling us both to the side as he curled himself around my back. I slid both my hands along his arms, never wanting him to let go of me. We lay in silence for a long time before he pulled away from me to deal with the condom. I flopped onto my back and stared up at the ceiling. I didn't know how anything could top tonight's sexual experiences with Gil, but I had a feeling he would manage it.

He sat on the edge of the bed a moment later and stared out over his room. I hadn't paid much attention to it when he'd brought me in here, but it was extremely neat and tidy. The walls were a pale blue, and his furniture was all black in contrast. The bed had light sheets with a dark blanket sitting at the end. It was rumpled from our... activities. There were big windows on two sides of the room, letting the light in during the day, but currently, it was dark outside.

"Gil..."

He turned his head to look at me over his shoulder. There was caution in his expression like he wasn't sure what I would say or how I'd react to what we'd done. I reached out a hand to him, wanting more physical contact. Needing his reassurance, he meant what he said about wanting me. He shifted and caught my hand with his, bringing it up to his mouth and placing a kiss on the heel of my palm.

"You want to talk," he murmured against my skin.

We needed to. I didn't know what page he was on. I wasn't sure what one I wanted to be on, either. I mean, I knew I wanted him, but in what capacity could we make this work? He was a mafia boss. I was a sex worker. Those two roles weren't exactly natural bedfellows in the real world outside of this little bubble we were in. Then there was the matter of my past... and the fact he'd killed three people in front of me.

He let go of my hand and stood up. It made me sit up.

"Where are you going?"

"To put something on."

"Oh."

He moved around the room, picking up our clothes and folding them neatly before placing them on his chest of drawers. Gil pulled on a pair of boxers, then selected a t-shirt from his drawers and brought it over to me. He sat on the bed next to me. I put my arms up and let him pull it over my head. It swamped my lithe form. I couldn't help pressing it to my face and breathing it in. Gil quirked an eyebrow. My face went red. I hid it behind my knees as I pulled them up to my chest. He reached out and stroked my arm with his fingertips. His touch was soothing. It made me feel good knowing he still wanted to be close.

"What are we doing here?" I asked.

"You mean us?"

"Is there an 'us'?"

He moved closer and wrapped his arm around my shoulders before leaning his head against mine.

"I've never done this before, but I'd like to explore the possibility… if it is a possibility."

I almost laughed. Did he not realise how enamoured I was with him?

"I like you, in case you hadn't noticed," I whispered.

"I had."

"Then you know there's a possibility."

He let out a breath and pressed his face into my hair.

"I needed to hear you say it."

My heart hurt. He needed reassurance. I let go of my legs and turned to him, wrapping myself around his body. He curled his arms around me, holding me tight against his chest. I didn't know how much I needed to be held by him until right at that moment.

"Are you sure about this, Theia? My life is…"

"Dangerous, I know. Did you forget you literally just killed three people in front of me?"

He let out a breath.

"No… but I don't know how you feel about that."

I pulled away to meet his eyes but didn't let go of him.

"Well, I don't know if I'm supposed to think you as a mafia boss is hot, but I kind of did."

Gil cocked his head to the side as if he was trying to work out whether I was joking. I licked my bottom lip and slid my hand from his back up into his hair.

"You thought it was… hot?"

"No, I think you are hot." I shifted so I could straddle his lap and wrap my arms around his shoulders. "The killing stuff didn't exactly bother me. I've seen a lot of violence in my life. Guess you could say I'm a little desensitised to it."

His brow furrowed as his hands gripped my hips and pulled me closer, so our chests were brushing together.

"I was my father's executioner, Theia. It's the only thing I'm good at."

I leaned closer, brushing my nose against his.

"I hate to break this to you, but you're very good at other things too. I can list them for you." I kissed his cheek before pressing my lips to his ear. "Protecting me. Whispering dirty things in my ear. Eating pussy, that one you should be particularly proud of because no one else has made me come with their mouth. Oh, and let's not forget sex. You're very good at that. I can attest to it."

When I pulled back, I noted his cheeks had a faint pink tinge to them. His eyes were lowered as if he wasn't used to being complimented. Well, he would have to get used to it if he wanted to be with me.

"Theia…"

I cupped his cheek with one hand and ran my thumb over his stubble.

"I'm not scared of you, Gil. The first time we met, you stabbed a guy in the hand. I didn't run away then and I'm not running now. Besides, I can't exactly go home under the circumstances."

Gil looked up at me, his expression darkening. I tried not to think about H and the sex traffickers who were trying to get me back.

"I'm going to keep you safe. They can't have you. You're *mine*."

He didn't allow me to say anything. His mouth met mine, kissing me with such intensity and passion. I was too busy melting into him to think about what he'd said. My hips rocked against his, seeking more friction. His hand slid from my hip under the t-shirt he'd put on me, skating across my bare skin.

"Theia," he growled in my mouth. "*Ti proteggerò con la mia vita.*"

I pulled back, knowing we should probably slow down. It was late, and we both needed sleep.

"What does that mean?"

He brushed his nose up my cheek.

"I'll protect you with my life."

Jesus, does he have any idea what he's doing to my heart?

"Gil…"

"Shh. We'll talk about it in the morning. *Voglio leccarti di nuovo la figa.*"

Now he was saying things to me in Italian on purpose, so I wouldn't know what was coming next. I couldn't quite bring myself to care when he pressed me down onto my back and buried his face between my legs. I couldn't think about anything at all long after he'd made me come because I fell asleep tucked up in his arms, safe and satisfied without a worry in the world. But I had a lot of things to be concerned about, not least of all, how Gil and I would navigate everything with the turmoil in our lives. One thing I knew for sure was I didn't want to let this man go now he'd found his way into my arms. I wanted to hold on tight to the one person who made me feel secure.

I'd never had anyone like Gil Villetti before.

And I needed to keep him.

My life depended on it.

TWENTY SEVEN

Gilberto

Theia was still tucked up in my bed with her hair a mess on my pillows when the buzzer for my door went. I shouldn't have been watching her from the doorway as she slept. I couldn't help myself. She was here. The beautiful woman I'd experienced so many firsts with last night, but it wasn't time to dwell on it right then.

I turned away from my bedroom and walked down the hallway towards the front door. I didn't even bother checking who it was as I pressed down on the button to let them in. Edric had sent me a text this morning informing me he was bringing breakfast. There had been no point in me arguing. He didn't take no for an answer. The only thing I had said was to bring extra for my guest. The message I'd received back didn't bear repeating.

I'd already set plates out on my kitchen island next to the stools, so I waited until he arrived at the front door. Edric didn't even bother saying hello as he walked in as if he owned the damn place. The little shit treated it like his own. It was why I'd never given him a key. He would come and go as he pleased otherwise.

He set the bags he'd brought down on the counter and turned to me with a huge grin on his face.

"Please tell me the reason she's still sleeping is 'cause you wore her out."

"Shut up."

His hazel eyes twinkled.

"Knew it. I'm impressed you managed to bag such a pretty little thing with your non-existent social skills. I mean, it's quite the feat."

"Do you want me to throw you out?"

He put his hands up. Edric wasn't exactly wrong. I wasn't good with people, but Theia wasn't like other people. I wanted to make the effort with her. Didn't mean I always got it right, but I was trying for her.

"Okay, okay, I get it. You don't want me leering at her, but fuck, Gil, she's a knockout. You kept that very quiet."

I walked over to the counter and started digging out what he'd brought with him so I wouldn't give in to the urge to deck him. I wasn't a jealous person, but I knew what Edric was like with women. He didn't stick around for long after he got what he wanted. He had an almost allergic reaction to commitment of any kind. I didn't know why anyone put up with his shit. Well, I suppose I did because everyone talked about how charming he was, but I knew the real Edric, not the happy-go-lucky façade he liked to put up.

"I didn't keep anything quiet. It was none of your fucking business," I muttered, looking over the array of food he'd bought along with coffee. I hoped Theia would be happy with this, but I had other things in the fridge if she didn't like anything he'd brought.

Edric took a seat on one of the stools and dragged a coffee towards him, taking a sip.

"I swear you spoil my fun with all your seriousness. You not even going to tell me how you two met?"

Did I want to explain to Edric that Theia worked at Zayn's club? Not particularly. He would get the wrong idea about her.

"None of your business."

"I'll ask her."

"Don't you fucking dare."

He wasn't going to leave this alone. In fact, he'd probably ask her to spite me. The man was not known for his subtlety.

I picked up my own coffee and sat down next to him.

"I'm only going to say this once. If you dare say one smart thing about what I'm going to tell you, I will throw you out and never allow you within ten feet of her ever again."

Edric merely looked amused by my threat.

"If you say so."

"Edric."

"Okay, okay, I won't say anything 'smart.' Jesus, never seen you so possessive over anyone. It's so cute. I'm going to savour this moment forever."

I ignored his comment. Nothing about me was "cute." He was just being a dick.

"She works for Zayn at the club, and she's going to be staying with me for the foreseeable future because she's in danger. As I can't be around all the time, I want you to arrange a protection detail so she can continue to go to work if she wants to."

While I might not have asked Theia what she wanted, I wasn't going to take any chances with her safety. I wanted her monitored twenty-four-seven until I could work out who the fuck these sex traffickers were. Then I would make sure I put them out of fucking business. In fact, I'd kill every single one of them. What they put people through was despicable.

"Okay, back right the fuck up. She works for your brother? As in she's a—"

"If you're thinking about calling her anything derogatory, I will hurt you."

He shook his head.

"I wasn't going to! Christ, Gil, you really have it bad for this girl."

"What's your point?"

Edric took his time as he sipped his coffee and dragged one of the breakfast sandwiches toward him.

"My point? Well, I'll handle the protection thing for you, no problem, but does your brother know you're dating his employee?"

My hand clenched into a fist on the counter.

"We're not dating. She's *mine*."

Edric's eyebrows shot up.

"Well, I stand corrected. Does he know she's your girlfriend?"

I hadn't exactly asked Theia to be my girlfriend, only that I wanted a chance to explore us. I wasn't going to call her my girlfriend until I made sure it was what she wanted.

"She's not…" I let out a sigh. "No, he doesn't know. I mean, I'm sure he knows I've been visiting her, you know what he's like about security, but he doesn't know about whatever me and her are."

The sound of footsteps made me turn my head. Theia was stretching as she walked into the living area. My eyes scanned over her body. She'd put a pair of shorts on underneath the t-shirt she'd worn to bed. She smiled at me when she noticed I was looking, then her eyes darted to the back of Edric's head. They widened slightly. I gave her a shrug. It wasn't as if I'd invited him over. Edric and I did need to talk about last night and what we were going to do now we had a name, but it could have waited until later.

Theia came over to me, looking a little nervous about the fact my best friend was here. I wrapped my arm around her waist the moment she got close and tugged her into my side.

"Good morning," I murmured, nuzzling her neck.

She shivered and let out a little squeak. Edric looked over at us with a grin.

"Well, hello again."

"Hi," Theia said in a quiet voice.

"Edric brought breakfast."

She looked over at the food, her blue-grey eyes lighting up at the sight of it.

"I didn't know how you liked your coffee," Edric piped up. "Gil has sugar and milk if you want to add to it."

Theia stepped away from me and went over to the fridge, pulling out the milk before she opened up the takeaway cup and poured some in. She replaced the milk and came to sit next to me on the other stool.

"Do you normally have breakfast meetings with him?" she whispered to me.

"No. He was too interested in you to stay away."

She hid her face behind her mug as her cheeks went pink. I turned my attention back to Edric. I wanted him out of my flat as fast as possible. Then I could talk to Theia about the protection detail and other things.

"The name Alvin gave us... we're going to have to be careful about how we approach him."

Edric raised his eyebrows and nodded at Theia. I gave him a sharp nod back. I didn't care if she heard us talking business. She wouldn't snitch. Besides, she'd seen me kill last night. If she wanted to run, she could have, but she'd stayed. I trusted her.

"You mean Devlin? Yeah, I know."

We'd never had any problems with Devlin Clarke before. He stayed in his North London territory, and never interfered with the mafia. The fact he was involved in my cousin's missing shipments made me incredibly suspicious. It was unusual for him to be interested in weapons, considering he was a drug king. Who the fuck knew if we could actually trust Alvin's word? He was dead, so if this didn't pan out, we'd be back to square fucking one. I couldn't have kept him alive. It would have been too much of a risk.

"We have Matteo's funeral in a few days, but we need to deal with this situation as soon as possible."

"Oh great, celebrating that old fuck's life. Thanks for reminding me."

I wasn't looking forward to it either, but as the mafia boss, I had to attend. And Edric wasn't getting out of it either. A mafia funeral was a big affair. I'd visited Matteo's wife not long after I'd executed him. She was none the wiser about the real circumstances under which he'd died. Mafia wives didn't get involved in their husband's business. Probably why Edric had been wary of talking in front of Theia. I wasn't like those traditionalists. Theia needed to know what she was getting herself into with me so she could make an informed decision about our relationship. I wouldn't hide anything from her. Not now I wanted her as my partner.

Finally admitting you want her in your life for good, are you? Maybe you need to tell her that too.

I told my brain to go fuck itself. It was way too soon to be thinking that, let alone telling Theia. I was still trying to wrap my head around the fact I wanted a serious relationship with another person. I wouldn't have taken her to bed last night if I had any doubts about my feelings. They might scare the crap out of me, but it didn't change facts. I wanted her by my side.

"You going to bring Theia?" Edric asked a moment later.

She looked over at him with a mouth full of the bagel she was tucking into. It wasn't something I'd thought about. To be honest, I hadn't planned on involving Theia in my mafia life, but it was unavoidable. She was a part of it, whether we liked it or not.

"I'll discuss it with her later."

"Might do your image some good if you arrived with a woman on your arm."

"Shut up."

"What? It's only a suggestion. Jesus, you're really fucking grumpy today, and here I thought you would have chilled out after you got some last—"

"If you say another fucking word, I'll break your nose."

I did not want Theia to think I'd been discussing the fact I'd slept with her last night with Edric. He'd made his own assumptions and there was no point in dissuading him. He was like a dog with a bone sometimes.

"So tetchy."

"If you're quite done pissing me off, I suggest you get the fuck out of my flat."

"I haven't finished eating!"

I huffed and turned away from him. Theia was staring at the two of us with a bemused expression on her face.

"I would apologise for him, but he never stops being a dick, so you're just going to have to learn to live with it as I do."

"I'm not a dick. Stop giving her a bad impression of me."

"You're doing a fine job of that on your own."

We both ignored Edric's sound of outrage as Theia leaned closer and placed her hand on my thigh.

"I like him," she whispered.

"You're the only one in this room who does."

She smiled. Fuck, she was so beautiful. I wanted to take her back to bed and force those delicious sounds she made while she writhed below me. Considering I'd barely thought about sex in the past, the fact I wanted her so much was unsettling. I wasn't sure what to make of these new urges and needs she brought out in me.

"Gil…"

"Mmm?"

"You have that look in your eyes."

"What look?"

Her cheeks went pink, and she looked away.

"The same one you had last night before... you know."

Our voices were low, but Edric was definitely listening. I leaned even closer to her, pressing my mouth to her ear.

"I'm thinking about last night and how I'd like to repeat it right now, but I can't as Edric is here."

I pulled away and caught the rather salacious look in her eyes. I'd momentarily forgotten how much Theia liked to be watched. Considering how much Edric was pissing me off, I decided he needed to be given an incentive to get out of my flat. He knew what he needed to achieve, so there was no reason for him to be here any longer.

"Are you done with that?" I asked, pointing at the half-eaten bagel in front of her.

"No."

"That's too bad." I slipped off my stool and picked Theia up, tossing her over my shoulder. "You can finish it later."

"Gil! What are you doing?" she squealed as I carried her across the living area and dumped her on my sofa.

I loomed over her, staring down at her flushed face.

"Repeating what I did to you last night."

"But—"

I knelt on the sofa, covered her body with mine, and kissed her. There was a sound of surprise from behind us, but I ignored Edric. He could leave if he was uncomfortable. I didn't give a shit any longer. He'd been driving me crazy since the moment he got here.

"Well, I know when I'm not wanted," he announced a minute later. "I'll text you later."

The front door slammed, and I pulled away from Theia. The two of us burst out into a fit of laughter. I'd given Edric a taste of his own medicine. He was clearly very unimpressed with me. No doubt I'd never hear the end of it. It wasn't like me to be playful, but Theia brought out new sides of me. I couldn't bring myself to hate any of it. She was the best part of my life. I planned on keeping her in it, no matter what it took.

TWENTY EIGHT

Gilberto

When we both settled down, Theia let out a sigh and looked away. I sat up, knowing we needed to have a discussion, even though I wanted to take her to bed. It could wait until this evening when I was back from headquarters. There were things I needed to deal with outside of me and Theia today, but first, I had to address everything going on with us.

"Are you okay?" I asked, sensing the change in her mood. She dragged a hand across her face and sat up.

"I am."

"But?"

"But I'm worried too." She rubbed her bare arm. "I never thought they'd try to get me back. It's been four years. I thought I'd escaped them for good." She looked at me, her eyes full of pain. "I can't go back, Gil. I can't ever go back. I'd rather…"

I knew what she was going to say. She'd rather die than go through that again.

"Come here."

I opened my arms. She crawled into my lap, resting her head on my shoulder, and allowing me to hold her close. Her hand curled around my neck, anchoring her to me. I never thought I would be okay with this type of closeness with another person, but everything inside me wanted to comfort Theia the way she needed.

"I'm scared of everything that's happening," she whispered. "Your life is dangerous and… and I don't know how I fit in it. I'm a sex worker. I don't want to give it up, but if I'm with you, doesn't it make everything complicated?"

Did she think I cared about what she did for a living? I wanted her for who she was, not for what she did.

"I don't have an issue with your job, and if anyone else does, they can go fuck themselves."

Theia looked up at me.

"Don't take this the wrong way, but I have to ask. Are you okay with me doing scenes with other people? If you're not, we need to talk about it."

Some men might have an issue with their partner being a sex worker. Theia had been very clear about who she did it with and why. It wasn't my place to tell her to stop. It was her choice.

"You said it's just with those three guys you work with, yes?"

"Yeah."

"Then I'm okay with it. If anything changes, we'll talk about it."

Her eyes went to my shirt collar. She was quiet for a long time. I didn't want to push her into speaking her mind, so I waited.

"I never thought I would meet anyone who would accept me for who I am and have no issues with what I do."

"Your work is your work. Outside of that, if anyone was to touch you, I wouldn't be so understanding."

Her eyes flicked up to mine.

"Why? What would you do?"

"They wouldn't be breathing for much longer."

Theia opened her mouth, then closed it again and looked like she had no idea how to respond. I wasn't a jealous person, but as far as I was concerned, she was mine. No one else could have her the way I did. They didn't get to see her let go and give up her control to me in a way I knew she couldn't do with anyone else. It was mine and mine alone.

"Okay, I'm going to pretend you didn't threaten to kill anyone who touches me," she muttered as her face flushed and she looked at her lap.

"But I would."

She shifted in my lap, squirming slightly. My eyes narrowed on her expression and the way she bit her lip.

"Stop saying that."

"Why? Does it scare you I'd kill for you?"

Her cheeks darkened.

"No. It has the opposite effect."

It took me a second to work out her meaning.

"Oh. Is that something you'd like me to whisper to you in bed? About how I'm going to gut anyone who tries to take you from me."

Theia buried her face in my shoulder as she squirmed again.

"Jesus, Gil, please stop. I can't think properly when you say stuff like that."

I wanted to make her surrender to me all over again, but I kept reminding myself I couldn't until later. I'd have to make plans for it instead.

"I take it that despite what happened last night, you want to continue going to work."

She didn't pull her face away from me.

"Yes."

"I've asked Edric to arrange a protection detail for you."

That made her stare up at me.

"A what?"

"My men will watch over you. Make sure no one can take you."

She blinked.

"You're giving me bodyguards?"

"Yes."

She placed both hands on my chest and pushed away from me slightly.

"That's crazy. I don't need bodyguards. They're not going to want to follow me around. And what the hell will my colleagues say when they see me turning up with a bunch of guys? Not to mention your brother. He's going to know—"

I wrapped my hand around the back of her neck so she couldn't go anywhere.

"I don't give a shit what Zayn knows. You're *mine*, Theia, you hear me? I'm not going to let anyone take you away or hurt you ever again. My men will do as I tell them because you're my girl. They protect what's mine."

The more I spoke, the more her eyes widened until she was looking at me like I'd lost the plot.

"I don't even know what to say to you right now." She wrestled herself out of my grasp and stood up. "I didn't ask you to rescue me or treat me like I'm... I don't know... a mafia wife locked in an ivory tower."

"That's not what I'm doing."

"Isn't it? Putting bodyguards on me twenty-four-seven isn't slightly excessive?"

I got up off the sofa and stared down at her. Did she think I was trying to restrict her freedom? It was the last thing I wanted, but Theia clearly didn't understand the world I lived in. This wasn't only about the people who were after her. The shit going on with my cousin's missing shipments and dead bodies made everything about my life precarious.

"Do you know why I killed those men last night?"

She crossed her arms over her chest.

"No, you didn't exactly explain that part."

"I've had two dead bodies turn up on my doorstep in the past few weeks. Both of them were my cousins' men. Someone is trying to pit me against them. If they find out about you, there is no telling what they will do to get to me. That's the reality of my life." I reached up and stroked her cheek. "I'm not trying to rescue you from anything. You don't need saving. Is it so wrong I want to keep you safe until I can find out who the fuck these sex traffickers are and deal with the mess between me and my cousins?"

She blinked, then frowned.

"You want to find the men who took me?"

"Yes. Did you think I was just going to stick my men on you and not deal with the source of the problem?"

"Maybe."

I almost shook my head. I should have explained that part to her when telling her about the protection detail.

"I don't want to restrict your freedom, nor do I want you to be a mafia wife. I don't believe in that shit. You're my equal, not subservient or a trophy to have on my arm."

She looked at the floor and dragged her toe across the rug.

"Now I feel stupid again."

"Why?"

"I should have known you weren't trying to restrict me." She rubbed her arms. "This is new for me, having someone care about my safety and accepting me for everything I am. And it's all happening so fast. One minute, I had no idea you even liked me. Now we're talking about being in a relationship, and I'm getting stuck with bodyguards because of all the shit going on in both our lives. It's a lot, Gil, it's just… a lot."

I hated the defeated look in her eyes. This was a lot for me too. I didn't know how to navigate a relationship with a woman. It was a terrifying prospect in all honesty, but Theia was worth it.

"Am I allowed to hold you?"

"Yes," she whispered, "you don't have to ask."

I tugged her against my chest and stroked her back. She sighed and buried her face in my chest, wrapping her arms around my waist.

"Do you have to work today?"

"Not until this evening."

"Then you can come with me and I'll take you to the club before your shift later."

I didn't want to leave her here alone today when she was feeling a little fragile over everything that had happened.

"Come with you where?"

"I have to deal with things at my headquarters."

She pulled away, making me drop my arms from around her.

"Won't I be in the way?"

"No."

"Can I grab a shower and finish my breakfast first?"

I nodded and pushed her towards the hallway. She was dressed and ready to go half an hour later.

Theia was quiet on the journey over to my building. She sat staring out the window with a pensive expression on her face, but she did let me hold her hand for most of it. I didn't let go when I took her inside the old printing factory. Her eyes darted around the place. She kept close to me as the men stared at us. Likely in their minds, a woman being here was the event of the fucking year, especially one that I'd brought, considering I never dated.

I was about to take her upstairs to my office when Edric rounded the corner with a grim look on his face. The moment he spotted Theia, his eyebrows raised.

"Well, hello again. Didn't realise it was 'bring your girlfriend to work day'."

I'm going to kill him. He's never learned to keep his mouth shut about anything.

"What do you want?"

He pursed his lips and looked at the ceiling.

"There's been another one."

"Another what?"

"B-O-D-Y."

For fuck's sake. Just what I needed.

"Take me to it."

He lowered his head and glanced at Theia.

"Are you bringing her?"

I was about to open my mouth to answer him when one of the men came up to us with an envelope in his hand.

"This came for you, boss."

I snatched it out of his hand and gave him a dark look. He backed away, perhaps realising it was not the time to get chatty. My eyes darted down to the envelope. It had my name on it in gilded lettering.

"Theia, do you want to come with us or wait in my office?"

"I'd rather stay with you."

I looked up at Edric.

"Then yes, I'm bringing her."

"Are you sure? It's kind of gruesome."

"She doesn't have to look. Now move."

He let out a huff, rolled his eyes, and turned around. Theia and I followed after him. I let go of her hand to open the envelope. Inside was an invitation to a gala. There was also a handwritten note from Dino's wife, Pippa, insisting I come to mend bridges with the family. I hated going to these functions. They were full of stuck-up fucks who had more money than sense.

Edric slowed down, so we were level and looked over at the invite.

"Ooo, a gala? That sounds like fun."

"Good. You're going with me."

"You're actually going?"

I showed him Pippa's note. His eyes narrowed.

"That's Dino's wife, right?"

I'd never introduced Edric to my extended family. There was never a reason to before now.

"Yes. *Papá* used to go to these things all the time, so I should go too. Besides, I want to know why Pippa decided to invite me personally."

Edric pushed open the door at the back of the building.

"Well, I'll get my nicest suit out for the occasion."

"If you dare wear that purple monstrosity, I'll kick you out of the event myself."

He looked mildly offended by the suggestion.

"I'll have you know women love that suit."

"It's an eyesore."

Theia was looking between us with a raised eyebrow and amusement painted on her features.

"Just because you have no fashion sense. It doesn't mean you can restrict mine."

"Edric."

He threw his hands up.

"Fine. Jesus. So bossy. I suppose you'll be telling her what she can and can't wear next."

He was wearing a ridiculously loud orange and white shirt today tucked into his beige chinos. I wondered if he'd gone raiding the charity shops for seventies throwbacks. Honestly, I didn't understand how he managed to attract women with his taste in fashion, but Edric could charm anyone he wanted, regardless of his appearance.

"Why would it matter what I wear?" Theia asked.

I glanced down at her as we stopped near the body that was slumped against the wall.

"You're coming to the gala too."

Her eyes widened.

"What? You can't take me to a posh gala, Gil."

"Why not?"

"People are going to ask me what I do. I can't tell them I'm a sex worker. They'll think you hired an escort for the night."

I'd already told her earlier that other people's opinions were irrelevant.

"If you're worried about that, you can tell them you're a dancer. Not like you'd be lying."

"That's not the point. I'll just embarrass you."

I wrapped an arm around her waist and tugged her against me. Theia let out a squeak of surprise.

"You could never embarrass me." I leaned closer until my mouth brushed over her cheek. "You're perfect the way you are."

"Now you're embarrassing me," she muttered, pushing me away from her.

I chuckled.

"Stay here. We can talk about it later."

I left her staring after me and Edric as we moved over to the body. He'd been tortured in the same way as the others. Now we had three fucking bodies. This was getting ridiculous.

"Do we know who it is?"

"I had to work it out on my own as Sal isn't here. He's another one of Dino's. Do you want me to take him to the safe house like the others?"

"Yes. This makes it even more imperative that we deal with Devlin."

Edric sighed and turned away from the body.

"How would you like to play that? A meeting perhaps?"

"No. We need to watch him to see what he's up to before we approach him." I waved at the body. "Get the men from last night to help you with this guy. They'll keep their mouths shut."

He inclined his head and glanced at Theia.

"Do you also want them on her?"

"Yes. We can discuss it when you get back. I'm going to take her upstairs now."

He gave me a knowing look. I ignored him. There was no fucking way I would be doing anything inappropriate with her in my office today. Didn't need my men having any more shit to talk about. I'd already set tongues wagging by bringing her in the first place. As far as I was concerned, they were going to have to get used to seeing her around. She might be afraid of this thing between us, but I was going to make sure I made it safe for us even if I had to fight tooth and nail to discover who the fuck was trying to mess with us.

It was time I showed everyone I was capable of being the boss. I was going to defend my own, no matter what it took.

TWENTY NINE

Theia

After spending the day with Gil, meeting my new bodyguards and working in the evening, I wasn't feeling any less overwhelmed with all the craziness of the past twenty-four hours. Gil had been quiet on the way to his after he'd picked me up from the club. I imagined it wasn't unusual for him not to be talkative, but I wasn't used to it. Besides, I could feel the tension rolling off him. Now I understood what was going on in his world, I could see the pressure he was under. And the fact he had me to protect as well was likely making it worse.

I hadn't asked Gil to do any of this for me, but I wasn't going to argue with him over it again. Not after this morning. If it made him feel better to have me protected by his men, I'd put up with it. It made me feel warm and fuzzy inside when he told me I was his equal. It wasn't as if I didn't know that, but it was nice to hear all the same. However, I was pretty sure he was getting a little sick of reassuring me my job wasn't an issue.

I never thought I'd ever meet a man who would be okay with it. Gil had his faults, but in that respect, he was a unicorn as far as I was concerned.

When we got into his penthouse, he walked over to his sofa and sunk into it, rubbing his hands across his face in a rather defeated manner. My heart lurched. I was walking over to him without thinking a moment later and sinking to my knees on the rug by his feet. My hands curled around his knees and pushed them open so I could fit myself between his legs. He dropped his hands and stared down at me with no emotion on his face.

"Why are you down there?"

I ran my hands up his thighs. I could feel the tension in his muscles, but it didn't stop me. The words I wanted to speak were on the tip of my tongue. There were still a million things we needed to discuss, but I wanted to forget about them for the rest of the evening.

"Theia?"

"I want to make you feel good."

He blinked. I had to press on. He wasn't going to judge me for this, just like he hadn't judged me or made me feel small for anything else I'd told him.

"And I have this fantasy about being on my knees for you with your fist buried in my hair while you tell me…" My eyes flicked down to his crotch, and I swallowed. "While you tell me to suck your cock with my dirty little slut mouth and stare at me with no emotion the way you're doing now."

I said the last part in an almost whisper. He knew I liked to be degraded, but I'm not sure he realised how far I wanted that degradation to go. This was actually the tamest of my fantasies when it came to him.

For a long moment he didn't speak, merely regarded me with his dark eyes. His scrutiny made me shiver, but I didn't press him. When he leaned closer and touched my cheek with his hand, I bit my lip.

"What am I going to do with you, hmm?" he murmured.

The next thing I knew, he'd gripped my hair tight in his fist and turned my face up towards him. With his other hand, he brushed his thumb over my lip, pulling it from my teeth.

"Is that what you thought about during our sessions at the club?"

"Yes."

I wouldn't lie to him about it. He knew about my hypersexuality. A part of it was these all thoughts and fantasies I had, but I'd always been too fucking terrified to carry them out... until him. Gil saw me for all that I was and wanted me anyway.

"I see."

His eyes darkened, but he kept any other emotion from his face. It made me shake in his hold.

"What a dirty little thing you are. If you're going to behave like a wanton slut, I'll have to treat you like one." He stuck his thumb into my mouth and pulled my jaw down, forcing me to part my lips. "Keep this open."

I obeyed when he removed his thumb. He sat back, keeping one fist in my hair as his other went to his fly. I watched him unzip it one-handed before he drew out what I wanted. His hand ran over his already hard dick. Clearly, I wasn't the only one turned on. Knowing I brought out this side of him made me feel so fucking special. It was no longer a one-sided infatuation. It was a real, tangible connection between two people who never expected to find someone they could be themselves with.

"Are you going to put that dirty mouth of yours to good work, Theia? I want you to get my cock nice and wet."

Gil drew me closer to him by my hair.

"Go on, wrap those lips around it."

Guided by him, I lowered my face and took him in my mouth, unable to help the moan sounding in the back of my throat. My hands remained on his thighs as he pushed me down further, making me take more.

"That's it, such a good slut. Taking it so well. *La mia bella sgualdrina.*"

I worshipped his dick with my mouth, taking my time to slide my lips down his shaft and using my tongue to caress him. When my eyes darted up to his, there wasn't a single emotion on his face.

"Good girl," he murmured, petting my face with his free hand.

In response to his praise, I sucked harder, drawing a grunt from his mouth. His fingers tightened around my hair, making me wince from the burn, but I wanted the pain. It made me feel alive. Made my pussy throb with need for him.

This was safety right here. I'd placed my trust in this man, knowing he wouldn't take it too far. He wouldn't hurt or abuse me the way I had been when I was held captive. Gil didn't make me feel shame for wanting this kind of sex. He understood why I needed it without me having to explain. I had a feeling it was something he wanted to explore too.

I pulled off him a moment later, panting a little as the ache between my legs grew unbearable.

"Please."

"Please what? Did my cock in your mouth make your pussy needy, slut?"

"Yes," I whined.

Without giving me any warning, Gil stood up and pulled me with him. I was dragged by my hair through his penthouse to his bedroom. His rough treatment only made me want him more. He bent me over his bed, pushing me face down into the covers before his mouth met my ear.

"You're lucky I want to fuck you, Theia. It's been on my mind all day, how much I want to wreck your pussy and make you cry out my name. I've never wanted this with anyone, but you... you make me crazy, and I can't stop. I don't want to stop. I want you so bad, it fucking hurts."

I choked out a breath. Knowing he wanted me and hearing him say it were two very different things. The intense need in his deep voice was intoxicating.

"Wreck me... please."

"Oh, don't worry, I fully intend to."

He was gone a moment later, striding over to his bedside table and pulling one of the drawers open. I heard the rustle of foil before he was back with me, peeling my clothes from my body enough to give him access. His fingers dipped between my legs, stroking through my folds and circling my clit. I moaned his name, arching into him, and received a smack across my pussy in return. It made me yelp, but he only did it again. It didn't hurt, just stung in a torturous way that only made me hotter for him.

"Please. Please fuck me."

"Not yet, slut."

I whined in response, but he didn't listen. Instead, he pulled the rest of my clothes off my body, leaving me naked in front of him.

"Hands up by the headboard. Now."

I crawled onto the bed properly and sat up, placing my hands on the top of the board. He climbed up behind me a few minutes later, after I heard him moving about the room. Taking one of my hands, he looped a tie around my wrist and secured it to the headboard before doing the same to the other. I knelt there with him behind me, feeling far more vulnerable and exposed than I ever had done in my life. And it unlocked an invisible cage wrapped around my ribs, keeping me from fully allowing myself to be free.

He skimmed his hands down my sides before he kissed my shoulder. I let out a sigh of pleasure. His hands wrapped around my hips, pulling me back so I landed in his lap. He held onto my neck before he pushed inside me. He didn't take it slow this time, thrusting up until I was squirming in his grasp from the way he filled me.

"Theia," he ground out through his teeth, "you feel so fucking good."

He wrapped himself around my back, holding me against his chest while he fucked me. There was nothing gentle about the way he hammered into my pussy. I held onto the headboard, taking it with pants and moans erupting from my throat. He nibbled my earlobe and pressed more kisses to my shoulder. I felt bereft because he abruptly pulled away from me. I let out a squeak of complaint. Gil ran a hand down my back before he shifted around and ducked under my arms. I stared down at him while he repositioned me until I was straddling his lap with my hands on either side of his shoulders.

"I want to see your face as you come for me," he murmured, pressing me down on his cock again.

Now I could see he'd undressed before he got on the bed. My eyes fixed on his bare chest and how much I wanted to run my hands all over it. However, I couldn't do a single thing as he wrapped his hands around my hips and began to move me up and down. I tried to match his rhythm using the headboard as leverage. When I took over, one of his hands left my hip and sank between my legs. I moaned when he stroked my clit, circling it with precision as if he knew exactly how much pressure I required.

"That's it. You're taking my cock so well."

His other hand left my hip and cupped my breast. He leaned over and took my nipple in his mouth, teeth grazing over my sensitive skin.

"Shit. Fuck. Gil, fuck."

He sucked away the sting, flicking his tongue over it in the most maddening fashion. It only made me ride him faster, wanting to push us both towards the edge. The way this man worshipped my body was feeding my need to be admired. He didn't do it with words, but with his touch. He made me feel wanted. Needed. Desired. He didn't make me feel like an object. When he complimented me, it wasn't for my body but for what I could do with it, and for my mind and soul. He made me feel beautiful inside and out.

I saw myself in a different light through his eyes. It helped me heal those broken pieces of my soul. I'd finally acknowledged the reasons why I was so fucked up inside. He hadn't tried to mend my fractured parts, nor did I need him to, but he'd given me a precious gift. A new perspective to view myself and the world with.

I shifted my hips, adjusting the angle of him inside me, and with the next thrust, he hit the spot that had my back arching.

"Fuck, there... right there, fuck, don't stop."

He released my nipple and looked up at me. Those dark eyes were practically black. The sight of his emotionless face sent me over the edge. I don't know why the fuck it turned me on so much, but it did. My vision narrowed to him as my body shook from my climax.

He's mine... I can't believe he's all mine.

From the moment I'd laid eyes on Gil, I'd been drawn to him. His aloof nature called to me on a fundamental level. Not to mention he was one of the most attractive men I'd ever seen. All that thick dark hair, a beautiful jawline, and those eyes... fuck those eyes of his. They were only expressive when he wanted them to be. And with me, he let himself go. He showed me who he was even if he didn't know it himself.

When I came down, I pitched forward slightly, resting my forehead on his shoulder as I caught my breath. Gil's hands slid to my back, holding me close while he rocked himself inside me. The sensation gave me little aftershocks. I pressed a kiss to his neck and breathed him in. His cologne had a woodsy smell to it.

"Will you untie me?" I whispered, desperate to touch him with my fingertips.

I raised my head from his shoulder as he shifted, twisting to untie each of my wrists. The ties dropped on the bed and my hands immediately went to his chest. I dragged my hands down his skin, revelling in the feel of him. He watched me without saying a word.

"Is this okay?" I said, realising I should have asked if I could touch him in an intimate fashion, knowing he didn't often allow anyone to get close to him.

"Yes."

My heart swelled and tears welled behind my eyes. What a fucking privilege. I don't know what it was about this whole thing that made me so emotional, but I let it out, allowing the tears to slide down my cheeks. Gil reached up and brushed one off my face.

"Theia?"

"I'm happy. For the first time in my life, I'm actually happy. There's so much shit going on around us, but I have you, and that makes it easier. When I'm with you, I'm safe. I don't have to hide behind all those walls I built around myself to survive. I don't have to pretend I'm okay or I'm not suffering inside. You're the light in all my darkness, Gil. And I know that's crazy considering the world you inhabit, but you are. I thought I was good, but the truth is I've been lying, telling myself it was okay for me to be alone because trusting anyone was terrifying after everything I'd gone through. But then I met you and now…"

More tears spilt down my cheeks. I sniffled and attempted to wipe them away, but Gil took a hold of my hands and held them to his chest. The way he looked at me like I was precious had me wanting to fall apart.

"And now I can't go back. I can't go back to a life full of nothingness, going through the motions and pretending I'm not hurting. I don't need you because you make it better. I need you because when I'm with you, I feel like myself. I feel like Theia. And I don't have to hide her away."

THIRTY

Theia

When Gil leant forward and kissed away my tears after my confession, I let out a choked sound and dissolved into sobs. I hadn't wanted to ruin the moment between us, but the emotional upheaval I'd been through since Gil had become my client was too overwhelming. Everything was attacking me at once from all sides. I didn't know what to do with myself any longer other than cry.

"Shh," he murmured, pulling me tight against him before running his fingers through my hair. "It's okay, *piccola mia*. I've got you."

"I'm sorry," I whispered, hiccupping on the word.

"Don't apologise to me for having feelings."

His words only made me cry harder, soaking his skin where my face was pressed against his neck.

"But… but we're in the middle of… of…"

I couldn't get my words out, but I hoped he understood what I was trying to say.

"Sex? I think you'd have noticed by now you and your feelings are far more important to me than that."

What did I do to deserve you?

I dug my fingers into his hair and gripped it tight.

"Stop saying all the right things."

"You want me to tell you to shut up, stop crying, and let me fuck you because I haven't got off yet?"

When I'd calmed down, I'd be perfectly content to let him lay me out and rail me, but right now, I wanted to be held by the man I was falling for. I had to admit to myself, even if I couldn't say the words to him. Why else would I not give a shit he'd killed people in front of me? There wasn't much Gil could do that would put me off him at this rate unless he got a personality transplant and started treating me like shit. I very much doubted that would happen, though.

"No," I mumbled.

He chuckled and nuzzled my hair with his face. Gil wasn't the type of man who would dismiss my emotional state for his own pleasure.

When I finally stopped crying, I pulled back and looked at him. His dark eyes were full of understanding, and it threatened to break me all over again. I was done crying. I wanted to pick up where we'd left off.

He let go of my hair to stroke his fingers along my chin.

"You're so beautiful," he whispered, smiling at me.

I wrinkled my nose.

"You think this is beautiful?" I waved at my face. "I'm pretty sure I look like a train wreck."

He smiled wider.

"You're my train wreck."

I slapped his shoulder.

"Oh, shut up."

His smile didn't fade, but he reached over to his bedside table to grab the box of tissues. Then, with patient care, he wiped my face and made me blow my nose. His gentleness had me wanting to swoon. As he was putting the sodden mess on his bedside table, I grabbed a hold of his face, turned it towards me and kissed him. He let out a little grunt of surprise, but he dropped the tissues and wrapped his hands around me, cradling the back of my head with one of them. I rocked my hips, making him growl into my mouth in response.

The next thing I knew, he'd flipped us over, so I was on my back, and he was holding me down on the bed. Our fingers laced together as he started to fuck me again. His mouth fused back to mine, kissing me like he never wanted to stop. The way he fucked me was a frantic rush to the finish line. It wasn't long until he was groaning my name and shuddering above me.

After the two of us cleaned up, Gil lay on his side and encircled me in his arms. I stroked his skin, staring at his hand curled around my stomach.

"Theia."

"Mmm?"

"Would you show me those letters you received?"

My stomach sank. I didn't want to read them again, but if Gil was going to find out who these people were, he needed to see them. I crawled out of his arms and went over to the bag I'd left by his chest of drawers, digging through the contents. Moving back over to the bed, I handed them to him as he sat up. I placed my head in his lap while he read each one. His body was tense underneath mine even as he stroked my hair with one of his hands.

"What is this?"

I looked up, finding him holding the raven charm between his fingers with a frown on his face.

"The place I was kept had ravens painted on the walls above most of the doors. I saw it every day in my room, but I don't know what it means. Maybe it's the symbol for the organisation."

He eyed the charm for a moment longer before stuffing it back in the envelope and setting it down next to us.

"You're probably right. It gives me something to look for unless you can give me anything else."

My eyes darted away from his.

"All the men went by initials. The one who came for me was H. He... he was..."

Flashes of the way he'd held me down seeped into my consciousness. I put a hand over my eyes, trying to escape them, trying to stop the tide from bursting through. Gil tangled his fingers in my hair and drew them in slow circles around my scalp. His touch was calming, reminding me I was safe. They hadn't got to me.

"He was particularly cruel," I whispered. "I remember him being the first one to... break me in. His words, not mine."

Gil leant over me and pressed his forehead against my hand.

"When I find him, I'm going to kill him. I'll kill all of them for hurting you."

"Does it make me a terrible person for wanting you to hurt them?"

"In my family, the only way justice is served is through death, so no, it doesn't make you a terrible person at all. Not to me."

He straightened, and I dropped my hand from my eyes.

"You said you were your father's executioner. Does that mean your brothers have killed too?"

He cocked his head to the side, but his expression remained neutral.

"Yes. I haven't kept count, but I was twenty when I became a made man. Zayn was like seventeen or eighteen, and Enzo… our father never made him kill. He thought Enzo was too soft to be in the mafia."

"I wouldn't exactly describe him as soft."

Enzo was a pain in everyone's arses at work.

"He was when he was a teenager, especially after our mother was put in a coma, and I had to take care of him. He puts up a good front, but Enzo has a lot of unresolved issues. It was a lot for both of us to deal with, losing her that way, but I think it was worse for him. At least *Papá* took an interest in me. He didn't give a shit about Enzo other than keeping him in line, so he didn't ruin our reputation. Our *Mamá* was the best part of our family, and… well, Gennaro took that from us."

He let out a sigh, his expression turning sad.

"What exactly happened to her?"

Gil let go of my hair and clenched his hand into a fist.

"Zayn didn't tell us until after our father died that *Mamá* tried to leave *Papá*. He tracked her down, beat her unconscious and kept her at the house on life-support for almost ten years. We were told she was in an accident, but the truth is, he wanted to punish her for leaving him." He blinked before closing his eyes. "She's in a better place now."

My heart broke for Gil, Zayn, Enzo, and their mother. They'd lived under such cruelty for so long. No wonder Gil was so closed off. He had to be to survive all of that.

"I'm sorry."

"It's okay, Theia. I only wish I'd known what he'd done, but Zayn didn't want me and Enzo to suffer with the knowledge like he had to. It's why he left the family and forged his own path. Why he opened Desecration. Our mother is the reason."

A lot of things clicked into place when he revealed that to me. Pretty much everyone at the club was a survivor of some description. Desecration was a place that gave us our choice back. And I'd be forever grateful to Gil's brother for giving us all a safe haven.

"I don't know where I would have been without the club after everything that happened to me. Zayn is kind of everyone's hero at Desecration for that reason alone."

Gil opened his eyes and gave me a sad smile.

"It's the one thing he doesn't get any credit for since it's not something he makes known to anyone outside those walls. He didn't tell me about *Mamá*, but he did explain what the club's purpose was after he opened it. I've always admired him for it, even if I've never told him." He rubbed his face. "I resented him when I was younger for leaving me and Enzo, but I understand why he did it. He couldn't stay around our father any longer."

"I think your father was a monster."

There were a lot of things I could say about Gennaro Villetti after everything Gil had told me. None of them were nice.

Gil's eyes clouded over, and his expression grew even more miserable.

"He was… and I don't want to be like him."

I sat up and turned around, seating myself in front of him before taking both of his hands in mine.

"You're nothing like him. You'd never hurt me the way he did your mother. Even though your cousins think you can't do this, you're still trying to fix their problems for them. I'm guessing they don't know about that part, but it doesn't matter. It's what you're doing that does. You told me you didn't want to disappoint Zayn and you want to keep your family safe. It's how I know you're not anything like Gennaro. You're Gil. And I happen to like him quite a lot. In fact, I'm kind of hoping one day I'll get to call him my boyfriend."

I could feel my cheeks heating up from my words, but I didn't care. Gil needed to know he wasn't a monster. He was his own man.

He bit his lip and rubbed his thumb over the back of my hand.

"You can call him that now."

"I can?"

He nodded.

"I want to be yours, Theia, just as you're mine."

I couldn't fight the smile forming on my lips.

"Well, you've just made this girl's whole entire year."

"Has it been that slow so far?"

Where the hell did this cheeky side come from? Maybe Edric has been rubbing off on him.

While I hadn't spent much time around his best friend, I was relatively sure he was the troublemaker out of the two of them.

"I'm going to give you five seconds to take that back."

"Or what?"

"Or I'm going to teach you a lesson."

I launched myself at him, shoving him backwards on the bed, and pinned his hands to the covers. The way Gil grinned up at me set my heart on fire.

"I'd like to see you try."

"I'll have you know I have many, many tricks up my sleeve. I may have to adapt them considering you're a rather dangerous mafia boss, but I'm sure I can manage."

His eyes glittered with amusement for a long moment. I squealed when he flipped us over and pinned me down instead.

"You were saying?"

I curled an eyebrow up.

"Maybe this is exactly what I was hoping for."

He leant closer, brushing his mouth against mine.

"Was once not enough for my little slut?"

I shook my head. He ran his tongue over my bottom lip, making me tremble beneath him.

"Careful what you wish for, Theia. For all you know, I could go all night."

Well shit…

"Promises. Promises."

I knew provoking him could well lead me down a dark path, but at this point, I would follow Gil to the ends of the earth. I'd already thrown myself headlong into this relationship with him. No way was I planning on disembarking from the crazy train any time soon... probably never. For once in my life, I didn't even care how far down the rabbit hole we went. Only that we were together.

"You're the one about to get a lesson. One you'll never forget."

And Gil certainly showed me how he could "go all night." I was going to be fucked in the morning in more ways than one, but I didn't care. Not when he'd given me the only gift I'd ever wanted.

Him as mine.

THIRTY ONE

Gilberto

My hand tightened around Theia's as we stepped on board the boat this gala was being held on. Fuck knows why Pippa had decided to host it on the Thames. I was already annoyed I even had to attend in the first place. Now I'd be stuck with a bunch of rich pricks for the next few hours, unable to leave even if I wanted to. It was a good thing I'd insisted on Edric and Theia attending with me, not sure I would survive without them by my side.

Thankfully, Edric had listened to me about his attire. He was in a three-piece navy suit with brown brogues, his signature wide-framed glasses and a cravat. An actual cravat. I decided not to comment on it because at least he didn't stand out like a sore fucking thumb in this crowd. And he wasn't wearing the purple suit. I thanked my lucky fucking stars he had taken me seriously when I told him he couldn't rock up in it.

Theia, on the other hand, I could barely keep my eyes off her. I'd had to smack Edric around the head when he wolf-whistled as he came to pick us up from the penthouse. The little shit thought my possessiveness over her was hilarious. Theia merely blushed and thanked him after he complimented her dress. In an effort to persuade her to come with me, I'd taken her out to buy it as, according to her, she didn't have anything appropriate. It was a flowy navy dress that went down to below her knees. The top part was a bustier. The fabric across her breasts was opaque, but the rest was see-through. It hardly surprised me Theia wanted a dress which showed off her beautiful form. And it was exactly why I couldn't stop staring at her.

She'd insisted we match each other, so she made me wear a navy suit that was similar to Edric's. Now we were all matching, but considering it could have been so much worse, I decided to go with it.

"You could make it a little more obvious she's yours," Edric murmured as we made our way inside from the deck.

"If you kept your eyes in their sockets, I wouldn't have to," I shot back.

"I don't know why you keep giving me shit when half the men on board are staring at her... and the women too."

My eyes darted over the assembly of people. He wasn't wrong. They were looking at us. When my gaze landed on Theia, I could tell she was enjoying the attention, so I let it be. They could look all they wanted. I would be the one peeling the dress off her body later, or maybe I'd fuck her while she was still in it against the glass window of my living room. It would be indulging in her exhibitionism kink, something I knew Theia would be on board with. The idea made me hide a smile. It would be the perfect way to end this evening from hell. We'd only just got on board, and I already wanted to leave.

"There's so many people," Theia whispered, leaning closer to me.

"Tell me about it."

Edric spied the waiters with drinks and grabbed champagne for the three of us. Theia clutched her glass between her fingers and took a sip. I watched her throat work, mesmerised by her every movement.

"So, who do we schmooze first?" Edric asked, leaning up against the window in a nonchalant way.

"I'd rather not have to speak to anyone."

"It's a gala. You can't hide in the corner and glare at people all night."

"That's why I brought you. Now I don't have to deal with small talk."

He snorted and rolled his eyes.

"Aww, Gil, don't you want to charm them all with your witty banter?"

Bringing Edric anywhere was a double-edged sword. On the one hand, he could be a social butterfly. On the other, he never ceased to give me a hard time over my lack of social skills. I swear, winding me up was some kind of sport for him.

"I'm going to throw you overboard before the end of the night if you keep that up," I hissed.

He grinned and waved his champagne flute at me.

"You certainly know the way to a man's heart. How could anyone resist such a romantic gesture?"

Theia was trying not to smile at our interaction. My eyes moved away from my girl, spying Pippa approaching us. She was in a skin-tight white dress with blood-red lipstick and heels. Her pin-straight chin-length blonde bob made her look severe. Dino wasn't with her, but I knew my cousin didn't always attend his socialite wife's events.

"Gil, I'm so glad you came," she said as she arrived in front of us.

"Pippa." I didn't plaster on a fake smile. There would be no point. "Thank you for inviting me."

She looked at Edric, who was eyeing her with interest.

"Who are your friends?"

He shoved off the window and stepped forward, sticking his hand out. She delicately placed her hand in his.

"Edric Russell, this one's underboss. And that beautiful lady over there is Theia, Gil's new flame."

Pippa's eyebrow twitched as she dropped Edric's hand and turned to Theia.

"Hello, it's a pleasure to meet you. I didn't realise you'd met someone, Gil, but I'm so happy for the two of you."

There was a certain level of animosity in Pippa's voice that had me tugging my girl closer. I wrapped my arm around her waist, not caring how possessive the gesture was.

"Hello," Theia said, glancing up at me with a frown.

"Pippa is my cousin's wife." I hadn't explained to her who Pippa was before we got here, but I should have. "Dino, her husband, is my first cousin once removed."

Theia turned back to Pippa.

"It's nice to meet you too."

Pippa didn't smile. Instead, she looked at Theia like she was a threat. Then her face cleared, and she clapped her hands together.

"Well, I best make the rounds, but do enjoy yourselves. Toodle-oo."

None of us had time to say another word as she turned away, swaying her hips as she walked over to another group of people.

"Damn, I bet she's demanding in bed. Probably dominates your cousin," Edric said, rubbing his hand over his face while he quite obviously stared at Pippa's arse.

"Did you really have to go there?" I asked, giving him a look.

"What?" He shrugged and waved at her. "Listen, I'm not saying I would... I mean, I would, but like it would be a one-time deal."

Why? Just fucking why?

"Bringing you here was a mistake."

Edric said something in response, but I wasn't listening as I spied one of my cousins on the opposite side of the room. With her dark blonde hair tied up in a slick ponytail and her black dress moulding to her body, Verona had her head thrown back as she patted the arm of the man next to her. Knowing I would never hear the end of it if I didn't say hello, I grabbed a hold of Edric's arm while keeping a tight hold of Theia and made my way over to my cousin.

"Where are we going?" Edric asked, brushing me off him with a huff.

"To see my cousin."

"Another one? Jesus, it's like meet the family night. I swear there are too many of you Villettis."

I ignored him because Verona had turned her attention to me. Her brown eyes narrowed as if she hadn't been expecting to see me here. I wasn't surprised she was in attendance considering she worked for a financier in Knightsbridge. I spied one of Zayn's men standing close by. Clearly, Verona had only been allowed out tonight with a bodyguard due to the threat against her family.

"Oh, hello, Gil," she said as we drew closer, giving me a tight smile. "Fancy seeing you at one of Pippa's dos."

"Evening, Verona."

Her eyes darted to Theia, giving her a cutting look before they landed on Edric, and disgust painted her features. I was in no doubt Verona was the last woman on earth who would ever let Edric charm her. She wasn't known for being nice to anyone. Being a bitch was pretty much her default personality at this point.

"Who are these two? Your friends or something?"

She said the word friends like she was surprised I had any. I didn't take it personally, considering my ability to maintain friendships was lacking.

"This is my girlfriend, Theia, and my friend, Edric," I said before turning to Theia. "Verona is my aunt, Martina's daughter."

"Well, at least you're dating an age-appropriate woman, unlike your brother," Verona said.

Edric almost choked on his champagne.

"I'm so glad you approve."

Verona's eyes narrowed as if she was trying to work out whether I was joking or not.

"So, what do you do, Theia? Hope you're not sponging off our family like Zayn's girlfriend is."

Theia looked up at me with wide eyes as if to say 'your cousin is blunt' before her expression cleared and her spine straightened. She turned to my cousin and plastered a bright smile on her face.

"I'm a performer at Zayn's club."

Verona blinked before placing her hand on her hip and giving Theia the once over. Then she looked impressed.

"Oh. Well, all the more power to you."

I don't know what I was expecting Verona to say in response, but it hadn't been that.

"Thank you."

Verona gave her a tight smile and looked at Edric again. He was staring at her as if he didn't know what to make of my cousin. It was the first time I'd seen Edric stumped by a woman.

"And you, what do you do? Ed-something?"

"It's Edric," he replied without any hint of the usual amusement in his voice. "And I'm Gil's underboss."

"You're his what?"

"Underboss. Second-in-command."

Verona looked at me with a raised brow.

"What is he talking about?"

Zayn clearly hadn't told our cousins about the new arrangement, considering they weren't involved in the mafia. I was sure Martina knew, but she kept her daughters away from the dangers of our life, just as her husband had when he was alive.

"I took Gennaro's place as head of the mafia," I said in a quiet voice since I wasn't going to shout it from the fucking rooftops.

"Zayn is letting *you* run things? Wow, okay. And this is your underboss?" Verona snorted. "I thought you were the sensible one, Gil."

Edric stepped closer to her.

"Excuse me, what is that supposed to mean?"

She crossed her arms over her chest.

"Well, my cousin here looks like he could kill a man without blinking, but you..." She waved at him. "You look like a fuckboy who couldn't tie his own shoelaces without help."

I'd never seen Edric's mouth drop open so fast. Verona gave him a nasty smile before she turned away to her boss, dismissing all of us. I took a hold of Edric's arm and pulled him away from my cousin, knowing if I didn't, he might cause a scene. By the time we reached the double doors leading out onto the deck, he'd shut his mouth and was glaring at Verona from over his shoulder.

"Well, she's... interesting," Theia said.

"More like a bitch," Edric muttered before turning to me. "You could have warned me."

I shrugged. I was so used to my cousin being mean to people it hadn't occurred to me to mention it.

"And ruin the surprise?"

"She called me a fuckboy!"

"Is she wrong, though?"

He put his hand to his chest and let out a huff.

"I am *not* a fuckboy. I should have known savagery runs in your fucking family."

I patted his shoulder, which I'm sure he thought was condescending, judging by the glare he sent my way.

"If it makes you feel any better, Verona is mean to everyone."

He pouted and shrugged me off.

"It doesn't."

He shoved his empty glass of champagne on the tray as a waiter appeared in front of us before barking at the guy to get him something stronger. Theia was watching him with her blue-grey eyes shining with amusement. I squeezed her side to get her attention.

"Is he always like this?" she whispered.

"Pretty much. Just watch. He'll sulk for the rest of the evening."

I leaned closer, pressing my lips to the skin behind her ear. She shivered, her hand snaking around my waist.

"Have I told you how—" I faltered when my eyes landed on a woman standing a few feet away. I'd never seen her before in my life, but something about her was strangely familiar. When I realised why, I swallowed hard and wondered if I was seeing things. She smiled at the person she was talking to. I knew that smile. There was a hint of playfulness along with a twinkle in her brown eyes.

She looks like Zayn's girlfriend. She looks almost exactly like Arianna Michaelson. What… the… fuck!

THIRTY TWO

Gilberto

The woman I couldn't help staring at had wavy dark brown hair with brown eyes and olive skin. Her face structure was very similar to Arianna's, but her nose was different. I hadn't met Ari's father, Bennett, but I imagined all of her other features came from him.

This wasn't any of my business, of course, but I knew Zayn's girlfriend had never met her mother, nor did she know who the woman was. Something inside me wanted to know if I was right. If this was indeed Ari's mother. She looked far too fucking similar for it to be a coincidence.

"Gil?" Theia prompted, shaking me from my reverie.

I straightened but didn't take my eyes off the woman. This might have consequences I wasn't prepared for, but I couldn't leave without knowing the truth.

"Stay here with Edric."

"What?"

I pushed her to stand next to my still pouting friend and turned my attention to him rather than answering Theia.

"Don't take your eyes off her, you hear me? I'm entrusting her safety to you."

Edric's eyes darted between me and Theia.

"Okay, you know I won't let anything happen to her."

"Good."

I made to step away, but his hand on my shoulder stopped me.

"Where are you going?"

Shrugging him off, I moved away without responding. I didn't have time to explain as I pulled out my phone and moved closer to the woman. I stuck it to my ear a moment later while listening to it ring.

"Evening, Gil," Zayn said when he answered. "Is this important? I'm right in the middle of something."

"Yes, it is. What's Arianna's mother's name?"

There was no fucking way my brother didn't know the answer to this question. Zayn knew everyone's secrets. It was how he'd become so powerful and taken over London. He used his knowledge to manipulate everyone into seeing things his way.

"What?"

"You heard me. What is her mother's name?"

"It's Julia McDonald."

"Thank you."

"Why do you want—"

I hung up on him before he could finish his sentence and stuffed my phone back into my pocket. He would no doubt try to call me back, but I'd put it on silent before we'd boarded the boat. I might have been pissed earlier I'd be stuck here the whole night, but now I was glad of it. She wouldn't be able to escape a conversation with me.

The woman was standing with two men, one of whom looked very similar to her, leading me to believe he might be her brother. If this was Julia McDonald, she was the eldest of five siblings. The headlines had been full of her youngest sister, Chelsea, recently. It was reported she'd committed suicide at her Knightsbridge residence. Who the fuck knew if that was the truth. I wasn't one to pay much attention to the wealthy, but it was hard to avoid it when stories like this were all over the news.

I didn't approach the trio, merely watched them from nearby. She caught my eye a moment later and frowned when she noticed I was staring. I nodded over at the double doors to the deck before retreating towards them and walking outside. My feet carried me over to the back of the boat. I leaned on the railings, staring out over the murky water. The sun was setting on the horizon, bathing the city in an orange and purple glow.

It took a few minutes, but she joined me with her back to the railings as she stared out over the party.

"Do we know each other?" she asked, her voice betraying her upper-class upbringing.

I turned to her. She was in a dark green dress that fell to her knees, and she looked to be in her late thirties.

"No." I stuck my hand out. "Gil."

She looked down at my hand for a long moment before taking it and giving it a shake.

"Julia."

I dropped her hand and looked out over the water again. There was no point in me beating around the bush since we were alone.

"Your father owns McDonald hotels, does he not?"

"Yes."

"This is going to sound like a personal question, but did you give up a daughter twenty-two years ago?"

I watched her stiffen out of the corner of my eye. It wasn't the most tactful way to ask her, but I didn't care. She leant closer, her brow furrowed and her eyes darting about the place to check if anyone was listening.

"Who are you? Is this some sort of plot to blackmail me? Because I won't stand for it."

"Blackmail? No." I flicked my hand out. "Let's just say I know your daughter."

"I do not have a daughter."

It was quite obvious she was lying by the way her face reddened and her brow twitched.

"I suppose that's true, considering you gave up the right to be her mother."

She let out a little sound of outrage before she reared back and stared hard at me.

"What do you want?"

I shrugged before turning to her.

"I don't want anything, Julia."

A confirmation was all I needed, and I had it now. This was Ari's mother.

"Then why are you asking about…"

"Arianna."

Her eyes softened and her expression fell.

"That's her name?"

"I take it that means you're not going to deny she exists any longer."

Julia looked away.

"I didn't know what Bennett called her. My parents... they..." She let out a sigh. "It doesn't matter. How do you know her?"

"Your parents, what?"

She scoffed and looked up at the sky.

"My parents made me give her up. They told me they'd cut me off if I didn't hand over all parental rights to Bennett."

My eyes narrowed. I hadn't expected her to open up and tell me outright what happened. I was a complete stranger. Then again, maybe she wanted to get this off her chest.

"I didn't want to leave my life behind to live on a council estate with his aunt and his brother. I was only with him because I knew my parents disapproved. You know how we all love to act out as teenagers. I didn't want to have a baby at sixteen, so I gave her to him without complaint and agreed never to contact either of them again."

"Did he want her?"

She nodded and stared at her hands.

"Bennett wanted her from the moment he found out. We never meant to get pregnant, but these things happen. She was always going to be better off with him."

Julia visibly shivered and wrung her hands out.

"I don't know whether to ask you about her. She's all grown up now, I guess."

I rubbed my fingers together, my gaze directed across the deck where I could see Edric and Theia standing inside. He was talking to her, but her eyes were darting around as if she was looking for me. It made my heart lurch. I wanted to be back with her, not talking to Ari's mother.

"She is."

"You're not dating her, are you?"

"Me? No. Definitely not. She's… it doesn't matter who she is to me."

She didn't deserve to know anything about her daughter. Not when she admitted she didn't want Ari. It wasn't my place to tell her, anyway. It would be between her, Bennett, and Arianna.

"I guess not."

Julia's expression was sombre when I glanced at her. I might not have wanted to know her reasons for never being in Ari's life, but I was glad she'd told me. Perhaps Ari would want closure regarding the topic. I could give her that without her ever having to be in contact with the woman who'd given birth to her.

"She's happy, and I'd personally like it to stay that way for her sake. I suggest you stick to your promise not to contact her. Arianna doesn't need someone who never wanted her in her life. She deserves better."

I didn't stop to wait for her reply, shoving off the railings and walking back towards the double doors. While I didn't know Zayn's girlfriend that well, I did respect her, especially since she made my brother happy. She was loyal to him. And she fit into our family. Our father may never have approved of her, and he would definitely not have approved of Theia either, but I did. I knew Ari was good for Zayn… just as Theia was good for me.

I didn't have the energy to continue speaking to Julia. I hoped I'd given her something to think about and she would keep her promise. Ari didn't need that sort of shit in her life.

When I got back inside, Theia spied me straight away. Her blue-grey eyes were full of concern. I made my way over to her and Edric. He had a whisky tumbler between his fingers and was still glaring at Verona. I ignored him, making my way straight over to Theia and wrapping my arm around her waist. Her hand went to my chest as she stared up at me.

"Is everything okay?"

"Yes."

The look in her eyes told me she didn't believe me, but I wasn't lying. Everything was okay. She was here, my beautiful girl, who brought me far more solace than she realised. It was all I needed right then.

"Gil…"

"I'm fine. I promise." I leaned towards her and pressed a chaste kiss to her mouth. "I have you."

The way she blushed at my statement made me smile.

"We should be more worried about him." I nodded at Edric. "Has he been glaring at her the whole time?"

Theia glanced at Edric, then across the room at Verona, who was laughing at something the person she was with said.

"Pretty much. He's been complaining too. Said she has no right to judge him when she doesn't know him, and other less than polite things about her."

Shaking my head, I poked Edric's arm. He whipped his head around to me.

"Oh, you're back. Good. Can we leave yet?"

"We're on a boat. How do you expect us to get off until this is over?"

His face soured.

"Fuck."

"Maybe you should stop glaring at my cousin and mingle."

He waved in Verona's direction.

"And have her think she's right about me? Fuck no."

Theia let out a snort, which only made him give her side eyes.

"I didn't think talking to people qualified you as a fuckboy. And why do you care about what Verona thinks?"

"Because she's wrong about me, Gil."

I wanted to roll my eyes, but I refrained, knowing he would only get even more irate if I did. Edric hated it when people got the wrong impression of him. People didn't often take him seriously because of his appearance and the way he conducted himself. He might be laid back and liked to crack jokes, but it didn't change the fact he was loyal to a fault and smart too. If I hadn't thought he was capable, I wouldn't have made him my underboss. He'd proven his worth by finding Alvin for me. Now we were monitoring Devlin Clarke, not that it had got us anywhere yet. Edric was determined to get to the bottom of this shit with my cousin's missing shipments. He'd find something, eventually. Then we'd make our move.

I'd kept Nino up to date with matters. He was keeping a low profile, not wanting to arouse suspicion with Dino and Gian, but he was glad I was getting somewhere. It meant this shit might be over soon.

"She can say whatever she wants. Doesn't make it true."

He didn't respond, merely turned his attention back to my cousin. Then I did roll my eyes and looked at Theia.

"He's not going to let that go anytime soon," she murmured.

"No. I'll have to keep an eye on it. Verona has never had any tact, nor does she hold back. Best way to deal with her is to give it right back. That's how you earn her respect."

"Is that why she didn't give me shit over what I do?"

I brought her closer to me, pressing my body against hers.

"Mmm, you weren't afraid of her. Edric's problem is he didn't fight back, but maybe he'll learn that lesson in time."

Theia didn't look entirely convinced, but I knew my cousin well enough by now. Verona didn't suffer fools lightly. The reason she still had it in for Ari was that she felt slighted by her, even though Verona had been the one to start it. Hopefully, the two of them would work their shit out in time. I doubted it, though. Verona held grudges like nobody's business.

"Well, I hope so, mostly for your sake."

"Why mine?"

Her eyes twinkled

"You'll have to listen to him complaining."

I groaned and rubbed my face.

"I'm used to it." Dropping my hand to her face, I stroked her skin. "What do you say we ditch Mr Miserable and dance instead? They're starting up over there."

Theia raised her eyebrows.

"You can dance?"

"No, but you can teach me."

She grinned and took my hand, pulling me over to where a band had started up, and people were beginning to congregate.

"Oh, this will be fun."

I shook my head as I followed her. If I got to see Theia smile like that, I'd just about do anything for her, including dancing, which I rarely ever indulged in. I had insisted she attend with me. The least I could do was make it fun for her. And maybe... just maybe... this evening might turn around for me too.

THIRTY THREE

Gilberto

3ayn had messaged me several times and left a couple of voicemails, so I decided to kill two birds with one stone the next day. Theia needed to go to work, and I needed a conversation with my brother. I took her in rather than leaving it to one of the men to do. She'd come around to having a bodyguard since they tried to be as unobtrusive as possible when they were with her. And so far, we'd had no more issues with the sex trafficking group.

I walked into Zayn's office after kissing Theia goodbye. Didn't matter to me if anyone saw us. Theia was mine. I wanted the world to fucking well know it at this point. I never thought I'd be possessive over another person, but I was with her.

Zayn was frowning at something on his desk. He looked up when I walked in, his eyes narrowing when he saw it was me. I shut the door behind me and went right up to his desk.

"So, you are actually alive, and just ignoring my calls."

I shrugged.

"I was busy."

"Clearly."

I leant a hand on his desk and looked over at the sofa on the wall, knowing he would broach the subject rather than me having to bring it up.

"Are you going to tell me why you wanted to know Ari's mother's name? You know I'm not very fond of guessing games, Gil."

My brother preferred to get straight to the point, as did I.

"I was at Pippa's gala last night, and I saw a woman who looked far too much like Ari for it to be a coincidence. Before you ask, yes, I did speak to her, and she told me what happened. Why she gave Ari to Bennett. And no, I don't think she has any intention of contacting Arianna, so you don't have to worry about that."

When I turned my gaze back to Zayn, his mouth was a thin line, and he looked troubled.

"I can tell you exactly what she said if you would like."

He nodded, so I did, making sure not to leave any details out. He sat back when I was done, folding both his hands over his chest before he looked up at the ceiling. I didn't say anything else, waiting for him to get his thoughts together. It wasn't like I would have ever kept this information from him. Zayn deserved to know. Ari did too. Julia was the one who had given birth to her. I didn't want to call her Arianna's mother, since she hadn't been in her life.

"I don't know what to say." He let out a sigh and met my gaze. "She's not going to like this."

"You're going to tell her?"

"How can I not? I've already kept the fact I know who her mother is from her."

I shifted on my feet.

"Dare I ask how you found out?"

He shrugged and lowered his hands from his chest.

"I asked Bennett. I wanted to make sure Julia wouldn't be an issue for Arianna in the future."

My brother was always twenty steps ahead of everyone else. Made him dangerous, especially to those who underestimated him and his wealth of knowledge.

"You know, I think this would be better coming from you since you're the one who spoke to Julia."

I stared at my brother for a long moment. I might have thought he was joking if I didn't know him so well. Zayn didn't say things like that lightly.

"Why? So you won't get in so much trouble for keeping something from her?"

"No. I can deal with her ire. Wouldn't be the first time I've pissed her off." He shrugged and placed his hands on his desk. "Ari would appreciate hearing it from the source rather than through me."

I could understand that, even if I still thought he wanted to avoid her getting too pissed off at him for keeping secrets. He'd confided in me about the last time they'd got into a fight, and how he'd been trying his best to have open communication with her. It was something I was trying to do with Theia too. She made it easy to tell her things, though. There was never any judgement between us. She was the other reason I needed to speak to my brother. It was time I dealt with the little issue of these letters and how someone had got through his security measures.

"Fine. I'll speak to her about it, but that isn't actually the main reason I came to see you."

Zayn raised his eyebrows, tapping his tattooed fingers on his desk.

"No?"

I set the letters I had in my hand on his desk.

"This is why I'm here."

He leaned forward and pulled them closer to him. His eyes narrowed when he read who the first letter was addressed to.

"Is this you coming clean about visiting the club under an assumed name to see one of my employees?"

"I didn't think I had to when you already know."

He smiled faintly as he pulled the letters from their envelopes.

"Are you going to explain what these are—"

Zayn didn't finish his sentence as he pulled the raven charm out. His expression darkened as he set it on the desk. I didn't ask him what he was thinking. It was clear he knew exactly what the charm meant. His face gave it away.

"That's not the only thing. Someone came to her flat and tried to take her. It was lucky I was still in the building to scare him off. She's not safe there, so she's staying with me, and I've given her bodyguards for protection."

He leaned his elbows on the desk, steepled his hands, and looked up at me.

"She's staying with… you?"

"Yes."

"Why would you do that for one of my employees?"

I rubbed my fingers together.

"Why wouldn't I? She's my girlfriend."

Zayn stared at me for a long moment without blinking. He shook himself before his gaze dropped to the letters. He spread them out on the desk, looking over each one.

"Right. Okay. You have a girlfriend now."

He nodded slowly before his eyes turned confused. He rubbed his temple as if he was having trouble wrapping his head around what I'd just told him.

"Is that a bad thing?"

"What? No, of course not. I was not expecting you to… it doesn't matter. Theia is a nice girl, and I'm very happy for you."

Zayn wouldn't judge me for dating a sex worker. Our father would have. He would have never allowed it, but I didn't care about what he thought any longer. He was dead. I was glad of it even if I shouldn't be.

"Are you sure about that?"

He met my eyes again.

"Yes. It's just…" He sighed. "Trust me, Gil, I have no issues with the two of you being together. Theia deserves to be happy, as do you. However, I have a lot to explain, and you're not going to like it." He waved at the letters. "Not to mention we need to look into who gave these to her and how they got into the building. I think you should sit down for this, though."

His words were slightly ominous. I did as he asked, taking a seat in front of his desk. Zayn let out a sigh and began to talk. The more he told me about what he knew, the more agitated I got about the whole situation. The things he knew were not what I expected at all, but what I didn't do was wonder why he hadn't done more. Why he hadn't done something about the person in charge of the sex trafficking organisation known as the Raven. It was the worst part… knowing it was the best-kept secret for a reason.

They were family. The Raven was fucking family. And they'd been doing this under all of our noses for years. Fucking years.

"I want to dismantle the organisation, but it's not that simple, and now you understand why. I'm doing what I can, rescuing the victims like Theia when possible and giving them a new chance at life. They deserve that much after everything they've been subjected to."

I had no words. It was all too fucking surreal. Like I was in a different reality.

"She doesn't know you did that for her."

"No. None of them do. I have to keep my identity and those who help me a secret."

It made sense. He didn't want the organisation to find out he was the one disrupting things. It would make his work more difficult.

"And it pains me to say this, Gil, but you can't touch them either. You can't go after her."

When he informed me the Raven was none other than Pippa, I'd known I couldn't do a single thing about it. Not when relations between me and my cousins were already at an all-time low. And not when I was investigating their missing shipments, and dead bodies had turned up on my doorstep. It was a fucking miracle we hadn't had another one. Three was enough.

I'd tasked Salvatore with finding more information about their families and what possible reason anyone could have had to kill them. I couldn't ask Nino as he didn't know we had the bodies. Sal hadn't discovered anything so far, leading me to believe they'd been scapegoats, tortured and murdered to paint me in a bad light. Perhaps the reason there hadn't been any more bodies was because I'd kept it all under wraps. They probably realised that approach wasn't going to work.

"I know. We can't do anything if you don't have evidence. Dino would bring down hell on us, and we don't need that. I have enough trouble with him already."

Zayn cocked his head to the side.

"He's still not accepting you as leader?"

"It's worse than that, but I'm dealing with it, so you don't need to worry about it." I leaned forward. "We might not be able to go after Pippa, but are you going to let this shit stand?" I waved at the letters. "I don't want Theia to be in danger, and someone is helping them. Someone who has access to your buildings."

He folded up the letters and placed them back in their envelopes before dragging his laptop closer and fiddling with it.

"Give me the date and time they arrived at her flat, and do you know the exact dates these letters turned up? I'll need those too."

Theia had told me. I gave them to Zayn, who wrote them down before I rose from my seat and came around to stand behind him. He was logging into a site to access the security footage from the building where the club staff were housed. The first thing he looked for was when the man Theia informed me was called H turned up. We found an angle showing the front door and him arriving. We watched him reach the intercom with the buzzers, and when he pressed down on one of them. He spoke to the person for a minute before he was allowed access through the front door.

"That can't have been Theia. She wouldn't have allowed him up," I said, pointing at the screen. "Do you have cameras on the front doors of the flats and the hallways?"

"Hold on."

Zayn fiddled with the program, going through the flat numbers until he reached Theia's. There was footage of me leaving, making Zayn frown, but he didn't comment. Minutes after I left by the stairwell, the guy turned up on her doorstep. We watched as Theia opened the door, then slammed it shut in his face. It was followed by him banging on it and making threats to her. It was followed up by me arriving, scaring him off and going back into Theia's flat.

"I took her back to mine that night. Well, after I took care of some business. She's been with me ever since. There's been no more notes that we know of, but she hasn't been back to the flat yet. I'm supposed to go later to get her some more clothes."

Zayn sat back and stared at the screen.

"Wouldn't you usually get Arlo to do this for you?" I asked when he didn't speak.

"He's taking some time off work after being stabbed."

"He got stabbed?"

He waved a hand.

"He's fine. Rina is taking care of him. It's a long story, but the situation with Martina and the girls is handled. I'll tell you about it later."

"Our cousin is taking care of him?"

Zayn smiled.

"Mmm. Seems being in close proximity forced them both to admit their feelings."

I'd been aware of Rina's crush on Arlo, but not the other way around. Then I registered Zayn's words properly.

"Did you purposely choose him to be Martina and the girl's bodyguard to push them together?"

"Maybe."

I shook my head. It shouldn't surprise me that Zayn had interfered in Arlo's love life. Arlo had been in our lives since we were all kids, and he'd been Zayn's constant shadow. Arlo might be his second, but they were also as close as best friends could be.

"Anyway, that doesn't matter right now. We need to find out who let this guy in. I'm going to bet it was whoever delivered this letter." Zayn pointed at the envelope that did not have an address on it, only Theia's name. "I can't imagine they persuaded more than one person who works here to do their bidding."

He checked the next date I'd given him and started searching the footage. We focused on the camera above Theia's door. When a man walked along the hallway and posted the letter after she'd left, my eyes narrowed on their features, and I felt sick to my stomach.

"I know him," I said, pointing at the man.

Zayn's expression was sour when I looked at him.

"So do I." He pushed back his chair and stood up, straightening his sleeves. "And he has some fucking explaining to do."

THIRTY FOUR

Gilberto

3ayn reached over to his office phone and pressed down on a couple of buttons. A moment later, a voice came on the line.

"Yes, boss?"

I recognised it as Liza, his manager's voice.

"I need you to prepare room five with plastic sheeting. When they're done, send Lynx in and make sure he's secure. Then I need you to reassign all of his clients to other people and cancel any appointments he has. Do not speak to anyone else about this, especially not him. I'll be dealing with it personally."

"Of course, I'll handle it right away."

The line went dead. Zayn cracked his knuckles, then his neck before he rubbed his hands together. Clearly, Liza had dealt with this kind of situation before since she hadn't asked Zayn any questions about why he was doing this. It hardly surprised me. They did work closely when it came to club matters.

"I take it you want to handle this," he said as he turned to me.

"You're letting me?"

He smiled at me before he pulled open one of his desk drawers and took out a gun.

"I'll be asking the questions as he's my employee. Depending on his answers, it will be up to you what we do with him." He placed the gun in my hand. "She's your girlfriend. You choose his fate on her behalf."

I hadn't brought my gun in with me from the car, having been too busy making sure my girlfriend got to work okay. Besides, I hadn't thought I would need it. I might have a lot of weapons, like the knife currently strapped to my calf, but I didn't get them out unless it was necessary. I could do enough damage with my bare hands if I was so inclined. I preferred not to get them dirty. It was more efficient to kill with a gun.

"I'm going to have to tell her about all of this, including what you did for her."

He nodded slowly.

"If she's with you, she's family, Gil. Just as Ari is, even though she'll never take the Villetti name. If you trust Theia, then so do I."

I knew all about Zayn's aversion to marriage. I didn't have the same feelings, but I'd also never put much thought into it either. It was a miracle I'd even found someone I was attracted to, so the idea of marriage hadn't seemed relevant. My father would have probably started on at me once he'd married Zayn off if he had his way. His wants didn't matter any longer. Mine did. All I knew was I wanted to be with Theia. The rest could come later.

"I do… trust her, that is."

"I meant it when I said I'm happy for the both of you. She's one of my best dancers, so you better not have any ideas about stopping her from working here."

"I'm not *Papá*, Zayn. It's her life. I would never stop her from doing what she wants."

"Just making sure. And for the record, I don't think you're anything like our father." He reached out and squeezed my shoulder. "You're a better man than he'll ever be. I'm proud of you, even if he never was."

"Thank you," I muttered, looking away as I was unsure how to feel about what he said.

"You're welcome."

Zayn dropped his hand. I slid the gun into my pocket, and to avoid thinking about what he'd said, I wondered what Theia would want me to do about her friend. She told me she wanted me to hurt the people who were after her. Did that include someone who had betrayed her? This was an act of betrayal in my eyes. It didn't matter if it had been innocent or not. He'd put Theia in danger. I wasn't going to allow it to stand. My girl had been through enough pain already.

Zayn looked at his watch before moving towards the door and opening it. He paused in the doorway to glance back at me.

"Coming?"

I nodded and followed him out.

"Will the room be ready yet?"

Zayn smiled at me.

"Liza is very efficient."

He pushed open the double doors that led to the private rooms. The light above number five was red, indicating it was occupied. Zayn nodded at me before he opened the door and stepped in. I kept my surprise out of my expression when we were confronted with a redheaded man sitting in the middle of the plastic sheeting on a chair with his ankles and hands bound by cuffs. Zayn didn't say a word as he shut the door behind us and turned to the man.

"Hello, Gael."

The redheaded man looked nervous as he eyed the two of us. I wondered how Liza was able to get him to go along with this. She'd probably told him it was a client request.

"Um, hello, Zayn."

My brother walked over to the drawers on one side of the room, squatted down, and pulled open a long, thin one at the bottom. There were various implements in it. Ones that had me wondering what kind of services they offered in this room. He selected a scalpel before rising and leaving the drawer open, the tools in full view.

"Can I ask what this is about?"

Zayn turned around and looked over the scalpel before his eyes went to Gael.

"This? Well, allow me to explain." He stepped closer. "You see, there's been threats made against one of the girls here, and I have reason to believe you are involved in whatever scheme these people have cooked up to get to her."

Gael's skin paled. His long hair was down, laying on his shoulders. He had a dark t-shirt with jeans on and looked like he hadn't even yet changed for his shift.

"What? Me? Why would I be involved?"

Zayn walked right up to him and placed the scalpel against his neck.

"Let's dispense with the 'I don't know what you're talking about' routine. We have footage of you delivering one of the threats, so you're going to explain to me why, after everything we've done for you here, you would think this was a wise course of action."

Gael swallowed and looked down at the knife in Zayn's hand. I moved closer to them. Gael's eyes went to me and narrowed.

"What is he doing here?"

Zayn glanced at me.

"Him? Oh well, I forget not everyone knows Gil." He removed the scalpel from Gael's neck and pointed it at me. "Let me introduce my brother, Gilberto, and he has every right to be here, considering it's his girlfriend you fucked with. Tut, tut, Gael, pissing off not only your own boss and the head of the mafia too. A very ill-conceived move on your part."

"W-what?"

Zayn gave him a bland smile and proceeded to dig the scalpel into Gael's arm. The guy let out a yelp and stared down at where blood started to pool around the wound.

"Oh no, you don't get to ask any more questions. Why did you give Theia those letters?"

Gael stared at the blood for a long moment.

"They promised me they would let my girl go free if I did what they asked."

Zayn narrowed his eyes.

"What is her name?"

"Raylin."

He snorted and dug the scalpel in deeper, making Gael cry out from the pain.

"I don't tolerate liars, Gael. You don't know this, but it was my people who set you free from that hellhole. I saved you, so you better start giving me real answers."

"How… how do you know that name?"

Zayn cocked his head to the side.

"She's recovering as we speak. My people freed her two months ago. Now, are you going to tell me the real reason or not?"

Gael looked between us, then his expression turned grim, and he looked a little put out about having to explain himself to us. Fucker should have thought harder about messing with one of his work colleagues when their boss was a Villetti.

"Fine. You want to know the truth? They were pissed off because your brother stabbed a guy in the hand when he was at the club. When his friend described the girl who started it all to H, the boss, he knew exactly who she was. They wanted her back, so they told me if I got them for her, they would leave me be. Said I didn't have to do much other than make sure she got the letters and let them into the building when they were ready to take her. That's all I did."

Zayn looked at me. I knew exactly who Gael was talking about. It was from the night I'd met Theia. That fucker who had started harassing her. All I'd known was Arlo had got rid of him and banned him and his friend from the club. H was the guy who tried to take Theia from the building.

I dug my hand into my pocket and drew out the gun before I stepped up to Gael and put it under his chin.

"You did this to Theia to save yourself?"

"Yes. And I would do it again. Listen, she's a nice girl and all, but it doesn't mean I owe her any loyalty."

"Does the Raven know who she is?"

Gael swallowed against the barrel. I wanted to know since Pippa had met Theia last night, and the way she'd looked at my girl had made me suspicious. If these men were trying to get Theia back, there was no way in hell Pippa didn't know about it.

"I don't know. They didn't talk about the Raven. No one ever does."

"Pity."

And without another word, I fired. The bullet sliced through his head, killing him instantly. Zayn let out a sigh and pulled the scalpel from Gael's arm. He had said I could choose Gael's fate. He'd put Theia in danger. He *betrayed* her. He was someone she trusted with her body after everything that had happened to her. What he'd done was unforgivable in my eyes.

"I never expected him to be such a selfish piece of shit," Zayn muttered as he wiped the scalpel off on Gael's t-shirt.

"He was one of the only people she trusts here. She *fucking* trusted him after all the shit she's been through, and this is how he repays her."

I shook my head, disgusted by this entire thing.

"I know."

"I hate people."

Zayn snorted.

"You and me both."

He patted me on the shoulder before digging his hand into his pocket and producing his phone. I watched him put it to his ear as I tucked the gun back into my pocket.

"Where are you?" Zayn asked, as the person on the other end answered. "I'm not even going to ask what you're already doing here. Come to room five. I have something I need you to deal with. And yes, you'll need a clean-up team."

He hung up and stuffed his phone into his pocket.

"Who was that?"

"My Fixer."

I'd never met the Fixer Zayn always used as we didn't run in the same circles and I had my own men to handle any clean-ups, but I was aware of his reputation. He was sought after by a lot of people, but he only worked with a few prominent clients he deemed worthy of his time.

"He's at the club?"

Zayn rolled his eyes.

"Yes. Probably watching Remi again."

"And you're not doing something about it?"

He rubbed his chin.

"No, she made me promise not to interfere in her life unless she asked for my help."

I almost laughed.

"That must be so difficult for you."

He scowled and moved away towards the door.

"Shut up."

Zayn wasn't known for letting things go when it came to the people he cared about. No doubt he was frustrated with Remi for wanting to handle things herself. He shouldn't be surprised. Remi was as stubborn as he was. Those two were like peas in a pod.

He opened the door, revealing a heavily tattooed man with a wide grin on his face.

"All right, Z?"

"Get the fuck in here."

Zayn took Penn by the arm and dragged him into the room, shutting the door behind him. Penn looked around the room, his eyes landing on the dead man next to me.

"Not as messy as your usual ones, Z. I'm disappointed."

"I did not kill him. He did."

Penn raised an eyebrow before his eyes landed on me.

"And who is this? I see the family resemblance." He put his hand to his chest. "Aww, Zayn, are you finally making me part of your inner circle?"

Zayn gave him a dark look.

"This is my brother, Gil. Gil, this is Penn."

Penn walked right up to me, his grin remaining in place before he looked me up and down.

"Well, well, I had no idea all of you Villetti boys were so easy on the eyes."

I stared at him without saying a word, wondering why he was in my personal space.

"Penn," came my brother's warning voice.

"Say, Gil, are you as ruthless as your brother over there?"

"I can be," I said, not knowing what to make of Penn at all.

He bit his lip and rubbed his hand over his chest.

"Oh, I bet you are. I can see you have this whole broody, stoic thing going on and I'm here for it." He waved at me. "I bet you have quite the fan club. Hell, I might even join it myself."

I wanted to step away, but I didn't want to seem rude. And I didn't understand what he meant about me having a fan club either.

"Shy one, are you? That's okay." He leaned closer in a conspiratorial way. "I'm good at making people talk, amongst other things, if you catch my drift."

He gave me a wink.

"Jesus Christ, Penn, stop flirting with my brother. He isn't interested in what you have on offer, and he has a girlfriend," Zayn barked.

I looked over Penn's shoulder at my brother, who was glaring at his Fixer. Penn ran his teeth over his bottom lip.

"Shame. I would have rocked your world."

Before I could respond, he stepped away from me and looked over Gael with a keen eye.

"This one shouldn't be too much trouble. My team is on the way, so you don't have to worry about it, Z. I'll let you know when you can have your room back."

Zayn shook his head.

"Good. I'll leave you to it then. Gil, let's go."

I stepped away from his Fixer, who gave me another wink before I walked over to my brother. The two of us left, Zayn rubbing his face with one hand, his features full of frustration.

"He was flirting with me?" I asked as we made our way back to his office.

"I despair of you sometimes."

"Why?"

He rolled his eyes.

"If you didn't notice that was flirting when he was being so fucking shameless about it, I don't know how you ever managed to work out Theia liked you."

I raised an eyebrow.

"How did you know she likes me?"

He scoffed.

"I watched the security footage, Gil. I saw the way she looked at you all starry-eyed like you hung the fucking moon, and there's you being completely oblivious to it as usual."

I could feel my face growing hot.

"I'm not... okay, fine, I didn't realise at first, but that doesn't make me completely oblivious. I worked it out in the end, didn't I?"

"Hmm, okay, whatever you say." He shoved the door to his office open. "Just remember that next time my Fixer decides to proposition you for the night because, for the record, that's exactly what he was doing."

I didn't know how to respond. It hadn't been clear to me, but maybe it should have.

"I thought you said he was interested in Remi."

Zayn scoffed as he went into his office.

"It doesn't mean Penn doesn't try to fuck anything that moves, Gil. He's not exactly picky. Anyway, come on, we have some more things to discuss, specifically when you and Theia are going to come over to dinner so you can have a talk with Ari."

I sighed and followed him in. Knowing Zayn, I wouldn't get out of having dinner at his house. Would Theia be okay with that happening, considering he was her boss? The only way I'd know was by asking, and I wasn't entirely looking forward to collecting her later. I was going to have to deliver a hell of a lot of bad news to my girl. I only hoped my being there for her would be enough to get her through it.

THIRTY FIVE

Theia

Gil was very quiet on the way back from the club after I finished my shift. He barely kissed me hello when he collected me, something that shouldn't have hurt my feelings, but it did. I'd got used to him being affectionate since we'd got together. To have that taken away all of a sudden had my heart aching in the most disconcerting way. The only thing he'd said to me before we got in the car was he'd got the clothes from my flat as I'd asked. I didn't know what was wrong. He hadn't been all broody when he dropped me off earlier.

When we arrived at his building, he pulled a bag from the boot before we made our way over to the lifts. He didn't even hold my hand. My fingers rubbed together as we rode up in the lift, bereft of his touch. I almost asked him what was going on but refrained, knowing Gil would only talk when he was ready. Something was clearly bothering him.

He strode out of the lift and unlocked the front door of his penthouse when the lift doors opened. I watched him take my bag with him towards the bedroom, leaving me standing just inside the door wringing my hands together after closing it. He was back a minute later, his expression neutral. He stopped by the sofa and met my eyes, frowning a little when he noticed I hadn't moved.

"Why are you over there?"

I fidgeted, feeling out of place at that moment.

"You've been acting weird since you picked me up, and I don't know what's wrong."

His expression softened a fraction.

"Come here."

I didn't want to obey him, but my feet moved all the same as if they were trained to instinctively respond to his commands. I cursed them internally, knowing they wouldn't listen to me even if I told them to stop. The truth was, I wanted to be near him. I wanted him to hold me and kiss me like he couldn't breathe without me. When he did, it reassured me he was right there, wanting me as much as I craved him.

When I stood in front of him, Gil placed his hand on my shoulder and made me sit down on the sofa. He sat in front of me on the wooden coffee table before taking one of my hands and holding it between his. I almost sighed at the contact, wanting to lean into it.

"I have to tell you something."

The note of concern in his voice made me swallow.

"You do?"

He inclined his head, those dark eyes of his growing sombre.

"Is it to do with us?"

"No. Not exactly."

Well, at least that was somewhat reassuring. I didn't think he was about to break up with me, but you never knew with Gil what he was thinking.

"Okay. Well, I'm listening."

He squeezed my hand.

"I spoke to Zayn today about the letters, and their attempt at getting you since it's his building and I had reason to believe someone helped them get in. The thing is, Theia, Zayn knows who is behind the sex trafficking ring."

My hand shook in his.

"Zayn knows? Why does he know? H-how?"

Gil took my other hand, enclosing both of mine in his and holding me tighter.

"He knows a lot of things. It's why he's as powerful as he is. You could call him a collector of secrets, but that's not really what's at stake here. This isn't going to be easy for you to hear, but he hasn't been able to challenge the person in charge directly because they're family. *She* is family. So instead, Zayn has been rescuing people from them for years. His people rescued you."

The person in charge of the sex trafficking ring is family? What the actual fuck?

"She?"

Gil took a breath.

"You were right about the ravens you saw being important. That's what the head of the organisation is known as. The Raven is Pippa, Theia. I want to take her down, I really do, but you understand I'm already in a precarious situation with my cousins, not to mention we don't have any evidence. Zayn hasn't been able to find proof, but he knows it's her."

It took a second for me to realise who Gil was talking about. The woman we'd met at the gala, the one hosting it, was the person who ran the ring. She'd given me a weird look when I met her. Did she know who I was? She must do.

Holy fuck.

I didn't know what to say. It wasn't like I expected this to be the thing Gil wanted to talk to me about. And I wasn't angry at him over not being able to go after her. With all the shit he was dealing with, it made sense. He couldn't rock the boat any further. I understood everything to do with his family had to be treated with delicacy. He couldn't go in all guns blazing with no proof either. It was the same with his cousin's missing shipments and the dead bodies. Gil needed to find out who was behind it first before he made his cousins aware he knew about it and was actively trying to deal with the situation for them.

"The woman at the gala. She's… she's in charge."

"Yes."

"Oh."

He let go of my hands to cup my face in both of his, making me meet his eyes. There was concern in them. Concern for me and my feelings about the whole situation.

"You understand why my hands are tied, right?"

"Of course, I do. She's family, and you have enough going on already with them. This is just another complication, isn't it?"

He had so much resting on his shoulders. I wasn't going to add to it.

"It is."

"Then I get it, Gil. I honestly do. I'm just processing. It's kind of a lot to drop on me, you know. I never expected you to find out who is behind it so quickly. And it's okay. I don't need you to avenge me or anything. Not really. All I want is to be safe. I don't want to go back. I can't."

"You're never going back. I swear to you, I'll never let that happen. I won't let them take you." He let out a sigh and kept his hands on my face. "But that's not everything."

I frowned.

"It's not?"

"No. There's something else. Something I'm having a hard time telling you because I know it's going to hurt you a lot more than this has."

What a way to sound even more ominous, Gil. Now I'm pretty fucking terrified about what you're going to tell me.

I would be brave and listen even if it was hard to hear. It was clear to me now why he'd been acting strangely. He was preparing himself to tell me something bad. But honestly, what could be worse than his cousin by marriage being the one responsible for my kidnapping and subsequent abuse? Pippa might not have been the one dealing it out, but she ran the organisation. She was in charge. I wasn't sure how someone could be okay with that. There were a lot of fucked up people in this world. Ones who didn't care about human suffering. They saw people as a means to an end. She was clearly one of those if she ran a sex trafficking ring.

"Hold on, Gil, you said Zayn's people rescued me?"

It just occurred to me what he'd said about his brother. It hadn't registered before, my mind too busy focusing on Pippa being the Raven.

"Yes, and you can't tell anyone he's behind it or it would disrupt his work. No one can know he's been helping set the people they take free."

My heart fucking hurt with the knowledge. Zayn had rescued me. Well, his people had, but he was still the reason I'd got out. I didn't know if I had the words to thank him for it. He had no idea how much I appreciated my freedom.

"Well, shit. I already thought what he does for people is pretty amazing, but now... I'm at a loss for words."

Gil let go of my face and rubbed the back of his neck. He was beginning to look distinctly uncomfortable. I was pretty sure it had to do with the other thing he needed to tell me. I reached out and put my hand on his knee.

"Gil, just tell me what the other thing is. I can take it."

He looked down at the floor.

"It's about who helped them get to you."

Who helped them?

"What do you mean?"

"Someone let H into your building, plus they delivered the last letter through your front door personally. Zayn and I found out who it was, and we dealt with... him."

I froze. It had occurred to me someone must have helped H get in, but I hadn't stopped to consider who. No one at the club had it in for me, did they?

"You dealt with him?"

Gil didn't look up. He kept his eyes fixed on the floor as if he knew this would break me in half.

"It was your friend, Gael. It seems he was also taken by the Raven and escaped, but they got to him. They wanted him to give them access to you, so they would leave him alone. He had no remorse for it. He told us he would have done it again."

My world dropped out from underneath me. I'd trusted Gael. He was the first person I'd been intimate with since the abuse. And for him to do this to me? To be okay with giving me back to them when he knew what it was like in that place? That was fucked up. He'd told me what he'd been through, but never mentioned the organisation that had taken him. I'd never put two and two together either.

"He... he... oh my god."

My heart hurt and tears sprung to my eyes. How could he? I understood why he didn't want to go back, but it didn't mean he had to throw me under the bus. It was just fucking cruel.

"Theia."

I blinked, tears blurring my vision as they spilt down my cheeks. I could just about make out Gil coming closer and him wrapping his arms around me.

"Shhh, it's okay."

He pressed my face into his shoulder as a sob erupted from my mouth. My hands clutched at his clothes, wanting him closer. Needing him because inside I was falling apart. I don't think devastated could quite cut it for what I was feeling. There'd been three men I trusted at the club. *Three.* And the one I thought cared for me the most hadn't thought twice about helping send me back to that place.

"He... he... he..."

"I know. He betrayed you."

Gil stroked my back before shifting off the coffee table and taking a seat next to me on the sofa. He pulled me into his lap, cradling me against his chest. I cried for what seemed like an eternity, purging all of my feelings of betrayal, heartbreak, and pain on Gil's chest. He held me the whole time, murmuring in my ear about how he'd be right there for me, and I could shed as many tears as I needed to.

What the fuck would I do without this man?

He'd given me so much. And he was still giving just by being there for me, even though I was a mess. He'd told me before that I was his train wreck. I don't know why it meant so much to me, but it did.

"Gil," I whispered into his wet shirt.

"Mmm?"

"What did you do to him? To Gael?"

He stroked my hair back from my face as I looked up at him.

"I want you to remember he not only betrayed you but Zayn too. Desecration is meant to be a safe space for all of you, and he betrayed that by giving you up."

"I know."

I had a feeling I already knew the answer to my question, but I needed to hear from Gil.

"Zayn questioned him, but he left Gael's fate up to me since you and I are together. What he did to you is unforgivable. I told you I would kill anyone who'd hurt you. That's what he got. He'll never hurt you again."

I swiped my fingers under my eyes, not wanting to cry any longer, and rubbed them on my t-shirt underneath my coat, which I hadn't taken off.

"Thank you."

Gil rested his forehead against mine. I closed my eyes, savouring the contact between us.

"I'm going to keep you safe, Theia. No matter what it takes. Eliminating him was necessary."

"I know, but Gil…"

"Yes?"

"Next time you have to tell me something difficult, can you maybe not hold me at arm's length? I thought something might be wrong between us."

He was silent for a long moment. When I opened my eyes, he had a pensive expression on his face as if he was trying to work out what he'd done to make me feel that way.

"I'm sorry," he said a moment later when his eyes met mine again. "I was too busy thinking about what I was going to say. Nothing is wrong between us at all… unless you have a problem."

I shook my head before I cupped his face.

"No. I promise there isn't. Everything's perfect. You're perfect."

"Well, I don't know about that last part."

You should. You're the best person in my life. Fuck… Gil, I'm falling in love with you. Well, actually I think I already am in love with you, but I'm not sure I can tell you that yet. Things are way too new between us.

"The most perfect boyfriend ever."

Gil frowned and pulled back.

"Did you even have a boyfriend before you got taken?"

"No, but I'm sure if I did have someone to compare you to, you'd still come out on top."

He shook his head. And before I knew what was happening, he stood up with me in his arms.

"Perfect," he huffed. "There's no such thing as perfect."

I held onto his neck as he carried me out of the living area towards his bedroom.

"In my eyes, you're perfect, so you better get used to me saying it."

Gil rolled his eyes as he set me down on the bed. He leaned over me and brushed my hair out of my face.

"I don't like compliments, but I'll put up with them for you."

"See? Best boyfri—"

He put his hand over my mouth and glared.

"That's enough for one night. What I want to know is if you're feeling okay and if not, then I'm going to undress you, tuck you up in bed and hold you for the rest of the night."

My heart. My fucking heart. How could he be any sweeter?

He let go of my mouth so I could answer him.

"Can I request this holding also includes kissing and an orgasm or two?"

He stared at me for a long moment.

"If that's what you want."

I nodded. I was still feeling pretty fragile, and I wanted a distraction.

Gil's hands went to my clothes, telling me he was onboard with that plan. He might not think he was perfect, but to me, he would always be. No one had ever made me feel more validated in my feelings and emotions than this man. And I couldn't help but be grateful he was fighting my corner with every inch of his being. Because I would do that for him too. Always.

THIRTY SIX

Theia

The next day, Gil took me to his headquarters with him. It was my day off, and he didn't want to leave me in the penthouse after yesterday. I was grateful for that. However, I wasn't expecting him to take me towards the back of the factory into a room that had thick metal walls. When I saw what was in the room, I turned to Gil and wondered why on earth he'd brought me in here.

"What is this?"

He frowned, letting go of my hand and walking over to a shelving unit where he placed a gun I did not know he was carrying down.

"It's somewhere the men use to practise shooting."

There were a lot of bullet holes in the walls and a few targets sitting around. Gil walked over to the other end of the room and started setting them up.

"I can see that, but why are we here?"

He looked back at me.

"I'm going to teach you how to use a gun. My life is dangerous, and I want you to be able to defend yourself if it comes down to it."

I opened my mouth, closed it and opened it again, unable to form a sentence. He wanted to teach me to do what? I'd never held a gun in my life, let alone wanted to shoot one. It wasn't something I ever thought about, considering handguns were illegal here, and I had no interest in shooting for sport.

"Are you mad? I don't want to fire a gun, Gil."

He walked back over to me, having finished setting the targets. I watched him place both his hands on my shoulders.

"I'm not expecting you to shoot anyone. It's a precaution, and it would make me feel better since I have a few around the penthouse. I don't want you finding one and not knowing how to handle it safely."

I swear I hadn't heard him right. He couldn't have told me he had guns in his penthouse.

"You what?"

"Well, I have knives, and a bat too. I'll show you where they are later."

I put my hands on his chest and stared up at him.

"Hold on one fucking moment. How many guns do you have in the penthouse?"

He let go of one of my shoulders to rub his chin.

"Five."

"Five! Why do you have five? Surely one would do."

He gave me a smile.

"That's not counting the one in the car."

I shook my head and pushed away from him.

"Jesus Christ. That's a little excessive, don't you think? Do I even want to know how many knives you own?"

He shrugged and walked back over to the shelves, picking up the gun he'd left there.

"I run the mafia, Theia. Unlike my father, I don't have bodyguards watching me twenty-four-seven. I can't be too careful when it comes to my own protection. And it's fifteen knives in total. Edric has been buying me them for my birthday for the past ten years, but I got a few of them myself."

I rubbed my face with my hands, hating how logical he sounded about it. What else had I expected when my boyfriend was a mafia boss? He'd already given me bodyguards. No doubt they were armed. I couldn't imagine Gil would let them be in charge of protecting me if not. Honestly, it hadn't even occurred to me until now they would have weapons. I should have known, considering I'd seen Gil kill three men with a gun. I hadn't been expecting him to be some kind of weapons hoarder.

"Come here."

My traitorous feet obeyed, walking right up to him without a second thought. Gil smiled at me again before he took one of my hands and placed the handle of the gun in it. It was heavier than I expected. He turned me to face the targets before standing behind me.

"Hold it out in front of you."

"You haven't even shown me how it works."

"I will. Just do as I say."

I rolled my eyes, thankful he couldn't see and raised the gun. He took my free hand and enclosed it around the handle, fitting his hands over both of mine.

"Widen your stance slightly."

I did as he said, feeling him move with me. His body was curled around my back, mirroring my pose. Gil's proximity did nothing but make me very aware of him.

"That's it," he murmured from above my head.

He lowered both of our hands before turning the gun over to show me the side.

"This is the safety. You click it off when you're ready to fire. And obviously, that's the trigger." He indicated each piece as he explained them. "I can teach you how to load and unload it, but the most important thing is you know how to aim and fire."

I let out a breath as he raised our hands again. While I hadn't exactly been on board with this to start with, having Gil wrapped around me this way was too hot for words. Not to mention the way his voice got lower as he told me about the gun.

"Now, take the safety off."

I did as he said, moving my thumb over it.

"I want you to aim for the middle of the target in front of us."

I adjusted my aim, squinting to make sure I got it right. It felt weird to do this, but if Gil wanted me to know how, I'd oblige him. Anything to keep him close to me this way. I fought the urge to rub myself against him, even though I was thinking about the way he'd buried his face between my thighs last night. And the way he'd fucked me after he made me come. I had no shame when it came to how much I wanted Gil all up in my pussy on a daily basis. Although, I'd quite happily have him all up in other places too.

"Now fire the gun."

I swallowed, placed my finger on the trigger and pulled it back, hearing the click, but the gun didn't go off. My head turned up towards Gil's. He was grinning down at me.

"Did I do it wrong?"

"No. It's not loaded."

I shoved my back into his chest.

"I thought it was going to go off."

He chuckled and nuzzled my hair with his face.

"I would have warned you about the kickback if that was the case."

"That's not playing fair."

He released my hands and wrapped his arms around my body, pulling me flush against him.

"I'm not interested in playing fair. Now, show me you can do it without my help."

How on earth did he think I could concentrate when his thumb was running a circle around my waist? I wriggled in his hold, but he merely tightened it.

"Theia," he all but growled in my ear, "do as you're told, or I might have to teach you a lesson."

"I like your lessons, especially the one where you fucked me until I was too tired to lift my head off the pillow."

I felt the rumbling of his chest as he made a noise of frustration. It was only when I felt what he was packing poking into my back I smiled and did as he asked, demonstrating to him I could fire the gun. Then I rubbed myself against him. Gil grunted, his fingers digging into my skin with the way he was holding onto me.

"Did I do it right this time?" I asked, keeping my voice innocent.

"Yes, but it doesn't mean your other behaviour has been as exemplary."

"Oh? Does that mean I'm in trouble?"

He took the gun out of my hands and stepped away from me. I turned, watching him place it on the shelf.

"Yes," was the only word he said before he was on me, digging his hand into my hair and pulling my head back.

I let out a pant when he ran his nose up my neck.

"I was going to wait until later, but now you've been a very bad little slut, I don't think I can let that slide."

Gil gripped my arm and dragged me from the room. I was hard-pressed to keep up with him as he tugged me across the factory towards the stairs leading up to his office. He didn't acknowledge anyone we passed, nor did he let up in pace until we were safely upstairs with the door shut and locked. He spun me around, making me face him before he loomed over me.

"Tell me, Theia, do you think it's wise to provoke me?"

I shook my head, my feet backing away from him. He followed me until I was pressed up against one of the glass windows looking out over the old factory.

"Answer the question."

"No," I whispered, trembling with need because this version of Gil was hot as fuck.

"I'm glad you agree. Turn around and face the glass."

My body did as he asked, while my mind was questioning what he was about to do.

"Put your hands on the glass and don't move them."

I obeyed, placing them by my head. My gaze went to the men below us, and I swallowed hard. Was he about to do this in full view of them?

Oh, fuck!

I didn't dare look behind me at what he was doing, worried he'd tell me off if I moved. There was the sound of a drawer opening and closing before I felt him at my back. His hands went to my jeans, unbuttoning them and tugging them down my hips along with my underwear. The window ended at waist level, but it still made me pant, knowing I could be seen.

Gil's fingers delved between my legs, stroking along my pussy.

"What were you thinking about to make this little pussy so wet, slut?"

"The way you fucked me last night."

He stroked my clit, making me whine in response.

"Well, it's much too bad for you, I don't plan on giving it any relief."

"W-What? You're not going to fu—"

He slapped my pussy, making me jolt, and shut my mouth.

"I didn't say I wasn't going to fuck you, Theia, but your pussy isn't going to be filled the way you clearly want it to be."

My legs almost buckled at his words. We hadn't done what he was insinuating yet, but it didn't stop me from wanting it. I had mentioned it one night in bed while discussing what else I was into. Whenever I told him about my sexual fantasies and desires, he took note and fulfilled them for me if he was interested in them too.

"Gil."

He stroked my neck with his other hand.

"Don't be scared. I won't hurt you."

"I know," I whispered, my breath misting the glass, "I want this."

His low rumble of approval had me shaking. When he removed his hands from me, I almost whined in frustration, but I had to be patient. He would give me what I wanted. I turned my head, watching him pick up a couple of things he'd left on his desk.

"Have you ever done this before?"

"No, but I did research." He held up the lube and a small plug before indicating the other larger ones sat on the desk. He came closer and pressed a kiss to my shoulder. "I've had this idea of a plug being inside you while I fuck your pussy in my head ever since you told me about your desires, but that's for another time. Right now, I'm going to prepare you so I can fuck you against this window while we watch my men below. I know you like being on show, my dirty little slut. And you're going to give me one because you've been a very bad girl."

THIRTY SEVEN

Theia

My legs felt like jelly with his words. How did he have the ability to say all the right things and make me melt into a puddle of need? I didn't have a fucking clue, but I was glad he wanted to explore so many things with me. It made me feel less self-conscious about my desires and hypersexuality. Although, it felt less like that with Gil and more like we were in a healthy relationship with well-matched libidos.

"Please," I whimpered, so desperate for him to get on with it I didn't care if I sounded wanton. He liked it when I begged.

Gil placed another kiss on my shoulder before he pulled away to coat the little plug in lube. He slid the bottle into his pocket for safekeeping before pressing the metal plug between my cheeks. The tip met my entrance, and I shivered. He made circles around it, not yet penetrating me, but it felt good regardless. He used his other hand to move my hair out of the way so he could nuzzle his face into my neck properly, pressing his lips to it. I moaned when the tip slid into me. He took it slow, inching the plug inside until I'd taken it to the base. Then he pulled it back before pressing it into me again.

"Does that feel good?" he murmured against my neck.

"Yes, yes, yes, please don't stop."

He chuckled, his breath heating my skin.

"We're just getting started, my little slut. You're going to have to take something much bigger soon enough. Then we'll see if you're still begging for it."

I moaned when he tugged the plug out, disappearing to get a larger one. He coated it in lube before pressing it against me. The stretch had me sucking in air. I was used to the feeling, having done this many times before. I wasn't going to rush him, though. It would be more pleasurable if we went slow and made sure I was ready to take him. I rocked against him as he fucked me with it, showing him how much I wanted it.

"You're taking it so well. Do you want me to use the largest one or do you want something else? It's your choice. I want you to be comfortable."

"I want you."

He didn't immediately remove it, continuing to fuck me to make sure I was ready. I didn't complain about it. My pussy ached with a need to be filled, but I wanted what he did. I needed him to fuck me up the arse with that beautiful cock of his I couldn't get enough of. I liked all my holes filled, and I wasn't ashamed of it.

Gil left the plug inside me as he shifted back. I heard his clothes rustling as he unzipped himself. He took his time to roll on a condom before coating his dick in lube. I stared down at the factory again, watching the men go about their business, having no idea their boss was about to fuck his girlfriend above them. It made me shift on my feet, the ache between my legs growing ever more pronounced. My favourite part of sex had never been orgasming. It had always been the act of getting fucked. Having a dick pound into you over and over again. That sensation was my ultimate goal. The coming part was a bonus.

"Gil, please, I want you so bad."

Pulling the plug out, he set it aside before he gripped my hip and lined himself up.

"Always so needy, Theia. My perfect little slut, so desperate for my dick. Is this what you need, hmm? Me all up inside you?"

"Please!"

Despite my pleading, Gil took his time as he pressed inside me. I choked on my own breath when the crown slid into me. My fingers curled against the glass. I wasn't uncomfortable. The sensation was intense in the best way possible.

"Fuck," he ground out through his teeth.

Fuck, indeed. I could wax poetic about how much it meant to me that Gil was sharing this moment until the cows came home, but the truth was, I felt alive. So fucking free because it was me and him. Two broken people who'd found an understanding partner in each other.

"Don't stop. I want you. All of you, please."

"So impatient," he murmured, pressing a little deeper. "Always demanding more. Has anyone ever told you that you're a greedy little slut, Theia?"

"I'm only a greedy slut for you."

His hand tightened around my hip.

"You're mine. All mine," he growled in my ear.

He punctuated his words by thrusting deeper. I moaned louder, closing my eyes as I pressed my forehead to the glass. Gil wasn't exactly small, but he felt so fucking good as he impaled me on his length. I was panting and whimpering when he finally seated himself inside me.

"Are you okay?" he whispered, pressing himself against my back.

"Yeah. Just give me a sec, okay?"

He stroked my hip to let me know it was. It wasn't so much I was struggling to take him, but I needed a moment to adjust to the fullness.

The hand he had been using to guide himself inside me curled around my behind, pulling my cheek open. I glanced at him, finding my boyfriend staring down at where his cock was buried in me. Perhaps it was a novelty to him since it was the first time he'd done anal with a woman.

"Do you like what you see?"

A small smile played on his lips.

"Seeing you all stretched out on my cock is…" He took a breath. "It's making me want to fuck you so hard, you scream. I want everyone to hear you and know I'm the one making you sound like that. No one else is going to fuck you as well as I do."

I pressed one of my hands to my mouth, trying not to combust on the spot. Not only was this man too attractive for his own good, but the mouth on him was something else entirely. I wouldn't tolerate anyone else telling me these things unless it was part of a scene. Even then, it never felt the same as when he did it.

"Make me scream."

"Oh, Theia… with pleasure."

I flattened my palm against the window again as he pulled back until only the tip of his cock remained inside me. When he thrust back inside me, there was force behind it, making me see double for the briefest of moments.

"Look at them. They have no fucking idea," he said to me a moment later, his breath against my ear. "They're going about their day while I'm buried all up inside you. Even if they did look up, they'd never know which of your little holes I'm fucking."

My knees did buckle then, but I was stuck between the glass and Gil's body. He was holding me up as he gave it to me, each thrust making me shake harder from the intensity.

"That's it. Take it like a good little slut. Let me make you feel good."

"Gil," I gasped, failing to remain remotely composed.

I was panting and arching into him, wanting more. Needing everything he had to give. He let go of my hip and laced our fingers together on the glass.

"Louder, slut. Let them hear you."

He tugged me back into him, adjusting the angle to allow him to fuck me even harder and deeper than before. I didn't bite down on my lip like I wanted to. No, I cried out, the sound echoing around my skull.

"That's my good little slut. Sing my fucking praises. They should know how well you take me, how much you need my dick pounding your little holes until you cry and come all over it."

"More," I panted, "more, Gil, please, fuck me."

The glass in front of my face was so misted up I couldn't see a damn thing, but it didn't matter. I was too far gone to care. Gil's pace was brutal. I closed my eyes and let the pleasure carry me away. I cried out until my voice grew hoarse. It was the most intense and frantic sex I'd ever had. He was relentless, leaving me utterly at his mercy. It was right where I wanted to be.

My free hand dropped from the glass, sliding between my legs. I rubbed my clit with my fingers, desperate to find that release with him. He growled in my ear with his approval. I was undone from that noise, rubbing little circles around my clit until I was hitting the right spot with every stroke.

It started deep inside me. This gnawing urge to fall apart. Spots started to form in my vision as the dam cracked. And when it burst through, I let out a voiceless scream, drowning in the intensity of my orgasm. This wasn't the same as the other times we'd fucked. Anal orgasms always felt different. It was why I enjoyed getting fucked this way so much.

My face smashed against the glass as I came down and my body went limp against his. Gil held onto me, continuing to fuck me. It left me with little aftershocks. I opened my eyes and stared at the room below us. No one had looked up. No one was even paying attention. It didn't matter to me. It was the thought of them being able to see that had turned me on.

"Good little slut," he whispered, pressing a kiss to my ear, "coming so prettily on my cock."

Would I ever get enough of the way he praised and degraded me at the same time? I didn't think so. It was my kryptonite. And the fact he was so willing to oblige was everything to me.

He said no more as he kept fucking me, his thrusts going more erratic. I pressed back against him, encouraging my man to take his pleasure from me.

"Theia," he grunted. "Fuck, yes, Theia."

The way he groaned when he came, emptying himself inside me, had me smiling. He slowed to a halt a few moments later, his breaths heavy against my skin as his chest rose and fell on my back. We stayed like that for a minute, both of us regaining our equilibrium.

"They can't actually see us if they look up," he murmured. "It's two-way glass."

I had a feeling that was the case, but the illusion of it was enough. I didn't want his men seeing us this way. Not really.

"Thank you for indulging in my exhibitionism."

"You still owe me a private show."

I smiled as he pulled away.

"Anytime, Gil. All you have to do is ask."

He didn't respond, but I knew he'd heard me. The man would store the piece of information away to use at his discretion. It was how we worked.

The two of us cleaned up as best we could in the small bathroom across from his office. When we were done, he took my hand and led me back downstairs. No one looked at us, but I was relatively sure they'd heard me being railed by Gil even if they couldn't see us.

"Where are we going now?"

"I didn't finish your lesson."

"I've had enough of those for today, don't you think?"

Gil chuckled and shook his head.

"Just wait until we get home. I was serious about showing you where all the weapons are."

I almost shook my head. It didn't actually bother me that he had a lot of weapons. And I would appreciate knowing where they were, so I didn't randomly stumble across them without meaning to.

"Okay, but it still doesn't mean I want to have to fire a gun, you know."

He ruffled my hair, making me scowl.

"I'd only expect it in a life or death situation, which I'm hoping you'll never be in."

"Yeah, me too."

He would never put me in such a position on purpose. It was other people I was more worried about. Like his cousins and all the shit going on with them. I trusted Gil to find a way out of this mess. He'd grown more confident in his role as the weeks went by. When he talked about himself being head of the mafia, it was with certainty. I don't know if he realised he was doing it, but I'd noticed. And I couldn't have been prouder of him for finding his feet. He could do this. He'd proven it, but only time would tell if Gil believed in himself enough to be the leader everyone else saw him as.

THIRTY EIGHT

Gilberto

Theia's hand tightened in mine, betraying her nerves about being around my family. I hadn't been able to put Zayn off with this whole dinner thing. She'd reluctantly agreed to come with me. I wasn't keen on leaving her alone at the penthouse, even though she'd be safe there.

Arianna answered the door with a bright smile on her face, her brown eyes glinting with happiness when she saw both of us. My skin prickled slightly with the memory of meeting her birth mother, and the fact I had to tell her about it.

"Come in, come in."

I pulled Theia inside. She would be fine. I knew she could handle herself. Ari shut the door behind us and turned to me.

"We'll get introductions out of the way in a minute. Come through."

She walked by us towards the kitchen at the end of the hallway. Zayn's partner was in a dark purple dress that fell to her knees, complimenting her tawny brown skin. Her curly hair was flowing freely over her shoulders, something I knew my brother liked. I'd seen him playing with her hair on multiple occasions when he thought no one else was watching.

"How old is she?" Theia whispered as we followed Ari.

"Twenty-two."

She blinked.

"Is that why Verona thinks she's not age-appropriate, because Zayn is like, what, thirty-four?"

I almost snorted.

"Pretty much."

"Well, it's a good thing there's only two years between us. We won't incur her wrath."

I didn't respond as we walked into the kitchen. The dining table was set for six. My eyes darted towards where my cousin Rina was standing next to Arlo. She was folded into his side, staring up at him with a smile. Zayn hadn't told me he was inviting them, but it wasn't a big deal to me. Theia, on the other hand, looked more nervous than ever.

My brother was in the kitchen itself at the stove. Our mother had taught all three of us how to fend for ourselves in the kitchen. She said she wouldn't have her sons growing up not knowing how to cook. He turned at our entrance. His hand whipped out to turn something off before he came out from around the counter.

"Good. You're here." He set his hand on my shoulder as he reached me before turning his attention to my girlfriend. "It's nice to see you, Theia. Thank you for coming."

I glanced at her, finding Theia blushing and looking awkward. I knew this was weird for her, considering Zayn was her boss.

"Thank you for inviting me."

Zayn beckoned his girlfriend over. Ari curled her hand around his waist when she arrived next to him.

"This is Ari. Ari, Theia."

Ari stuck her hand out.

"It's so nice to meet you."

Theia shook her hand.

"Likewise."

Zayn looked at me before indicating my cousin and his best friend.

"Can I get you a drink, Theia? We have wine, beer and soft drinks since I know this one doesn't like to drink." Ari waved at me. "Unless you want something stronger…"

Theia waved a hand.

"No, no, wine is fine with me."

"We'll go sit down," I interjected, before guiding Theia away.

I could feel the awkwardness radiating off her, and I wanted to make her more comfortable. I glanced back to find Zayn pressing his face into Ari's hair and squeezing her waist before he moved towards the stove again. She went to fetch Theia a drink.

We got to the table where Rina and Arlo had already taken their seats. I pulled out a chair for Theia before taking my own seat. She gave Arlo a little nod.

"How's the stab wound?" I asked him.

He raised an eyebrow and looked between me and Theia, who was staring at the cutlery on the table.

"Healing. Zayn forced me to take time off, says he can manage on his own."

"I'm sure the break will do you some good."

Arlo rolled his eyes but didn't respond. He was a workaholic and loyal to a fault. I didn't blame my brother for mandating he take it easy while he was healing.

I turned to Theia and nudged her with my shoulder.

"This is my cousin, Rina." My eyes darted across the table. "Rina, this is my girlfriend, Theia."

She already knew Arlo, so I didn't have to introduce them.

I watched Arlo wrap his arm around Rina's shoulder and whisper something in her ear. Rina nodded at him before turning to Theia.

"I-I-It's n-n-nice to m-m-meet you. I'm v-very h-happy Gil has f-found s-s-someone."

Rina rarely spoke. We all knew she had trouble because of her stammer, but to hear her make an effort with Theia made me reach out and take my girlfriend's hand under the table.

"You too," Theia said, her eyes softening as she came to the realisation too.

I'd explained my family tree to Theia, so she understood how we were all related after I'd shown her where all the weapons in the penthouse were. She wasn't so keen on the gun thing, but I felt better knowing she could handle one herself.

Ari and Zayn joined us at the table not long after that, and dinner got underway. They both engaged Theia in conversation, which I was pleased about as she began to relax next to me. Rina came out of her shell during it, even if she didn't say a lot.

When dinner was over, I nudged Ari, who was sitting at one end of the table closest to me. She looked at me with curiosity in her eyes.

"Can I talk to you in private?"

Her eyes narrowed slightly as she looked towards the head of the table at Zayn. He gave her a nod, knowing exactly what I was about to do.

"Okay."

We got up to excuse ourselves. I pressed a kiss to Theia's hair, stroking her shoulder to soothe her when she grew tense.

"I won't be long," I whispered, knowing she would be okay without me, but wanting to reassure her all the same.

She nodded, but her expression told a different story. Her nerves were back. There wasn't much I could do about it since I had to have this conversation with Ari. It was important.

I followed Zayn's girlfriend into his office. She turned to me, her brown eyes wide as I stopped by the fireplace.

"Is everything okay?" she asked when I didn't speak.

I nodded slowly.

"I'll get right to the point. Zayn and I agreed I should be the one to tell you this. I met the woman who gave birth to you last week at a gala, and we had a conversation about you."

All of the blood drained from Ari's face. She wrapped her arms around herself as if the news was shaking her right to her core.

"You met my mother?"

"I'd hardly call her that, but yes."

She took a step toward me.

"Dad never really talks about her. He wouldn't even tell me her name."

"It's Julia McDonald. Her father owns the hotel chain."

Ari nodded slowly. Her feelings were written all over her face. She was conflicted by this news.

"What did she say about me?"

I almost sighed. Instead, I stepped closer to my brother's partner.

"Do you want the whole truth?"

"I think so."

"I need you to be sure, Ari."

She took a breath, released her middle and shook out her arms.

"I can take it."

I paced away, finding this more difficult than I expected. It was easy to tell Zayn since I knew he wouldn't be emotionally affected by it in the same way. After I'd had to tell Theia the truth about Pippa and her friend, it hit me hard. I'd been learning how to deal with emotionally charged situations because of her. It made me uncomfortable, but I coped for her. I realised emotions made us human. I couldn't shy away from them for the rest of my life. Especially not when it came to Theia. She was my everything, not that she knew. I wasn't entirely sure how to tell her. The feelings I had towards her were still new to me. I didn't know how to explain them. All I did know was I cared deeply about her, wanted to be around her at all times, and found her ever more endearing and engaging every single day I spent with her.

I took a breath, knowing the best way to approach this was to be honest. Ari would appreciate it.

"She told me her parents made her give you up to Bennett, but she also didn't want to be a mother in the first place. Her relationship with your dad was an act of rebellion. She was never going to leave her life of wealth and privilege to raise you. The agreement between her and Bennett was that she could never contact you or be involved in your life. She gave away all her parental rights to him. I'm guessing they kept her pregnancy a secret since it's not public knowledge that you're hers. She looks like you for the most part. It's how I knew when I saw her."

Ari stared at me for a long moment before her eyes dropped to the floor. Then she pulled out her phone and fiddled with it. Her hand went to her mouth. I peered over at the screen, finding she'd brought up a photo of Julia.

"I always wondered what she looked like. Dad told me I'm biracial, so I knew, but I didn't realise I would look so similar to her." She let out a little sigh. "I suppose it all makes sense now why he never really said much about her."

"I'm not sure you'd like her."

Ari looked up at me with curiosity in her eyes.

"No?"

"She was rather self-important, and posh... very posh. The way she talked about your father wasn't complimentary in the slightest. The thought of having to live on a council estate made her lip curl up with disgust."

She let out a snort.

"She sounds like she would have got along with your father with all his working-class hatred."

I smiled.

"Most likely."

She slid her phone into her pocket before reaching out and placing her hand on my arm.

"Thank you for telling me, Gil. I feel like I don't have to be curious about her any longer now I know who she is."

"You're not upset she never wanted you?"

Ari shook her head.

"I have Dad. He wanted me enough for both of them. I've never been under any illusions about her. If she wanted me, she would have been there." She let out a breath. "This gives me… closure."

I inclined my head. What she said made sense. She was very rational about the situation. It made me realise why she and Zayn were well suited. She certainly wasn't shy or retiring, but she picked her battles carefully.

"I'm glad you brought Theia, though she seems a little nervous about being here."

"Zayn's her boss. It's weird for her."

Ari gave me a smile.

"Okay, yeah, I can see how that would be awkward, but she doesn't have anything to worry about. Zayn likes her." She squeezed my arm. "Does she make you happy? You seem happier in yourself."

I didn't know what to make of her observation. Edric told me I came across as aloof and stoic to everyone. Had being around Theia brought out a different side to me? I certainly didn't feel so conflicted about myself any longer. Talking things out with her helped me because she never judged me. Well, she'd been a little weirded out by how many weapons I owned, but she hadn't told me to get rid of them or anything. Guess she understood why I had them.

"She does."

"Well, good, because Zayn's been worrying about you, not that I should be telling you this, but he is your big brother, so I guess it's not that shocking he'd worry. He's far more concerned about Enzo than you, though."

It wasn't surprising in the slightest. Zayn took his responsibility as head of the family very seriously.

"Enzo is being a little shit."

Ari laughed and shook her head.

"Yeah, but he's endearing in his own way, at least when he chooses to be. Sometimes I think he deliberately pisses Zayn off to get a reaction out of him, but he rarely ever rises to the bait. Not like with me, but that's different."

I nodded before I moved towards the doorway of the office, meaning to go back into the kitchen to see Theia. I was worried about leaving her for too long. Pausing in the doorway, I looked back at Ari.

"I'm pretty sure *daddy* would be rather put out if you didn't brat him."

I caught her blush before I walked out of the room. If she thought I hadn't noticed what she called him and their relationship, she was mistaken. I didn't judge them for it, just found it funny how they tried to keep it under wraps when everyone close to them knew what was happening. Zayn had always taken care of everyone he loved, so to see him in a caregiver relationship with his girlfriend was unsurprising. I hoped they realised they didn't have to hide it from us sooner rather than later.

THIRTY NINE

Theia

The moment Gil left the kitchen, I panicked inside. I was stuck with my boss, his second-in-command, and Gil's cousin, who didn't talk all that much. Rina and Arlo had their heads together, quietly whispering to one another, making them entirely unapproachable. Zayn was watching the doorway Gil and Ari had left by as if he was concerned about what they would be discussing. I looked down at my empty plate and fiddled with the dark tablecloth, trying not to bring attention to myself.

Why did he have to leave me on my own?

I already knew. Gil had explained to me why he needed to talk to Zayn's girlfriend before we came here, but it didn't make it any easier on me. What the hell did I even say to Zayn? I'd mostly made small talk with him when we passed each other in the hallways of Desecration, but now I was dating his brother. And I knew he was the reason I'd been rescued. It made it supremely awkward for me. I didn't know whether to bring it up or thank him. A part of me wanted to. He'd set me free from the nightmare that was being kept as a sex slave for people who were cruel and cared little about me. He had to understand why it was significant for me, but would it be strange if I did thank him? Gil had said Zayn kept this part of his life a secret, but he knew I knew.

Fuck, why did this have to be so difficult? I should be able to thank the man who'd helped me without it being awkward and weird.

I need you to come back as soon as fucking possible, Gil.

I was so lost in my own thoughts, I didn't realise Zayn had moved from his spot and had taken Gil's vacated seat until he set his hand on the table. My body jolted, my head whipping up to meet his dark eyes. He looked so much like his brother it was almost uncanny. Of course, the neck tattoos gave him away, but it still took me a second to register it was him rather than my boyfriend.

"You looked a little lost," he said, keeping his voice low.

"I did?"

"Mmm. It's okay, Theia. I know it's weird for you with me being your boss, but I want to assure you nothing will change at work."

"I wasn't worried about that."

He cocked his head to the side.

"No?"

I dropped my hands into my lap, wringing them together under the table.

"I was trying to work out if it was okay to… to thank you."

Zayn was silent for a moment, his eyes assessing me before he leaned closer.

"You don't need to do that, but I appreciate it all the same."

My eyes went to the table. He knew exactly what I was thanking him for.

"I think I do. You're responsible for saving my life. I mean, I know it was technically your people who did, but if it wasn't for you… I don't know what I would have done if I had to stay in that place."

My voice broke a little with my words.

"What you do for people you don't even know is… well, it's everything." I placed my hand on my chest, trying to stop the pounding of my heart. "I… I wanted to die every single day I was there, and when I was rescued and cared for, it gave me hope that not everyone in this world was as cruel as everyone in that place. Then I felt like I had a new chance at life when I was able to work at Desecration. It helped me cope with everything I'd been through. I just wanted you to know what you do matters to everyone you save. It's a lifeline for them."

Zayn blinked as if he wasn't expecting me to be this grateful for what he'd done for me. He reached out and took my hand from my chest. I could see my words had affected him from the way his eyes grew warm and full of wonder.

"I don't do any of this for recognition, Theia. I can't stand the idea of people being trapped in places like that with no choice or freedom. No one deserves that."

"Gil told me about your mother."

Zayn bowed his head slightly.

"She's the reason I started it all, the club, my team of people, everything. It's easier to work in the shadows when no one knows you're behind it. We can do more good that way."

He shook his head. "One day I'll be able to set everyone she's hurt free."

He was referring to Pippa.

"I know."

He let go of my hand and leaned back.

"Not that I think he would, but if my brother does ever fuck you over, I'll sort him out."

I bit my lip. Gil had been nothing but protective, understanding and good to me.

"You'd be on my side?"

Zayn shrugged.

"He should know better."

I grinned.

"Trust me, he does."

He nodded slowly.

"Good." He rose from his seat and looked down at me. "You're family now, Theia. Villettis protect their own."

He patted my shoulder and moved towards the kitchen. I stared at the place he'd been standing in. Gil and I hadn't been together long, and yet his brother still saw me as part of their family. It made my heart ache. My parents hadn't cared about me, but these people did.

Gil walked back in, his eyes immediately going to me. He was by my side the next moment, taking his seat and lacing his fingers with mine.

"Theia?"

I blinked back the tears forming in my eyes.

"I'm okay."

He leaned closer and dropped his voice.

"You don't look okay."

I gave him my best smile.

"I am."

He frowned, his eyes darting across my face as if he didn't believe me. I dropped his hand and cupped his face.

"I'm perfect, I promise."

There was a look in his eyes that told me he wasn't going to drop this. His worry for me made my already aching heart squeeze harder in my chest. How could I tell him all I ever wanted was to feel like I had a place in the world, and he'd given that to me just by being with me? I hadn't thought I was capable of loving someone the way I did him. I hadn't said those three words yet, but I needed to soon because he should know how I felt. How I wouldn't let go, no matter what happened between us.

Gil's phone going off interrupted my thoughts. He pulled away and took it out of his pocket. He stood up and paced away as he answered it. He spoke in low tones, so I couldn't make out everything. He didn't look particularly happy when he ended the call. In fact, his expression grew conflicted. Then he was walking into the kitchen to talk to his brother, who nodded at him before squeezing Gil's shoulder.

Gil came back over to me with a grim expression on his face.

"We have to go. I have business."

I nodded, immediately getting up from my seat, and hurrying over to say goodbye to Zayn, thanking him for dinner. I hadn't noticed Ari had come back into the room, so I gave my goodbyes to her before I approached Rina and Arlo. Gil was talking to his cousin.

"Are y-you going to v-visit Merry and Pippin s-s-soon?" Rina asked with a shy smile.

"Are your cats missing me?"

She nodded.

"If I promise to come over very soon, can I bring Theia to meet them?"

"I'd l-l-like that."

"Consider it done. I'll see you both soon."

I made my goodbyes to Arlo and Rina before Gil whisked me out of Zayn's house and down to the car. I turned to him when we were settled, and he'd set off.

"What's happened?"

"Edric said something is happening at Devlin's, a meeting of sorts. I need to be there. I don't have time to take you back to the penthouse."

"Okay."

Gil reached over and squeezed my hand, giving me a tight smile. I wasn't going to complain about having to go with him. I understood this was important. He had Edric and his men monitoring this guy, and they were hoping it would give them a lead. It was becoming more and more imperative they found out where his cousin's missing shipments were. One of his cousins, who he'd told me was called Nino, had been in touch with him, saying another one had gone missing yesterday. Gil was a little on edge because of it. He didn't want more bodies turning up, either.

"I don't think we'll have to intervene, but if we do, stay down and keep close to me."

"I will."

He pulled his hand away to change gears. I sat back and watched the buildings pass us by. It was dark out now. The city was bathed in the light from the streetlamps, with people going about their night without a care in the world. I'd never be like them. Not with the life I had. And I didn't want to be either.

I used to wish I could have a simple life back when I longed for freedom. Now, I wanted a life with the man beside me, no matter how complicated and dangerous it was. We would protect each other. Even if I couldn't physically keep Gil safe, I'd be his mental shield, helping him through the emotional side of things. He needed someone in his corner, fighting his battles with him. And loving him for who he was.

I wanted to tell him how I felt. With all the shit going on, it didn't feel right to blurt it out. Was there ever a right time to tell someone you loved them?

The car pulled up behind another one, jolting me out of my thoughts. Gil reached over me, opened the glove compartment and pulled out a gun. I didn't flinch at the sight of it. He'd told me it was there. He tucked it away on his person before undoing my seatbelt and placing a kiss on my forehead.

"Just stay close, okay?"

"I promise."

"Good girl."

I shivered at his praise and caught him smiling before he got out of the car. He knew exactly what he'd done by saying that. Shaking myself, I got out, finding him and Edric talking by the bonnet of the car. Tucking my hands in the pockets of my dress, I made my way over to Gil. Edric's eyes widened when he saw me.

"You bought your girlfriend?" he asked, giving Gil a frown.

"We were at Zayn's, I didn't have much choice."

"You couldn't have left Theia with them?"

Gil gave him a dark look.

"No. I need her where I can see her."

Edric rolled his eyes.

"So possessive," he muttered.

My boyfriend gave his best friend a slap around the back of the head. Edric rubbed it and pursed his lips.

"That was unnecessary."

"We need to get inside before they arrive," Gil said, ignoring Edric's comment.

"There's a fence around the perimeter. I haven't been able to get in."

Gil nodded before retreating around the back of the car and opening the boot. He grabbed a few things out of it before closing it and coming back around with a bag. He dug into it and handed Edric a pair of heavy-duty wire cutters. I didn't even ask why he owned those and kept them in his car. Gil was the type of man to be prepared for anything. It was why he had a stupid number of guns hidden around his penthouse, not to mention the knives.

"Let's go."

Edric shook his head but followed Gil as he crossed the street. I kept close to them, glad I'd chosen flats. Tottering around on heels would have been a pain right now. The three of us snuck down the fence line until we got around the corner and were at the back of the building. Edric squatted down and used the cutters to make a hole in the fence. Gil grabbed a hold of the side and pulled it back, nodding at me to duck through.

Edric went next, followed by my man. He tucked the fence back into place to make it look like it hadn't been disturbed.

The three of us dashed across the small open area and huddled behind the back of the building. It was a tall brick warehouse. Gil looked at Edric.

"Okay, how long until the meeting?"

Edric checked his watch.

"About twenty minutes. Devlin is inside, but his guest isn't. I have our men monitoring the entrance. They'll let us know when they're here."

"Right, we get in, scope the place out as best we can, and then find a place to watch them."

Edric eyed me warily as if he was worried I'd be in the way. I had a feeling Gil was less anxious because I was there next to him. His attention wouldn't be divided. I intended to stick to his side the whole time.

"You sure about this?"

Gil nodded. His mouth was a grim line.

"I'm done getting played. One way or another, I'm ending this shit tonight."

FORTY

Gilberto

Edric clearly disapproved of me having brought Theia into this situation, but I didn't care. Having her close was important. I would have been stressed out if I'd left her with my men while Edric and I infiltrated the building. Edric had scoped it out, but I'd been wary about us going in while we were monitoring Devlin, not wanting to arouse suspicion. Edric was sure this was the only place the shipments could be. Devlin didn't own any other warehouses.

"Let's go."

I tucked Theia behind me as we approached the backdoor. There was no one about, but it was locked. I set the bag down and picked the lock with ease. Edric stuffed the wire cutters back into the bag while I opened the door slowly and peered in. The hallway was empty, so I dragged the two of them inside, closing the door silently behind me.

"This way," I whispered, pointing towards the double doors at the end.

We hurried down towards it. I checked through the windows, eyeing the warehouse floor warily. I could see a few of Devlin's men standing around, but they weren't close to the doors. There was an upper level. One man was lounging against the railings, looking over the area where the other guys were.

"We need to get up there."

Edric looked up at where I was indicating and gave me a sharp nod. Carefully opening the door, I slipped inside, with Edric and Theia behind me. I tucked my hand into hers, wanting to keep a hold of her. We skirted around the stacked crates, finding the metal staircase that led up to the upper level. It was hidden behind more large crates so they couldn't see us, but I was still wary about the noise we might make. We had to take our chances with it because time was ticking down.

There was the persistent murmur of voices followed by laughing. I took the opportunity to move towards the stairs and creep up them. Theia stayed behind me, with Edric bringing up the rear. We went slowly, making sure our feet were as silent as possible on the metal. When we made it to the top, I paused, checking the area. No one else apart from that one guy was up here, but he was on the other side of the building from us. It was darker up here, making it harder for them to see us if they looked up.

I took the left path, further away from the guy watching the scene below. Some of the crates were stacked high enough that they hid us from view. We found a spot where we could mostly see the cleared area where the men were hanging out, including Devlin Clarke. He was on the phone with someone, and he wasn't keeping his voice down. I tuned him out as the three of us crouched down. I watched what was going on while Edric pulled out the small camera from the bag and plopped it down next to him. He set it to record, pointing it towards the men. I checked my watch. We had a few minutes to spare.

Edric drew out his phone and checked it before handing it to me. Our men had noted a couple of vans and a car pulling up at the gates. They'd been let through with no issues. I gave Edric his phone back and settled in to keep an eye on everything. We weren't here to stop the meeting, merely to observe. I didn't want to put Theia in danger by starting something.

There was a bunch of noise and footsteps sounding from beyond where we could see. Devlin and his men straightened, and then Devlin smiled a moment later.

"Didn't expect you to come in person."

"And miss out on seeing my favourite business associate, I think not," came a voice that sent a fucking chill down my spine.

The moment she came into view, I clenched my fists at my sides. This was the very last person I expected Devlin to be having a meeting with.

What the actual fuck?

Beside me, Theia stiffened. She was pressed against my side. I hadn't noticed when she'd moved closer.

"Besides, this will be the last one. We'll be out of your hair very soon."

Devlin gave her a bright smile.

"Long as I get paid, I don't give a shit." He waved a hand at the crates behind him. "They're all safe, as agreed. No one suspects anything."

She came closer, her blonde bob severe as usual, and patted him on the shoulder.

"I wouldn't be so sure of that if I were you. I suggest doubling your security. I'll pay, of course. Can't be too careful now my husband's cousin is sniffing around."

Devlin's eyes narrowed.

"Which one?"

"Oh, don't worry, he's a problem I intend to fix."

He crossed his arms over his chest.

"Which cousin?"

"Gil Villetti."

Devlin tipped his head to the side.

"You mean to tell me I have the new mafia boss on my tail? Shit, Pippa, you could have told me." He slapped a hand on his chest. "I already answer to his fucking brother. I thought this was just about getting leverage over your husband, saving the day and all that shit, not pissing off the most powerful men in the city."

She didn't smile. In fact, she tapped her high heel against the concrete floor.

"This is about taking that little upstart down so my husband can be on top. We've had to live under Gennaro's shadow for long enough. He's dead, so it's my time now."

Devlin looked at her like she was mad. To be honest, I thought she was batshit fucking crazy too. Did she really think she could get away with stealing Dino and Gian's shipments without anyone taking notice? They'd already kept it under wraps, which made me suspicious. Devlin's pronouncement about it being to get leverage on her husband told me he didn't know, but what if he did? Was that why he'd done nothing about it? It was a question I didn't think I would get answers to right now.

"Whatever. I'll double security, but you need to get this shit out of here soon. If Zayn finds out I was helping you, I doubt I'll be alive much longer."

She stepped closer to him and patted his cheek with one hand.

"Let me worry about Zayn and Gil." She waved at the men behind her. "Give him his money and unload the crates. I'll be seeing you soon, Dev."

She turned and sauntered away towards the entrance. Her men came forward with two bags and threw them down at Devlin's feet.

"Check them," he said to his own men.

I shifted, turning to Edric, who had a grim expression on his face. He gave me a slight nod. We both knew what had to happen next. He pulled out his phone, firing off a text to our men as I nudged Theia, indicating we needed to move. The sooner we got out of here, the fucking better. While Devlin's men were distracted with unloading the shipment, we could leave without anyone being the wiser.

Edric packed up the camera before the three of us crept away. I was livid, of course, but I kept my temper in check. It was not time to explode and go off on one over what we'd learnt. I had to remain focused and make a plan for what needed to come next.

We retraced our steps until we were out of the building and beyond the fence. It was only then I turned to Edric.

"Did you make sure they're going to follow them?"

"Yup, they're still unloading, and Pippa is on the phone outside the car."

"I had no fucking idea it was her, but it makes sense. All of it fucking well makes sense." I ran a hand through my hair. "She's been running the trafficking ring and now this… she wants to take me out to make way for Dino."

Edric's eyebrows rose up into his hairline.

"Trafficking ring?"

I hadn't told him about that. Hadn't been relevant before.

"She runs a sex trafficking ring."

"The one that held me and is trying to get me back," Theia added.

I turned to her. She looked unnerved by what we'd found out.

"Hold on, that's why he's protecting you?" Edric asked, looking at us. "Holy fuck, it's all connected."

"Yes, it makes it even more imperative we put a fucking stop to this shit. Make sure the men follow the vans. I'll bet they'll be returning to wherever her headquarters are. I'm betting it's the same place they keep their… victims." I waved at the two of them. "Come, we need to get Theia back to the penthouse, then we're going after Pippa. I don't give a shit if she's family. She's fucked all of us over with this shit. I'm not standing for it any longer."

I took Theia by the arm, pulling her back the way we came towards the car. Edric followed us, carrying the bag and fiddling with his phone. When we reached the car, he stuffed the bag in the boot and got into the passenger seat. I helped Theia into the back, giving her a quick kiss before I got in the driver's side. Edric had got a lift with one of the men while he was monitoring the place, so hadn't brought his own car.

"Get Sal to mobilise everyone. Once we find out where the fuck her headquarters are, we're going in."

"Shouldn't we think about this?" Edric asked as I set off towards the penthouse. "I thought you didn't want to start a war between you and your cousins."

"You heard her. She's been fucking with their businesses too. It's not up for debate, Edric. I don't care what happens. I'm not letting her get away with this shit any longer."

Edric didn't respond as his phone went off.

"Yeah? What do you mean, the car went another way? No, stay on the vans. We need to know where they're headed."

Pippa was going somewhere else. That didn't bode well, but I didn't have time to dwell on it. Our resources were limited since we'd only put a few men on monitoring Devlin. I wanted them on the vans.

Edric hung up and looked over at me.

"Where do you think she's going?"

"Fuck knows. We find her headquarters first, then we'll deal with Pippa."

Right now, my focus was on getting Theia back to the penthouse, where I knew she would be safe. It would give the men time to find out where the vans were going. We were going to shut Pippa's ring down and force her out into the open. I had proof she was behind the missing shipments. And I would get proof of her other activities. Then Dino and Gian would have no choice but to listen to me. Even if they knew about the shipments, they didn't know about the sex trafficking. Dino wouldn't have been okay with it. He might not be the most stand-up man, but the Villettis didn't deal in human trafficking. I was sure of that much.

I checked Theia in the rearview mirror. She was staring out of the window with a pensive look on her face. I'd check in with her before I left her at the penthouse. This whole situation was fucked up, but I'd make it better. We were going to end it tonight. If I removed Pippa from power, I'd make Theia safe too. She wouldn't need constant watching to make sure no one took her. Our lives could be normal again. Well, I'd never have a normal life as a mafia boss, but I didn't want her to live in fear.

I swear I'll make it safe for you, Theia, if it's the last fucking thing I do. You deserve that. You deserve everything. I'll give you that and so much more. I promise.

FORTY ONE

Theia

My mind was a riot of feelings. I was most concerned about what was going through Gil's head. He was calm on the outside, but I knew the knowledge Pippa was behind all the shit with his cousins weighed heavily on him. I didn't blame him for being done with it and wanting to take her down. She'd betrayed the family in more ways than one.

When we got back to his building, he hustled me into the lift and took me up to the penthouse himself. He hadn't given me a spare key yet, so he needed to let me into the flat. He didn't say anything to me until we reached the door. Then he took me by the arm and turned me towards him.

"I don't want to leave you here alone."

I smiled up at him.

"I'll be okay. You have to go be the boss."

His lip twitched, but he didn't smile back.

"I'm not looking forward to it."

Stepping closer, I wrapped myself around him and pressed my face into his chest.

"I know."

He curled his arms around me and rocked me from side to side.

"I wasn't expecting it to be her, but it's all making sense now." He sighed and buried his face in my hair. "You'll be safe here. I need you to be safe so I can do this."

I hugged him tighter. He would be strong and handle it. I had every faith in him.

We held each other until his phone went off. He pulled away to check it, his expression turning grim.

"They have the location. I need to go."

I nodded. He leant down and pressed a kiss to my cheek. Then he stepped by me and unlocked the front door, holding it open for me. I walked through, placing my hand on it. Turning back, I stared at him as he let go. Something inside me protested at the fact he was leaving, but I knew I couldn't go with him. Gil gave me a sharp nod before he started to walk back towards the lift.

"Gil!"

He stopped halfway there and turned back to me. The next thing I knew, I was running towards him, and the door slammed shut behind me. I faltered when I reached him. It was the wrong time. There were so many reasons why I shouldn't have stopped him, but I couldn't hold back any longer. Things might go to shit tonight. No matter how much I believed in him, I couldn't account for what other people would do. He was going after Pippa. She had proven herself to be dangerous. No one could afford to underestimate her.

"I… Gil, I…"

He stared down at me, waiting patiently for me to get my words out.

"I love you."

I fidgeted on the spot, my hands wringing together. I'd never told anyone I loved them before, but I couldn't allow him to leave me tonight without knowing how I felt.

He didn't say a word, but his nostrils flared as he exhaled. It was the only sign my words had affected him.

"I just needed you to know before… before you—"

Gil reaching out, grabbing me by my hair and tugging me against him, had my words dying in my throat. Then he was kissing me, his tongue shoved in my mouth and his arm wrapped around my back. I gripped his clothes, kissing him back with the same intensity he gave me. The relief I felt was palpable. He hadn't freaked out on me.

"Theia," he whispered against my lips, "*mia bellissima ragazza, tornerò presto per te.*"

He kissed me one more time before releasing me. He had to unlock the door for me again. This time I let him leave without complaint, even though I still watched him from the door.

"Get inside," he told me before the lift doors shut.

I closed the door and turned on the light. Shrugging my coat off, I hung it up along with my bag and kicked off my flats. I trudged into the kitchen to pour myself a glass of water. I turned and set it on the kitchen island before I looked up to find I wasn't alone.

"Hello, Theia."

I swallowed hard as everything came crashing down around me. Standing in Gil's living room was Pippa Villetti flanked by four men I recognised, including, strangely enough, the guy from the club whose friend Gil stabbed in the hand. How I remembered him, I don't know, but I guess he stuck out in my brain as it was the first night I met Gil.

I froze when a hand wrapped around the back of my neck. The touch made my skin crawl.

"Would you look at that? It's my favourite whore," came a voice from behind me.

I clenched my fists, realising the person who had a hold of me was H.

"Let's go."

He hustled me out from behind the counter, pushing me towards an armchair before forcing me to sit down. He kept a hand on my shoulder and cold steel pressed into my temple. I glanced at the gun and swallowed again. This was bad. Really fucking bad.

Pippa stepped closer, giving me a bland smile.

"Get her phone," she told one of the men who were with her.

I'd left it in my bag, as I didn't think I'd need it. He moved away towards the door. The armchair faced it so I could see him digging through my shit and pulling it out. He brought it back over to Pippa, who walked right up to me with it.

"Unlock it."

I shook my head. No fucking way I wanted to do anything she said. She leant closer, forcing me to meet her eyes.

"I don't think you realise how this works. I own you. I always have even when you were off playing house at Zayn's club. I have you back now, Theia, and you're going to obey me. Now unlock the phone."

I tucked my hands under my thighs. Was it fucking terrifying I had the woman who'd been responsible for my abuse in my face along with a gun? Yes, yes it was, but I wasn't going to show her I was afraid. I wouldn't let any of them see it. They didn't get to terrorise me all over again. Not after the pain they'd put me through for two long years.

"Fine." She looked up at H. "Make her."

Before I could do a single thing, two men came forward and wrestled my arms from under my thighs, forcing me to put my hand out. One of them pressed my finger to the screen to unlock the phone. They released me and pushed me back against the armchair. The gun dug harder into my temple. Didn't they know I'd rather die than go back with them?

"Good," Pippa said, walking away with my phone in her possession.

She put it to her ear a moment later.

"Hello, Gilberto, I hear you're looking for me."

She knew. She'd fucking known Gil was getting close to finding out. That's why she was here. It all fell into place. Pippa had deliberately gone to Devlin's this evening. She wanted Gil to know it was her. Now she was luring him here to end it all.

"Oh, your little girlfriend? Well, she's fine… for now, but you forget, she was mine first and I intend on taking her back."

Pippa let out a nasty laugh at whatever Gil had said. I wanted to launch myself at her. I wanted to tear her stupid blonde hair out and smack that smug look off her face. This woman had ruined so many lives. And she was trying to do it to me all over again, along with my boyfriend.

"I'll see you very soon."

She hung up and threw my phone down on the sofa beside her. Then she turned to me.

"The boys have missed you, Theia. They're very eager to get you back where you belong."

I gritted my teeth, not wanting to rise to the bait. The gun at my temple kept me from doing anything stupid or reckless.

"Cat got your tongue? I suppose that's normal under the circumstances. Poor baby has to go back to her prison, doesn't she? Pity I don't care what you want."

"Go. Fuck. Your. Self."

She merely laughed.

"I see you've become rather spirited since you left. No matter. I'm going to break you, but this time it will be worse." Her eyes narrowed and her smile dropped. "I'm going to take away the only person you care about. He's in my way, Theia, and I don't take kindly to anyone interfering in *my* business. I'm starting with him, then I'm going to get rid of his fucking brothers. Zayn has been a thorn in my side for too long, and little Enzo has to die too. Then no one will have a claim to their kingdom. It'll be *mine*."

My fingers curled around the arms of the chair. The thought of losing Gil permanently had tears welling in my eyes. Not to mention going back to that place where all they'd done was abuse me. I bit the inside of my cheek.

Do not cry in front of this woman. Do not fucking do it.

Satisfied she'd made her point to me, Pippa turned away and spoke to one of her men instead. I tuned her out and tried to work out what the fuck I was going to do. Gil was coming for me, that much I knew, but he'd only had Edric with him.

The rest of the men were still mobilising. It would be two against six. I didn't like those odds regardless of how efficient in killing I knew Gil was.

I wasn't sure how much time passed when the front door slammed open. Edric walked in first, followed by Gil. Both of them had their guns raised, their eyes assessing the scene. The moment Gil saw me, his eyes went dark with rage. It wasn't directed at me but seeing the way me being held at gunpoint affected him made a tear roll down my cheek.

"Well, those are a little unnecessary," Pippa said, waving at their weapons.

"I beg to differ," Gil said, his voice devoid of emotion. It hardly surprised me. Gil was always calm under pressure, even if this was likely testing his limits.

I couldn't see Pippa's face from where I was sitting, but I watched her flick her hand out. The men around her raised their own weapons, pointing them right at Edric and Gil. I flinched, and another tear split down my cheek. We were outnumbered, and I was unarmed. If Pippa carried out her threat to kill them, she'd take me back to the life I'd escaped. To the hell I'd lived in for too long. I couldn't go back. I just fucking couldn't. I would rather die. I'd rather fucking die.

"I swear you men never want to do anything the easy way," Pippa said. "Do you think you can win against me?" She shook her head. "This is only going to end one way, Gil. They're going to kill you and I'm going to take your little plaything back where she belongs. I always win in the end."

"Do you? Is that how you've kept this from your husband all this time?"

Pippa shrugged.

"Dino isn't the sharpest tool in the shed. When Zayn gave you Gennaro's empire, I knew I had to pave the way for him. You had to go make it difficult for me."

"The staged bodies at my headquarters. Those were your handiwork."

She scoffed.

"Of course. Not me personally, but I ordered them."

"And the shipments?"

She waved a hand.

"Oh well, those were to teach my dear husband a lesson. And when I give them back to him, he'll have no choice but to listen to me. I'm going to make us great, more powerful than you and your brother. More powerful than Gennaro ever was."

Power-hungry people always stepped on everyone else to get to the top. They didn't care who they hurt in the process.

"Now, I suggest you lower those weapons and hand them over to my men. Don't make this any harder on yourselves unless you want to watch your little plaything die. It'll be a waste of her talents, of course, but if you want that to be the last thing you see before you die, then by all means."

Gil let out a breath as two of Pippa's men approached him and Edric. His best friend glanced at him. Whatever he saw on Gil's face had him handing over his weapon. Gil did the same. The men backed off. The other two kept their weapons trained on Gil and Edric.

Pippa clapped her hands together.

"Well, since you proved to be quite the adversary, I'll give you a choice of how you'd like to die. How does a single bullet to the skull sound?"

Gil's fists clenched at his sides, but he didn't respond to Pippa. I almost broke down into more tears. I didn't want to watch him die. I couldn't. It was too much. Too fucking much. I took a deep breath, trying to steady myself, but my emotions were running riot inside me.

I can't go back. I can't let any of this happen. Get it together, Theia. You have to do something. You can't sit here like a lemon. DO something!

My eyes darted up towards H. He looked more relaxed now Gil and Edric had been disarmed. The gun he had pointed at me was laxer in his hand, and it was no longer pressing so hard against my temple. He was distracted. Could I use that to my advantage?

It was right then it occurred to me where I was sitting. I was reminded of the conversation I'd had with Gil right by this chair. I'd given him shit over the fact he had knives strapped underneath all of the armchairs and the sofa.

There's a knife underneath me.

My eyes darted back to Gil, who was staring right at me. My hands shifted in my lap, dropping to the soft fabric beneath me. There was a slight twitch of his mouth as if he knew what I'd remembered. Then he gave me a subtle bob of his head. And I knew exactly what I had to do.

This was a life or death situation. Either we'd get out of this alive or we'd go down trying. Regardless of the outcome, I was never going back to that place Pippa wanted to take me. Hell would have to fucking freeze over before I allowed that. If I had to save us, so fucking be it. I'd do anything for the man I loved. And I'd do it for myself too.

FORTY TWO

Gilberto

Remaining calm was growing ever more impossible the longer I stood there, helpless to fix the situation we were in. Edric and I had been disarmed. I didn't have access to the knife in my boot. Any wrong move right then could result in both of us being gunned down. I couldn't afford to do something stupid.

"No? Would you rather feel a little pain before you die?" Pippa asked when I didn't say anything to her earlier question.

I angled my head towards Edric, who was standing right next to me.

"When I say duck, do it," I whispered.

Before he had a chance to respond, Theia dropped her body forward, letting out a rasping sob and dislodging the gun from where it was pressed against her temple. From where I was standing, I could see her hand fumble underneath the armchair she was sitting on.

"Hey, sit up," barked the guy holding the gun.

Pippa didn't turn around, but her mouth thinned into a grim line at the distraction.

"Get her under control," she ground out.

The guy put his hand on Theia's shoulder and pulled her upright. My girl gave me a smile as her face came into view. The guy glared at Theia, but she merely turned her head up towards him. Before he could react, she swung her arm up and stabbed him in the chest with the knife she'd retrieved him from under the armchair. He let out a loud grunt of pain, which Theia used to launch herself at him. She grabbed a hold of his gun, trying to get it out of his hand. When that failed, she wrapped her own hand around his, spun around, took aim, and forced him to fire. The gun going off echoed around the room.

The other men looked stunned as Pippa dropped to the floor. Red blood seeped out of her back into the white fabric of her dress.

"Duck."

Edric and I dropped behind the sofa in front of us before any of them could register what had happened.

"What the fuck?" Edric hissed as he glanced at me.

I was busy with my hand under the sofa, reaching for one of the knives.

"Stay down until I tell you to move."

Pulling out the knife, I peered over the top of the sofa. Theia was still grappling with the man she'd stabbed. The other men were trying to aim at her, but there was no clear shot. I didn't want to give any of them the opportunity to take her out. My hand raised, and I threw the knife at one of them. It embedded itself in his back, making him yelp and drop to the floor. The noise distracted the others.

"What the fuck? Hey, he's got—"

I slid the knife from my boot and threw it at the one who was talking. It hit him square in the chest. He stared down at it. I didn't stop, moving further along the sofa to grab another knife. That one sailed through the air and hit the third man in the back.

"Jesus fucking Christ," the only uninjured one barked, turning his gun on us.

Edric and I ducked back down behind the sofa.

"What now?" he hissed.

The sound of a gun going off had me flinching. I peered over the sofa, finding the man Theia had been grappling with slumped over the armchair while she'd disappeared. Assuming she was hiding behind it, I checked on the other four men. Their attention was on the guy she'd killed.

"There's a gun in the top drawer of the kitchen island," I whispered to Edric. "If you can get that, we can get out of this. Go now while they're distracted."

He didn't hesitate, shifting to the edge of the sofa, checking the coast was clear before he squat ran and slid behind the island.

"HEY!"

I grabbed a large candle in a glass off the table next to the sofa and threw it at the guy who'd shouted. His attention was on where Edric was, so didn't see me. The candle sailed through the air and smacked him on the side of his head. He cursed and staggered back.

"Get them," the one with the knife in his back shouted.

He was too late. Edric stood up from behind the counter, gun in hand, and fired. The guy with the head injury went down first. The other one was turning as the second man went down. Edric fired another shot to take down the last guy. Then he looked over at me and winked.

I stood up, watching the last one collapse before I vaulted over the sofa.

"Theia!"

My girl peered out from behind the armchair, her blue-grey eyes widening at the sight of the bodies. She stood up, holding the gun she'd stolen from the man she'd killed in her hands. There was a noise behind me as I moved toward her.

"Get down," she screamed.

I didn't hesitate, dropping to my knees as she raised the gun and fired. My head turned to find a man behind me with his arm raised, clutching a knife in his hand. He stared down at the blood pooling on his clothes before Theia fired again. This time, the bullet embedded itself in his skull. His eyes went dead, and he fell to the floor.

It was the first guy who'd gone down when I'd thrown a knife into him. I wondered when he got back up, but it didn't matter because Theia was scrambling out from behind the armchair and running towards me. She slammed down on her knees when she got to me, letting go of the gun which clanked as it met the floor.

"Gil."

I reached out, grabbed a hold of her and pulled her to my chest. Theia let out a sob, burying her face in my neck as her arms went around me.

"It's okay, I'm right here," I whispered into her hair, "I've got you. We're okay. It's over. I promise."

The sound of the buzzer going off made both of us jolt. I didn't let her go, trusting Edric to answer it. A group of our men were on the way over here. I'd rung them from the car on the mad dash back here. The rest of them were congregating at the location of Pippa's building, where I was pretty sure they were holding all the victims of her sex trafficking ring. I'd phoned my older brother too and told him to get his people over there as fast as possible. I would have to explain all of this shit to him, but I didn't have time in the car. He seemed to take that in his stride when I explained Theia was in danger.

Now we were okay. Pippa and the men she'd brought were dead. Theia had been so brave and fought for our lives. She hadn't hesitated when we were all facing execution.

I pulled her away from my neck, cupping her wet face with both my hands. She blinked and stared up at me.

"*Ti amo.*"

The words were out before I could stop them. When she'd told me she loved me earlier, I'd been surprised, but so overwhelmed with happiness, I barely knew what the fuck to do other than kiss her. It was only when I got back to the car and had set off, I realised I felt the same way too. I loved her. There was no other explanation for my feelings towards this woman. She was my everything.

"What does that mean?" she whispered, her voice all croaky.

I smiled.

"I love you."

She let out a little choked sound, her chest stuttering with it. I tugged her closer, brushing my mouth across hers.

"I love you, Theia, and I'm never letting you go."

I caught her mouth with mine, not caring she was still crying. Her hands wrapped around my wrists as she kissed me back. Then she was so overcome with emotion that she practically collapsed on me, sobbing into my chest as her hands gripped my clothes.

"Shh, it's okay," I murmured before I picked both of us up off the floor, cradling Theia against my chest. I carried her towards the sofa and sat down with her.

The front door opened a minute later as I sat there stroking her hair and allowing her to purge all of her feelings out on my chest.

"Well, you missed all the fun," Edric said to the men assembled outside. He ushered them in and put his arm out. "As you can see."

One of them looked at him with a raised eyebrow.

"What do we do then?"

"What do you do? Clean this shit up, that's what you do."

"We're not fucking cleaners," another one piped up.

Edric turned to him with a bright smile.

"Did you just disobey a direct order? I'm pretty sure I didn't hear you tell me no when we're standing in our illustrious leader's penthouse in full view of the man himself."

The men spied me, and several of them went pale.

"Um, no, Jim was joking, weren't you?" the first one said as he slapped Jim around the back of the head.

"Yeah, yeah, of course. We'll get right on it, boss," Jim said, rubbing his head.

Edric clapped his hands together.

"Good."

I waved Edric over, wanting to have a word with him about the plan. He nodded at the men before sauntering towards me.

"Yes, boss?"

I stroked Theia's hair again.

"Don't care what you do with the men but preserve Pippa's body. I want to send Dino and Gian a little message with it, and the others we've been keeping."

Edric raised his eyebrow.

"I like the way your mind works."

"You can make sure we have all the evidence against her gathered for me to send with the bodies."

He saluted.

"On it." His eyes darted to Theia. "Is she…?"

I looked down at my girl. She'd stopped crying and was holding onto me like she never wanted to let go.

"She'll be fine. Unless you need me, I'm going to put her to bed."

He waved a hand.

"Nope. You do what you need, Gil. I'll sort this out."

I trusted him to have a handle on it. The men would deal with the mess in my penthouse and tomorrow, we could address everything else.

I stood up with Theia and carried her from my living area down the hallway to my bedroom. Shutting the door with my hip, I set her down on her feet. She stared up at me as I unzipped her dress and helped her out of it. A few minutes later, she was tucked up in bed with one of my t-shirts on after I'd cleaned her face, and me beside her. She buried herself in my arms and pressed her face against my chest, snuggling close.

"Do you really love me?" she whispered into my bare chest.

"I'm beginning to think you like questioning me every time I tell you something, since you don't believe me at first."

She wriggled in my grasp.

"I do not."

"Yeah, you really do."

"Shut up."

I snorted and hugged her closer, burying my face in her hair.

"Are you sure you don't need to be out there dealing with them?" she asked a moment later.

"Edric can handle it. It's what he's there for." I pulled back to look at her face. "You're more important to me, Theia."

She let out a sigh.

"I'm just glad we're both okay. I was so scared, but I couldn't go back to that place."

"You saved us all instead."

Her cheeks went pink.

"She was going to kill you."

I stroked her hair back from her face.

"I know. I'm proud of you for what you did. Guess you're not so upset with me for making you learn how to shoot."

She didn't exactly scowl at me, but her mouth thinned.

"Doesn't mean I want to go around shooting people on the regular. I'll leave that to you and Edric."

Leaning closer, I pressed a kiss to her lips.

"I'll never make you shoot anyone again."

"You can't promise that. You're a mafia boss. Who knows what danger you'll get mixed up in next."

"Are you sure you want to spend your life with such a dangerous criminal?"

Theia shook her head and shoved me.

"You're not dangerous to me."

I rolled her over onto her back and towered over her. Theia stared up at me with a twinkle in her eyes as I gripped both her wrists, pinning them to the bed.

"I'm going to make you take that back."

She squealed when I pressed kisses to her jaw, wriggling against me. We'd been in a life or death situation, and I wanted to reaffirm things between us. Judging by the way she was moving against me, Theia wanted that, too.

I hovered my mouth over hers a moment later, staring down into her beautiful blue-greys.

"*Ti amo,* Theia."

"I love you too, Gil," she whispered.

I knew we'd be okay after everything we'd been through together. Theia and I were stronger together. We'd proven that tonight. Tomorrow, I'd set about making sure my cousins were aware of who was the fucking boss around here.

Me.

FORTY THREE

Gilberto

Edric and I were sitting in my office talking about what we needed to deal with next when one of the men knocked on the door to inform me my cousins were waiting downstairs. I smiled at Edric before clearing my features and cracking my knuckles.

"Let's go see what they want."

He rolled his eyes.

"As if you don't know."

It had been two days since the incident at my penthouse with Pippa. The men had been busy clearing up the mess she'd left behind. Zayn's people had helped by taking in all the sex trafficking victims they'd found at Pippa's building. All the men involved had been rounded up, questioned, then disposed of. It was better to clean it up ourselves. We didn't need questions being raised about what had gone on.

Last night my men had dropped off the bodies we'd kept in our mortuary, along with Pippa and the whereabouts of their missing shipments at Dino's headquarters. We'd provided the evidence of her betrayal, of course, but I knew they'd be on my doorstep the moment they found out.

"How's Theia?" Edric asked as we made our way out of my office.

"Fine. Happy to be free of her bodyguards."

She'd taken what had happened in her stride. I think the knowledge it was all over helped. She was dealing with the aftermath of having killed three people, but at the end of the day, she was glad Pippa was dead. She couldn't hurt anyone else now.

"You sure?"

"She'll be okay. We take care of each other, so she'll get through it."

Edric paused at the top of the stairwell, raising his eyebrow.

"I'd never thought I'd see the day you would willingly take care of another person."

"Why wouldn't I? She's my girl, and I love her."

I walked down the stairs, ignoring his wide-eyed look. He knew I was serious about Theia. I wasn't going to give her up for anything, especially not now she was no longer in danger.

When I got to the bottom of the stairs, I was met by Dino, Gian, Nino and a few of Dino's men. My cousin did not look happy. His wife was dead, so it was hardly a surprise, even if she had been a shit human being. Nino gave me a subtle dip of his head. We'd spoken the day after Pippa had died. I'd told him everything that had gone down, but he'd decided to keep quiet about what he knew. He wanted to know how Gian and Dino would react before he said anything about his involvement in setting me on the case.

"Hello, cousins. What can I do for you?" I asked as I stuffed my hands into my pockets.

"What can you do for me?" Dino barked, his face going an ugly shade of red. "You can start by explaining why the fuck you killed my wife."

I waved a hand at my men. They scattered like the wind, going back to what they were meant to be doing, leaving me, Edric, and my cousins alone. They weren't a threat to us. If they tried something in my headquarters, they wouldn't walk out of here alive. I didn't care if they were my cousin's men. This was *my* house. No one fucked with me here unless they had a death wish.

I stepped closer to Dino.

"Did you not look at the evidence?"

"Of course I fucking did."

"Then I would have thought the answer would be obvious. Well, that and your wife would have quite happily killed me if I hadn't got to her first." I shook my head. "A threat to me and my own can only be dealt with one way, regardless of who they are."

It didn't matter if Theia was the one who pulled the trigger. Edric and I were taking personal responsibility for what happened in my penthouse. She didn't need to be wrapped up further in my mafia world, even if she was well aware of what went down in it. There was no telling what Dino would do if he ever found out my girl had killed his wife. I wasn't going to take that chance. Pippa had got what was coming to her, anyway.

Dino opened his mouth. I put my hand up, silencing him.

"Did you know what she was doing?"

"If you're asking if I knew about the sex ring? No, no, I fucking didn't." He clenched his fist at his side. "We don't deal in people that way. It's not what we stand for."

"And the missing shipments?"

Dino looked away.

"No. I didn't know about that either."

I knew it took a lot for him to admit his wife had got one over on him.

"Then what do you want, Dino? The way I see it, I did you a favour by uncovering the truth, something neither you nor Gian seemed capable of doing. One of your own had to come to me for help after the two of you decided it was 'under control.' Were you just ignoring the problem and hoping it would go away? That's what it looked like to them."

Gian looked at Dino, who was frowning heavily.

"What do you mean, one of ours? Who the fuck told you?"

I wasn't going to out Nino to them, that was his choice. He was staring at his father with no discernible emotion on his face.

"Do you think I'm going to betray their trust to two men who can't find their way out of a fucking paper bag? If you were as competent as you clearly think you are, you would have found out who was stealing your goods long before now, but no, I had to intervene. And to think you turned your noses up at me running my father's empire. You still want to tell me I'm incapable now? The way I see it, you two are the ones who are running your own empire into the ground."

I glanced at Edric, who was having a hard time keeping a straight face. I was glad he was amused, since this situation was far from fucking funny to me. These idiots had no legs to stand on. Dino could be as angry as he liked at me, but he knew I was right.

No one said anything. Dino and Gian glared at me, clearly turning my words over in their heads. The silence was only broken by Nino crossing over to me and taking his place by my side. His father and uncle looked at him with joint surprised expressions on their faces.

"I was the one who told Gil about what was going on. I gave him the information 'cause neither of you could get your acts together."

"You did?" Gian said, staring at his son like he'd gone mad.

"Yeah, I did. I'm tired of you acting like my opinions and concerns don't matter. You treat me like I'm a child." He shook his head. "I'm done, *Papá*." Then he turned to me. "Gil, would you accept me as *famiglia*?"

I heard his father's sound of outrage, but I ignored Gian and Dino. It had not occurred to me that my cousin would defect, but considering he'd come to me over his father and uncle's decision to bury their heads in the sand, it shouldn't have surprised me.

"You're family, Nino. You have a place here if you want it."

He gave me a sharp nod. As if I wasn't going to let him join me. He had proven to be resourceful, and he knew when to ask for help.

"Set me wherever you like. I'm willing to learn."

"Let me see your father and uncle out, then we'll talk."

I stepped toward Gian and Dino, who were completely dumbfounded by what was happening.

"Gentlemen, I believe our business is concluded. I suggest you take a long hard fucking look at yourselves, what it means to be *capo* and decide whether you're really qualified for such a role. I'll be waiting when you're ready to acknowledge who is the better leader here."

I gestured to Salvatore, who was nearby. He came over with several of the men.

"Please see my cousins and their men out. They've overstayed their welcome."

Salvatore gave me a slight nod before gesturing to my cousins. Dino glared, and Gian looked at his son like he was at a loss for words. It served them right for being useless pricks.

My cousins and their men followed Salvatore out. I waved at Edric and Nino, who followed me back upstairs to my office. I dug my hands in my pockets and stared out of the window at my warehouse. It made me smile as my thoughts drifted to when I had Theia up against it, begging for me. I almost couldn't wait to see her later. I was due to pick her up from work. She'd not wanted to go back to her flat yet. I'd told her she was welcome to stay with me as long as she wanted.

"Well, that was quite the show," Edric said, eyeing my cousin.

"Mmm. It was. Nino, this is Edric, my second-in-command." I waved at Edric. "Edric, go get Sal."

He merely gave me a look but retreated from the room. I turned to Nino. He had a pensive expression on his face as if he was wondering what I would say next.

"I know you were training under your father."

"Yeah, but I can't say he was the best teacher."

Gian was more interested in boasting about himself and his children than actually giving them usable life skills.

"Even so, I have a vacant position I'd like you to fill. How would you like to be my *capodecina*?"

Nino's eyes widened.

"Me?"

"Yes, unless you don't think you can lead the men."

He waved his hands.

"No, no, I can. I promise."

"Then consider it done."

The men Salvatore had suggested to me weren't suitable. I didn't trust them enough, but my cousin, he was worthy of it. Besides, he was family, and having another Villetti by my side felt right.

"Thank you. I won't let you down."

I smiled at him as Edric returned with Salvatore. I introduced them, leaving Nino in his capable hands to meet the men and get settled in. They left Edric and me alone in the office.

"Well, who'd have thought your cousin would tell his dad to go fuck himself. Man, your cousins' faces were a picture."

I shrugged.

"They're incompetent."

"Do you think they'll cause you more trouble?"

I shook my head.

"Doubt it. And if they do, I'll pull a Gennaro and take over their *famiglias*."

He blinked behind his glasses.

"You serious? I thought you didn't want to be dear old dad."

I walked over to him and wrapped my arm around his shoulder.

"My father wouldn't have shown them mercy. They have a chance to reform themselves. Things around here aren't going to run the way they did when my father was alive. The era of Gennaro is over. It's time we do things the Gil Villetti way. And you're going to help me make sure we stay on top."

"The Gil Villetti way, huh? I like the sound of that."

I ruffled his hair.

"Good. Now let's get down to actual business."

Edric grinned at me.

"Yes, boss."

I might have been questioning myself a couple of months ago, but now I was sure of who I was. I didn't need to be my father. All I had to do was be me. A fair but ruthless mafia boss who didn't take fools lightly. Zayn was right when he gave me the keys to our father's empire and told me to run it my way. He trusted me. And now… now I trusted myself to be the man he always knew I could be.

FORTY FOUR

Theia

As I unlocked the door to the flat, I almost couldn't believe it would be my first night of officially living here permanently. It had taken me a month to even go back to my own flat after everything went down. And only two weeks after that to tell Gil I missed sleeping next to him every night for us to make the necessary arrangements. We might not have been together long, but I was sure of one thing. Gil was it for me. I was never letting this man go. I didn't care if he was a mafia boss and led a dangerous life. As far as I was concerned, he was perfect for me.

The day we told each other we loved each other had been tumultuous. I chose to focus on the positives. Yes, I had ended up taking three lives that night, but it was a life-or-death situation. I'd saved myself, Gil and Edric. That was the important part. Besides, after all the shit H had put me through, killing him felt like justice. As had ending Pippa. Getting rid of them meant all the people they'd hurt were free.

Gil and Zayn's men had rescued everyone, giving them a safe place to recover and a new chance at life. What were three lives when you'd helped stop the sex trafficking ring that held you captive? Nothing in the grand scheme of things. I was safe now and didn't have to live in fear I'd be taken away again. The price of freedom was heavy but ultimately worth every sacrifice I'd made.

We had to attend Pippa's funeral. The official cause of death given was she'd taken an overdose. Only a few people knew about the bullet I'd put in her back. Gil was still at odds with his cousins since Gian's son had defected, but they stayed out of his way. Nino was wholeheartedly welcomed into Gil's side of the family. He wasn't on speaking terms with his father, but I'd met his mother, younger brother and sisters a couple of weeks ago. They were a lot of fun. I think Gil appreciated having me as a buffer between him and his extended family as I took on the bulk of making conversation with them. He would never be a people person, but he was open with me. I cared more about that than anything else.

Through all of this, I was most grateful I had him beside me to help me cope with everything. He was my rock, my solace and my safety. The only person in this world I trusted above all else. I loved every moment I spent with him. My stoic mafia boss boyfriend, who wouldn't hesitate to kill for me. He was my forever.

When I stepped into the penthouse, I almost jumped out of my own skin. Gil was standing right by the door, waiting for me. He caught me by the arm and steadied me before I fell backwards.

"Jesus, give a girl some warning before you just appear like that."

He merely smiled at me. Gil was notorious for sneaking up on me. I don't know how a man his size was so damn sneaky and silent, but he was always scaring the crap out of me with his antics.

"I wanted to welcome you home."

"Well, next time make some damn noise, so I know you're there."

He pulled me closer and cupped my cheek.

"I'm sorry. How can I make it up to you?"

"You could kiss me hello."

He leant down and caught my mouth with his, kissing me deeply and making me melt into him.

"Better?" he murmured against my lips.

"Much."

He pulled back and smirked.

"So, you don't want my surprise, then?"

"What? You have something for me?"

He inclined his head. He didn't need to buy me presents. I never expected anything other than his time, but he always gave me that in spades.

"Of course I want it!"

"Close your eyes then."

I almost rolled them but did as he told me. He moved behind me and directed me forward into the living area. We came to a stop, and Gil leant his chin on my shoulder as he wrapped his arms around me.

"Open them, Theia."

Letting out a breath, my eyelids fluttered open. It took a second to register what was in front of me.

"Do you like it?"

My head turned so I could look at him.

"You bought me a pole."

"I thought you would appreciate somewhere to practise. And I'll admit, it's for me too."

I raised a brow.

"Does my big bad mafia boss want his girl to perform just for him?"

"Always."

I pushed out of his arms and stepped over to the pole. It was in one corner of the room that housed Gil's bookcases. There was a comfortable armchair nearby where he could sit and watch.

I grabbed a hold of the pole and spun around it. Whoever had installed it had made sure it was fully secured to the ceiling and floor. I looked at Gil and smiled.

"It's perfect. Thank you."

He came closer, reaching up to cup my face.

"Anything for you, my love. I want you to make this your home too. This is only the start. We're going to build a whole life together."

My insides flipped. Gil wanted forever with me. I already knew that, but hearing it always made me happy. He was just as invested in this relationship as I was.

"Oh yeah? What do you see this life including?"

He grinned and caught me up in his arms.

"You and me." His hand dragged down my back. "The rest we can decide together in time. All I want is you, Theia."

"I just want you too."

He kissed me, making me feel safe and secure in his arms. It was my favourite place to be.

I was the one who pulled back when an idea came to mind. He'd got me a present. It was my turn to give him one in return.

"Go sit."

I waved at the armchair. Gil licked his bottom lip, giving me a devious smile, but he did as I asked. I hurried away, stripping out of my coat and bag before wandering along to our bedroom. My clothes were gone soon after and I put my hair up in a ponytail before doing a couple of stretches.

When I came back out, he had moved the armchair, so it was facing the pole. His dark eyes roamed over my naked body, his lip curving up at the sight of me. He'd told me once he wanted to watch me dance when I had nothing on. Well, now I would make one of his fantasies come true after he'd brought so many of mine to life.

I got my phone out of my bag and put some music on, casting it to his speakers. Setting it down on the coffee table, I approached the pole. The routine I started was something new I'd been working on for a few weeks. Gil could be my sounding board when it came to my dances now we had the pole at home. Dancing had always been my favourite part of my job as much as I enjoyed the sex work part.

I began my routine, making sure to keep my eyes on Gil the whole time, watching his pupils dilate as I moved. The way he rubbed his hand across his thigh was the only indication this was turning him on. It might be weird to some people, but the fact he rarely showed emotion did something to me. It made me want to be good for him, then I got rewarded for it. Gil's sexual rewards were the very best kind.

My body twisted around the pole as I bent back, putting all of my assets on show. Gil shifted in the armchair. I could tell he wanted to say something, but he kept silent. When I moved again, shifting my pose, he let out a low growl as if his control was beginning to fray around the edges. I didn't say a word, merely continued twirling around the pole until I finished my routine. Then I jumped off the pole and stalked towards him. I leant over my man, placing my hands on the arms of the chair, swaying my body to the beat with every movement I made.

"Open your legs," I demanded.

He did as I asked, spreading them and allowing me to step between them. I spun around and lowered myself until I was almost sitting on him. My hands landed on his knees to steady myself as I gave him a lap dance. I could feel his attention on me, watching my every movement. It made me feel alive, knowing I was his sole focus. He wanted me and only me. All I desired was him watching me, touching me, fucking me until I was a mess of pleasure, undone by his mouth and his body pressing into mine. We'd become so in sync in the bedroom, each giving the other exactly what they needed. He pushed. I pulled. And together we made beautiful fucking music.

He gripped my hips and tugged me against him, my back meeting his chest. He ran his tongue down my ear.

"That's enough teasing, my little wanton slut," he murmured, nibbling the lobe before his hand drifted between my thighs. "I want this. And I want it right now."

He ran his fingers along my slit, making me let out a moan. I pressed myself into his hand, wanting to feel him everywhere.

"Mmm, I see you liked showing off to me, didn't you? Your needy little pussy doesn't lie, slut. I can feel how much you want to be impaled on my cock."

I spun around in place, forcing him to release me. Then my hands were at his shirt, undoing the buttons. When I got to the bottom, I worked on his fly, unable to control the desire to have him inside of me. I wanted it so fucking bad. My hand dug into his boxers to draw his cock out. It was hot to the touch. He watched me the whole time, his dark eyes full of wickedness.

I straddled his lap, positioned him at my entrance, and sunk down on him. Gil and I had abandoned condoms. I'd always been on birth control, and we were all regularly tested at the club.

His hands went to my hips, gripping them tight. His eyes drifted down my body to the place we were joined.

"So beautiful."

I shivered, placing both of my hands on his bare chest to give me leverage to ride him. He watched me the whole time, keeping a tight hold of me to guide me along. I let go and gave in to the pull between us, letting his attention drown me. This was what I wanted. Just me and him this way. I loved this man so much. The connection we shared. How we always talked things out and made each other happy. It was a perfect balance. The relationship I never thought I could have.

Before all of this, I didn't think I deserved to find someone who loved me for me. Gil had shown me that wasn't the case. He wanted me for my mind long before he ever was attracted to my body. It helped me change my perspective on myself and the world, setting me free from the cage I'd been trapped in.

Gil and I were the better versions of ourselves now. The ones we were most comfortable with. He'd found his way. I'd found mine. And together, we were a force to be reckoned with. The mafia boss and his exhibitionist sex worker. Who would have thought that could ever work? I hadn't, but the world worked in the strangest of ways. A chance encounter at the club had set us on a different path, one we could now follow together. I'd helped him find himself, and he'd given me safety and a family. It was more than I could have ever asked for.

"I love you," he whispered, pulling me down for a kiss.

His other hand fell between us, his fingers working on my clit until I was panting and gasping into his mouth. He groaned as I tightened around him with my climax, spots forming in my vision from its intensity. Gil thrust up into me, increasing his pace until he fell off the edge too, the two of us drowning in ecstasy.

I pressed my forehead against his and closed my eyes while I caught my breath. When I opened them, he was staring at me with so much love and affection, my heart threatened to burst. I wrapped my hand around the back of his neck, keeping him anchored to me.

"I love you too. Forever."

He smiled, joy lighting up all of his features.

"Forever, my beautiful little slut. Forever and always."

ACKNOWLEDGEMENTS

A huge thank you to my besties Ash and Amber. I couldn't do any of this without you. Both of you have brought so much light into my life. I've had a lot of hardships this year but having you to rely on when things got tough has been everything to me. Your support has given me the time and space to grow as an author and for that, I will be forever grateful. Pack Bailey for life!

To the Society of Sarah Bailey Stalkers and all my readers – thank you for all your support! You really do make me smile every day and I'm grateful you all love my words so much.

To my mother – thank you for all your help and the support you give me with my writing career.

To my wonderful husband – thank you always being there for me no matter what life throws at us.

ABOUT THE AUTHOR

Sarah writes dark, contemporary, erotic and paranormal romances. They adore all forms of steamy romance and can always be found with a book or ten on their Kindle. They love anti-heroes, alpha males and flawed characters with a little bit of darkness lurking within. Their writing buddies nicknamed Sarah: 'The Queen of Steam' for their pulse racing sex scenes which will leave you a little hot under the collar.

Born and raised in Sussex, UK near the Ashdown Forest, they grew up climbing trees and building Lego towns with their younger brother. Sarah fell in love with novels as teenager reading their aunt's historical regency romances. They have always loved the supernatural and exploring the darker side of romance and fantasy novels.

Sarah currently resides in the Scottish Highlands with their husband. Music is one of their biggest inspirations and they always have something on in the background whilst writing. They are an avid gamer and are often found hogging their husband's Xbox.

Made in the USA
Monee, IL
11 August 2023

40833435R00236